SAVAGE

———— ALSO BY ————
THOMAS E. SNIEGOSKI

The Fallen Series
The Fallen 1: The Fallen and Leviathan
The Fallen 2: Aerie and Reckoning
The Fallen 3: End of Days
The Fallen 4: Forsaken
The Fallen 5: Armageddon

SAVAGE

THOMAS E. SNIEGOSKI

SIMON PULSE
New York London Toronto Sydney New Delhi

This book is a work of fiction. Any references to historical events, real people, or real places are used fictitiously. Other names, characters, places, and events are products of the author's imagination, and any resemblance to actual events or places or persons, living or dead, is entirely coincidental.

SIMON PULSE

An imprint of Simon & Schuster Children's Publishing Division
1230 Avenue of the Americas, New York, New York 10020
First Simon Pulse hardcover edition May 2016
Text copyright © 2016 by Thomas E. Sniegoski
Front jacket photo-illustration by Sammy Yuen Jr.
Jacket photographs copyright © 2016 by Thinkstock
All rights reserved, including the right of reproduction in whole or in part in any form.
SIMON PULSE and colophon are registered trademarks of Simon & Schuster, Inc.
For information about special discounts for bulk purchases, please contact Simon & Schuster Special Sales at 1-866-506-1949 or business@simonandschuster.com.
The Simon & Schuster Speakers Bureau can bring authors to your live event.
For more information or to book an event, contact the Simon & Schuster Speakers Bureau at 1-866-248-3049 or visit our website at www.simonspeakers.com.
Book designed by Karina Granda
The text of this book was set in Adobe Garamond Pro.
Manufactured in the United States of America
2 4 6 8 10 9 7 5 3 1
This title has been cataloged with the Library of Congress.
ISBN 978-1-4814-4373-9 (hc)
ISBN 978-1-4814-4375-3 (eBook)

This book is for Christopher Golden.
Thank you so much for all the knowledge, insight, and excitement that you share not only with me, but many other writers out there, and most especially, thank you for being a friend. (Cue Andrew Gold song!)

This book is also dedicated to James Herbert, and all the other writers out there from my childhood who entertained the crap out of me with their tales of animals running amok.

PROLOGUE

An Island in the South Pacific
Two Weeks Ago

The absence of birds crying in the trees and the incessant buzzing of insects on this tropical island told the scientist it had happened again. He could hear only the gentle whispering of the breeze and the distant crashing of waves on the beach behind him, and he knew that every bird, every bug, every warm- and cold-blooded thing that had called this island retreat home was dead.

He took a deep breath, steeling himself for what he would find, knowing it wouldn't be pleasant, and began to follow his team toward the resort itself. Carefully he stepped over the dead birds and monkeys rotting in the newly risen sun, not wanting to disturb anything that could give him a clue as to what had happened here.

"Sir?" a female voice called out from somewhere up ahead.

He moved toward the sound, finding a set of wooden stairs that led up from the beach. The first human corpse, a middle-aged man, lay at the bottom of the steps on his stomach, arms reaching out, fingers dug deep into the sand as if attempting to drag himself toward the water.

The scientist knelt to examine the body. Even at first glance he could see similarities to the previous incidents, and a numbing chill ran down the length of his spine.

"Sir?" came the voice again, closer this time, and the scientist turned his gaze toward the woman standing at the top of the stairs.

"Just a second," he called up to her. "I want to check something here."

He reached into his pocket and pulled out a pair of blue rubber gloves. He tugged them on over his hands, then grasped the body by the shoulder and pushed, balancing the stiffened corpse on its side. The smell was horrible, but that wasn't what caught his attention.

"Jesus," the scientist said as he caught sight of seven Polynesian rats pushed into the sand, eyes wide in death. He guessed that they had been killed when the man fell on top of them, but that didn't explain why they were gathered at the foot of the steps.

The scientist leaned in closer, examining the rodents' teeth and claws.

"Anything interesting?" the woman asked.

He didn't answer at first, gazing from the crushed rats to the front of the stiffened corpse. Then he gently lowered the body back to the ground.

"I suppose you want me to see what you've found," he sighed, rising to his feet.

"Why should we be the only ones to have nightmares later?"

the woman questioned sarcastically as the scientist climbed the wooden steps.

Heaven's Breath was an exclusive, high-end resort on one of the smaller Polynesian islands in the South Pacific. It had catered to the wealthiest of businesspeople and their families looking to escape the day-to-day pressures of their hectic existences, but the scientist doubted that this was what they had expected for their three thousand dollars a day. What had been quite beautiful before the event was now just grotesque.

The stairs led up to a circular stone patio, in the center of which was a hot tub. A fully clothed woman's body floated there, a tiny Yorkshire terrier still on its leash floating beside her. The water was a disturbing rust color.

"Do we know how many?" the scientist asked, counting at least nine bodies within sight of where he stood. One in particular caught his attention and held it in a steely grip—a young girl, his daughter's age, arms and legs splayed, a cell phone just out of reach of fingers with chipped pink nail polish. He tried to imagine what it must have been like for her and felt his pulse quicken, his eyes begin to burn.

At the moment he wanted only to call his daughter, to hear her voice, and to tell her how much he loved her.

"The desk register said that there were twenty-five guests." She gestured toward the main building where other members of the team were moving about. "We're checking the rooms now, then we'll move on to the surrounding jungle."

"Anything different?" the scientist asked, noticing a shattered sliding glass door stained with drying blood.

"Not that we can see," she answered. "So far, it's pretty much the same as the others. Estimated time of death for the bodies we've already examined coincides with the typhoon."

The scientist gazed at the corpses strewn about, trying to imagine the horrors that had driven them out into a raging tropical storm.

A sudden thump from nearby was as startling as a shotgun blast.

"What the hell was that?" the woman asked, her hand going to the firearm she wore in a holster on her hip.

The scientist was already moving toward the sound, his body tensed, prepared for almost anything.

"Dr. Sayid," the woman cautioned, but he quickly raised his hand, silencing her.

There was another sound, muffled. . . .

His eyes quickly scanned the area, finally focusing upon a dark teak chest in front of what looked to be a maintenance shed. He glanced back at the woman and motioned for her to follow him. She did as he ordered, weapon at the ready.

They stopped before the chest, ears straining for a sound of life amid all of this death.

"Want me to open it?" the woman whispered, squinting down the barrel of her pistol.

"I'll do it," Sayid said. He reached out and grasped the handle. "Ready?" he asked the woman, who grunted her reply, her finger now twitching on her weapon's trigger.

The scientist took a deep breath, then pulled open the lid. The chest was filled with supplies for the hot tub, plastic bottles of chemicals, a coiled hose, brushes, and a heavy green tarp.

The tarp moved.

Sayid tensed as the armed woman beside him bore down with her gun, ready to fire at the first sign of hostility.

And then they heard the sobbing, a soft cry filled with so much fear it was almost palpable. The scientist could not help himself. He reached down into the chest, pulling aside the rough green material to reveal the source of such immeasurable sadness.

She couldn't have been any older than five; the My Little Pony T-shirt she wore was stained with spatters of blood. Her wide, brown eyes were filled with more fear than the scientist had ever seen.

"It's all right," he said in his kindest, gentlest voice. "Everything is going to be fine . . . we're here to help."

The woman had lowered her weapon and returned it to her holster. She stepped forward and reached for the child. "Let's get you out of there," she said.

But the little girl began to scream, grabbing hold of the tarp and attempting to bury herself beneath it. "No!" she screamed over and over again. "You can't! We gotta hide. . . . Mama said we gotta hide or they'll get us!" Her eyes were frantically darting around, and then her gaze turned toward the sky. Sayid didn't think it was possible, but she looked even more scared.

He followed her gaze up and saw a pattern of dark clouds forming above; a low rumbling thunder from the swirling configuration implied another storm was inevitable.

"What is it, honey?" Sayid asked. "What do you see? Is it the storm?"

The child was frantic. "They'll come again," she wailed pathetically, her face a fiery red from emotion.

Her fear made him again think of his own child, when she was just a little girl, and he reached down into the chest to scoop the frightened girl up in his arms, whispering assurances to her.

"Shhhhhh, it's going to be okay," he said, but she fought him, arms flailing, legs kicking, her eyes fixed on the sky above.

"They're gonna get us," she cried as he tried to hold her tight. She was like a wild animal fighting to escape. "They come in the storm!"

Fighting for its life.

"They come in the storm!"

CHAPTER ONE

There must be a storm coming.

Sidney Moore opened her eyes to the morning and groaned, the beginnings of a sinus headache throbbing inside her skull.

Great, she thought as she lay in bed, staring up at the ceiling. For the briefest moment she felt a rush of panic that she might have overslept and that she was going to be late for school. But that was immediately followed by an incredible sense of relief when she remembered that school was over for the summer, never mind the fact that she had graduated. The pressures of high school were over and done, and the wonders of an unknown future were laid out before her eighteen-year-old self. But the thrill quickly soured, any potential this particular day might have in store for her dissolving as a knot of discomfort formed in her belly and she remembered the inescapable things that had lately been the source of her troubles.

The things that haunted and distracted her from the excitement of her future.

She rolled over with a heavy sigh and reached for her phone just as the large white head of a German shepherd loomed up from beside the bed and planted a wet kiss on her face. A kiss that smelled like the glue on an old envelope.

Lovely.

"Morning, Snowy girl," she said, looking deep into the dog's icy blue eyes. Snowy's bushy tail began to wag wildly, and she pawed the bed for more attention.

"All right, all right," Sidney exclaimed. "I'll get you some breakfast in a minute."

Snowy sat down, watching with eager, hungry eyes as Sidney checked her phone for messages.

"Unngh," she groaned, seeing that one of the dreaded *things* that held back her anticipation had called while she slept.

Her boyfriend—*ex*-boyfriend—had left another message.

"Cody, why can't you just leave me alone?" she whispered sadly as she threw back the covers and climbed from bed.

Snowy excitedly leaped to her feet.

"Yes, yes, go on." Sidney motioned the dog from the room with the hand that still held the phone, and Snowy bounded down the hallway toward the kitchen.

Sidney knew what she should do—delete the message and forget that he'd even called. She would be better off, she was sure of it, although there was still a part of her that cared for him. But that was the part of her that obviously wasn't dead set on leaving Benediction for college in Boston.

The part she was trying her damnedest to ignore.

The kitchen smelled deliciously of French roast, and half a pot sitting in the coffeemaker filled the air with the aroma that she'd always loved, even though she could barely stomach the taste. *One of these days,* she told herself as she picked up Snowy's water dish from the place mat on the floor and proceeded to rinse it clean before filling it with fresh water. Sidney had taken to imagining herself in deep with her college studies, pulling all-nighters with cup after cup of steaming hot coffee to keep her awake. Developing a taste for the stuff was one of the many things she was going to have to do while getting used to being on her own.

She set Snowy's dish down and went to the strainer by the sink for her food bowl. There was a plastic container in the corner beside the fridge that held the dog's food, and Sidney unscrewed the lid and poured a measured cup into the bowl.

"Here ya go, girl," Sidney said as she carried the dish across the kitchen. "Made it up fresh myself."

Snowy wasn't looking, so she did not know that Sidney was speaking to her. The dog was standing in front of the sliding glass doors, looking out onto the deck where Sidney's dad was sitting, enjoying the early morning, as well as a smoke.

"Dammit," Sidney cursed, bending to set Snowy's food bowl down. Sidney stomped her foot on the floor to get the dog's attention.

Feeling the vibration, the white shepherd turned to look at her.

"Here's your chow," Sidney said as the dog dashed to her meal.

"That's a good girl." She patted her side lovingly, suddenly experiencing a strange wave of emotion over the idea that it wouldn't be long before she was gone and wouldn't be here to feed her special friend.

"I'm gonna miss you something fierce," she said, continuing to stroke the dog's gorgeous white coat. The two had had a special bond from the first day her father had brought her home from the mainland as a special birthday gift, the bond only intensifying when she learned of Snowy's unique disability.

Her dog was deaf.

Snowy looked up from her bowl of dry food, chewing happily but empathically sensing the shift in Sidney's mood.

"That's all right," she reassured the dog. "You keep eating."

The shepherd did as she was told, digging her pointed snout into the bowl for the remaining kibble.

Sidney left the dog and went to the sliding doors, her mood shifting back to one of annoyance as she let herself out onto the deck.

"Hey, you're up," her father said.

"Yeah," she agreed. "Watcha doing?"

"Enjoying what's left of the summer," he said, reaching with his left hand for his coffee mug. There wasn't any sign of a cigarette, which meant that he'd already disposed of the evidence. He lifted his chin and looked across the expanse of backyard to a house that could just about be seen through a section of woods. "I think the crap in the Mosses' yard is multiplying," he said, and chuckled.

He was making reference to their neighbors across the way that they believed were hoarders. He knew that they always got a good chuckle talking about Caroline, her son Isaac, and the ever-increasing collection of stuff that piled up in their backyard. But she didn't feel like chuckling at the moment.

"Can I get you another cup of coffee?" she asked.

He finished his sip and then offered her the cup. "That would be awesome."

She took the cup from him and started for the door. "Would you like another cigarette, too?" she asked, standing in the doorway from the deck into the kitchen.

Her father didn't answer.

"And I'll bring the phone out to you too so that you can call nine-one-one when you finish."

"When did you get to be so fresh?" her father asked. "I remember that well-behaved little girl who wouldn't dream of disrespecting her father. Whatever happened to her?"

"She went away when her father almost died of a stroke from too much smoking and stress."

"So who are you again?" he asked, trying to coax a smile from her.

"I'm the daughter that'll be making your funeral arrangements if you keep doing this crap."

"So I had a cigarette, big deal," her father said, a touch of petulance in his tone.

"You know that's not good for you."

"Yeah, yeah," he said, waving her off.

Snowy pushed past her out onto the deck and to her father's side.

"There's a good girl," her dad said, patting the shepherd.

Sidney watched him with a wary eye, paying extra attention to his right-hand side and how he avoided the use of it. Though he had regained some use since the stroke, it still wasn't all that strong.

"I should have her bite you," Sidney said.

"She'd never do that. Would you, girl?" he asked the dog, staring lovingly into her focused gaze. "We're the best of pals."

"I'm sure she'd be as mad as I am if I told her that you were killing yourself."

"I had one cigarette," he said. "Don't make such a big deal out of it."

Snowy had brought him a ball, dropping it into the right side of the chair. He squirmed a bit, trying to grasp the ball with the hand on that side, but frustration won out, and he reached across with his left. He threw the ball and smiled as the dog bounded across the deck and leaped into the yard after it.

"You've only had one cigarette? Look me in the eye and tell me that."

"Are you going to bring me that coffee or . . . ?"

"Thought so," she said, going inside before she could say anything that might make the situation worse. Her mind raced as she stood at the kitchen counter. *What can I do?* Her father was a grown man and could do anything he wanted despite what she told him he could and couldn't do.

Her memory flashed back to the horrible day when he'd had the stroke, and how the world had suddenly become a lot scarier than it ever had been before, and she was forced to look at life through more adult eyes. It had always been just the two of them, her mother having walked out before she was even five, but after her dad got sick, she had no choice but to grow up.

The doctors hadn't been sure that he was even going to make it, but her father had surprised them, regaining his speech and most of his ability to walk. Sure he had to use a cane, but that was better than nothing. Better than being stuck in a bed.

But it wasn't enough for him. Her father wanted to be back to the way he was before the stroke, and that was something that couldn't be guaranteed. His recovery after getting out of the hospital had been slow, physical therapy only doing as much as the patient was willing to put into it. She couldn't even begin to count the number of times that they'd talked about him working harder—lots of tears and yelling, followed by promises that he'd do better, and he would . . . for a time.

It was like he'd decided that if he couldn't be 100 percent better, it wasn't worth the effort. And if it was bad now, how awful was it going to get once she went off to school and couldn't keep an eye on him? She imagined another phone call, and a ball of ice formed in her belly.

This was that other nagging concern preventing her from truly getting excited over her future plans. The other thing that held her back.

She heard the door sliding open behind her and the sound of her father's efforts to come inside.

"Do you still want that coffee?" she asked, taking the carafe from the coffeemaker.

"Yeah, that would be good," she heard him say.

She filled the cup and was turning around to bring it to the small kitchen table in the center of the room when she saw that he was having some difficulty getting his right leg in through the doorway.

"Wait a sec," she said, not wanting to spill the drink as she carefully set it down.

"I got it," her dad said, but she could hear the frustration already growing.

She turned to see Snowy outside on the deck, tennis ball clutched in her mouth, as her father continued to struggle.

"Dad . . ."

"I'm fine," he barked, his anger providing him with enough fuel to actually haul the semiuseless leg up over the lip of the slide and get himself inside.

That was when Snowy decided she and her ball were coming inside as well, her large and quite powerful eighty-pound body pushing past Sidney's father impatiently, throwing off his balance and sending him backward.

Sidney was on the move before her father hit the floor, reaching and grabbing at anything that might lessen the fall. Her father went down wedged into the corner of the kitchen, knocking some plants from the metal plant stand as his good arm flailed.

He swore as she got to him.

"It's okay," she said, not wanting to make a big deal out of it. "I've got you."

His breathing had quickened, explosions of expletives leaving his mouth as he settled. She squatted down, put her hands beneath his arms, and attempted to haul him to his feet. Sidney didn't consider herself weak by any means, but even though he had lost some weight since the stroke, her father was still pretty darn heavy, and not having the full use of his right side only made matters all the more difficult.

The first try was a failure, with her slipping to one side and him falling to the floor for a second time.

"Leave me here," she heard her father say. The anger was gone now, replaced by something that sounded an awful lot like disgust.

"Yeah, right." She tried again, getting a better hold beneath his arms, and managed to at least get him upright. "A little help here," she said, chiding him. "That's it. You got it."

He was helping now, though she could tell that he was tired. This only made her think of the man that he used to be. The guy who would be out of the house and off to one of his contracting jobs at five in the morning, only to return later that day to do even more work around their own house. She hated to see him this way probably as much as he despised being it, but what choice was there? The alternative was not an option she cared to consider.

Though she was certain there were nights that her father had considered it.

The idea of him being gone—*being dead*—nearly took her strength away, and she was afraid that she would drop him again. Snowy, ball still clutched in her mouth, stood across the kitchen, watching cautiously, tail wagging ever so slightly, the look in her icy blue eyes asking if everything was all right.

Then, at that very moment, Sidney wanted the answer to be yes, yes, everything was going to be fine. Pushing all the sadness and concern aside, she managed to pull her father up to his feet and, balancing him against her shoulder, dragged one of the kitchen chairs over close enough that she was able to assist him in sitting down.

"No gym for me this morning," she joked, feeling out of breath from the struggle. She could tell he was exhausted as well, sitting slumped, head back. Snowy had come to him with her ball, checking the situation out, making sure that everything was as it should be. He petted her silently, the action helping to calm him.

"You good?" she asked, rubbing his back.

He didn't answer as she picked up his cane, leaning it up against the kitchen table. She then reached over and slid the mug of coffee closer to his reach.

"Here's your refill."

He just nodded, letting the good hand that was petting Snowy reach for the coffee.

Sidney had been planning on having a cup of tea and maybe something to eat before getting ready for work, but glancing at the clock on the microwave told her that wasn't going to be possible if she didn't want to be late.

"If you're okay, I've got to get ready," she told him.

He was mid-sip but finished and carefully brought the coffee mug down to the table. "I'm good," he said as the mug landed without spilling a drop, and then he looked at her.

But in his eyes she could see how sad he was, and how tired.

And that he was lying.

CHAPTER TWO

Janice Berthold savored mornings like this.

They'd been coming to their home on Benediction Island during the summer months for as long as she'd been married, but there was still nothing better than when all was entirely quiet, and she was alone.

When *he* was gone.

It wouldn't last for long, and she knew it but tried not to remind herself. She wanted to savor each and every minute—every second—of these precious moments of solitude.

Imagining how wonderful it would be without *him*. How every day would be just like this if *he* was no longer around.

She felt the muscles around her mouth contract and a smile begin to form. It felt strange.

Janice couldn't remember the last time she had genuinely smiled, the misery of her days with *him* blocking any recollection of past joy.

And as quickly as it had come, the smile was replaced with an expression reflective of the grim reality in which she lived.

Her eyes slowly opened to the exquisite view from the sunroom window, but the undulating blue gray of the Atlantic could do nothing to recapture that so elusive bliss she had been experiencing.

Once again, *he* had ruined it.

She decided to try again, closing her eyes, feeling herself lulled by the natural sounds of the million-dollar summer home: the ticking of the grandfather clock in the library study, the humming of the refrigerator from the gourmet kitchen, all wrapped up in the muffled rhythmic ebb and flow of the ocean outside.

Yes, she was almost there . . . almost . . .

The sound of the door coming open and then slamming closed tore her from the embrace of peace and dropped her back into hellish reality.

She could already feel it happening, all brought on by the sounds of his arrival and the knowledge of his presence within the once-peaceful house. She could hear him moving about, the irritating thump of his footfalls, the clamor of his car keys carelessly being thrown upon the granite countertop in the kitchen, the refrigerator door pulled open, its contents rummaged through, before the heavy door was slammed close.

She could feel her panic setting in, wanting to run and hide herself away someplace where he could not find her—could not affect her with his poisonous being.

But he would always find her.

"Janice!" his voice bellowed, shattering what remained of her blessed silence like a brick thrown through plate glass.

He expected her to answer, but that would just be foolish as he would find her all the faster. She stood up from the couch, steeling herself for the inevitable. His steps were coming closer, and she could see his grotesque shape as he shambled down the short corridor somehow sensing and being drawn to the room she was in.

"Janice, where are you?"

His voice caused her flesh to tingle and itch as if covered with insects, the sound of her name coming from his mouth so sickening that it made her want to change it to something else entirely. But then he would eventually know it, and speak it, and it, too, would be corrupted by his foul mouth.

She could feel him there in the doorway behind her, the poison of his very presence radiating from his body.

"There you are," her husband, Ronald Berthold, said, followed by the sloshing of water and the sound of him swallowing.

Though she would have preferred to look out the floor-to-ceiling windows at the undulating expanse of ocean, she braced herself and turned to look at him.

Her husband was drinking greedily from a bottle of water. He had been out for a morning run and still wore the sweat-stained T-shirt, running shorts, and sneakers upon his feet.

She could smell him now, smell his sweat, and almost became sick, breathing through her mouth to counter the nausea.

"Hey," he said as he brought the bottle down from his mouth, screwing the cap back in place. "We should think about getting out of here sometime today. There's a pretty big storm coming."

She'd heard the weather report earlier but had been distracted from the news by the fact that her husband had been getting ready to leave for his run. That was all she could focus on at that moment, the sweetness of him not being there. She would have tolerated the most destructive of natural disasters if it meant he wouldn't be there.

"I'll start to pack," she said, hating to speak to him because it would only lead to him talking to her more.

She sensed his movement and turned to see that he had left the entryway and was approaching her.

Oh God, she thought, feeling her revulsion rise. She turned to face him. The smell coming off his body was nearly too much, and she felt herself grow light-headed.

"I should probably get started if we want an early start" she was able to get out without gagging, trying to move past him, but he reached out and gently took hold of her arm.

The feeling of his hand on her flesh was beyond awful, and it took all that she could muster not to scream. And to think that at one time, so very long ago, when she was too young and naive, she had actually invited his touch.

She fired a withering glance at his hand upon her arm, and he released her as if laser beams had shot from her eyes to sear his flesh.

"Let me shower and I'll go pick up Alfred from the vet," he suggested.

"No, I'll do it," she said quickly, seeing it as a way to remove herself from his loathsome presence, if only for a time. Yes, she would have to spend some of the time with the dog, but at least Alfred was somewhat tolerable.

"Are you sure?" he asked, his voice like nails on a blackboard. "I can do it . . . just let me clean up a bit and—"

"No," she said with finality, already on the move to get away from him. "I'll do it. You stay here and get the house ready for the storm."

She could feel his eyes following her as she was leaving the room.

"Okay," he said. "See ya when you get back."

Janice was already starting to feel better being away from him when she heard him call out from the sunroom, words that were like poison-dipped blades thrust into her flesh.

"Love you," Ronald Berthold announced.

It was all she could do to keep from vomiting.

CHAPTER THREE

Sidney had hoped that a warm shower would have helped her headache, but that wasn't the case. It felt as though she had a steel band wrapped around her forehead and somebody was slowly tightening it.

She sometimes had problems with sinus headaches, especially when the weather was going to get bad, so it didn't surprise her one bit to hear that a pretty serious storm was on the way.

Before leaving the house, she'd taken two Advil, but it hadn't done much of anything to cut the nausea-inducing pain, so she figured that maybe some caffeine might do the trick. At this stage in the game she would be willing to try just about anything. She wondered if it was entirely the weather's fault for her nasty head pain, or if it also had to do with what had gone on earlier at the house with her father, and the message she still hadn't listened to. Her eyes darted from the road to quickly glance at her phone on the passenger seat.

Snowy whined from the backseat of the Jeep, realizing where Sidney was going. Charter Street was unusually crowded for a week day, and it took her longer to find a parking spot. An SUV pulled out of a space directly across from the Sunny Side Up Diner, and she thought maybe there was the chance that today wasn't going to be as bad as she'd originally thought.

The dog started to pace in the back of the Jeep, going from the window on one side to the other, whining the entire time. Sidney turned in the driver's seat, motioning with her hand for Snowy to pay attention to her. She hadn't intended on bringing Snowy to work with her today, but seeing as her father wasn't having the best of days, she thought maybe it would be a good idea.

Sidney snapped her fingers, even though the dog could not hear, but the movement was enough to capture her attention.

"You be good for a minute, and I'll bring you a corn muffin, all right?" Sidney said, giving the hand signal that informed the shepherd that she was leaving for a moment but would be right back.

The dog sat obediently, watching her with a steely gaze as Sidney got out of the Jeep and crossed the street to the diner.

Jillian, a classmate of hers since kindergarten, was working the to-go counter and greeted her with a smile, and immediately asked how she and Cody were doing. Sidney thought about just blowing it all off and saying they were fine, and leaving it like that, but she just couldn't bring herself to do it, the words much harder to get out than she expected.

"We're not together anymore."

The expression on her friend's face went from shock to sadness and sympathy.

"Oh my God, what happened?"

Sidney just didn't want to get into it right now and attempted to simplify. "It was just one of those things. We'd grown apart, and with me leaving for school, we thought it would be best if . . ." Sidney paused, and Jillian accepted this as an invitation to put in her two cents.

"That really sucks; I'm so sorry. I didn't think you two would ever break up."

"Yeah, but . . . ," Sidney said, eager to wrap the conversation up.

"I thought for sure that you two were like, permanent. I could totally see the two of you married and stuff, and . . ."

Sidney's headache had grown much worse, and her stomach wasn't doing too good at the moment either.

"Things change," Sidney said firmly, but then managed to smile.

"Well I think it sucks," Jillian added. "But who knows? Maybe you'll get back together."

Sidney wanted to tell her *no*, that they wouldn't be getting back together, and the fact that they *had* been together for so long didn't necessarily mean that they *were* going to be together for eternity. It was just over; things like this happened.

Instead she just smiled again, saying "Who knows," and ordered up a large black tea to go, momentarily forgetting the corn muffin that she'd promised Snowy. But she quickly rectified the situation, putting the order in when Jillian brought her drink.

Waiting for the muffin, she distracted herself by watching the flat-screen televisions on the wall above the counter and the weather forecast that was predicting doom and gloom. From what she could see, the storm was going to make a direct hit on Benediction with some heavy rains and high winds and might even stay a hurricane instead of being downgraded to a tropical storm, which is what usually happened.

Great, Sidney thought, remembering the last bad summer storm and how they went without power for six and a half days, and that one *had* been downgraded.

Jillian returned with her muffin and said again how sorry she was. Sidney thanked her through gritted teeth, leaving the diner with a wave while sipping from the steaming cup of tea. She decided to leave the tea bag in the boiling hot water, wanting the tea to be as strong as it could be to help alleviate the pressure in her head.

She stopped on the sidewalk for an opening to cross, darting out when all was clear. Snowy was patiently waiting, eyes fixed on her as she approached the Jeep. Sidney could see that her tail was wagging like crazy, somehow knowing that a special treat would soon be hers.

"Were you a good girl?" Sidney asked as she slid into the driver's seat.

Snowy didn't wait for an invitation, climbing from the back into the passenger's seat, snout having already found the bag that contained the muffin.

"All right, you gotta sit," Sidney said while making the hand gesture that the dog was quite familiar with. Snowy sat, trickles of drool already leaking from the sides of her mouth in anticipation.

The dog watched as Sidney rummaged in the bag, first breaking off a piece of muffin for herself, and then another for the dog, which was gently plucked from Sidney's fingers. It wasn't long before the corn muffin had completely disappeared, most of it making its way into Snowy's belly. She didn't give the German shepherd people food all that often, but every once in a while Sidney liked to give her special pup a treat.

"There," she said, crumpling up the bag. "How's that?" She rubbed the dog's head and pointed ears affectionately, then signaled for Snowy to return to the back before they could go.

Sidney turned the key in the ignition, starting the Jeep up, but before putting it in drive, she unconsciously reached for her phone, checking for new messages.

The message from Cody was still there, begging to be listened to.

She thought she was stronger than that, strong enough to put the phone away—maybe even delete the message—before heading on to work, but in a moment of weakness she called up the voice mail to listen.

"Hey, it's me," Cody's voice began. *"I know you said that you didn't want to talk anymore about . . . about us . . . but I think we should—"*

Sidney gasped, startled as somebody rapped a knuckle against the driver's-side window. Lowering the phone, she saw an all too familiar smiling face at the window, motioning for her to put the window down.

"Hey, gorgeous," Rich Stanmore said cheerfully. He leaned into the car, reaching back to pet Snowy. "And how's my Snowy girl?"

"She's good," Sidney answered. "What are you doing here? I thought you went back to Boston."

"I did, but I'm back," he said. He was holding a coffee from

Sunny Side Up and took a swig. "My folks left during the week. Dad had to head back for some meetings, so they asked me to come this weekend to close the place up." He had some more coffee.

"Just in time for the storm."

"Mmmm," he hummed, swallowing his sip. "Which makes you the perfect person to see."

"Oh yeah, why's that?"

"Not only am I closing up the house, but I've got to take care of the sailboat," he said.

"Yeah . . . ," she said, still unsure what he was getting at.

"Well, I need to get it out of the water, especially if there's a storm on the way, and Dad has the truck . . ." He waited for her to catch on, but it still hadn't sunk in yet. "I was wondering if Cody could . . ."

She felt her stomach plummet at the mention of her ex-boyfriend's name. She had no desire to go again through the fact that she and Cody had broken up, and even less to answer the inevitable follow-up questions as to why, and how she was holding up, and blah, blah, blah. . . .

She just couldn't do it right then.

"I don't know; I guess I could ask him," she said, having no idea why she would even suggest such a thing since they hadn't spoken since the breakup, and the fact that Cody hated Rich, having always suspected that the older boy had harbored a secret crush for her.

"Yes!" Rich said, pumping his fist in the air. "If you could do that for me, I would love you forever—seriously."

"Let me see what I can do," she told him, regretting each and every word. "But I've got to get to work."

"Call me later?" he asked.

"Will do."

"Okay," Rich said, stepping back from the car.

She said good-bye, rolling up her window as she pulled out of the parking spot. Rich's reflection waved to her in the rearview as she headed down Charter, where she would take a left onto Lafayette.

The day just kept on getting better.

And Sidney seriously began to consider if it was too late to call in sick.

CHAPTER FOUR

Caroline Moss could not bear the thought of anyone in her home touching her things.

The woman sat in her favorite recliner, surrounded by the accumulation of years: stacks of newspapers and magazines, piles of junk mail, receipts, empty cat food cans and take-out containers. Furniture once covered in plastic to keep it clean had been swallowed up by mounds of stuffed animals, baby dolls, record albums, VCRs and VHS tapes, CDs, milk cartons, and clothing—piles and piles of clothing. To anyone else it would have looked like the town dump, but to Caroline, everything was something of value.

But now somebody was threatening to come and take her treasures away.

As she sat in the comforting nest of her things, Caroline quivered with anger, remembering the unexpected visit from her daughter,

Barbara. Caroline managed to hold back another bout of tears, of which there had been many of late, all brought on because Barbara chose to stick her nose into business that didn't concern her. Caroline sneered with the memory of her daughter's overwrought emotional response, pleading with her mother to seek help, if not for her own sake, then for the sake of her brother, Caroline's son, Isaac.

Caroline had argued a blue streak, telling Barbara that everything was perfectly fine, that she and Isaac were getting along very well and didn't need her involvement in their lives. But Barbara was always a stubborn thing, and when she got an idea into her fat head, there was nothing that was going to change it.

As if sensing their owner's distress, Caroline's cats—her fur babies—emerged from various places of concealment about the room, meowing and chirping as they approached. Some leaped up onto her lap, while others walked across precariously piled stacks of equal parts books and rubbish.

She'd lost count of how many there were now. All she knew was that they were her friends, her furry children. This was as much their home as hers, and she wasn't about to let anyone take it away from them.

But she'd agreed to her daughter's demands, agreed to let a television program about filthy people and their filthy, cluttered houses come see her home. It was the only way to shut Barbara up, to get her to agree not to call Adult Protective Services on her and Isaac.

The presence of her feline friends calmed her. She stroked them as they walked upon her or passed by on their way to some other area of the house also bursting at the seams with stuff.

Just the idea of somebody coming into her home, to judge her . . .

Caroline seethed, an anger that she worked so hard to control over the years bubbling to the surface. It was the kind of anger that could get her into trouble . . . the kind of anger that made her do things she always regretted later.

Sitting there in her chair, surrounded by her cats and by years of accumulation, she imagined how easy it would be to set it on fire. She bet that would make Barbara happy. It would certainly take away all her concerns.

Caroline saw herself burning with all her things and almost convinced herself that this was what she should do, but then she thought of her cats, her babies, and how they would suffer.

And then there was poor Isaac.

He was her other baby, her special boy. Hit by a car when he was only four and developmentally challenged as a result of extensive head injuries, he had brought her nothing but joy these sixteen years.

No, she could not do that to him.

But what to do?

A Maine Coon cat called Mrs. Livingstone got right in her face, meowing questioningly, before head-butting her.

"I don't know, pretty kitty," Caroline said, running her hands down the length of the enormous cat, right down to the end of her fluffy tail. "Perhaps you could tell me?"

The cat abruptly turned around, sticking her furry behind in Caroline's face, making her laugh. "I'm not sure that would be effective," she told the animal, who suddenly snarled and sprang from

Caroline's lap with a hiss, angrily attacking the other cats meandering around the chair.

"Is that what you'll do to those horrible people coming to our house?" she asked the big cat. A full-fledged fight had now erupted, with Mrs. Livingstone spitting and swatting at the other cats.

"Maybe you've got a point," Caroline said to her furry friends, deciding that there might be another option besides burning her house down or giving in completely to her daughter's whims.

Mrs. Livingstone leaped upon the back of an equally large male tabby called Manx, biting down into his shoulder blades and sending him scurrying away with a shrieking wail, books and stacks of paper falling from where they'd been precariously perched in his wake.

Maybe she could make it so difficult for them that they wouldn't want anything to do with her or her house.

Maybe she could fight them at every turn.

Maybe.

The cats were fighting again.

Isaac quickly reached up to both his ears, playing with the volume of his hearing aids so he would not hear them. He hated the sound of their fighting. The screeches, hisses, whines, and wails gave him scary thoughts and put horrible pictures inside his head.

He did not like that, not one little bit.

The young man played with the tiny controls. There was a sharp crackling followed by some low hums that tickled his throat, but it seemed to cancel out the noise of the battling felines.

He wasn't supposed to play with his hearing aids, but no matter how many times he promised his mother he wouldn't, he would still find his sneaky hands reaching up to play with the tiny knobs of the plastic devices. Without them he could barely hear at all, one ear almost completely useless. He called that one Steve, after his father whom he barely knew, but his mother always told him that the man was no good and completely useless.

Today Steve was ringing oddly, and it kind of hurt. Isaac's hands again went up to the hearing devices, fiddling with the controls, hoping to stop the strange sound in his Steve ear. He was tempted to pluck them both out, to surrender to the silence, but he could never do that. What if his mother needed him?

Isaac decided that he would rather deal with the cats, and was about to try and adjust the volume in his ears again, when Steve suddenly went quiet, the disquieting, unfamiliar sound now gone. The young man cocked his head to one side and then the other, listening for anything out of the ordinary, but things seemed to be back to relative normal. Even the cats had stopped, and he could just about hear the sound of the television from outside his room. *The Price Is Right* was on. That was his mother's favorite show.

He considered going to join her for the Showcase Showdown, but first he had to make sure that his room was in order. Turning very slowly where he stood, Isaac took in the details of his space. It was the exact opposite of the rooms outside his—very sparsely furnished with only his bed, a bedside table with a lamp on it, and a chest of drawers with a mirror. Everything that he owned was in a very specific place. He did not care for the messiness of the rest of the house and often tried to get his mother to clean it up, but he was finally getting to realize after all these years that it was just too hard for her.

For a moment he wondered how other boys and girls dealt with their messy parents and felt a familiar frustration begin to arise over the fact that he seldom had the opportunity to interact with people his own age, his mother having decided to homeschool him due to his disabilities.

Isaac's anger flared. He hated that word—hated to be reminded of the fact that he was different. As far as he was concerned, everybody had something that set them apart. Even Sidney, his neighbor across the way who he thought was the most perfect person in the whole wide world, had something that set her apart from everybody else at close inspection.

She never seemed to smile, Isaac mused, attempting to remember each and every time he and Sidney had seen each other. Sure, there had been attempts to smile, the corners of her pretty mouth going through the motions politely, but Isaac knew that it wasn't real.

She's just too darn serious, is what his mother said. And he had to agree.

He noticed that his hairbrush was askew ever so slightly and stepped over to the chest of drawers to align it perfectly. Happy that he had found the imperfection, Isaac stepped back to the room's center, and checked his surroundings once again. He looked at his reflection in the mirror, standing perfectly still so that he could check how he looked. His eyes moved over his image; his button-down shirt was fine, his hair combed just right, his scar . . . Isaac reached up to the left side of his head where the scar was, where his head had been opened when he was only four, and ran a finger along its puffy length. He hated the scar and wished it wasn't there, but it served as a reminder to him. He didn't remember the car running him over and crushing his head, but the scar did. It told him to always be careful.

Things looked good at the moment, and he slowly backed up to his door, reaching behind him for the doorknob.

He kept his eyes on the room and all his belongings as he opened the door behind him and stepped out into the chaos of the hallway.

Taking a deep breath, he took it all in. The amount of stuff stacked and lying on the floor of the hall path nearly sent him into a panic, but it was always this way after leaving the ordered universe of his room. It would take him a little while to get used to it. To adjust.

But he always did.

As he stood and adapted to his surroundings, his mind wandered, and he thought of the strange sound he had heard in his Steve ear back in his room. Reflexively his hand shot up to the ear and the device there. He was tempted to play with it again, but—

"Isaac?" his mother called from the living room, though there was very little room for living there. They could barely even watch TV.

He quickly took his hand away.

"Yes?" he called out.

"Come watch *Price Is Right* with me," she said. "The Showcase Showdown will be coming on."

Feeling a bit more at ease, Isaac navigated the uneven surface of the hallway floor to join his mother, the disturbing sound he'd experienced in his bad ear forgotten.

For now.

CHAPTER **FIVE**

Sidney wasn't sure she'd ever seen the parking lot of the Benediction Veterinary Hospital this crowded before.

She drove down to the back of the lot where the hospital staff was supposed to park and walked up with Snowy obediently by her side. The way the morning was going so far, she really didn't know what to expect inside, and the tea had done very little for her headache.

Removing Snowy's leash from her back pocket, she fastened the clip to the dog's collar and reached for the door, opening it into chaos. It was as if everybody in Benediction had decided to bring their animals in at the same time. Not only were there barking dogs, held tightly on leashes against their owner's legs, and crying cats inside the confines of pet carriers, but there were squawking birds and wire cages filled with guinea pigs, rats, hamsters, and what looked to be a chinchilla.

Pam, one of the front-desk workers, looked up from her computer, where she was finishing up checking out a woman client, comically widening her eyes and making a twisted face.

Sidney approached the counter and asked, "What's going on?"

"I haven't a clue," Pam said, handing the woman her credit card and receipt. "It's been like this since we unlocked the doors."

Michelle, another of the front staffers, was busily checking folks and their pets in. "It's appointments, but it's also walk-ins, like everybody decided at the same time to pay us a visit today. It's crazy."

"I'll be right out to give you a hand," Sidney told them, navigating the meandering crowds with her dog.

"Excuse me," the woman Pam had been helping suddenly said. "Exactly how long am I expected to wait before you bring me my dog?"

Pam, who was already finishing paperwork for another client, spoke up. "I sent one of the techs to get him, Mrs. Berthold," she said as pleasantly as she could. "He should be right out."

Berthold, Sidney thought as she rounded the counter and approached the door that would take her to the back area of the animal hospital. *Why is that name familiar?*

Just as she and Snowy reached the door, it flew open from the other side. Sidney saw who was standing there, and it all became clear.

Berthold. She'd seen the name on paperwork that she'd worked on quite a few times.

Alfred Berthold.

Alfred Berthold was a large male, brindle French bulldog with some serious aggression issues, and he was standing just inside the door no more that three feet away from them.

Normally it wouldn't have been a big deal, all the staff at Benediction Veterinary Hospital having been trained on how to handle aggressive breeds, but every once in a while a situation would arise. . . .

This was one of those situations.

Alfred saw Snowy, and Snowy saw Alfred. Although usually perfectly obedient, Snowy had no patience with outright nastiness. Sidney's special girl had no problems defending herself or protecting Sidney if necessary.

The problem that Sidney could see in that split second was that Alfred was being brought out to his owner by Maynard. Maynard was a good kid, everybody liked his easygoing style, but he was a bit of a stoner, and sometimes, well . . . sometimes he just wasn't paying enough attention. And she could instantly see the problem with Alfred's leash.

One needed to be on guard 100 percent when dealing with Alfred because he could be tricky. One minute he was completely fine, and the next he was trying to chew off some other poor dog's ear. Alfred was bad news, and now here he was, at the end of a leash being given way too much play, with Snowy right in front of him.

Sidney knew that things were about to go from bad to worse when Maynard uttered the words "Oh shit."

She couldn't have agreed more.

It was as if somebody had fired a starter's pistol.

She saw it all in slow motion. Alfred's dark, beady eyes had locked onto Snowy, a stripe of brindled fur suddenly rising upon the Frenchie's back telling her that he was going to strike. Snowy had stiffened protectively, her own white hackles lifting on her neck and back as she readied herself. Sidney yanked back on Snowy's leash, trying to put herself between the two dogs and eliminate the challenging eye contact, but it was too late. Alfred lunged with a guttural snarl, striking her leg with his front paw and causing her to stumble back. Snowy reacted instinctively, moving around Sidney's recovering form to let Alfred know that he had gone too far. The bulldog sprang to meet the shepherd's attack, mouths filled with many teeth coming together in a snarling, ferocious mass.

"Pull him back!" Sidney screamed to Maynard, who seemed to be in a kind of surprised stupor.

Sidney was attempting to pull Snowy away, but she and Alfred were still entangled in their angry tussle. The animal hospital had erupted in sounds of panic, with all the pets voicing their concerns at once.

A human voice rose above the cacophony.

"Alfred!" it cried out in panic, and Sidney saw Mrs. Berthold reaching into the mass of snarling and snapping dogs to separate hers from the other.

Sidney knew what was about to happen. She pulled back on Snowy's leash with all her might, dragging the dog away from Alfred, but it was too late. Alfred reacted as if Mrs. Berthold was part of the threat against him, and he snapped at her hand, his small, crooked teeth sinking into the tender flesh.

Mrs. Berthold's scream was piercing and startled Alfred enough that he let go of her hand, his fleshy face frozen as he realized for the first time that she was there. Thick trails of slobber dripped from both sides of the bulldog's jowls, and Sidney noticed that it was tinted pink with blood. A quick assessment of Snowy showed that she was fine, that there were no puncture wounds, the blood belonging to either Alfred or his owner.

The woman's hand was bleeding, the front of her blue silk blouse stained with drops of dark crimson.

Maynard had already begun to apologize to anybody with whom he could make eye contact, holding tightly to Alfred's leash as he should have been moments before.

"I'm so sorry," the young man stammered. "He got away from me and . . ."

There would be time for apologies later. They needed to help this woman with her injuries. Spatters of red dappled the linoleum floor beneath her bleeding hand.

Pam was already moving around the counter with a towel.

"Could you take Snowy," Sidney said, handing her dog's leash to Michelle, who took Snowy and led her outside as Sidney grabbed the towel from Pam. "Cover it with this," she said, stepping closer to hold the towel beneath the woman's dripping hand.

The woman looked at Sidney with a dazed expression.

"Here you go, Mrs. Berthold," she said, starting to wrap up the bleeding hand. Sidney took a moment to check out the wound and saw that it didn't look too bad, just a few punctures with some torn skin. "Apply pressure to stop the bleeding."

Mrs. Berthold then looked at her, that dazed expression gradually morphing into one of absolute rage.

"Take your hands off of me," she said with a snarl, causing Sidney to step back. The look on her face reminded Sidney of Alfred, just before he lunged.

"We're so sorry," Sidney began. "Let me take you out back, and we can clean that up before—"

"I'm not going anywhere with you," she stated. "Where's my dog?" She looked around at the faces watching her. "Where is he?"

Maynard was standing in the corner by the door with Alfred when her eyes locked on him.

"Give him to me," she ordered, reaching for the leash with her good hand.

Maynard did as he was told.

She wrapped the leash around her uninjured hand and started to leave, Alfred walking by her side.

"Mrs. Berthold," Sidney called to her. "You might want to have that bite checked out at the hospital."

The woman stopped just before the door, turning to glare. Sidney noticed that Alfred was glaring as well.

"Thank you so much," she said calmly, coldly, pulling Alfred closer to her side. "I'll be sure to mention your concern to my lawyer when we speak this afternoon."

She then abruptly turned, taking herself and her animal from the building.

"Have a nice day," Sidney muttered beneath her breath, unsure if she would be able to survive the surprises the remainder of the day might have in store.

CHAPTER **SIX**

"What was all the racket about?" Doc Martin asked, spinning her chair around from the desk where she sat working on the computer in the back office of the clinic. She took her black-framed glasses from her face and let them hang from a fluorescent-green croakie around her neck.

At a closer look, Sidney saw that she was working on a particularly challenging game of solitaire.

"Snowy and one of the discharges had some words," Sidney said, kneeling down beside Snowy to better check her over.

"Bring her here," the old vet said, leaning forward in her chair and motioning with her hands to bring the dog over. Sidney guided the dog to the woman. Snowy responded with a happy wag of her thick tail.

"How's it going, girl?" Doc Martin asked, placing her heavily veined, calloused hands beneath the dog's big head and tilting it upright to look into her eyes. She put her glasses back on her face and then proceeded to check out the splotches of crimson that stood out prominently on the shepherd's white fur.

"Looks like we've got some minor scrapes, but no punctures," Martin said.

"Yeah, thought so," Sidney said, stroking her dog's side.

"Who'd she go up against?" Martin asked.

"Alfred the Frenchie."

"That evil son of a bitch? That bulldog's got a mean streak a mile wide." She finished looking Snowy over. "She's fine. Clean the scratches with some antiseptic and she'll be good as new."

Doc Martin started to rub the dog's ears, causing Snowy to make a low, grumbling moan of pleasure.

"How was the other one?"

"Alfred was fine. Maybe some scrapes too, but his owner's hand got bit."

Martin's eyes widened. "Who did the biting?"

"Alfred. And we've got plenty of witnesses."

"Phew," Doc Martin said, leaning back in her office chair. "Lot harder to sue when it's your own beast that bites."

Sidney used some antibiotic swabs to clean her dog's wounds and to wipe away the bloodstains.

"That's a good girl," she said, looking into the dog's eyes, then kissing her on the nose.

"How's it going out there otherwise?" Doc Martin asked as she saved her solitaire game.

"It's a madhouse." Sidney gestured to Snowy to go lie down, and the dog padded obediently across the room to curl up on a square cushion against the wall, beside a coatrack. "A lot of walk-ins. I'm going to see if there's anything I can do to help clear out the lobby."

She went to the coatrack and took a lab coat from one of the hooks and put it on.

"When you're done with that, I've got some blood work for you to run, a few heartworm blood tests and a kidney function," Doc Martin said.

"What are you doing?" Sidney asked as she headed for the door and the mob scene beyond it.

"After I finish my solitaire game?" Doc Martin asked with a smile. "I've got a spay and a neuter waiting for me, and a basset that swallowed five fifty in quarters."

"You have fun with that," Sidney said, pulling open the door.

"How could I not?" the old vet called after her. "I'm livin' the dream."

CHAPTER SEVEN

Sayid watched as the child slept.

Her physical injuries had been minor, but not the emotional ones; he wasn't sure if the five-year-old would ever properly recover. The little girl whimpered pathetically, and his heart broke. It again reminded him of his own daughter back home, no longer a little girl, and the mysterious threat to their safety and the safety of so many others.

The child's stuffed bear fell from her grasp, and Sayid retrieved it, gently placing it in the crook of her arm. She reacted, embracing the bear as she rolled onto her side, pulling her knees up into the fetal position.

They had gotten very little from Heaven's Breath's lone survivor, but what they had begun to pull together from the evidence left on the island filled him with increasing dread.

"Dr. Sayid?"

The man turned to see his head of security, Brenda Langridge, in the doorway.

"How is she?" Langridge asked, her usual steely resolve replaced by a look of genuine concern. He believed that finding this child with him on the island had activated some sort of maternal instinct in the security head.

Stranger things have happened.

"Still sedated," Sayid said. "They've tried weaning her from the sleep meds, but the night terrors are still quite strong."

"Her entire family is dead, and we can only imagine what she witnessed before ending up in that chest. I wonder if it wouldn't have been better if . . ."

"It will take some time, but she'll survive," Sayid said quickly. He reached out and laid a hand upon the child's foot beneath the blanket. "I think she's quite strong."

"She's going to need to be," Langridge said, the softness in her gaze suddenly turning quite hard.

"Do you have something to report?" Sayid asked.

"I do." The woman held out a stack of papers. "The National Weather Service is currently tracking four tropical storms."

He took the papers and began to study them. "Anything that might suggest these will precede an event?"

"Not yet. Three are likely to occur out at sea, but one is causing some concern."

He continued to read the pages and found what Langridge had been referencing as she began to describe it.

"It's moving up the Eastern Seaboard," she reported, "and is likely to make landfall somewhere on the coast of Massachusetts."

The little girl in the hospital bed moaned woefully in her sleep, as if sensing Sayid's sudden feeling of dread.

CHAPTER **EIGHT**

The lobby was still full when Sidney came out from the back room, and she threw herself head-on into the chaos, helping the staff of the front desk as best she could by answering questions about medications, signing folks with their pets in for appointments, and checking them out once they'd finished. She'd even managed to answer a couple of medical questions that really didn't require Doc Martin to get involved. It was all good prep work for when she would someday have her own veterinary practice.

    Sidney had always known her life would somehow involve animals. She remembered how convinced she'd been that a show on the Animal Planet channel was in her future, even going as far as having her father record video of her interacting with local wildlife and sending it to the cable network to spotlight her talents. Needless to say, the network never called, and she began to rethink her career opportunities. It was the summer that she turned nine when she decided she was going to work for the Benediction Veterinary Hospital and pedaled her bike in ninety-degree heat across the island to the hospital to inform Doc Martin of that fact.

Sidney smiled at the recollection of how Doc Martin had put her to work feeding and watering a litter of kittens that had been abandoned on the doorstep of the hospital that morning. Martin had even given her a ride home that afternoon, tossing Sidney's pink Schwinn in the back of her Subaru wagon, and speaking with her father, who, truth be told, hadn't noticed she was gone. Doc Martin had told Dale Moore that Sidney was welcome to come and help at the hospital anytime she liked. That was all Sidney needed. She'd shown up just about every day, voraciously absorbing everything she could about the hospital, even going as far as to take Doc Martin's veterinary textbooks home to read and study.

There was no wonder that she'd wound up where she was today: top of her high school class and heading off to Tufts University, where she'd eventually enter the veterinary science program. It was like she'd been preparing for it all her life.

She'd just waited on a woman buying flea-and-tick medicine for her cat when she realized that the lobby was empty.

"Hey, look at that." She glanced from the empty lobby to the clock, noting that she'd worked through lunch and still had those tests to run for the doc. Pam and Michelle were giving each other high fives for surviving the ordeal as she headed for the back.

"Give me a holler if things get nuts again," she called out.

Snowy bounded from her bed in greeting, and Sidney gave her

some appropriate loving before getting to work on the tests that Doc Martin wanted.

She had just finished the last heartworm test when she felt her phone vibrate. Making sure that everything was done with the test first, she pulled the phone from her back pocket to see a text from Rich.

What's the word?????

She'd completely forgotten that she was supposed to ask Cody about that favor. About to send a text back saying that she was working on it, Sidney stopped, deciding that she should probably get in touch with Cody first before saying anything more.

Cody.

Again, she felt that horrible weight in her belly that threatened to grow, spreading through her limbs, dissolving her resolve and leaving her little more than a statue firmly rooted to Benediction and watching the world go by.

Dramatic, she knew, but at the same time there really was a part of her that would be willing to let her dreams of leaving the island go, to embrace the old and comfortable, and not have to think about troubling things like leaving her father and the person who, until not too long ago, she thought she loved.

It would be so much easier.

Sidney felt herself getting angry for even thinking such things. She'd wanted this for as long as she could remember, and she wasn't about to let guilt and doubt eat away at her dreams.

She considered calling Cody but doubted that he would answer while working, and the same for texting. When at work he was pretty focused on the job. Plus his father the hard-ass had a thing about cell phones.

What she had to do was obvious, but not what she wanted to do at all. She guessed that she could contact Rich and tell him Cody said no, but that would just end up contributing to the giant pool of guilt she was already carrying around. No, she pretty much knew what she would do.

A moment later Doc Martin came out from surgery, pulling off her bloody gloves and depositing them in the special waste container.

"Everything good?" Sidney asked, tidying up her work space.

"Yep, everything's fine," the doc said. She pulled a pack of cigarettes from the pocket of her lab coat and tapped one out. "Except it was five fifty in change, some aluminum foil, chicken bones, half a tennis ball, the eraser end of a pencil, and three hair barrettes inside the basset." Doc Martin put the unlit smoke in her mouth. "He was like a friggin' hairy piñata," she said, lips tight around her cigarette.

Sidney laughed.

"Hey, I've pretty much caught up here, and the front has calmed down. Would you mind if I took off early today? I've got to take care of something."

"I don't see any problem," Doc Martin said. "I was planning on closing early today anyway on account of the storm."

"Thanks."

"Everything all right?" Doc Martin asked. "Your dad doing okay?"

Sidney shrugged as she removed her lab coat. "As good as can be expected I guess." She hung the coat on one of the hooks. Snowy was watching her expectantly from her bed.

"Us old folks can be a real pain in the ass," Doc Martin said, making her laugh some more. "You'll be old yourself someday. How old are you now? Thirty-two?"

"Eighteen," she answered, suppressing a smile.

"Going on thirty-two," Doc Martin said with a nod. "So . . . Cody. Anything new with that?"

Doc Martin knew that they'd broken up, and why, and seemingly supported her decision.

"Nothing new. We're still broken up, but I'm going over to the boatyard to ask a favor for Rich Stanmore and . . . unngh." She made a face and laughed uneasily.

"Is that a smart thing to do?"

"If I didn't have to do it I'd be ecstatic, but I told Rich I would. And besides, I can't avoid seeing him forever."

"Yeah, you're probably right," the old vet said as she walked to the back door, turned the knob, and pushed it open.

The door was practically torn from her grasp in a gust of wind.

"Crap!" she said, attempting to hold on. "The wind's really picked up. You be careful out there; do what you have to do and then get home."

Snowy jumped up and was now standing attentively by Sidney's side, knowing that they were about to leave.

"If you need any help closing up, call my cell," Sidney said.

Doc Martin had used her foot to keep the door from blowing wide open again and was trying to smoke, but the wind kept pushing the smoke back in her face.

"I'll be good," she said. "I'll see you in the morning."

Sidney gave her a wave and headed out the other door to say her good-byes to the front-desk staff.

"Heading out for the day," she told them. "Everything cool?"

"A-okay, captain," Pam said. "Going anyplace good?" she asked as Sidney placed her back against the door, ready to push her way outside.

Again she made the face. "Rather be going to a funeral," she said, opening the door wide as she and Snowy left the building, escorted out by the laughter of Pam and Michelle.

But in all honesty, she really would have.

CHAPTER **NINE**

In a way, Cody Seaton was glad about the coming storm.

It had little to do with what the damaging high winds, rain, and pounding waves could do to the marina, and everything to do with the amount of work he and his harbormaster father had to do to maintain the safety of the boats still moored there.

It had everything to do with being distracted.

Cody moved down the docks. All the boats that could be removed had been yesterday—hauled back to homes or stored in the nearby boatyard. The remaining crafts were too big to move, and although ultimate responsibility for the safety of those boats rested with the owners, Cody still took it upon himself to make sure that they had been properly prepared. As he walked, he checked that all the lines were doubled and that chafing protection was in place where the dock lines passed through the fairleads and chocks or over the sides of the vessels. He checked to be sure that all the boats had ample fenders to protect their hulls when the waters became increasingly choppy.

Everything was looking pretty good, and he desperately started to go through his mental checklist to find the next thing that he could do to occupy his time.

To keep from thinking about . . .

Too late. He'd already opened that door. Before Cody knew it, his mind was racing, bringing him back to that night when his girlfriend did the unthinkable.

Just the thought of Sidney and what she had done to him filled him with equal parts anger and hurt. She had said that she didn't want to hurt him, but then turned right around and ripped the heart from his chest and threw it into the harbor.

She might as well have just shot him in the head.

Sure, they'd had their problems over the years. Who didn't? No one's relationship was 100 percent perfect, but he was at least willing to work on things.

She had said that she needed a clean break, a fresh start. But what about him? Had she even taken the time to think about what *he* might want? They had been together for so long, he couldn't imagine their lives separately, and that just made him feel sick to his stomach.

The wind was picking up, and rain had started to spatter him and the docks. Cody pulled the hood of his Windbreaker over his head and reached into his back pocket for his phone. He'd promised himself he wasn't going to do this—constantly checking to see if

Sidney had called or texted—but he did anyway. She hadn't, and it made him feel all the more terrible.

All he wanted was a chance to explain his side, how he would do anything to be with her. Things didn't have to change so dramatically just because she was heading off to college. He wanted an opportunity to be a part of that life, for them to experience it together.

He looked around the marina. His father expected him to take over as harbormaster once his dad retired, but if he had the opportunity to leave the island with Sidney . . .

His father opened the door of the office at the end of the main dock and motioned for Cody to join him. The young man slipped his phone back into his pocket and jogged over.

"Everything all right?" his father asked, squinting into the rain-swept wind.

"Yeah, everything looks good," Cody answered.

"I was watching you from the window, just standing there in the rain. You sure you're all right?"

His father knew the situation. Sidney hadn't been one of his favorite people even before the breakup, and now . . .

"Yeah . . . just thinking."

"I'm sure." His father stared at him for a moment with those eyes that always seemed to know more than they should. "Hungry?" he asked finally.

"No," Cody answered. His stomach hadn't felt right for days. He had no interest in eating.

"You need to eat."

"I know."

"Did you have anything for breakfast?"

"Yeah."

"You're lying," his father said matter-of-factly, pulling his wallet from his back pocket. "Go on to the diner and get us some lunch. Cheeseburger will do it for me; get yourself whatever."

"I'm really not hungry," Cody said as he took the money.

"You'll be surprised when you have something."

"Maybe." Cody shrugged.

"I'll hold down the fort till you get back," his father said as he shoved his wallet back into his pocket.

Cody was already heading toward his truck when he heard his father's voice again.

"Has she called you back?"

The young man stopped but did not turn. "No . . . not yet."

He braced himself, waiting for what the man would say next: *Maybe it's all for the best. . . . You can do better anyway. . . . You were always more serious than she was. . . .* But he said nothing, which in Cody's mind was the best thing he could have done.

CHAPTER TEN

Isaac's mother had found some walnuts.

She had been moving a box of cookbooks that she'd bought at a church flea market a few years back and knocked a plastic bag that had been wedged beneath a pile of aluminum pie plates and plastic take-out containers onto the floor. When she bent down to pick up the bag, she'd found the whole walnuts inside.

She had no idea where they'd come from or how long she'd had them, but she couldn't imagine that they weren't still good, and the perfect treat for her squirrel friends in the backyard.

Isaac did not want to go outside. He could hear the wind pounding at the house, the rain spattering against the windows, but his mother insisted.

"Our friends need their treat," she told him as she put on the yellow slicker that she'd found beneath ten other coats hanging over the back of a dining room chair.

Isaac knew enough not to argue with his mother, especially these days, especially since his sister Barbara had come back into their lives. Instead, he went to his room and grabbed his own raincoat from where it hung neatly in his closet.

His mother called for him again, and Isaac pulled on his coat as he hurried down the hallway to the kitchen, careful not to slip on any of the debris that was in his path. She stood at the back door, hood over her head, plastic bag of walnuts in her hand.

"Hurry up," she ordered, turning to open the door. There was a rush of wind into the kitchen, and it picked up stray pieces of paper and debris to create a mini tornado of trash.

"Hurry! Hurry!" she repeated. "Before the wind messes everything up!"

Isaac thought things were pretty messy already, but he did as he was told, passing through the swirling litter and closing the door firmly behind him as he joined his mother on the stoop.

From where he stood, Isaac could just about see Sidney's yard and house. He craned his neck to see if she might be out, but then quickly chided himself. Why would she be outside on such a horrible day? Sometimes, like his mother often said, he just wasn't thinking straight.

The backyard was as chaotic as the house. They picked their way over toys and flowerpots as they descended the steps into a large yard overgrown with weeds and wildflowers. Rusty bicycle frames, old tires, car rims, and garden statuary were nearly swallowed up by the overgrowth, and there were enough birdbaths to keep all the birds that called Benediction their home very clean indeed.

Isaac found that thought amusing, picturing cartoon birds scrubbing their backs with tiny brushes as they took their evening baths, but his musings were interrupted as a gust of wind picked up a blue kiddy pool and sent it hovering across the high grass toward them like a UFO.

"You should probably put some rocks in that," his mother said. "Don't want it blowing away." She was holding on to the back stairs' metal railing so she wouldn't lose her balance in the wind.

Isaac looked around and found a stone cherub lying on its side in the grass beside the house. One of its wings had been broken off, something his mother was going to fix, but never quite got around to. He walked over to the stone angel, lifted it up, and placed it atop the pool, looking up to see if his mother approved. But she'd already moved on, making her way through the grass to a metal bench just beside the run-down garage.

"Come over here and help me," she called to him, motioning with a hand. "We've got a lot of hungry mouths to feed."

He carefully navigated the yard, not wanting to trip on something hiding in the brush. But as he was concentrating so hard on his feet, another powerful gust took him totally unawares, and he stumbled after all, his shoe catching in the metal frame of an old bike and sending him to all fours in the high grass.

"Isaac!" his mother called out with concern.

But he could barely hear her, for the sound—that strange sound that he had heard primarily in his Steve ear—had come back and was louder now, making his head hum and his teeth rattle. He brought a dirt-covered hand up to his ear to turn down the sound, but only managed to make it squeal and crackle all the louder.

"Don't play with your hearing aids!" his mother yelled. "Come here and let me take a look at you."

He wanted to do as she asked, but the sound had frozen him in place, stealing away his ability to act. The sound had become like a voice, but a voice he could not understand, drifting in and out among the static, like a bad radio station. It was just as much inside his head as it was in his bad ear.

It was like the sound was trying to tell him something, but no matter how hard he listened, he could not understand.

The rain was starting to fall harder now, the moisture of the damp ground under his knees soaking into his pants. He didn't like the fact that he was getting wet, but he could not concentrate enough to move. Even though he knew he was not supposed to touch the hearing aids, Isaac decided that he couldn't stand it anymore. He reached up to his Steve ear to tear the device from his head.

A hand wrapped around his wrist, stopping him. He looked over and saw that his mother now stood there.

"What did I tell you?" she asked, annoyed with him. "Do you know how much those hearing aids cost us?"

He wanted to apologize, to explain what was happening, but he was unable to speak, the sound inside his brain stealing away his ability to communicate. His mouth moved noiselessly as he tried to tell her. She continued to hold on to his wrist, preventing him from reaching his Steve ear.

The sound was growing in his brain, making him feel *wrong*.

It made him feel angry. The kind of special angry that he felt when one or more of the cats got into his room and messed things up. The kind of angry that made him want to hurt things. The sound continued to fill his head with bad feelings, and he could stand it no more.

With a cry of desperation he tore his hand from his mother's grasp, grabbed at his Steve ear, and pulled away the hearing aid. The sound coming over the hearing device was silenced at once, and he could move again, his mind no longer filled with such angry, horrible thoughts.

"You better not have broken that," his mother snarled.

Isaac looked at his hand, and at the hearing device that he was holding, and hoped that he had broken it.

He never wanted to hear those horrible sounds again.

CHAPTER ELEVEN

Janice Berthold held her breath as she ran her still-bleeding hand beneath the cold water from her bathroom sink. She could feel her heart beating in the wounds, as if the powerful muscle had somehow relocated from her chest to her hand, each pulse accompanied by sharp, stabbing pain.

She squirted liquid soap into her good hand and gently rubbed the antiseptic around and into the wounds. That would be all that she would need, for the bite to get infected. Janice looked through the doorway of the bedroom bathroom at Alfred sprawled upon the floor, gnawing relentlessly on one of his toys. There was a part of her that felt a spark of anger toward the dog, but another that felt bad. The poor thing didn't know he had bitten her. He thought he was protecting himself.

Didn't he?

The French bulldog saw that she was watching him and locked eyes with her. She tried to find a sign that the dog was concerned for her, sorry for what he had done, but she saw nothing. It was like looking into the blackness of a doll's eyes.

But she knew that he loved her in his special way.

A faint noise from somewhere downstairs made Alfred bark, and she started, whacking her injured hand on the faucet. She swore at the explosion of pain, removed her hands from beneath the water, and turned the faucet off. Alfred had run off to investigate the sound, but she had already guessed what it was.

Who it was.

She could feel herself getting immediately angry, the anger using the pain of her hand to fuel its severity. Grabbing a towel, she wrapped her throbbing hand, listening for the sound of his approach.

"Honey?" her husband called from downstairs. "You up there?"

No, I'm not. . . . I've gone away someplace where I never have to hear your awful voice again, she wanted to scream, but instead—

"Yeah, I'm in the bathroom."

She dried her hand while listening to hear if he would come up to bother her further. First there was the sound of multiple paws coming up as Alfred returned, followed by Ronald's heavier footfalls.

Janice didn't want him to see her like this—injured, in pain. She could just imagine the indignities she would suffer because of it.

From a cabinet in the corner of the master bathroom, she removed some bandages and antibiotic ointment.

"Honey?"

She didn't answer, willing herself invisible—*NO,* willing herself to another part of the world. *Another planet,* if it were possible.

Ronald pushed the door open wider with a creak. She could sense him standing there, hear the sound of Alfred breathing alongside him, and again she wondered how she could have gotten here.

How she could despise another human being so much.

She must have loved him once, but in all honesty, she could not remember. The hate was so strong now it had burned away all memory of their past life, but what she did remember was what her life wasn't.

It wasn't what it was supposed to be like in the fairy tales, or in the movies. Love so satisfying that you didn't even need to eat to continue to live. He was supposed to give her that, but she came to eventually learn that it was all a lie. Ronald was supposed to give her this fantasy, but instead he gave her the monotony of life.

He wasn't a prince, or an action hero, or even a college professor.

He was a middle-aged, balding, certified public accountant, and he had tricked her into giving away the best years of her life.

Janice closed the cabinet door, catching a reflection of herself in the mirror over the sink, and wondered who the old lady was looking back at her.

"It's really starting to blow out there," Ronald started. "Got the lawn furniture into the shed before it could blow away."

"That's good," she said, watching the old woman's mouth move as hers did.

"Everything go all right at the vet? Alfred's teeth look good—nice and clean. Did he behave himself?"

She must've moved a certain way to show him her wrapped hand.

"What the hell's wrong with your hand?"

"Nothing," she said, tearing her eyes from the old woman in the mirror. "Just a little accident."

He was suddenly there beside her, taking her hand in his, unwrapping the towel. His nearness made her flesh crawl, the painful throbbing of her hand becoming almost unbearable.

"It's nothing," she told him, trying to pull her hand away.

"It's not nothing," he corrected her. "That's a bite. Who bit you? Did one of the dogs at the vet . . . Did Alfred bite you?"

Alfred was sitting on the bathroom rug, watching closely with his dark doll's eyes.

"It was an accident," she said, getting away from him before she started to scream. "There was a fight, and I got bit as I was trying to break them apart."

She left the bathroom as quickly as she could, the closeness of him like poison to her body. Alfred followed her into the bedroom, as did Ronald.

"Did you call the doctor? Maybe you should go to the emergency room . . . you're probably going to need a tetanus shot, and maybe rabies."

"I'm fine," she said, even though the pain was worse now than before. "I'm just going to bandage it up and keep it clean." She hoped that her assurances would get him to leave.

She had put the bandages and tube of antibacterial ointment down on her makeup table and thought she saw him leaving the room—

But he came up suddenly behind her.

"Let me help you with that," he said, taking the ointment from the table and grabbing her wrist.

And that was when she knew it was going to happen.

That was when Janice Berthold knew she would kill her husband.

CHAPTER **TWELVE**

The poor weather conditions were starting to intensify. Sidney held tightly to the wheel of her Jeep, struggling to keep control as the wind and rain threatened to push her from the road.

Snowy whined in the backseat, and Sidney reached back to scratch her nose, keeping her eyes on the road ahead of her. "It's all right, girl," she said, as much to reassure herself as the dog.

The visibility was bad, but Sidney finally spotted the turnoff for the marina through the driving rain. The lot was nearly empty; she didn't even see Cody's truck. Had she come all this way for nothing? The lights were on in the main office, and since she was there, she decided she might as well find out.

Throwing the hood of her light jacket up over her head, she opened the door and motioned for Snowy to exit, and the two of them ran across the puddle-filled lot to the front door of the office and quickly entered.

Cody's dad looked up from a stack of papers on his desk.

"Hi, Mr. Seaton," Sidney said, removing her dripping hood. "Is Cody around?"

"No," he said, standing and taking the papers to a file cabinet on the other side of his desk up against the wall. He pulled open the first drawer and dropped the stack of papers into it.

Snowy walked across the room to greet the man who slammed closed the drawer and turned, holding his hand out for the shepherd to sniff.

"Anything I can do for you?"

"That's all right," Sidney answered, feeling very uncomfortable. Cody's father had never been one of the most talkative of people, and he gave off an air of sternness that by instinct forced her to be on her best behavior. "I'll try and get in touch with him later." She motioned for Snowy to follow her as she flipped the hood back onto her head.

"Are you here about the two of you?" Mr. Seaton asked.

Sidney froze as she was reaching for the door. "Excuse me?"

"About the two of you," he repeated. "I know that you ended your relationship with my son the other night, and I'm wondering why you're back."

Sidney had never felt more on the spot, as if a bright light shone directly on her and alarms wailed in the distance.

"It's nothing about that," Sidney said, pulling her hood back down and playing with her hair. She wished she didn't do that when she got nervous and quickly took her hand away. "I've just got something that I need to ask him. A favor for—"

"Maybe that isn't such a good idea," Mr. Seaton interrupted.

"What do you . . ."

"Maybe it isn't a good idea for you to see him . . . talk to him, right now."

She didn't know how to respond.

"Cody was pretty broken up," Mr. Seaton explained. "He actually talked to me about it when he came home late the other night."

Mr. Seaton was standing very stiff in front of the file cabinet, as if attempting to keep everything that he was feeling from leaking out of his body, but she could see it on his face. He was angry.

At her.

"My son and I don't talk about things," he continued. "Especially things like this—personal things. It was probably something better suited for his mother, but . . ."

Cody's mom had passed away from breast cancer their first year of high school.

"He came into the house that night, and I've never seen him like that before. He's a strong boy, a good kid, but the person who came into my living room that night . . ."

Mr. Seaton stopped, and Sidney could see that he was remembering.

"That wasn't my son," he said, shaking his head. "That was just a shell."

She felt even more uncomfortable, wanting to quickly open the door and run out into the storm. Yes, she would rather have been out in the storm than in the office.

"It was a tough night," Sidney agreed. "But it had to be said."

"You were done with him," Mr. Seaton said. "It was fun while it lasted, but now it's time for you to move on."

"It's not like that."

"Accepted to a fancy college on the mainland, all kinds of new doors will be opening for you, so why would you want to have anything to do with what's back here?"

"Mr. Seaton, I don't think . . ."

"Clean house, tie up loose ends, move on, and start fresh. I get it. I'd probably do the same if I was like you."

The words hit her like a blow to the stomach.

"Like me? What's that supposed to—"

"I never could understand what he saw in you," Mr. Seaton went on. "I always figured you were just hanging around until something better came along."

"You know what?" Sidney could feel the anger surge, and her eyes burned with tears. As if sensing her emotion, Snowy moved to stand with her. "I think I've heard enough."

"Watching my nineteen-year-old son cry made me think of all the things I've lost, and how I'd never wanted Cody to ever feel as bad. And yet, I think he felt worse." His voice trembled with emotion.

Sidney managed to get the door open.

"I won't tell him you were here," he added as she and Snowy stepped out into the storm, slamming the door behind them.

Sidney stood trembling in the rain, not from the raw dampness, but from hurt and anger. Things she wanted to say raced through her mind, and she was tempted to go back inside and really let him have it, but something held her back.

Was he right?

Sure, she had loved Cody as much as any fifteen-year-old high school girl was capable of loving somebody, but that love had changed as she'd gotten older and began to realize that the world was a much bigger place than Benediction Island. Was it sad that their love had lessened? Sure it was, but it didn't mean that what they'd shared had been a lie. They'd loved each other once and that was great, but now . . .

She reached up with a trembling hand to wipe away the scalding tears that were running down her cheeks. Snowy was watching her with curious eyes.

"I'm all right, girl," she lied to the dog. "Let's go back to the Jeep."

She had just started to jog with Snowy by her side when she heard the car horn. A red Honda Accord was coming down the drive, and she watched as it pulled into a parking spot not far from where she'd left her Jeep.

Rich Stanmore climbed from the car, pulling the collar up on his jacket as he approached.

"Hey," he said. "Did you talk to Cody?"

"No," Sidney started, just as Cody's blue pickup truck pulled up in front of the marina's office. Could things get any worse?

"Hey, there he is," Rich said cheerfully.

The door to the pickup swung open, and Cody climbed out, holding a large white bag.

"Hey, bro!" Rich called out, waving.

"Don't," Sidney warned, already getting a sense that things were about to become very bad.

Cody started toward them, his pace quickening the closer he came. When he dropped the lunch bag onto the wet parking lot ground, she realized that her biggest fears were about to come true.

Cody had never liked Rich or her friendship with him. It had always been a sore spot in their relationship. He had even accused her of breaking up with him to date Rich. Having Rich here now was a recipe for disaster.

"I asked Sidney to talk to you, but since I'm here—"

Before Rich could finish, Cody lunged at him with a curse-laced growl, grabbing him by the front of his coat and pushing him back onto the hood of his car.

"Dude!" Rich yelled in surprise.

"Cody, no!" Sidney cried, trying to pull her ex from atop her friend, as Snowy barked frantically.

"I knew it!" Cody lifted Rich up and slammed him down onto the hood again.

"What the hell are you . . ." Rich asked, still trying to figure out why he was being attacked.

Sidney grabbed at Cody's hands.

"That's enough, Cody," she said firmly.

"I can't believe you two," he said, lost in his anger. "Coming here to rub my face in it."

"It's not what you think," Sidney said, and she managed to rip one of his hands from Rich's jacket, slapping it away as Cody attempted to grab it again.

"It's not what you think!" She screamed this time, thinking maybe the louder she said it, the better chance it might have of sinking in.

He batted her hand away and she shrieked. It hurt like hell, and for a second she was afraid of him, afraid of the boy she used to love.

It was her scream that took things in another direction. Cody stopped for a second, concern appearing on his face, giving Rich a chance to collect himself.

Pushing off from the hood of his car, Rich punched Cody in the jaw, sending him stumbling to the right. Snowy was going wild, barking and growling crazily, trying to involve herself in the violence, wanting it to stop. Sidney grabbed the dog by the collar, pulling her away from the fight. Rich didn't let up, following through with another punch before Cody could recover.

"What is wrong with you?" he shouted, hitting Cody again. "I didn't do shit to you!"

Cody blocked Rich's next swing, coming in low in a tackle, sending them both to the wet ground in a heap of swinging fists.

"You ruined everything," Sidney heard Cody say as he crawled atop Rich, directing punches at his face.

She couldn't stand it anymore, again going in to try and break it up. She also let Snowy go, and the dog darted in, snarling and snapping threateningly at the two.

"Get off of him," she commanded, wrapping her arm around Cody's neck in a headlock and using all her strength to pull him off. Rich managed to get his leg under him and kicked out, hurling Cody away.

She hadn't seen Mr. Seaton come out of the office, and he was suddenly there, between them, cell phone in hand.

"Am I going to need to call the police?" he asked, loud enough for them all to hear.

"You son of a bitch," Cody spat, getting to his feet.

"C'mon," Rich urged angrily. "Let's see how good you are when I'm ready."

"Did you two hear me?" Mr. Seaton asked. He got in front of his son, thumping him back with his chest. He then turned around to face Rich.

"I'll have you both thrown in jail for fighting on my property without thinking twice."

He glared at them, one and then the other.

"Go ahead . . . try me."

No one moved, and Mr. Seaton abruptly turned and headed back to the office.

"Cody," he called as he walked. "Where's my lunch?"

Cody managed to tear his gaze away from Rich, then walked to the rain-saturated white bag and picked it up carefully, bringing it to his father and leaving Sidney and Rich alone outside.

"What the hell was that all about?" Rich asked, touching his lip and checking his fingers for blood.

"We broke up the other night," Sidney said, watching the door to the office.

"You broke up?"

"Yeah, and he thinks it was because of you."

"Because of me? Shit."

The door of the office opened, and Cody stepped out. Sidney had to grab Snowy's collar to keep her from running to him.

"No more, Cody," Sidney warned.

"Go," he said, waving them away with his hands. "My dad wants you both off the property immediately, and so do I."

Sidney couldn't stand it anymore.

"What is wrong with you?" she demanded, not bothering to hide her anger.

"Back off, Sid," he told her. "Take your new boyfriend and—"

"Cut the shit, Cody," she screamed. "You know full well that Rich isn't my boyfriend."

"It's true, Cody," Rich said. "The only reason I'm here is that I asked Sidney to find out if you could give me a hand with my sailboat."

Cody looked at her hard, she could see that his eyes looked hot—moist. He was on the verge of tears.

"You can tell me. I'm a big boy."

"There's nothing to tell, Cody," she said, bringing the volume down. She let Snowy go, and the dog went to him, hungry for his affection.

"Dude, if I'd known the two of you weren't together I never woulda asked," Rich said sympathetically.

"So why are you both here . . . together?" Cody asked.

"Because I came to ask you the favor alone so something like this wouldn't happen, but you weren't here. I had a lovely chat with your father, by the way," she added sarcastically.

"And I hadn't heard from her, so I thought I would come down and ask myself. Then I saw that Sid was here and . . ."

"Shit," Cody said, lowering his gaze and focusing his attentions on Snowy, which was fine by her.

"Yeah," Sidney agreed.

"I called you, and you didn't get back to me," Cody went on. "So my imagination was already running wild when I pulled into the parking lot and saw the two of you. . . ."

"Understandable, I guess," Rich said.

"No, it isn't," Sidney answered angrily. "I told you why we were breaking up, and it had nothing to do with anybody else, but you still didn't believe me and had to come up with some reason to make me look even worse in your eyes than I already do."

"Sid," he started, looking up into her angry gaze. "I'm sorry."

"You should be," she shot back. "And you hit me back there."

"I was slapping your hand away and—"

"You hit me," she said more forcefully. "If you even think about doing something like that to me again I will most certainly press charges. Do we understand each other?"

She could see the shock in his expression, and she genuinely did believe that he was sorry, but she needed him to know that it wasn't cool in the least to put his hands on her. *Ever.* No matter the situation.

"Yes," Cody said. "I'm so sorry." Nervously he started to pet Snowy again.

"Then we don't need to mention it again," she said.

Things then got awkward as they stood there in the rain, each of them hoping that the other would say something to shatter the uncomfortable silence.

Sidney concentrated on the weather. It was getting worse, the wind and rain picking up, the clouds in the sky above them moving and swirling about so quickly they could have been smoke.

She was just going to comment on it when—

"Sorry I attacked you," Cody finally said to Rich, eyes darting about nervously. "There was no reason for it, and I feel like a complete ass."

"It's cool," Rich said, then stepped forward and extended his hand.

Cody looked at it for a moment before taking it in his. They shook firmly then quickly let go, stepping back. Sidney doubted the two would ever be best friends, but it was a start.

"This weather's getting not so nice," Sidney said to change the subject, squinting as she looked up into the ferocious sky.

"The weather guys said that it would be getting bad in the afternoon," Cody added.

"Which makes the timing on that favor even more crucial," Rich said.

"What's the favor again?" Cody asked. "Probably the least I could do after kicking your ass."

"You kicked *my* ass?" The favor was suddenly pushed aside by his ego. "If there was any ass kicked today it was me firmly placing my foot against your—"

"C'mon, don't you think I've had my fill of this crap today?"

Sidney asked with disgust. "Ask your favor please, before I lose my patience," she told Rich.

"I was hoping that you could help me get my sailboat out of the water before the storm," Rich said.

Cody looked up into the angry sky. "Looks like you might be a little late."

"Yeah, but if we hurry we might be able to miss the worst of it. What do you say?"

Cody looked to Sidney. "Probably the least that I could do, huh?"

Sidney agreed. "Probably."

Yes, Rich mouthed, pumping the air with his fist.

CHAPTER **THIRTEEN**

The storm had grown from bad to even worse in a short amount of time. Sidney was having a difficult time seeing through the deluge assailing her wipers. She was following Rich's car back to his parents' place, with Cody following her in his truck. For an instant back at the marina, Sidney had considered leaving the boys to handle this on their own, but something told her that might not have been the best of ideas, the potential of a fight breaking out all too real. So here she was.

"Really coming down, eh, Snowy?" she asked her dog, who leaned forward from the backseat, peering through the torrential downpour. It was like somebody was spraying a hose directly onto the windshield.

Up ahead she saw the flash of Rich's brake lights, followed by a left-turn blinker, which told her that they had arrived. Rich pulled his car over to a spot in front of the large two-story house, and she took one right beside it. She waited, listening to the incessant sound of pelting rain as Cody parked his truck near the two-car garage where the boat's trailer had been left.

When Cody had asked why the sailboat hadn't been taken from the water sooner, Rich had said that he and his parents had hoped to have at least a few more weekends of sailing before the inevitable end of the summer season. Normally his dad would have taken care of removing the boat, but he'd been called away by bank business, which meant that Rich could either take the risk of leaving the boat out during the hurricane or do something about it. He loved the boat and decided a quick weekend trip to Benediction, and hopefully some assistance from friends, would be in order.

"Do you want to stay here or come out in the rain?" Sidney asked Snowy.

"Woof!" the shepherd said.

"I thought so." Sidney rubbed the dog affectionately behind the ears, then she opened the car door, and they both got out into the pouring rain.

Cody was already backing the truck up toward the trailer so Rich could attach it.

"That's good!" Rich yelled, and the truck came to a stop.

He began to attach the trailer to the hitch as Cody jumped out of the truck and headed back to help. Sidney was glad to see them getting along so well, for the moment anyway.

"Anything that I can do?" she asked, voice raised to be heard over the heavy rainfall.

"We're good," Cody said, inspecting the connection. Rich gave her a thumbs-up as the two of them returned to the truck cab.

Why am I here again? she thought, becoming more and more rain-saturated each passing second. *Oh yes, so my ex-boyfriend and my friend don't kill each other. That's it.*

The truck pulled away with the boat trailer in tow, and she considered going back to her car to wait until they'd finished, but since she was already soaked . . .

"C'mon, girl," she said, motioning to Snowy for her to follow. "Let's go see if the guys are gonna be able to do this." She followed the side road, which went down to the beach and to the Stanmore's private dock. The wind was really getting intense, and a few times she thought for sure that it might topple her over. She considered that the weather might have gotten too bad for the guys to pull this off.

They must have sensed that their time was limited as well. The water of the bay looked almost black, reflecting the anger in the shifting clouds in the sky above, and Sidney felt the concern for her friends growing as they began to interact with the rough waters. She moved closer, watching carefully as they worked, Rich now on board the sailboat, its masts already removed, as he used the engine to carefully drive the boat onto the partially submerged trailer.

Sidney held her breath as the boat was secured, with Cody turning the winch that gradually pulled the boat onto the trailer. The sky had grown even darker, the blackness of it all seeming to be pressing down, coming closer to the land. There was a feeling in the air that she didn't like, a growing apprehension that seemed to foreshadow that something terrible was about to happen. A sudden tingling across the surface of her flesh made the tiny hairs on the back of her neck stand at attention. Snowy had begun to whine, telling her that something was most definitely up.

"Are we almost done, guys?" she yelled as she moved closer. They of course ignored her, as they finished hauling the sailboat from the water.

"Guys?" she called again.

"Yeah," Rich said, pulling on the straps that secured the boat on the trailer.

"Almost," Cody answered over the increasing wail of the wind.

It felt as though there was an electrical current suddenly running through her arms and legs, and she stamped her feet on the saturated ground to try to dispel the strange, tingling sensation.

"Something isn't right," she said as she noticed Snowy suddenly tensed, hackles raised, lips peeled back in a savage snarl as she, too, reacted to the bizarre atmospheric change.

Sidney didn't know what to do or how she should react. The sky was black and churned and swirled above her, and at the moment she didn't believe that there was anyplace where she would be safe.

She was about to call out to them again when she noticed that Rich and Cody were both returning to the truck, Rich now giving her the double thumbs-up as they climbed into the front seats. The engine of the vehicle revved loudly, and the truck slowly advanced, pulling the trailer and sailboat from the water. She had started to walk back up the road toward the house when it happened.

When the heavens roared, and there was a searing flash that stole away her sight, and for a brief moment Sidney thought it could very well have been the end of the world.

CHAPTER **FOURTEEN**

It was like the storm was speaking to her—*screaming at her*—telling Janice to do it—*do it now*—or the moment would be lost forever.

The sound from outside was all encompassing, surrounding the house completely in its furious message.

Alfred yelped loudly as the lights flickered, and the power went out.

"Great," Ronald said, standing beside her in the darkness.

Yes, yes it is, she thought, listening to the urgings of the storm. She reached out toward the top of her bureau for the bronze statue of a French bulldog that she had gotten from a dear friend the week Alfred had come to live with them.

"Do we have a flashlight up here, or is the one downstairs the only . . ."

Janice followed the sound of his disgusting voice, the promise of never ever hearing it again adding an almost preternatural strength to her arm as she smashed the bronze statue into the side of his face. He went down with a yelp of surprise, and she stood above him still clutching the bronze Frenchie. She could smell something strong and coppery—her husband's blood. Even the stuff that coursed through his veins disgusted her beyond belief.

It was dark in the room, and through squinted eyes she tried to find where he had fallen, finally zeroing in on the sound of his labored breathing. He lay on his stomach, legs moving as he attempted to crawl. Janice straddled her husband, at first disappointed that he was still alive, and then strangely excited.

That meant that she would get to hit him again.

Ronald rolled over onto his side, and she could just about make out the wide whites of his eyes as he looked up at her.

"Why?" he managed as she found the strength to lift the bronze dog up over her head.

"Because I hate you," she answered in all its cruel simplicity as she brought the statue down upon his head.

CHAPTER **FIFTEEN**

Sidney had never heard a clap of thunder so loud or seen a lightning flash so bright.

On instinct, she had immediately dropped to her knees in the rain, blobs of undulating color writhing before her eyes in reaction to the nearly blinding flare.

"Sidney!" she heard Cody call out to her. She could just about make out the shape of the truck ahead of her and her ex-boyfriend leaping from the driver's seat to help her up and bring her and Snowy back to the car.

"What the hell was that?" she asked, both scared and a little embarrassed.

"I have no idea, but I don't think we should be out here anymore," Cody said, sliding into the driver's seat as she squirmed closer to Rich.

"Take us up to the house," Rich said. "We'll stay there till this dies down."

Cody brought the truck up to the front of the building with the sailboat in tow. The rain was falling in what seemed to be a single sheet. Even though they were no more than ten feet from the house, they could barely make it out in the drenching torrent. After putting the truck in park, Cody turned off the engine. They all sat there, listening to the nearly deafening hiss of the storm. Their visibility was zero through the truck's windshield; they might as well have been underwater.

"Are you okay?"

Sidney realized that Cody was talking to her, and she looked at him.

"I'm fine."

"You're shaking," he said.

She realized that he was right and chalked it up to being wet and cold, although she knew it was more than that.

"I'm soaked," she said, throwing her arm around Snowy and giving her a quick hug. "Let's get inside and dry off."

They exited the car into the ferocity of the storm. If it wasn't for being directly behind Rich as he ran, she could imagine herself getting lost and wandering off in the opposite direction. It was crazy; she could honestly say that she'd never seen rain like this before.

They all stood behind Rich, urging him to hurry as he fished his keys from his pocket to open the door. Then they rushed in, desperate to be out of the wet.

"Shit," Rich said, flicking a light switch up and down. He

walked down the hall and to the left, peering into the room beyond. "Power's out. No clock on the microwave."

"That's all right," Sidney said. "Just as long as it isn't raining on us, I'm fine."

Snowy shook violently, and Cody leaped back with a squawk.

"Do you mind?" he asked the dog, who wagged her tail lovingly as she looked at him.

"Do you have an old towel that I can use to wipe up?" Sidney asked Rich.

"Yeah, sure," he said, walking into the dark kitchen.

He returned with a flashlight and a roll of paper towels.

"Catch!" he said, tossing the roll to her.

Sidney pulled off a few sheets and went to work drying the hardwood floor.

"So was that really just thunder that seemed to shake the planet?" she asked.

"I don't know what it was," Cody said. He motioned for the paper towels and pulled off a length to dry himself. "It sounded more like a bomb went off."

"I'm surprised it didn't shatter any windows," Rich said, perusing the living room on the opposite side of the foyer, his flashlight beam moving from window to window.

He returned to where they were all standing.

"Well, that was fun," he said, and smiled in typical Rich fashion.

"Yeah, it was a blast," Cody replied with a taint of sarcasm, rubbing a wad of paper towels over his dark, wet hair.

They found their way into the kitchen and gathered around the granite-topped island in the middle of the room. Rich left the flashlight in the center of the countertop to give them some light.

"Still sounds pretty nasty out there," he said, leaning against the island.

They all listened and could still hear the pounding rain and wind, but strangely enough there wasn't any more thunder.

The sound they heard next was more localized and sounded like a cartoon spring being let go. Sidney's hand went to her stomach.

"Oh crap," she said, and laughed. "Did you hear that?"

"Oh my God," Rich said, laughing. "I didn't know what the hell that was."

"I'm starving," she said, defending herself.

"I'm pretty hungry too," Cody agreed.

"Shouldn't have thrown your lunch in the parking lot," Rich said with a smirk.

"Screw you."

"You got anything to eat?" Sidney asked hopefully.

Rich looked around the kitchen. "House was pretty much closed up for the summer," he said. He went to the cabinets and began opening the doors. "I don't think there's anything up here."

He slammed the last of doors and lowered his hands. Sidney noticed him reacting to something as he reached into the pocket of his jacket.

"Aha!" he said pulling something out and dropping it in the center of the granite island. "Boom!" he added. "Who's the man?"

It was a half-eaten package of Starburst candies.

"I do believe there are three left."

"Looks good to me," Sidney said, peeling away part of the outer paper to help herself to one of the candy pieces. She was hoping for cherry but got lemon instead. *Beggars can't be choosers,* she thought as she unpeeled the candy and popped it into her mouth.

"Go ahead," Rich said, gesturing for Cody to help himself.

"Nah." Cody stepped back. "I hate friggin' Starburst."

Rich rolled his eyes, reaching for the remaining candy and choosing one.

Sidney studied Cody as she chewed the sour candy.

"I never really noticed before," she said in between chews, staring at him.

"What's that?" Cody asked.

"That you can be a real jerk a lot of the time."

CHAPTER SIXTEEN

She'd only had the chance to fully cook one of the microwave dinners before the power went out.

Caroline peeled the plastic covering back on the one that had only partially cooked, sticking her fingers into the mashed potatoes to see how hot they were. They were barely warm, with areas of cold. She didn't hold out much hope that the Salisbury steak was any hotter.

"This one only got cooked halfway," she said to her son, who was holding a glass jar with a candle burning within.

"That's all right," Isaac said. "I'm not hungry."

His free hand twitched at his side as he held back the urge to fiddle with his hearing aid.

"Well I'm not going to waste it," she said. "And don't even think about touching that hearing aid again. We're very lucky that you didn't break it. There's no way to fix it if you do, you know—so leave it."

"Yes, Mother," he said, not making eye contact with her.

She knew he was upset with her for yelling at him, but if she hadn't, he would have broken those hearing aids. He'd had problems with that ear in the past, and the audiologist had adjusted things so it should have been working fine, but who knows what he had been up to when she wasn't watching him.

"Here," she said, handing him the colder of the meals. "Eat what you can. I don't want you complaining later that you're hungry."

With his twitchy hand he took the dinner from her.

"I'm going to eat in my room," he told her.

"No, we're going to eat together," she corrected. "Just like a family should."

She could see him looking about the kitchen, and the less-than-clutter-free environment that existed. Yes, she was well aware that the house was a bit messy, but she was working on it.

That made Caroline think of her daughter again and the strangers coming into her home to film how filthy she was for all the world to see, and that just made her angry.

"We'll eat in the living room," she stated firmly, taking her dinner and plastic silverware and making her way from the kitchen.

Normally she would have enjoyed some television while eating, but with no power there wasn't any chance of that. She knew that she had some batteries around someplace and considered sending Isaac to look for them, but decided that could wait, that maybe the power would return shortly, and there would be no need for batteries.

"Hold that candle a little higher," she ordered her son, who was walking behind her. "I can't see when you hold it so low."

"Sorry," Isaac mumbled.

She hated to be cross with the boy, but as he'd gotten older, he'd become more defiant, wanting things done his way. She let him think he was the boss when it came to his room, but that was as far as she let him go. Isaac thought he was a man, but to her, he would always be her little boy and would always need her to care for him, even if he thought otherwise.

She carefully made her way across the uneven landscape of the living room, not wanting to tip over any of the stacked boxes or piles of important belongings on her way to the area of the room that she liked to call her nest.

"You can set the candle right there," she told her son, motioning with her microwaved dinner to a relatively flat surface on top of magazines that had been stacked on the coffee table. She'd been meaning to go through those.

Isaac did as he was told, placing the candle down and partially illuminating the semiopen area where she liked to enjoy her television programs.

Caroline lowered herself into the chair at the center of her nest. She grunted as her butt sank into the cushion, the springs barely able to support her weight anymore. She would have to think about replacing it someday.

Someday.

Placing the serving tray of her dinner on her lap, she proceeded to peel away what remained of the plastic covering. She looked up from her steaming plate to see Isaac just standing there.

"Aren't you going to sit?" she asked her son. His face was eerily illuminated in the light of the candle.

He looked around. "There isn't anyplace."

"Of course there is," she corrected, annoyance in her voice. "Just move some things. Find a place." She waved her plastic fork around in a general area.

Isaac seemed to be looking where she was pointing. He then turned and placed his own meal on a stack that looked relatively stable.

"You won't get angry if I move this?" he asked about a mound of things that she could not discern.

"I won't be angry," she said, eyeing the pile as she popped a piece of Salisbury steak into her mouth and began to chew.

Isaac bent over, grabbed hold of the heap, and lifted it up from the floor. He gasped as living things quickly scurried away from the sudden exposure.

"What was that? What's wrong?"

Isaac dropped the armful and stepped back. "Mice," he said, catching his breath.

"Mice?" she asked incredulously. "How could there be mice? Are you sure? Maybe it was just a trick of the candlelight."

"I know what mice look like, Mother."

"But how could there be mice? We've got cats and . . ."

And that was when she noticed something peculiar. Perhaps it was because the lights were off, but Caroline suddenly realized that there weren't any cats around.

"I know we have cats, but those were most definitely mice," Isaac went on.

"Where are they?" Caroline asked, looking around the room, the dark corners made even darker by the fact that there was little light. "Where are the cats?" Even Mrs. Livingstone, who was always there to beg for a piece of her meal, was nowhere to be seen.

Caroline started to make the noises that usually brought her fur babies to her.

Had they somehow gotten out? Did Isaac leave the door open, and they all escaped out into the yard?

Panic began to set in.

She placed the remains of her meal on the cluttered floor and began to stand, wanting to search the room for herself. She felt something cold poke her hand, and before she could see what it was, there was a sharp stab of pain.

Caroline cried out, falling back down into her nest as she pulled her hand away.

"What is it?" Isaac asked.

"Something bit me," she said, examining the bleeding wound in the fleshy part of her hand before bringing it to her mouth to suck on.

"Probably a mouse," Isaac said, eyes darting around the room.

"We don't have mice," she said, taking her hand from her mouth. "We have cats."

The concern for her babies began to rise again, and she pushed herself up from her seat. "I have to find them," she said. "Help me, Isaac." She motioned with the noninjured hand for him to take it so she would not lose her footing on the debris-strewn floor. "We have to make sure that none of the doors were left open."

"I don't think we left any—"

"We have to check," she barked at him, desperate to find her cats.

They were making their way across the uneven surface of the living room when they heard unfamiliar sounds.

Caroline stopped, looking around, attempting to zero in on the rustling noises. They seemed to be coming from all around them.

"Pretty kitties," she said in a high, squeaky voice. "Is that you?" Again she made the noise that normally brought them to her. "Why are you hiding from Mommy?"

Mrs. Livingstone was the first to appear, her large head emerging from the shadows atop the china cabinet in the corner of the room.

"There you are," Caroline said happily. The cat just stared at her with large, unblinking eyes, and as Caroline stared back, she noticed something of concern. Perhaps it was a trick of the light, but it was something that she was going to need to check once she had the chance.

Is that some kind of a film coating Mrs. Livingstone's right eye?

Binky, Shadow, Cavendish, and Nero were the next to appear, each of them silently emerging from their hiding places.

Are their right eyes looking funny too?

She was about to mention this to her son when she noticed the strangest of things, odd at first and then, as the realization of what she was looking at sank in, *disturbing*.

"Do you see that?" she asked Isaac, wanting to be sure that it wasn't a trick of what little light was being thrown by the candle.

"I do," he answered, his hand going up again to play with his hearing aid. This time she did not stop him. She was more concerned about what she was seeing.

Her cats were perched atop pieces of furniture, boxes, and years of accumulation, watching her and her boy with unwavering gazes.

Around the cats, in numbers too great to comprehend, were mice.

And the mice were watching them too.

CHAPTER SEVENTEEN

"Did you hear what I said?" Janice Berthold asked her husband, who was lying dead upon the floor. "I hate you."

Her eyes had adjusted to the darkness, and she could just about make out the shape of her husband's body. She pulled back a foot and kicked him as hard as she could.

It felt surprisingly good, but not as good as the sensation she'd experienced when she'd smashed the statue into his face. She felt a flush of warmth on her cheeks and needles of sweat breaking out over her body.

Janice looked down again at the body before her, searching for any sign of movement, but she saw nothing.

Have I actually done it? she wondered.

It was something she had dreamed about doing for far longer than she cared to think. There had even been times when driving with him that she'd been tempted to reach across and grab the wheel, to send them careening off into space with the hope that he would die horribly, but she would survive.

She'd never wanted to take the risk that he might survive as well.

Continuing to watch the body at her feet, she still saw no signs of life, but she had to be sure. Janice squatted down to the floor, tentatively reaching a hand out to grab his wrist and check for a pulse. Her hand landed in something warm and thick puddling on the floor beneath her husband and quickly recoiled. She could see the dark, nearly black blood covering the side of her hand and almost cried out in disgust but managed to hold it together.

A little blood was a small price to pay to guarantee that he was actually dead.

Pulling herself together, she reached out again, taking hold of his limp wrist, feeling for a heartbeat. As far as she could tell, there was nothing, but she still didn't trust it. Letting his hand drop back to the floor, she reached up to the collar of his shirt, her fingers searching for his neck, where she would again attempt to verify if he still lived.

And what if he does?

Janice's mind raced. She supposed that she could always hit him again with the statue or maybe just pinch his nostrils closed and cover his mouth. She imagined that would do the trick as well.

His skin was going clammy as she pressed the flesh around his neck for signs that his heart was still pumping. As with his wrist, there was nothing that she could find.

A giddy laughter bubbled up from somewhere deep and dark; she might have actually done it.

But her happiness was short lived, almost immediately replaced with wondering what she was going to do now. Different scenarios began to play within her mind. She could call the police and say that there had been an attempted burglary, and that there had been a struggle and . . . If she used that one she was going to have to be certain to either dispose of the murder weapon or thoroughly wipe it down. She could always dispose of the body, and then report him missing. Disposal possibilities danced through her fevered mind.

Janice had been thinking about these things for a very long time, and now all she had to do was pick the one that guaranteed she would not be suspected of any wrongdoing.

She was trying to remember where Ronald stored their saws and plastic leaf tarp when she experienced the eerie sensation that she was being watched.

Still squatting by her husband's body, Janice slowly turned toward the bedroom doorway.

Alfred sat there, perfectly still, watching her.

"It's all right, baby," she told the dog. Janice reached out her uninjured hand, trying to coax the Frenchie to come closer. Alfred remained in that spot, large dark eyes fixed upon her.

At first she thought it was just light reflecting unusually off the surface of the dog's right eye, but the longer she stared . . .

"Alfred, is there something wrong with your eye?"

She climbed to her feet, slowly approaching the animal, not wanting him to run.

"Let me see," she said, focusing on what appeared to be some kind of glistening—almost metallic-looking—film over his right eye.

Looks like another trip to the vet, she thought, annoyed that this latest ailment hadn't manifested until after his last visit to the veterinarian's office.

Alfred suddenly sprang at her, forty pounds of French bulldog connecting with her midsection and knocking her backward into the room, where she tripped over her own feet and landed upon the corpse of her husband . . .

. . . who turned beneath her with a low, horrible moan and wrapped his arms around her.

Not a corpse at all.

CHAPTER **EIGHTEEN**

Rich reached the bottom of the wooden steps and stepped onto the dirt floor, his flashlight beam playing over the cellar space.

"Find anything?" Sidney called from the kitchen upstairs.

"Give me a freakin' minute, would you?" he asked, annoyed.

They were all still hungry, even after the Starbursts, and he told them that he thought he remembered seeing some canned goods down in the basement.

Sidney thought it was a great idea for him to look, so what choice did he have? If it had been Cody's idea, he probably would have just told him to choke the last Starburst down or suffer.

But it had been Sidney who'd asked, and he would have gone out into the hurricane to pick her wild berries if she'd asked. Rich had secretly harbored a crush on Sidney for the last two years or so. He had never done anything about it, her being with Cody and all, but now . . .

"Anything?" Sidney called playfully to him again.

"Will you shut it?" he said as he walked across the unfinished cellar to where his parents had set up some shelving to store emergency items for times very much like this. The storm was still going pretty fast and furious outside, and he hadn't a clue how long they might be holed up there, so he hoped that there was something on the shelves even remotely appetizing, or they were screwed.

Rich navigated the cramped space. The place had pretty much become storage for junk; stacks of old patio furniture, boat cleaning supplies, and boxes of beach toys were scattered about the room, placed upon wooden pallets to keep them up from the damp dirt floor.

The edge of his flashlight beam caught movement, and he shined it down to the floor to see the segmented body of a good-size centipede disappearing beneath a pile of garden tools. A shudder of revulsion went through his body as he reached the shelves.

"Bingo," he said, finding that there were more cans on display than he expected. He shined the flashlight beam onto the cans to read the contents. There were lots of vegetables—peas and green beans making up the majority—but he doubted that was what Sidney had a hankering for.

And that had been the problem for years.

He'd wanted to talk to her about how he felt, but he was never quite sure how she would react. There were times when he thought he was getting a clear message and would psyche himself up to tell her his feelings, but then she'd say something about Cody and her relationship, and the wind would get totally taken out of his sails.

That was just how it had been, and he'd pretty much given up on anything ever happening, until this afternoon in the marina parking lot when things suddenly changed.

"You'd better not be eating all the good stuff," Sidney warned from the kitchen.

He ignored her, reaching for more cans and hoping for something other than vegetables. On the shelf below the veggies he found a can of SpaghettiOs with meatballs and felt as though he'd hit the lottery.

"Oh yes," he said, taking the can, discovering that there were other delectable meals on the shelf as well—cans of cheese ravioli and corned beef hash. He tried to take them all into his arms while still holding the flashlight, which resulted in the SpaghettiOs falling to the ground.

"Shit," he muttered, bending down carefully so as not to cause the other cans to tumble, and felt around for the wayward canned feast. His fingers touched it but also something else—something that tickled the flesh of his hand before the incredible sting of pain.

"Yarrrah!" Rich screamed, dropping all the cans as he pulled his hand away and held it up before the light. The skin had already started to redden and swell.

Something had bitten him.

The image of that centipede crawling beneath the tools filled his head, and he shuddered. Whatever it was that had bitten him, it hurt like hell.

"What's going on down there?" Sidney called out.

"Nothing," Rich said, feeling embarrassed. "I'm coming up with a feast fit for royalty."

He shined his light around the fallen cans and saw that there was nothing in their immediate area. But as he squatted down to retrieve them, the dirt seemed to come alive.

"What the f . . . ," he began, the beam of his flashlight still illuminating the ground.

There were bugs coming up out of the dirt. Not just one or two, but lots, hundreds, and it wasn't even just one particular kind. He saw carpenter ants, centipedes, earwigs, and some kind of beetle that he wasn't at all familiar with.

There were all coming up out of the damp earth of the cellar floor and crawling toward him.

Rich backed up, deciding to leave the cans, and felt a sudden pain beneath the collar of his shirt.

"Ahhh!" He slapped his hand to his neck and felt something crunch and squirt with the impact. Bringing his hand away from his neck, he shined the light on his fingers and saw the remains of a pretty large spider.

"That's it," he said, turning for the stairs. The beam of his light briefly touched the floor, where in every inch of dirt crawled some kind of disgusting bug.

He didn't understand what it was that he was seeing, telling himself that maybe the storm had something to do with it, the foul weather somehow stirring up the bugs that lived beneath his house. Before reaching the stairs, he glanced up to the ceiling and saw that it wasn't just the floor that was crawling with life.

Spiders. There were spiders everywhere that the light of the flashlight touched, and they all seemed to be heading toward him.

Rich ran for the stairs. He could feel the bodies of the harder-shelled insects crunching beneath his sneakers as he ran across them, but that was nothing compared to the absolute horror that he experienced as he saw the spiders dropping down on their silken lines, some landing upon him and crawling up toward his face at incredible speeds.

Crying out, he flailed his arms crazily, slapping at his body, diving for the first step, and nearly smashing his face as he fell, sprawling across the ascending stairs.

"What's going on?" Sidney asked, appearing in the doorway above. He had dropped the flashlight and had no intention of looking for it.

"Get out of the way," he said, trying to keep the panic from his voice as he got his feet beneath him and sprinted up the steps.

"Rich, what is it?" she asked, obviously concerned. He gripped her by the shoulders and moved her out of the way as he slammed the cellar door closed.

Cody was smiling nervously by the granite island. "What?" he asked. "I thought you said you found food?"

He was about to tell Cody what he could do with the food when he felt movement just beneath his hairline, followed by sudden pain.

"Damn it!" he screamed, slapping at the back of his neck.

"What the hell is going on?" Sidney asked.

A spider the size of a quarter landed on the floor and started to crawl toward Rich's sneakered foot. He stomped on it, grinding it into the tile floor.

"Gross," Sidney said. "That was huge."

"They're all over the cellar," he managed, his voice sounding raspy and out of breath.

"Spiders?" Cody asked.

"Everything!" Rich shouted.

He thought he felt more movement and reacted violently, tearing his shirt up and over his head and shaking it out.

"Are you all right?" Sidney asked.

He could see that she was smiling, trying not to laugh.

Cody didn't have that willpower. "Dude, you should see yourself."

"You should see what it's like down there," Rich said. "The place is infested."

"Infested?" Sidney asked. "Did you ever have a bug problem before?"

Rich shook his head. "No, nothing like this." He was starting to calm down a bit but still shook his shirt some more just in case.

Cody was really laughing now, and it was taking just about everything Rich had not to go over and smack him, but Sidney was laughing as well, even though she tried to hide it by covering her mouth with her hand.

"Yeah, laugh it up you two," he said, angrily. "I'd like to see the two of you go down there and . . ."

Sidney was looking around him to the cellar door, and he turned to see that Snowy was pawing at something.

"What have you got, girl?" Sidney asked, going over to the dog to see.

The white shepherd had her nose close to the bottom of the cellar door and had started to whine, backing away with a growl.

"What is it, Snowy?"

There was suddenly a steady flow of insects coming from beneath the door.

"Shit," Sidney exclaimed, reaching for her dog to pull her away. "Do you see this?"

"I told you," Rich said, watching in horror as the multitude steadily increased, the floor now writhing with insect life.

Insect life that seemed to have a purpose, crawling across the kitchen floor toward where they stood.

"What the hell is this?" Sidney demanded. It was all so strange she was having a difficult time wrapping her brain around the moment.

She found herself walking around the flow of insects, pushing past Rich, who was busy stomping on the bugs as they advanced, and grabbing hold of the doorknob of the cellar door.

"What are you doing?" Cody asked from where he stood behind the kitchen island.

She needed to see in order to begin to understand the situation. It was one of her more bothersome traits. Even after she'd been summoned to the office and told that her father had been rushed to the hospital, that they suspected that he'd had a stroke, she really hadn't believed a word. She'd needed to see him for herself. What if they were wrong? What if it had been nothing, and he would have been fine? She would have been upset all for naught.

It hadn't been nothing, but what if?

Rich had stopped stomping bugs long enough to spin around just as she started to turn the knob.

"You don't want to—" he called out just as she pulled the door open, wide enough to peer down into the darkness.

She needed to see if this was something.

Sidney's cell phone was in her hand, and she hit the button to turn on the light feature, illuminating the stairs in a harsh white glow.

It was something.

The stairs were invisible, every inch covered in squirming, climbing, skittering bodies, a moving carpet of insect life flowing up from the cellar's dirt floor.

Sidney barely had a moment to move herself from the opening as Rich's shoulder plowed into the door, abruptly slamming it closed.

"Oh my God," she managed as she stared into her friend's frightened eyes.

"Yeah, oh my God," he answered.

Cody was coming around the island now, an excited Snowy following him.

"No!" Sidney ordered, holding out her hand to them. "Keep her over there." Cody instantly grabbed the dog by the collar, peering around the island to see.

The floor was covered in bodies of the living and the dead.

"What the hell?" Cody began, but Sidney was already directing.

"Find something to stick under that door," she said, on the move, opening kitchen drawers.

Rich continued to stomp on the bugs that squirmed their way out from beneath the door, while Cody began to help Sidney with her search.

Snowy nudged her hand with a cold nose, and she took a moment to connect with the shepherd, making eye contact with her. "Good girl, Snowy," Sidney said, raising her hand and making the gesture for the dog to sit and stay put. "That's a good dog," she praised.

"How about this?" Cody asked, holding up a green quilted place mat.

"That might do it," Sidney said. "Are there any more?"

"Hey, guys, you want to step it up a little? It's getting bad over here," Rich cried out, and Sidney could hear the beginnings of hysteria in his voice, along with his heavy footfalls and the wet crunch of breaking bug bodies.

Cody approached with a handful of the place mats. "I found five of them," he said.

Sidney grabbed them and moved toward the cellar door, Snowy beginning to follow.

"Keep her back, would you, Cody?" she said as she stared at the sight of bugs as they wriggled and squirmed for their freedom from the cellar and into kitchen. It seemed to take them a moment to get their bearings—to think of what they'd come up here for—then they made their way toward Rich, and her.

Weird didn't even begin to describe it anymore.

Sidney knelt down, shoving the first of the place mats underneath the space between the door's bottom and the floor. Some of the insects that managed to escape went right for her—a centipede at least eight inches long squirmed onto her hand, wrapping itself around her middle finger before finally making its way to the back of her hand, where it sank its pincers into her flesh.

"Ahhhh! Shit!" she cried out, shaking her hand savagely. She was tempted to take off, to leap back before any more of the bugs could bite her, but she knew that she had to get this done. The first of the cloth mats was in place, and she was starting on the next. She couldn't grasp the number of insects that were coming under the door, never mind the fact that they were all together, hanging out as if they were somehow friends. A big insect block party. It didn't work that way, she thought as a spider and cluster of ants went after her fingers.

Cody crushed the spider with his thumb, pressing its body into the floor with a disgusting sounding pop. He dropped down beside her with another of the place mats, starting to cram it beneath the door next to her last.

"My hero," she said, and he just grunted, obviously as freaked out as she was by the situation.

"Guys, what the hell is going on?" Rich asked, his dance of bug death finally able to slow down some. He was looking at the soles of his sneakers with disgust.

Sidney got another of the mats shoved beneath the door, which pretty much closed up the opening.

"Are we good?" Cody asked, grimacing as he wiped his arms clean of straggler ants with the last remaining place mat.

"I think so," she said, standing up, but keeping her eyes riveted to the row of green quilted cloth sticking out from the bottom of the door.

"This is just . . . ," Rich said, and they looked over to see him staring down at the kitchen floor in front of the door, which was covered and smeared with the crushed bodies and guts of literally hundreds of dead insects. "This is just freaking disgusting. What's happening?" he asked in all seriousness, without a trace of his usual jokey persona that was normally present.

Cody looked to Sidney as Rich did the same.

She realized that they were looking to her for answers.

"You're asking me?" she said, eyes darting to the bottom of the door to make sure that the mats were still holding. They were. "I haven't a clue." The wind howled outside, the rain upon the windows sounding like the pattering of thousands of tiny feet. "Maybe it has something to do with the storm," she offered.

"How is that?" Rich asked, finding some bugs still alive and stepping on them with a crunch. "Why would a storm make bugs go crazy?"

"I don't know," Sidney said, frustrated over the fact that she didn't have a good enough answer. "It was just a friggin' theory."

"Best one we got, unless you've got something better," Cody said, his attitude toward Rich rearing its head again.

"I'm not the animal expert," Rich retorted, having picked up on the attitude. "I've just never seen anything like this before and—"

They all jumped at a thumping sound. Sidney believed, as likely they all did, that something had just been blown against the side of the house, but then it came again.

And again.

"What now?" Rich asked, slipping in the bug guts that covered the floor, but grabbing hold of the island's edge before he actually went down. If things hadn't been so tense at the moment, it almost might've been funny, but right then it just made the situation all the tenser.

There were multiple hits now. Loud thumps and bangs that seemed to be coming from all around the house.

Rich let go of the island and made his way toward the front of the house, careful not to slide. Sidney, Snowy, and Cody followed as the loud sounds continued.

Standing in the entryway, Rich listened.

"Is it just the storm?" he asked them.

The noises continued to pummel the home.

"I have no idea," Sidney said, eyes traveling to the various points of impact.

"Maybe it's hail," Cody suggested.

"Seriously?" Rich asked. "Hail? That's the best you could come up with? It's the freakin' summer. I don't think you can even have hail in the summer."

Something hit off of one of the living room windows, broken glass tinkling to the floor beneath.

"Are you shitting me?" Rich said, heading toward the window where one of the curtains now billowed.

Sidney didn't really know why she reacted the way she did, but she called out, "Rich, no!"

He turned ever so slightly but continued toward the broken window. He grabbed the long, billowing material of the curtain to pull it away, but something was waiting for him behind it.

Rich let out a scream, jumping back as a raccoon, crouched among the broken pieces of glass, sprang at him.

CHAPTER **NINETEEN**

Janice cried out in a mixture of rage and absolute disgust, thrashing wildly atop the body of her husband as he attempted to put his arms around her.

His movements were weak, spastic, flailing, giving her the opportunity that she needed to escape his clutches. She would rather not have remembered, but the memory was suddenly there in her mind, a time when she actually welcomed Ronald's strong arms around her. But that was a long time ago, before the hate and revulsion.

Janice drove her boney elbows into her husband's ribs with all her might to break his hold on her, and to drive the disgusting memory away. An awful moan escaped the man, and all she could think of was a ghost roaming the halls of some ancient English castle.

Rolling off the thrashing man, she scrambled to her knees and began to stand. The fact that her husband still lived was a problem, and she at once began to formulate how she would finish what she had started. The pain in her hand was incredible, each rapid-fire beat of her heart like somebody taking a hot poker and driving it into the meat of her palm. She held the bandaged hand to her chest as she rose, keeping her distance from the man who twitched and flopped upon the floor of their bedroom. Perhaps he would still die, she thought as she watched him there in the darkness. Maybe he just needed a little more time.

The smell was instantly revolting, but familiar. A smell that she'd grown used to since purchasing Alfred, the pungent and incredibly strong smell of French bulldog farts.

Janice turned in the black of the bedroom to find the dog standing behind her, staring at her intensely. She again noticed the strange glassy shine over his right eye.

"Who wants a cookie?" she asked in the calmest of voices, not wanting the dog to pick up on her tension. There wasn't much that the dog wouldn't do for a snack. She figured that was all she needed to distract him from what she had done.

Alfred continued to stare at her intensely.

"Do you?" she asked him, again with little reaction.

She noticed that Ronald had gone completely silent and turned her attention from the dog to see that her husband now lay perfectly still.

Dead, she hoped.

Janice could not stop the smile from coming, her spirits lifted by the possibility of her husband's demise.

But her happiness was short lived. As she turned back to her dog, she found that he was right there in front of her, mere inches away, having silently come closer.

She actually gasped as she found the French bulldog looking up into her eyes.

"Let's go get that cook—" she started, but never finished. The dog silently lunged, his sharp, crooked teeth sinking into the flesh of her thigh.

Janice cried out, pulling away from Alfred's attack but tripping over the body of her husband and falling to the floor once more. The dog continued to come at her, powerful jaws widening for another bite. Janice kicked with her legs, attempting to drive the bulldog away, but it had little effect. Alfred snapped crazily, willing to bite at anything near his mouth. She tried to get up, to run away, but he kept at it, keeping her down at his level. Alfred dove at her side, going for the flesh of her stomach. She tried to grab hold, to wrestle and perhaps immobilize him, but the dog was too fast and strong, squirming from her grasp before lunging and snapping again.

Janice tried to get him to listen, screaming out commands, but her attempts at authority were falling on deaf ears.

Arms flailing, she managed to grab hold of some of the looser flesh and fur on the side of Alfred's face, yanking him back and holding him at bay. The dog silently twisted in her grasp, seemingly unaware of the pain that he must be causing himself as he tried to bite her. He brought one of his paws up as he twisted, trying to scratch her with his claws. With her bandaged hand she batted the paw away, but it still managed to dig bleeding furrows into her wrist. Her arm was getting weaker, and the dog seemingly stronger. Janice knew that it wouldn't be long before the dog grew so incensed and twisted so violently that he would cause the furry flesh on the side of his face to tear, and Alfred would again be free to bite at her.

Holding the dog at a distance as it thrashed in her grasp, she looked around the room for some sort of solution. In a flash of lightning followed by a nearly deafening crash of thunder, she saw the bathroom across from the bedroom and made her decision. Janice didn't waste any time and began to drag the struggling dog across the room toward the door. His movements were getting more wild and frantic, and she could feel the sides of his chomping teeth now rubbing against her hand furiously as he continued to fight and shake in her grasp in an attempt to bite her.

Alfred planted his paws, but the hardwood floors of the bedroom were not a bulldog's friend, and he was easily dragged. The dog fought even more wildly now, as if realizing where it was that she was taking him. Alfred thrashed his muscular body and continued to try and gouge her with his claws, but Janice held tightly, for the alternative was something that she would rather not think about.

She made it through the doorway out into the hall, but the dog managed to get his claws dug into the wood of the door's threshold, and she found her grip on the dog's face sliding off just enough so that . . .

Alfred went wild, his savage jaws snapping crazily, like some kind of mechanized animal trap. Janice screamed as she pushed herself back with her legs toward the open bathroom doorway as

Alfred came at her. Her hands shot out in front of her to hold him back, and the dog's mouth chomped down upon her fingers. She felt the fragile bones snap beneath the closure of his unrelenting jaws. The pain was blinding, and she saw brilliant explosions of red before her eyes as she struggled to retain her consciousness. Rolling over onto her knees, Janice furiously began to crawl her way into the bathroom. An incredible weight landed upon her back, driving her flat to the floor, and she felt Alfred's hot breath upon her neck. Scrunching up her shoulders, she reached behind her to try and knock the animal away. Her fingers touched on something cold and metal, and she at once knew that she was touching the dog's choke collar. Grabbing the chain, she yanked with all her might, flipping the dog over her right shoulder as she pushed off from the entryway floor to the bathroom.

Alfred rolled from her back into the side of the bathroom's trash can, barely pausing a second before he was charging her again. She'd managed to stand and reached over to pull a wicker hamper into the dog's path, blocking him. Janice used that moment to turn herself around and grab hold of the bathroom door to start to close it. Alfred sprang off the body of the hamper, wedging his head in the doorway just as she tried to pull it shut. The bulldog was wild, attempting to shake his blocky head free and force more of his muscular body through to get at her. Janice pulled the door with both hands, even though the pain from her injuries was excruciating. But she was willing to endure it to prevent what would surely be worse if the dog managed to get out of the bathroom.

Still pulling on the doorknob, she raised her foot, kicking the dog in the face once and then again. Blood dribbled down his dark nose onto his yellowed teeth, giving them a new, horrific look as they continued to snap and grind. Summoning all her strength for one final push, Janice lifted her leg and drove the heel of her sensible shoe square into Alfred's snout and managed to drive his head back into the bathroom and allow her to pull the door closed.

She stood there shaking, head pressed to the door. Alfred was going wild in the bathroom, repeatedly hurling his muscular body against the door. She actually started to laugh, a kind of release from the intense emotions that had been gradually building since smashing her husband's skull in. The door felt cool against her brow, and she closed her eyes, giggling insanely as the tension began to slowly leave her.

Alfred angrily continued to throw himself at the door, and she seriously began to worry that the French bulldog might be strong enough to punch his way through. She turned herself around, her back pressed to the vibrating surface of the door, and opened her eyes to the darkness of the room . . . and her husband standing mere inches from her.

Janice tried to scream, but the sight of him, the way his head was grotesquely misshapen where his skull had been smashed in, and how he looked at her, head cocked strangely to one side, with dark, dead eyes that seemed to bore into hers . . . it stole away her ability to cry out.

Then she noticed it, just as she had on Alfred. A shiny reflective coating over her husband's right eye. She wondered what it might mean as he lunged at her, his mouth agape.

Janice tried to escape, darting to go around him, but he was too fast. Ronald collided with her, slamming her back against the hallway wall, and lowered his face to her neck to sink his teeth into the tender skin and rip a huge chunk away. Her hands went to the spurting wound as she cried out; there was so much blood. Janice tried to push her husband away with one hand, but the blood from the neck wound had made the hardwood floor slippery, and she found her feet sliding out from beneath her.

Ronald stiffly lurched in her direction, his spastic movement reminding her of the mechanical historical figures at the Hall of Presidents in Disney World. Her head was becoming light, and she tried to use the wall to prop herself up, to make her escape toward the stairs and hopefully to freedom out into the storm, but Ronald caught her, driving her down to the floor again. Janice tried to fight him, but he was too strong. Again he lowered his bloodstained mouth toward her exposed neck.

He sank his teeth into her throat with a sickening pop, tearing the tender flesh away with a savage yank.

The man who had been Ronald Berthold watched the woman die.

No longer did he remember that he had once loved her, cared for her. Nor did he remember that she had tried to kill him.

Ronald Berthold was gone, and only the body remained.

The blood that had been gushing from the woman's gaping throat wound had slowed to a mere trickle as her heart ceased to pump. The man stared, watching for further signs of life, but there were none.

Satisfied, he struggled to stand, slipping in the coagulating puddle of blood and almost falling to the floor.

Almost.

The man caught himself against the closed bathroom door, a bloody handprint smeared across the white surface. The door suddenly vibrated menacingly as something on the other side threw itself against the obstruction.

The man stiffly stepped back from the door, staring at it with a questioning eye. It shook violently again.

Tilting his head from one side to the other, the man determined that something was on the other side and wished to come out. The man studied the door as it continued to vibrate and be pounded upon, his eyes fixing on the doorknob.

It took a moment, but the body remembered what it was for, reaching out with a blood-covered hand to grip the cool metal of the knob and squeeze it tightly, before slowly turning it to the right and—

Click!

The bathroom door swung inward with a prolonged creak, exposing the muscular figure of the dog standing there.

Waiting.

The man locked eyes with the beast, a kind of invisible communication seeming to pass between them.

The dog left the bathroom, briefly staring at the cooling corpse of the woman in the hallway before coming to stand beside the man.

They stood for a while, as if waiting for something—a message perhaps—and then began to walk toward the stairs.

Side by side, the man and the dog descended the steps to the first floor. At the front door, they paused momentarily before the man reached for the doorknob and, recalling what he had done just moments before, turned it.

He pulled the door open. There was a heavy gust of wind and rain, but the man and dog were unfazed by the fury of the elements as they walked together through the doorway.

Out into the storm.

CHAPTER TWENTY

Doc Martin should have left the clinic and gone home hours ago, but there she was, still puttering, having little need or interest to head home.

This was where she truly lived. This was where she was alive, and it had pretty much been that way since she'd first opened the practice nearly thirty years before.

The animal hospital was her life.

She was craving a smoke but dreaded the idea of going outside. The storm was raging and sounded like it could have gotten worse. The weather guys had said that this one was going to be a beaut, and for once it wasn't all hype. She seriously considered spending the night at the clinic. It wouldn't have been the first time that she'd sprawled out in her office chair, covered in blankets meant as donations from one of the mainland's many animal shelters.

She was about to start flipping through the first of at least twenty veterinary medical journals that she'd let pile up when she heard them.

It sounded as though a full-scale riot was going on in the kennels.

"What the hell is that all about?" she muttered, leaving her seat and heading to the door that led to the dog kennels.

Doc Martin opened the door to the sounds of the wild. It seemed as though every animal inside the caged compartments was in the process of losing its mind.

"Whoa! Whoa!" she called out as she stepped inside the room. "What's going on?"

The dogs inside their recovery cages were extremely agitated, barking and scratching at their compartment doors. The strong smell of urine and feces filled the air.

She stopped at the first cage to check out Lilly, the basset hound who'd had stomach surgery that afternoon. The dog was up on all fours, frantically pawing at the bottom of the cage door, and when she saw Doc Martin, she immediately threw herself at the door, biting ferociously at the metal.

"What's gotten into you?" she muttered to herself, concerned that the dog's frantic activity might cause her stitches to pop. Doc Martin was considering getting some medication to calm her down when she noticed similar activity in the cage beside the basset hound.

Rufus, a cute corgi/Labrador mix who had come in to have some teeth pulled, was spinning around inside his cage so fast that Doc was afraid he was going to hurt himself.

"Hey," she said, approaching the cage. She laid her hand against the front of the cage door and tapped it to get his attention. "Knock it off before you break your friggin—"

The dog stopped on a dime and shoved his face against the metal grate of the door so hard in an attempt to bite her hand that blood actually squirted from his nose.

Doc Martin quickly pulled her hand away, and Rufus immediately went back to spinning. Feeling eyes upon her, she glanced across the way to see Beau, the standard poodle who had come in for neutering, staring intensely at her, teeth bared in a sign of absolute aggression.

She didn't know what was going on, but clearly something was up. It would have been easy to blame it all on the storm, to come up with some bullshit connected to atmospheric conditions, or even something as simple as intense fear caused by the sound of thunder, but she knew that it wasn't right.

Something was seriously wrong.

A glint of light from one of Beau's eyes caught Doc Martin's attention, and she moved closer to the poodle's cage. The dog reacted as aggressively as the others had, ramming his face against the metal cage door.

"What's wrong with your eye?" she asked the dog.

Beau's right eye seemed to be covered in a shiny, metallic film. She stared at it, moving one of her hands in front of the cage in order to get the dog to move his head around so that she could check it out better. She hadn't a clue as to what it was. The fact that it was only covering one eye was interesting as well.

Doc Martin was just about to check out the other dogs to see if they, too, showed any signs of this ocular malady when there was terrific crashing sound from the end of the row of cages. All the dogs went suddenly silent as the door of the last cage in the row exploded outward, twisted and hanging on by a single hinge, followed by the huge form of a bull mastiff named Bear who had been recently operated on for an ulcerated lower intestine. The two-hundred-pound dog resembled his namesake, lumbering down the aisle toward her, picking up speed and moving far quicker than an animal that had experienced that kind of surgery should have been able to move.

Just before turning toward the door, she caught a hint of it—a silvery glint coming from the dog's right eye. A cold chill of dread raced up her spine.

She was pulling the door open when Bear sprang, his two hundred pounds slamming her against the door and shutting it. The mastiff's massive head came down, jaws open to bite. She could smell the stink of his breath, a rotten, meaty stench mixed with a hint of anesthesia. The veterinarian rolled onto her back, wedging her forearm beneath the behemoth's throat, preventing his mouth from coming down. The dog was furious in his assault, pushing against Doc Martin's arm, jaws snapping, and all the while she was fighting for her life, she couldn't help but stare into the dog's right eye, at the silvery film that covered the dark, and normally quite soulful, orb.

Doc Martin knew that it was only a matter of time before the powerful animal broke through her defenses and likely tore out her throat. Remembering the surgery that she had performed on the dog, the veterinarian pulled up and lashed out with her legs at the animal's underbelly and at the fifteen-inch-long incision held closed with multiple metal staples.

Bear paused momentarily, grunting and starting to back away, before lunging at her again. This time she was able to plant one of her feet against the dog's chest and kick him back.

The mastiff awkwardly fell to his side, twisting upon the slick linoleum floor before climbing back up to his feet. Doc Martin noticed blood on the floor, spattering down from beneath the dog. The mastiff charged again, and pushing herself back up against the door, Doc Martin used all her remaining strength to kick him in the side.

The sound that followed was nasty, tiny pops followed by a wet tearing sound just before the dog's internal workings spilled out from the now-opened incision onto the floor.

The mastiff hesitated, swaying slightly as if attempting to discern the extent of the damage. Doc Martin tensed as the dog stood there, his muscles and limbs trembling as he started toward her again. She was ready to kick out, but there was little need. Bear took steps toward her before his front legs gave out, his huge head snowplowing along the floor, coming to a final resting stop between her legs.

Doc Martin pushed herself up along the wall, her entire body trembling. The dog twitched and moaned, his back legs kicking out, sliding him forward as if he was still attempting to come at her.

The animals inside their cages were even wilder now, as if Bear's failure to kill her was driving them to even further madness. They threw themselves savagely at the cage doors, blood from their frantic attempts to escape spraying the floor outside their cages.

Unable to stand the sound and the sickening sight of their inexplicable insanity, Doc Martin quickly left the kennel, escaping to the safety of the office.

The kennel door now at her back, Doc Martin reached into the pocket of her lab coat for her cigarettes, taking one out and lighting up with a trembling hand.

What the hell is going on?

CHAPTER **TWENTY-ONE**

Cody couldn't help it.

He started to laugh.

It was like something out of a cartoon it was so outrageous. Rich was yelling at the top of his lungs, stumbling backward as he tried to pull the attacking animal, a raccoon, from the front of his shirt, but the raccoon was holding on, snapping at Rich's face.

It wasn't that it was actually funny—in fact it was pretty terrifying—but the insanity of it all, bugs by the thousands swarming up from the basement, raccoons breaking through a window gave Cody only two choices: either blow off some of this awful tension by laughing or scream like a crazy person and risk never stopping.

So he laughed, but only for a second.

Because then he saw the blood.

Cody ran to the scene, his eyes fixed on the wildly digging and snapping animal on the front of Rich's blood-spattered shirt.

"Hold still!" Cody screamed as he reached for the thing snapping, digging, and biting at Rich's chest. He grabbed a handful of fur at the back of the creature's neck, feeling its muscles tense as it tried to turn its head to bite him. But he just held on tighter, squeezing with all his might and pulling the raccoon away from Rich.

It was wild in his grasp, thrashing, clawing, and snapping in a desperate attempt to sink its teeth into him. It twisted its body in such a way that its back legs caught the underside of Cody's arm, and he cried out, feeling the flesh tear. He lost his grip, and the raccoon fell to the floor, immediately turning, fixed on Cody, preparing to attack.

And there was nothing funny about that at all.

It was taking all of Sidney's strength to hold back Snowy.

When the raccoon attacked Rich, the German shepherd had tried to make her move, but Sidney wasn't having any part of that, practically jumping onto the dog's back and throwing her arms tightly around her neck. She hadn't a clue as to what was going on, but she wasn't about to let anything happen to Snowy.

Snowy watched the struggle with the raccoon with a laser-beam focus, straining against Sidney's arms. And when Cody dropped the raccoon, the dog lunged, pulling Sidney to the floor as she broke the girl's grip and went for the ferocious animal just as it was about to go at Cody.

"Snowy, no!" Sidney cried, even though she knew that her dog couldn't hear her.

Snowy pounced on the large raccoon, clamped her teeth around the maddened animal's neck, and began to furiously shake the beast. It was never a pretty sight to watch, but it was nature, and there was very little to be done to curb the dog's natural hunting instinct.

Blood spattered the floor and walls as Snowy savagely shook her prey, at last releasing the animal, its body flying across the room, where it actually seemed to try and get up again, but then grew very still.

The three teens simply stood there, staring at each other in shock. Then Sidney rushed to Snowy, checking her over to be sure she wasn't hurt.

A part of Rich wished that she cared as much about his well-being, but that thought was quickly tossed aside when he heard more scrabbling at the broken window.

"What now?" Cody moaned, trying to examine the bleeding furrows in his tricep.

Rich moved toward the window and stopped just before the curtain, the sounds outside growing louder. "We've got to block that hole," he said, on the verge of panic.

"Here!" Cody tossed him a small pillow he had grabbed from a nearby chair.

Rich cautiously pulled the curtain aside. Something was trying to crawl onto the edge of the broken pane of glass, but it fell backward into the darkness. He leaned closer to the window and peered out through the rain-swept glass. It was as if the shadows had somehow come alive.

Quickly he turned his attention to the broken windowpane, shoving the pillow into the square to block the opening.

"What were you thinking?" Sidney said to Snowy, checking her for injuries for the second time that day. There was blood around her mouth and on the fur of chest, but it didn't seem to be hers. Thankfully, she appeared to be fine.

The dog was panting, her dark eyes fixed on the corpse of the raccoon lying on the floor across the room.

"Don't you even think it," Sidney said, holding Snowy's head to be sure the shepherd was looking at her. "You stay right here with me."

She looked over at Cody and Rich, who stood by the window. The thumps and bangs upon the house continued, even as the winds howled and the rain whipped against it. "Everything all right over there?"

"Yeah," Rich said, making sure the pillow was secure before turning away.

"No!" Cody said. "No, everything isn't all right. What the hell is going on?"

Sidney started to answer but stopped, shaking her head.

Frustrated, Cody strode over to the corpse of the raccoon, looking at the gouges beneath his arm and then at the dead animal. He nudged it with the toe of his boot. "Maybe it's rabies or something," he said.

Sidney motioned for Snowy to lie down, gave her a quick pat on the head when she did, then walked over to join Cody. She squatted down for a closer look at the raccoon. It was a little mangy in appearance, but that wasn't necessarily a sign of anything.

"Guys," Rich called out, a tone in his voice that Sidney didn't like.

She stood and turned to see Rich standing by the entrance to the kitchen. She and Cody quickly glanced at each other, then stepped toward Rich, only to come to a fast standstill. Insects had managed to push past the rolled-up place mats and were once again streaming up from the cellar.

"I don't think this is rabies," Rich said, a tremble of fear in his voice.

"No," Sidney agreed. "I think it's something worse."

CHAPTER TWENTY-TWO

"That isn't right, Isaac." Caroline's grip was very hard on his arm. "That just isn't right."

Isaac had to agree.

They were standing amid the severe clutter of the living room, staring at the piles, boxes, and stacks of stuff that had created dark pockets and corridors of shadow from which the cats and mice—*hundreds and hundreds of mice*—now stared out at them.

"I'm scared," his mother said, and something told Isaac that she had every right to be.

She suddenly screamed, yanking furiously on his arm. "Something bit me!"

Isaac felt it as well. Sharp, burning sensations in his ankles, as things—hundreds of things—moved about his shoes. He started to turn, to pull his mother out of there, when Cavendish sprang from his perch. Without a sound, the cat landed on Isaac's chest, claws digging through his shirt to the tender flesh below. Isaac let out a yelp of pain, instinctively swatting the clinging cat away.

"Stop it! You'll hurt him!" his mother screeched, pulling on his arm.

"No, Mother," Isaac cried, somehow knowing that things were about to get even worse. "I think they want to hurt us."

His sense of foreboding was intensified by the strange sensation he was picking up in his Steve ear. It made the flesh on the back of his neck tingle, his hair stand on end. He remembered the time he'd rubbed a red balloon on the top of his head and how his hair had stood up. This was something like that, but it wasn't fun like the red balloon had been.

Mice were leaping from the shelves, tiny bodies dropping down upon them, hanging from their clothes. His mother was screaming hysterically, flailing her arms, knocking over towers of books, dirty plates, and magazines. He saw at least two of the candles that his mother had lit when the power went out tumble out of view and knew that wasn't a good thing at all.

But he couldn't help her. There were mice on his head, and they were biting him. He grabbed at the tiny attackers. They bit at his fingers, and he tried to ignore the stabbing pain as he tore them away, throwing them to the floor, where they simply began climbing up his legs. Isaac kicked out with his limbs and stamped his feet. He could see blood on his hands and on his clothes, and that just made him all the more frantic. He thought of his room—his perfectly clean and structured room. In there he could clean away the blood from his body and change his clothes.

He was preparing to make a run for his special place when his mother let out the most horrible of screams. Isaac turned to see that she had fallen sideways onto bags of old winter clothing. She'd often talked about how she was collecting them for a charity. She'd said that somebody was really going to appreciate those winter things, but nobody ever had.

Isaac rushed to help her up, ignoring the nibbling mice that were scaling his body. He gasped at the horrifying sight of her as he drew closer. The cats—Binky, Nero, Shadow, Cavendish, and Mrs. Livingstone—were all on top of her, clawing and biting as she struggled to get up, but she was unable to get her footing beneath the shifting bags of clothing.

"Get away from her!" Isaac yelled.

The cats did not seem to hear him, continuing to savagely scratch and dig at his mother as she moaned beneath their onslaught. He'd never seen them act this way toward his mother. Sure they'd fought among themselves, but they loved his mother, often all lying with her on the mattress that acted as her bed, purring loudly.

"Get away from her now!" he yelled again, reaching down to swat at the all-black cat named Shadow. His fingertips roughly brushed along the cat's back, and it instantly spun around, jumping onto his arm, biting and clawing, back legs kicking and ripping through the fabric of his long-sleeved shirt, drawing blood.

Isaac whipped his arm back and forth, but the cat still hung on, sinking his claws and teeth into his flesh. The pain was incredible; his shirt was reduced to bloody tatters. And for the first time, Isaac began to fear for his life.

All the while, the sound in his Steve ear was growing worse, spreading to the area where the doctors had put the metal plate. He forced himself to ignore these sounds and strange feelings that made him scared and angry, and concentrated on trying to save himself and his mother.

Isaac plowed through the piles of clutter, knocking aside two card tables placed tightly together to accommodate a jigsaw puzzle of two kittens in a flower basket. He reached the huge china cabinet made from dark, heavy wood, drew back his arm, and slammed it as hard as he could into the doors, the cat, still clinging to his flesh, taking the full brunt of the hit. Isaac felt Shadow's grip loosen then tighten again, the biting even more vicious. Again he slammed his arm into the front of the cabinet, this time shattering three of the glass panes. The cat finally lost his grip, and Isaac quickly pulled his arm back, leaving Shadow inside the cabinet, his body broken and covered with shards of glass.

Isaac's arm burned and throbbed, but at least he was free of the cat, and he turned his attention back to his poor mother. Caroline had managed to roll onto her knees, huddled within the confines of her stuff, trying to protect her head and face from the remaining cats who tore at her back and buttocks. She cried hysterically, trying to push herself deeper into the layers of her belongings for protection.

Isaac lumbered toward her, spying a desk lamp that stuck out from the top of a box filled with items left when his sister moved out ten years before. The box had been destined for the trash but never made it there. Mother had wanted to look through it, in case his sister was throwing out something that could still be used. And for once, she was right. Isaac grabbed the lamp, pulling it from the box like Excalibur from the stone.

He didn't want to hurt the cats, even though there were times when they would get into his room and mess things up. He knew that he could be quite strong if he wanted to be, and his mother had always taught him to control his temper. But now she was being hurt, and to make that stop he had to do something that he didn't want to do.

Focusing on his mother's cries, Isaac swung the square stone base of the desk lamp and connected with Binky. Without a sound, Binky soared across the room, crashing into a stack of green plastic milk crates before disappearing beneath a sea of clothing and stuffed animals.

Only for a second did Isaac think it odd that the animal didn't cry out. Nero was now digging at his mother's hands as she attempted to protect her neck. The cat turned his gaze on him and bared needle-sharp teeth. Isaac swung his makeshift weapon and smashed it into the cat's face. But Nero still clung to Caroline's back, even though his jaw hung crookedly and a stream of black, blood-tinged drool dripped from the side of his mouth. Isaac lashed out again, this time hitting the animal so hard that his head was practically torn from his body, blood spattering nearby boxes in a crimson streak.

Mrs. Livingstone and Cavendish had darted for cover when the battle with Nero started. There were no signs of them, but the mice were swarming.

"Mother," Isaac said, bending toward the cowering woman. "Mother, we have to go."

She was crying hysterically, the words that were leaving her mouth unintelligible. Something about the cats, and how could they hurt their mother this way.

Isaac didn't understand it either, but he knew that it wasn't the time to wonder. He reached down, grabbed hold of her arm, and yanked her to her feet. Her face was a mess of blood and deep scratches. He could feel the panic starting to rise but managed to hold it together, knowing that he had to be strong for the both of them.

"We have to leave," he said again.

She looked around, flinching as mice continued to fall from various high places around the room.

Still clutching his lamp weapon, Isaac tugged on his mother's wrist, attempting to lead her from the living room. He didn't look down as he walked but could feel the mice being crushed with each footfall. They were not his concern.

"Why?" Caroline was asking behind him. Isaac had only seen her drunk once in his life, and the way she sounded now reminded him of that time. She had won a bottle of champagne at a church raffle and drunk half of it one Saturday afternoon. He remembered that she had cried a lot and had said that she felt sad for him because of his injuries. That maybe it would have been better if he hadn't lived after the car accident.

"Why would my fur babies want to hurt us?" she asked him through the tears.

He didn't answer, just continued to drag her over the piles of material that had tipped during their struggle.

"Maybe they're sick, Isaac," she suggested.

Still he moved forward. They were almost to the kitchen.

"Isaac!" she screamed, suddenly stopping and ripping her hand away from his. "Are you listening to your mother?"

"We have to go," he told her, averting his gaze. He hated to see her bloody like that.

"But what if our babies are sick? We can't just—"

Mrs. Livingstone attacked from out of nowhere, flying through the air and landing on Caroline's shoulder. Caroline screeched as the cat sank her needle teeth into the soft flesh of her neck. She managed to grab Mrs. Livingstone by her fluffy Maine Coon cat tail and yanked. The cat came away, eerily silent, but so did a large chunk of Caroline's neck. She flung the cat away and clamped her hand over the spurting wound, trying to stem the flow of crimson. She dropped to her knees, and Isaac could see a swarm of eager mice already heading for her.

He rushed toward her, stomping on the mice. As he did, he caught sight of Mrs. Livingstone calmly watching the scene from a nearby sewing machine cabinet. A shudder of terror passed through him. *What's the matter with her eye?* he wondered.

But he had no more time for thought. His mother was covered with gray and black mice. They were in her hair and moving beneath her clothing, and she twitched and moaned pathetically as they bit her repeatedly.

"No! No! No!" he cried, grabbing handfuls of the tiny life forms, squeezing them with all his might before throwing their crushed corpses among the other refuse.

His mother's hand was still clamped to the bite on her neck, and he could see the blood oozing from beneath her closed fingers, running down her neck, and soaking her shirt. She was trying to speak, her mouth moving strangely as her eyes bulged.

He hauled her to her feet. She was heavier now. He pulled one of her arms around his neck and placed one of his around her waist and began to drag her toward the kitchen. As they passed the sewing machine cabinet, he saw that Mrs. Livingstone was gone.

They were finally in the kitchen, and Isaac couldn't help himself. He stopped and turned his head to see if he could see Mrs. Livingstone. His heart jumped painfully in his chest at the sight of not only Mrs. Livingstone, but Binky, Cavendish, and Nero following closely, with what could only be described as a sea of mice flowing over the clutter, heading directly for him and his mother.

Isaac fixed his sight on the back door, hauling his mother across the trash-strewn floor with renewed vigor, knocking things from the kitchen shelves as he navigated the best he could. He could hear the storm raging outside and briefly considered stopping to grab his raincoat but realized that was probably not the smartest idea.

For a moment he thought his hearing aids were acting even more strangely, as the sound of a high-pitched alarm suddenly filled the home, but then he saw the trails of smoke wafting from the living room and realized that the smoke detectors were letting him know there was a fire. He remembered the candles and how they had fallen over in the struggles.

From the corner of his eye he caught movement and instantly lashed out with his lamp club, catching Cavendish as he sprang. The overweight cat fell into a shelf above the sink, filled with decorative teacups. There was a deafening crash as shelf, teacups, and cat fell into the trash-filled sink. Isaac actually felt a twinge of sadness as Cavendish lay still in the wreckage. He had liked Cavendish best; that one had never made a mess in his room.

Caroline had fallen from his grasp and was curled in a tight ball on the kitchen floor. Isaac reached down to pick her up, never taking his eyes from the living room doorway. Mice were pouring into the room, scampering up onto the counters, and streaming across the uneven surfaces toward them. His mother was making awful sounds now, and her skin had taken on a strange grayish color. Her hand fell away from her neck, the wound continuing to bleed quite badly. Isaac thrust his arm around her waist again and managed to get her up, then balanced her weight against his hip as he opened the door to the outside.

The cats came from opposite sides, Mrs. Livingstone descending from the top of the refrigerator, and Binky from the kitchen island, both landing on Isaac's back. Fighting through the pain, he opened the wooden screen door and pushed his mother outside, closing it tightly behind her.

Then he spun, swinging his lamp. The pain in his back was so bad that he thought he might pass out, explosions of color like fireworks blooming before his eyes as Mrs. Livingstone continued to gnaw and claw at his back, while Binky ripped at the flesh of his legs and stomach. Isaac fell to his knees, hearing the wind rattle the screen door behind him, feeling the spray of rain as it blew through the screen. He had been so very close.

So. Very. Close.

He felt the life going out of him as the cats continued to bite and scratch.

Then something exploded in a rush of fire just outside the kitchen doorway; tongues of flame reached into the kitchen to stroke the water-stained ceiling.

It was if the fire gave him life, the sight of orange flame and thickening black smoke allowing him to tap into some reserve of strength that he wasn't aware existed.

With a surge of energy, Isaac screamed and threw himself toward the storm door, not even slowing down to unlatch it. He barreled through the woven screen and over the metal railing, where he landed in a heap beside his mother on the rain-soaked ground.

He felt Mrs. Livingstone squirm fitfully beneath him and pushed himself up from the ground to find the cat's crushed body, her head bent at an awkward angle but still trying to snap at him.

Already soaked to the skin by the driving rain, he managed to get to his knees and crawl to his mother. She was lying on her side, facing away from him, her face pressed to the ground. Gently, he took her arm and rolled her onto her back.

A blood-covered Binky looked up from the hole he had burrowed into Caroline's chest. Isaac gasped, falling heavily backward onto his butt. The cat glared at him, a glint of something silver over one of his bulging eyes. He seemed to consider Isaac for a moment, then continued to tear into Caroline's still form.

Isaac was horrified. His hand found a rock in the mud beside him and he grabbed it, forcing himself to stand on shaking legs.

He was about to bring the rock down on Binky's head when movement from the corner of the yard distracted him. The undergrowth was moving, a wave of animal life—squirrels, chipmunks, snakes, bugs, and mice—flowing through the grass toward him.

A tiny voice in his head told him to run. He looked down at his mother. He didn't want to leave her, but even he understood it was too late for her, and if he stayed, he would die too. Isaac cried out with rage as the lightning flared and the thunder crashed. He threw the rock with all his might at the swarm of life, but it was like tossing a pebble into the ocean, if the ocean was a living thing that wanted to chew the skin from his bones.

Not wanting to see what the wave would do to his mother, Isaac turned and raced across the yard into the woods.

As the storm raged on.

CHAPTER **TWENTY-THREE**

Sidney wanted to try something.

She stood in front of a line of insects that had made it up the stairs and through the place-mat barrier they'd shoved beneath the door. She was fascinated by the spiders, ants, centipedes, beetles, millipedes, and some bugs she had never even seen before coming toward her.

"What are you doing?" Rich asked incredulously. He was stomping on even more bugs as they came out from beneath the door while Cody attempted to reinforce their barrier with some dish towels.

"I'm curious," she said. She took one step back and then a wide step to the right. Within seconds the bugs had changed course to follow her.

"You're shitting me," she said.

"What?" Cody asked. He stood up and crossed the kitchen toward her.

"Watch," Sidney ordered. The bugs were almost upon her. She moved around toward the back of the flow.

It took only a moment for the flow of insects to follow, heading directly for her once again.

"That's crazy," Cody said.

"Ya think?" Rich said, coming to stand beside Cody.

Sidney tried it again a few more times, and each time the bugs changed course, coming menacingly toward her.

"They're actually coming after me," she said as she pushed her foot toward the front of the mass. A spider lunged forward, striking at the toe of her shoe, as a swarm of ants climbed up onto her foot. She quickly shook them off. "They've become incredibly aggressive."

Rich approached, and as if sensing his presence, the flow of insects turned toward him. "But why?" he asked. He started to step on the bugs, grinding them into the floor as they continued to come at him.

Cody helped with some strays.

"I don't know," she said, petting Snowy's head as she thought. "What could affect insects, as well as mammals?" She looked over to the dead raccoon.

"You said it might have something to do with the storm," Cody offered. "That sounds as good as anything."

There were more bangs and slams against the house, but they'd grown used to the sounds by now.

Sidney walked over to the raccoon and dropped to her knees next to it. "Maybe some sort of toxin," she said, thinking out loud. "Maybe something in the runoff from the storm."

Cautiously she touched the raccoon. Pushing up the loose skin around its mouth, she examined the gums for any discoloration or evidence of a toxin. At a glance everything looked relatively normal, and she moved on to the raccoon's eyes, first checking the left and then . . .

"What the hell is this?" she muttered.

"What?" Cody asked. "Did you find something?"

"Yeah," she said, pulling the skin wide above and below the animal's orb. "Maybe I have."

She studied the eye and the strange, almost reflective cataract that covered it. The shiny substance appeared to be breaking down, partially sliding off the eye. She'd never seen anything quite like it before and wondered if it might have something to do with—

A thump and crashing sounds came from upstairs.

"What now?" Rich moaned, and headed toward the stairway, peering up through the darkness to the landing.

"What is that?" Cody asked Sidney as he squatted beside her for a closer look at the raccoon.

"I don't know," she replied, "but I'd like to find out."

The silvery substance was sliding across the surface of the eye and pooling at the bottom of the raccoon's eyelid.

"Hey, Rich," Sidney called out. "Do you have a trash bag I could put this in?"

"I think there's a box under the sink." Rich turned toward the kitchen, but more noise from upstairs distracted him, and instead he climbed the first few steps.

Cody stood and went to check under the sink. Sidney could hear the sounds of bugs crunching beneath his feet as he walked. He returned with a green trash bag and snapped it open.

"Do you want me to do it?" he asked.

"You're such a gentleman." She lifted the raccoon by the tail and dropped it into the empty bag. Cody smiled at her, and despite the strangeness of the situation, she smiled back as she took the bag from him.

"What are you planning to do with it?" he asked.

"I'd like to get it to Doc Martin," she said. "Maybe she can run some tests and see what's—"

Sidney was interrupted as Rich nearly fell down the stairs and rushed toward them.

"What?" Sidney asked, moving toward the foyer.

"Don't!" Rich screamed.

There was movement in the dark at the top of the stairs, and she gasped at the sight of multiple fur-covered bodies amassing on the landing.

Squirrels. Hundreds of squirrels.

They began to descend in a wave, their tiny claws scrabbling across the wooden surface.

"Shit, we got to go, guys," she said, backing up quickly toward her friends.

"Go? Go where?" Rich asked. "There's a freakin' storm out there!"

"Someplace," she screamed, waving the trash bag. "Anyplace . . . but we can't stay here."

Snowy began to bark crazily as the squirrels flowed down the steps into the foyer, heading for the kitchen.

"Oh my God," Cody said. "OhmyGodohmyGodohmyGod . . ." He stood frozen, watching as the animals moved toward them, just like the flow of insects from the basement.

"Move!" Sidney shouted. She grabbed Snowy's collar and pulled her, but the path to the back door was blocked by yet another swarm of insects from the basement. Instead, she led the shepherd into the nearby bathroom, the guys close behind her.

"What are we doing?" Rich asked, his voice loud and high pitched.

"I don't know," she snapped. "But at least we should be safe for a while in here. It'll give us a chance to figure this out."

Cody slammed the bathroom door on the wave of angry life swarming behind them.

CHAPTER TWENTY-FOUR

Doc Martin dragged Bear's body across the threshold from the kennel, a wide smear of crimson on the linoleum floor marking their passing.

The animals in their cages were still throwing their bodies mercilessly against the doors, trying to escape and get at her. With a grunt she pulled the mastiff into the office and allowed the kennel door to close, muffling the sounds of the crazed animals beyond.

She leaned against the wall to catch her breath.

"You're a big boy, aren't you," she said to the dead dog. She reached into the pocket of her lab coat and removed a pack of cigarettes, at that moment not really giving two craps about office rules. *I'll be sure to fine myself in the morning,* she thought, popping a smoke into her mouth and lighting up.

They'd always told her that the cancer sticks would be the cause of her death, and typically she'd believed them. Now she stared at the massive dog at her feet. Never had she thought one of her own patients would do her in.

She took a long drag on the cigarette, feeling her nerves start to settle.

Then, cigarette sticking from the corner of her mouth, she bent down, took the big dog by his front paws, and pulled him to the nearby examination room. Lifting with her knees, she managed to haul the dead beast up and flop him onto the metal table.

"Holy crap," she said breathlessly. "What the hell were they feeding you?"

She took a few more puffs on her smoke before throwing the butt into the metal sink, then she plucked two rubber gloves from the box on the counter and turned back to the mastiff.

"All right then," she said, pulling on the gloves. "Let's see if we can figure out what's happened."

She started by feeling the animal's body, looking for any odd lumps or lesions, but other than the gaping surgical wound, she felt nothing. Next, she placed a hand against the dog's massive head and pulled open his eyes. She shined the penlight from her lab coat pocket into the left eye and then the right.

"Well, what do we have here?" she asked aloud as the beam of light reflected off a metallic, almost spiderweb-like covering on the right eye.

The vet took a scalpel from another drawer in the supply cabinet and began to poke at the covering. At first she believed it to be some kind of cataract, but the more she examined it . . .

Holding the flesh around the eye wide, she peered even closer. From the looks of it, the cataract—or whatever the hell it was—appeared to completely encase the eye.

Doc Martin wanted an even closer look. Flipping the scalpel around and using the rounded end to wedge beneath the eyeball, she forced it upward, eventually popping it from the skull.

She held the still-attached eyeball in her rubber-gloved hand, slowly turning it. The foreign material did indeed cover the entire orb and then entwined around the optic nerve, going farther up into the skull cavity.

"Huh," she said, letting the eye dangle against the mastiff's face. She stepped back and removed her rubber gloves, tossing them in a nearby trash can.

Doc Martin knew what she wanted to do next, but in order to do that she was going to need to take a look inside the dog's skull. A slight smile formed on her face as she left the examination room, remembering how they told her she was crazy when she'd invested in the bone saw.

CHAPTER **TWENTY-FIVE**

Dale Moore sat in the darkness, listening to the sounds of the storm raging outside.

He picked up the cell phone that rested on his thigh, looked at the time, and dialed Sidney's number again. The call, as the twenty or more calls before it, didn't go through.

Maybe a tower's come down with this wind, Dale thought as he hung up and placed the phone back on his thigh.

But that didn't explain where Sidney was.

He racked his brain trying to remember if she'd said anything to him about her plans for the day and evening. They hadn't talked much after the business of that morning, each annoyed with the other. The only thing he knew for sure was that she was going to work. He picked up his phone again and looked at the time.

Something thumped outside, and he looked in the general

direction of the sound. The wind howled like a hungry wolf, and he could hear the hissing patter of rain against the windows.

It sounded pretty bad out there, which just made him worry all the more. He figured she was probably hanging out at the animal hospital, helping Doc Martin until the storm calmed down. That's just how she was, but still, he'd like to know for sure.

When Sid's mother had left them, his daughter had suddenly become his focus; everything he did was somehow connected to her, her well-being, and her happiness. It had become his job to make sure that she had everything she needed to live her life in the best way possible. Dale recalled, with a twinge of guilt, the amount of time he'd spent away from his little girl, the special jobs that he'd sometimes taken on the mainland, leaving Sidney to fend for herself. But truth be told, it had all been for her. A lot of the money he'd made had gone to her college fund, to help her with her dream—with her future.

His right arm began to ache, a dull throbbing pain to remind him that it was still there. How could he forget? Too many cigarettes and stress.

He'd thought he was going to die, to leave his little girl all alone, but then he'd gotten better—*if you want to call it that*—and he began to worry that it would have been better if he had died.

Sure, it would have been tough for her at first, but then she would have gone on with her life and on to to great things. Amazing things.

But with him alive—*if you want to call it that*—Sidney was left with the burden of his care. He remembered the days following his release from rehab and the things that his daughter had had to do for him.

Things that a daughter should never have to do for her father.

Dale felt that familiar anger again. He and it had become old friends, the anger usually rearing its ugly head when he was feeling sorry for himself. It was the kind of anger that resulted in him doing something he knew he shouldn't. Something that both he and his daughter knew was completely stupid, like smoking cigarettes or changing the batteries in the smoke alarm or flipping the mattress on his bed.

He wondered what sort of stupid thing he would do now.

His mind raced with a number of really dumb things, but instead, he just sat on the couch and stewed, waiting for his daughter to come home.

His thoughts drifted to the near future when Sidney wouldn't be there anymore, when she'd be living in Boston and going to college. He decided that he'd probably miss moments like this, worrying about where she was in the storm.

The house shuddered in a blast of wind, and his concern began to amplify. He grabbed his cane and maneuvered himself off the couch, slowly crossing the living room to the window that looked out at the road. Pulling the shade aside, he squinted through the glass at windswept darkness outside. It was as bad as it sounded, the rain blown sideways by the intensity of the wind. It was no surprise that they'd lost power and cell signal.

For a brief moment he considered trying to pull out the old generator in the garage and starting it up, but then he heard his daughter's angry voice in his head and decided against it. Bitterness at being an invalid began to surge through him, but something outside caught his eye, mercifully distracting him from his rage.

At first he believed it to be debris caught up in the exceptional flow of rainwater that was running like a river past his house, but as he watched, it changed course, moving against the flow of water and heading directly for his home.

"What the hell is that?" Dale muttered. Whatever it was, it had moved out of the road and into the grass before the white picket fence. He left the window and went to another, hoping for a better angle. Through the rain he could see something moving around the fence and through the grass, coming up toward the front—

The front doorknob violently rattled, startling him.

Dale went to the hallway and stood, staring at the front door, listening.

Again the knob rattled.

It has to be Sidney, he thought, moving toward the heavy wooden door. *But why would she use the front door when she always uses the back?*

His brain was already formulating reasons as he moved his cane from his left hand to his weakened right and reached for the door chain. He slid the chain across and popped it from its track, then undid the lock above the doorknob before taking it firmly in hand, turning, and pulling it open.

"Where the heck have you been?" he found himself asking the man who stood on the doorstep. The man who was most definitely not his daughter.

"I'm sorry," Dale started to apologize, about to ask if there was something he could do for the stranger, but the next words didn't come as he noticed the odd way the man was standing, the way he swayed, and the way his head tilted weirdly to the left.

Then lightning flashed, and Dale saw the paleness of his flesh, the blood that covered his face, and the unnatural contours of his skull.

The ghoulish stranger seemed to smile as he lurched forward, wedging himself in the doorway, even as Dale attempted to close the door. Dale struggled to push the door closed, but the man pushed harder, causing Dale to lose his balance and fall backward to the floor.

The door had swung wide in the struggle and wind, and the assailant just stood there, as if waiting for something. Dale floundered upon the floor, searching for his cane. He found it and pulled it toward him, rolling onto his side and using it to push himself up onto his knees.

He heard a strange, snuffling sound from the entryway behind him and turned his head to see that an ugly bulldoglike dog had joined the stranger in the entryway.

Now Dale knew who this was. He was one of the summer folk, those who usually came out to the island at the end of May and left on Labor Day. Dale remembered because before his stroke this man had called him for a construction quote on his summer house. While at the house, Dale had had a less than pleasant encounter with this nasty bulldog.

Berthold was the name. Alfred, he believed the dog was named.

"What are you doing here?" he demanded as he fought to his feet.

The dog moved into the hallway, the man following him. The way they moved made Dale think of the walking corpses in that zombie show that was so popular on television.

He actually managed to right himself and turned toward the intruders. "Get out!"

Instead of leaving, the dog sprang at him, knocking him backward with the weight of his thrust. Dale managed to stay on his feet by angling his body in such a way that he fell against the hallway wall. He raised his cane to club the dog that crouched before him, but the man, as if responding to some inaudible command, came at him next, his hands reaching out . . .

Cold fingers wrapping around Dale's throat . . .

And he began to squeeze.

CHAPTER **TWENTY-SIX**

Isaac ran through the thick underbrush that separated his family's property from his neighbor's, driven by the terror he had just experienced.

The ground was wet and slippery and fraught with hidden dangers. It was hard for him to see in the dark and pouring rain, and he found himself stumbling over trash covered by years of rotten leaves, sticks, and tree branches. There were rusted bike frames, rotting wooden doors, and even an old dollhouse that looked as though it had erupted up from beneath the slimy ground cover.

Something snagged his ankle, and Isaac went down on all fours, his fingers sinking into the rotting detritus. He began to panic, thinking that a snake had tripped him up, but as he pulled his foot away, he saw that it was in fact an old garden hose. Feeling relieved, and just a bit foolish, he freed his foot and pulled his hands from the sucking mud. But as lightning flashed, he saw that there were things moving on his hands; worms entwined around his fingers as earwigs traversed the muddy flesh of his hand and up his arms.

Isaac shook his hands crazily, wiping away the filth and crawling things as he again began to run. He wasn't sure exactly where he was going, just that he had to get away from his house.

He tried to remember what this area of the yard looked like when it was light and not in the midst of a hurricane. Finally, he stopped for a moment in the hissing rain, closing his eyes to picture the backyard.

In his mind he saw her, Sidney, his neighbor and his friend. Just the thought of the girl who didn't smile was enough to bring him some measure of solace. She had always been nice to him, even though she never seemed to be all that happy.

Isaac looked through the thick underbrush in the direction he believed Sidney's house to be. Maybe she would help him. He could tell her about the cats and the mice.

And his mother.

Images of his mother lying dead in the backyard, a cat burrowing deeply into her chest, made him want to fall to the ground in a tight little ball.

But things rustled in the wet leaves and squirmed upon the ground, and he knew that whatever they were, they were coming for him. If he didn't move, they would get him.

The hearing aid in his Steve ear began to make that sound again, as if picking up some frequency broadcasting nothing but fear, menace, and unspeakable violence. If he chose to listen, he knew that he would be lost to it, falling into the embrace of the sound that was nothing but bad.

Like a bad radio station playing in his ear, wanting him to do horrible things like the cats and mice and creepy crawlers in the dirt.

Isaac's hand shot up to his Steve ear, fiddling with the settings of the hearing device. For a brief moment he could have sworn that he heard his mother screaming his name over the sound of the howling winds, and he quickly pulled his hand away, listening carefully as he peered through the darkness.

"What are you doing here?" yelled a voice that Isaac realized wasn't his mother but was close by. Carefully he moved closer to the sound, only to hear the voice again, angry and insistent.

"Get out!"

Lightning flashed, illuminating the angry sky as well as his surroundings, and he saw that he was standing near the back of Sidney's house. He realized then that the voice he was hearing was coming from inside his friend's home.

And it sounded like someone needed help.

Isaac ran across the yard, toward the sounds of struggle becoming more pronounced over the raging of the storm . . .

Over the sound of the bad radio whispering horrible things in his Steve ear.

The bad, bad radio.

CHAPTER **TWENTY-SEVEN**

Dale stared into the eyes of the man who was trying to kill him.

The eyes were wrong, one bloodshot and horribly dilated, the other covered with a silvery film.

Then things started to go black, and he felt himself begin to slip away.

He tried to fight back, using every single bit of strength he could manage, but his attacker—*attackers*—were too strong.

The dog had taken hold of Dale's cane in his powerful jaws and was attempting to wrench it from his grasp. Dale held on with all his might, believing that if the cane was lost, he would most assuredly follow.

He flapped his arms wildly as his legs weakened and he began to slide down the hallway wall, the stranger's hands still wrapped tightly about his throat. He felt the fingers on his left hand begin to loosen as the dog tugged on the cane, and panic set in. The dog temporarily released the cane to take a better grip, and Dale used the moment to lash out with his leg, kicking the bulldog square in the face and driving him back. He managed to bring his cane up and swing it into the man's horribly pale, blood-covered face, hitting him right above the nose and opening a huge, oozing gash.

The man grunted, his hold on Dale's throat weakening, allowing Dale to squirm free and slide to the floor, where he began to wildly swing his cane in an attempt to keep his attackers away. The bulldog suddenly emerged from the shadows, moving lightning quick to sink his nasty teeth into the meat of Dale's left arm. Dale cried out. Reflexively, his hand opened, and he heard the sound of the cane hitting the floor. He tried to retrieve it, tried to recapture the only thing that might save his life, but the dog held tightly to his arm, dragging him away from the prize.

Berthold kicked the cane away as he lumbered closer, then dropped on Dale's back, pinning him to the floor.

Dale tried to throw the man off, bucking and thrashing wildly, but his attacker was too heavy and the bulldog still held on to his left arm, while his useless right arm flopped pathetically against the floor. He felt the man's cold, bloodstained hands wrap around his jaw from behind and begin to savagely pull upward. With intensifying horror Dale wondered which would snap first, his neck or his back.

Berthold continued to pull, and Dale screamed in agony, the tendons and muscles in his neck and back strained to the point where they would soon tear, and then the bones would—

"What are you doing to him?" a voice boomed from someplace close by. "What are you doing to Mr. Moore?"

Dale managed to twist his body to see the familiar form of his neighbor, Isaac Moss, standing soaking wet just inside the doorway. Dale tried to warn him away, but found that he was only capable of making a strangled, gargling sound as his neck was about to be broken.

"You let him go!" Isaac shouted, coming farther into the house.

The bulldog released Dale's arm and moved to jump over his prone body to get to the youth. Dale reached out as the dog leaped over him and took hold of his muscular back leg.

The dog fell, then tried to spin around, jaws snapping savagely. Dale held tight, even as the dog's razor-sharp teeth ripped the flesh from his knuckles.

Isaac rushed closer. He kicked the dog savagely, knocking him across the room.

"Get out of here, you bad dog!" he yelled. Then he grabbed hold of the man atop Dale and wrenched him back, throwing the attacker to the floor.

"And you get off Mr. Moore!"

Dale scrabbled across the floor and pushed up against the wall. He'd never realized how strong Isaac had become as he'd gotten older, still remembering the quiet youth who rarely left the house in all the years that he and Sidney had lived here.

Isaac stood, watching the man he had thrown to the floor slowly start to get back up. The bulldog was stalking in from the living room, the pair seeming to act in tandem.

"What should I do, Mr. Moore?" Isaac asked, his voice nervously high pitched.

Dale wished that he could do more to help the young man, but in his current condition he was next to useless. "We have to get them outside," he croaked, still feeling the effects of his neck being crushed.

Berthold silently lunged at Isaac, attempting to put his hands around the teen's throat. Isaac backed away as the man grabbed for him. Dale saw that the dog was maneuvering around behind Isaac to attack and managed to bend down and snag his cane from the floor. He hobbled as quickly as he could toward the scene unfolding before him, raised the cane with his left arm, and brought it down hard on the dog's head before he could attack the boy. Dale found it incredibly strange that the bulldog barely made a sound as he collapsed to the floor and lay there motionless.

Isaac's attacker paused as the dog fell.

"Throw him out, Isaac!" Dale cried. "Grab his clothes and toss him out!"

Isaac immediately reached out, grabbing the man by the back of his shirt, spinning him around, and hurling him toward the open front door and the storm that raged outside.

The man stumbled but stopped at the doorway, appearing to collect himself as he slowly turned.

Dale made it across the hall in time to club the man in the forehead, then fell to his knees. Berthold seemed stunned by the blow, falling backward onto the outside landing, where he lost his footing and tumbled down the stairs to the soaking concrete walkway.

Dale leaned on the cane and turned to where the dog still lay prone upon the floor.

"Grab its collar, Isaac!" Dale yelled. "Drag it to the door by the collar!"

With a tentative hand Isaac grabbed the dog by the chain choke collar and began to drag him across the floor toward the door. "Like this, Mr. Moore?"

"Just like that, Isaac," Dale said. "Quickly now."

Dale looked out to see that Berthold was recovering on the walkway.

Isaac was almost to the door when the dog began to awaken. The animal tossed his head savagely to one side at the youth's wrist, and Isaac let out a loud squawk, letting go of the collar to avoid being bitten.

The man outside was slowly rising. They didn't have much time.

The dog's head was apparently still rattled from the hit. He attempted to climb to his feet but slumped back down to the floor.

"We have to get it out the door—fast!" Dale said.

"It'll bite me," Isaac said.

"It'll try to kill you if it gets a chance to wake up," Dale added, hobbling closer to the animal. Dale quickly reached down, grabbed the dog by the collar with his left hand, and tried the best he could to drag it. The dog traveled less than a foot before he was trying to bite him again.

"Damn it," Dale hissed.

Dale looked over to see that Isaac looked very upset, one of his hands up at his ear where Dale could see that a hearing aid had been placed.

"Isaac?"

The young man's hand was at the hearing aid, his eyes locked on the dog as he started to get up again.

"The bad radio," Isaac said, his face grimacing as if he were in pain. "The bad radio is inside my head."

Dale didn't know what that meant but looked over toward the open door to see Berthold coming up the stairs. They had to do something right away, or things were about to get very bad once again.

The man was coming in through the doorway when Isaac lost it. The teen began to scream at the top of his lungs, going for the still-recovering dog, snatching him up from the floor, and running with him toward the doorway.

Dale barely had the chance to get out of his way, stumbling over to one side and almost hitting the floor. He watched as Isaac ran, thrusting the squat body of the dog at the man, knocking him backward, the two of them tumbling down the three brick steps to the wet sidewalk.

Isaac was wild-eyed, standing just outside the doorway panting. His hand was at the hearing aid once again, snatching at it with clawed fingers as if the device was somehow hurting him.

Dale moved as quickly as he was able, careful not to fall as he got to the door, watching as the bulldog clambered to all fours, Berthold right beside him.

"Isaac, get in!" Dale yelled.

The youth turned around slowly to look at him, and then obeyed, coming in from the landing.

Dale slammed the door closed and locked it, leaning his trembling body against it as fists pounded on the other side.

"It's the bad radio," Isaac said. "It's all the bad radio's fault."

Dale had no idea what the young man was talking about as he leaned his aching body back against the wall, but as far as he was concerned, it sounded like as good of a reason as any.

CHAPTER TWENTY-EIGHT

If it was fifteen years before Sidney saw another bug, it would still be way too soon.

It amazed her how they could get themselves through the smallest cracks. Almost immediately, spiders, ants, and centipedes began to find their way under the bathroom door, heading to the first person in line, which was her.

"Give me some towels," she ordered. She'd dropped the trashbag with the raccoon inside by the tub and was crushing the next wave of attacking insects beneath her sneakered feet.

Rich reached into a small cabinet above the toilet and pulled some out before tossing them to her.

She began to shove them tightly against the bottom of the door. She yelped as a centipede slithered over her sneaker and under the cuff of her jeans, and she stomped her feet and swatted at the leg of her pants until the thing dropped out. Half of its body was crushed, but that didn't stop it from trying to get at her again.

"So now what?" Cody asked as Sidney jammed the last of the towels against the door.

"Now they won't be getting in," she said, double-checking her handiwork.

"Sure," Cody agreed. "But in case you haven't noticed, it's a little cramped in here."

Sidney stood and gave the bathroom a good looking over. She noticed the frosted glass window directly opposite the door.

"Where does that go?" she asked Rich.

"Backyard," he answered.

Something larger than an insect pounded on the door.

They looked at each other, a spark of fear evident on all their faces.

Whatever was outside the door hit it again, causing it to shake. And then it began to scrape on the door, claws scratching furiously at the cheap wood.

"That door isn't going to last," Sidney said matter-of-factly. "We're going to have to go out the window." She pushed past Rich and tried to open it, but it wouldn't budge. She checked to see if it was locked and found that years of paint had made the latch inoperable. She turned to look at Rich.

"We never opened it"—he shrugged—"so when Dad painted—"

He was interrupted by the sound of splintering wood.

"We have to break it." Sidney's eyes scanned the bathroom and stopped on the metal towel rack attached to the wall. "This'll do," she said, grabbing the rack in both hands and giving a savage yank.

"Hey!" Rich objected as she pulled it again. "You're wrecking the place."

The rack came loose, plaster raining down to the tile floor. "Seriously, Rich?"

"Guys!" Cody's gaze was fixed on the bottom of the door, where the wood had started to pock and crack above the barrier of towels.

Snowy sniffed at the towels, then barked wildly. The noises on the other side of the door stopped for only a moment before beginning again all the more furiously.

"You were saying?" Sidney said to Rich as she began to bang on the center of the window with the end of the towel rack. She was surprised it didn't break. In fact, she was barely scratching it.

"Let me try," Rich said, taking the metal rack from her. He hit the window squarely in the middle, and a fine crack appeared. "It's all about the muscle," he said, hitting it again. More cracks spiderwebbed through it, but still it didn't break.

Snowy was barking again, her snout jammed into the towels at the bottom of the door, where pieces of wood were beginning to fleck away.

"What the hell is this made of?" Rich asked, preparing to strike the window again, but Sidney was too impatient.

"Give it to me," she said, yanking the towel rack away from his hands.

Rich looked shocked and maybe even a little hurt, but she didn't care. Time was running short.

She planted her feet and mustered all of her strength before swinging the end of the rack into the window like a baseball bat. The glass splintered, and several pieces fell away into the yard outside. Wind and rain whistled through the opening as she continued to bang away at the glass.

"Hold off," Rich said, reaching to carefully pry away the jagged glass with his fingers. Sidney handed him the towel rack and went to see what she could do about the door.

She couldn't do much. The bottom of the door was being gradually broken away. From the sounds of it, there was more gnawing now than digging.

This was getting way too freaky for her.

"Whatever is on the other side is going to be able to get under there soon," Cody warned. He nudged the towels farther beneath the door with the toe of his shoe.

"Yeah," Sidney agreed, looking behind her to the window. Rich was doing a good job, and almost all the glass was gone from the frame, but the opening looked much smaller now.

Rich peered out into the stormy darkness as he pulled the last of the glass from the frame. "Got a bit of drop back here," he said as he turned to face them.

"Are we going to fit?" Cody asked.

"We'll fit," Sidney said firmly. There wasn't any question—no other option.

From the corner of her eye, she caught a flash of fur on the floor and gasped as a small, black, clawed limb reached through an opening in the door, ripping even more of the cheap wood and drawing it away. The scratching and gnawing sounds were intensifying by the second.

"Go," she said, pushing Cody toward the window. Then she grabbed Snowy by the collar and hauled her toward the window as well. "You're going to have to help her."

"You first," Cody said, "and we'll pass her to you."

Sidney shook her head. "No, you first, then Rich and I will get Snowy out. Rich will go next, and then me."

"I don't think—" Rich began.

"I do the thinking in this group and that's my plan."

"What if we don't like it," Cody said as Rich nodded emphatically.

A squirrel forced its head through the hole in the door, flashing sharp yellowed teeth before retreating.

"Not enough time for a new plan," Sidney said. "I win. We have to go now." Sidney pushed Snowy closer to her ex.

Cody looked as though he wanted to argue some more, but common sense prevailed, and he started to move. He stepped up onto the toilet and pushed himself through the window, his broad shoulders barely clearing the frame.

"Give me a shove," Cody shouted over his shoulder as he kicked his legs and wriggled, trying to maneuver through the tight space.

Sidney and Rich each grabbed a leg and began to push, and a moment later Cody dropped out of sight, followed by a slight thud and a grunt.

Sidney stood on her toes to peer outside. "You all right?"

She saw him climbing to his feet, muddy and wet.

"I'm good. Get Snowy out here." He raised his arms, preparing to catch the large dog.

Sidney squatted down in front of the dog to capture her attention.

It was obvious that the shepherd was quite nervous by the streams of drool that were dripping from her jowls as she panted. Sidney rubbed the dog's ears lovingly and looked into her eyes. "You're going to be all right," she said as calmly as she could, hoping that the dog would pick up on her intent.

The door was breaking away; she could hear the crunching and splintering of wood but refused to turn around.

"Ready?" Sidney asked Rich, who nodded.

She rose from her squat and placed her hands beneath the dog and began to lift. Rich joined her as Snowy began to wildly squirm.

"It's okay—it's okay," she said to the dog as she looked into her dark brown eyes. "We've got you."

They lifted her head through the window first. She was still squirming like crazy but quickly seemed to put two and two together as she must have seen Cody outside and below.

Snowy's back legs were scrabbling for purchase, and Rich assisted by placing them up onto the sill.

"There she goes," Rich said as Snowy disappeared.

There was a brief yelp of pain, and Sidney immediately panicked, sticking her head out into the rain to see what happened.

"Is she all right?" she called, holding her breath as she waited for the answer.

"She's good," Cody said. "I think she might've landed on a paw funny, but she's good," he added.

Sidney could see Snowy excitedly circling Cody, looking up at the open window space. He was rubbing her head and praising her for being a good girl. Snowy loved Cody, which was just one more reason that Sidney felt like such a terrible person for breaking up with him.

"Sid, look," she heard Rich say behind her, and turned from the window to look at the bathroom door.

Something bigger than a squirrel was trying to push its way beneath the door, fighting the insects that swarmed in around its struggling head. She didn't know what it was, but it had some nasty claws and was making short work of what remained of the bottom of the door.

"You next," she said, grabbing hold of Rich's arm and pulling him toward the window.

"No, you," he said, fighting with her.

"We've already had this discussion and I won, remember?" she said. "I'll be right behind you."

He looked at her hard for a moment and must have realized it would do no good to argue. Time was running very short. Without another word, he grabbed the trashbag and climbed atop the toilet. He shoved the bag out the window, then hoisted himself through the opening and disappeared.

"All right?" she called out, now facing the disintegrating bathroom door.

"We're good," she heard Rich reply.

The bottom of the door was pushed inward with a loud cracking sound, and a groundhog forced its bulk through, allowing a swarm of insects and an assortment of rodents—she saw mice, ground squirrels, and even some chipmunks—to flow in to attack her.

She could see that they would be on her in seconds and decided that she wouldn't take any chances of not making it through the window. Her eyes touched upon a lighter sitting on the back of the toilet tank next to a candle.

Flame. Fire. Something to drive them back.

She squatted down quickly and opened the cabinet beneath the sink and found what she was looking for.

A can of bathroom deodorizing spray.

Yeah, this will do nicely, she thought, remembering her younger days, hanging out with friends and matches.

The groundhog was looking at her with one cold, dead eye and another that glistened as if covered with some sort of reflective cover, just like the raccoon.

She pointed the can of deodorizer at the bottom of the door, and all the things that were now squirming inside to get at her, and pushed down on the spray head while bringing the lighter flame toward the chemically sweet spray streaming from the nozzle.

The vapor ignited in a rush of fire and intense heat, engulfing the flow of life as it squeezed beneath the door. Sidney kept her finger on the nozzle, moving the orange flame from left to right, driving some of the larger life back and igniting the towels wedged beneath the still-intact sections of door. She found it odd that none of the animals made any noise when burned, no hisses or squeals or cries of any kind at all, making something that was already incredibly strange and disturbing all the more so.

The animals had retreated temporarily, but she could already hear movement, guessing they were about to attempt to come through again. Sidney released the canister plunger, stopping the flame, and turned back toward the window, ready to make a run for it. The groundhog, or whatever the hell it was, with fur blackened in places and eyes seared red and oozing, shoved its head back beneath the door and again begin to drag itself inside, pushing the smoldering towels aside and opening up a larger passage.

And opening the floodgates.

The space beneath the door gaped wide, and a steady swarm of insects and vermin flowed into the small bathroom, moving immediately to attack her. Sidney jumped back, away from the swarm, stomping on and swatting at the animals and bugs. The back of her foot came up against the bottom of the bathtub, and she nearly lost her balance, grabbing on to the shower curtain so as not to fall. As if sensing an opportunity, the rodents sprang, moving with incredible speed up her body, seeking out any areas of soft, exposed flesh to scratch and bite. She reacted as best she could, grabbing at the warm, biting bodies, crushing them in her hand and tossing them away. If she weren't fighting for her life, the feeling of the tiny, hollow bones of the rodents breaking beneath her fingers probably would have made her throw up. Hopefully, there'd be time for throwing up later, if she got through this.

The burned groundhog and three raccoons were forcing their way in beneath the crumbling wooden door, and she knew that it was probably only seconds before they were at her. Her eyes darted over to the open window as the boys called to her from outside. She had to get to them.

The animals' numbers were growing. It was completely insane, but there wasn't any other way to look at it. They wanted to kill her.

Climbing into the bathtub, she used the shower curtain as a

shield against the encroaching onslaught, yanking both the plastic liner and the cloth curtain down from the rod and throwing them over her head like a cape to cover her body.

The groundhog leaped over the lip of the tub, mouth agape, squared yellow teeth ready to take a bite. She lashed out with her foot, knocking it away. The raccoons came next, springing at her but sliding from her body as they came in contact with the slick material of the shower curtain. She could hear the smaller critters as they attempted to attack her, their bodies pattering off the plastic covering her body. It was a good idea but one that she was sure the animals would eventually find a way through.

She wasn't going to give them the chance.

The guys were yelling to her from the backyard. She stuck her head out the window briefly, seeing that Cody was attempting to climb back in.

"I'm coming now," she called, using the toilet to give herself the leg up she would need to crawl through.

Something heavy struck her from behind, and Sidney lost her balance, her foot sliding off the plastic toilet lid and making her collapse to the floor. Still mostly covered, she lay there, collecting herself, listening to the sounds of claws sliding across the plastic covering her while trying to keep anything from crawling beneath.

Ready to rise, she was struck again by something heavy, and she found herself being slammed against the bathroom wall. She had no doubt that it was the raccoons working in tandem with the groundhog to keep her from escaping.

How is this even possible? Her panicked thoughts attempted to understand the insanity of the situation.

She moved toward the window again, listening to the sounds of clawed feet scratching upon the tile floor, and braced herself. The weighty body of one of the varmints struck again, but she was ready, bracing herself against the onslaught.

"Sidney, where are you?" Cody yelled up from the yard below the window. "C'mon!"

She used his voice as a beacon, sliding along the wall until she reached the window again. Mice and squirrels and chipmunks landed upon her plastic cloak, sliding back down to the floor, where they quickly resumed their attack upon her.

Lifting the makeshift cape over her head and face, she saw the opening and made her move, leaping up onto the sill of the window, squirming within her cocoon of plastic. The wood of the window frame was rough against her stomach, scraping away what she thought to be layers of skin, but that was the least of her concerns. Sidney wriggled her body through the opening, inspired to move all the faster by the sounds of multiple clawed feet clicking upon the tile floor of the bathroom. She imagined the sight of them in her mind, a wave of bugs and vermin surging toward her across the bathroom floor desperate to claw and bite—

To kill.

Shedding her plastic skin, Sidney squirmed into a position where both her legs were now sticking outright into space, and she brought one leg and knee up, pushing off on the small windowsill to finally send herself flying over the edge.

The ground rushed up to meet her, and she braced for the pain of impact. There was a flurry of movement just before she hit, and she found her fall halted by the arms of her friends catching her.

"What took you so long?" Cody asked as he and Rich lowered her to the ground. Snowy jumped up onto her chest, licking at her face happily.

She didn't answer, looking up to where she'd just fallen from. There were animals leaping onto the sill, spilling over the edge to land in the grass at their feet.

"We should go," she said as she stood, motioning to her dog to follow when she started around the house toward their cars.

And then she remembered.

"The raccoon," she said, stopping short and turning.

Rich and Cody stopped and stared.

"The trash bag with the dead raccoon," she explained.

Rich turned and ran back to the yard where he'd dropped the bag.

"Are you all right?" Cody asked.

She looked at him strangely.

"I'm as good as I can be," she said. "Given the circumstances."

Rich returned, and she grabbed the bag from him before continuing around the house to the front drive, Snowy trotting by her side.

Even above the pouring rain she could hear something and stopped to listen.

"What now?" Rich asked, watching her.

"Listen," Sidney said. "Do you hear that?"

It was sort of a rustling sound, but from all around them, growing louder than the heavy rainfall. The hair on the back of her neck stood on end, and an icy chill ran down her spine as the sounds intensified, coming closer.

From every open space around the yard, from around the house, they saw movement. Things making their way toward them.

"You're shitting me," Rich said, already on the run.

Cody was running too, though he continued to look back to where they had just come from.

Sidney looked as well. At first she didn't understand what it was that she was seeing. It was like a wave of water, like a river that had overflowed its banks and was coursing in through the woods of Rich's backyard. But that would have made some sort of sense.

What she was seeing made no sense.

Instead of water there were living things—mice and rats, and cats and squirrels. She even saw some smaller dogs within the wave of life rolling toward them.

"Sidney, move!" Cody screamed, and she hoped that this was all some sort of crazy dream.

But it wasn't. It was real.

The wave of animals flowed across the lawn, obliterating any sight of grass. It was as if a living cover was being slowly pulled over the entire expanse of Rich's backyard.

Sidney managed to tear her gaze from the terrifying sight to see that Cody and Snowy were waiting for her. They urged her on, Snowy barking excitedly and Rich waving with his hands as they ran alongside Rich's house toward the driveway.

The bushes and trees to the left of her rustled, but she refused to look there, knowing full well what she would see and afraid that her brain just might completely shut down from the sight of it.

"Get in the truck!" Cody screamed to Rich.

The ground was crunching beneath her feet, and Sidney looked down to see that it was covered with the glistening bodies of june bugs—hundreds and hundreds of june bugs writhing en masse, crawling upon each other and now attempting to crawl on her. She kicked out with her feet, clearing a swath in front of her, continuing to follow her dog and friends to Cody's truck.

The ground before the driveway was moving, the living flow spreading there as well. They all reached Cody's truck, grabbing hold of the door handles to pull open the doors and—

The doors didn't open.

Sidney looked across the truck to see Cody reaching into his pockets.

"Locked? Are you kidding me?" she asked.

"What the frig is wrong with you—you locked your truck in the driveway of my house—in a freakin' hurricane?"

Cody didn't answer, ripping the ring of keys from his pocket and dropping them to the ground.

"Damn it!" Sidney heard him scream.

Hand still clutched to the wet metal of the door handle, she looked about her and felt her terror grow. There were larger things among the small ones, almost as if the smaller animals and insects had failed in their duty to kill them and now . . .

She heard the car lock pop and yanked on the door, crawling up into the front cab, with Snowy and Rich right beside her. Cody sat behind the wheel, feeding his key into the ignition.

"Lock the doors," she said, eyes scanning the night outside the vehicle. "Please lock the doors."

Cody hit the switch that made his and the passenger-side doors lock up tightly, and she found that she really felt no better. All around them, the night was moving.

The truck engine roared to life, and the headlights of the vehicle illuminated the darkness before them.

No one in the car said anything. Their voices had been taken from them by the horror of what they saw.

The row of cats in the headlight beams was growing, more and more of the water-drenched felines casually emerging from the darkness of the woods that surrounded the house.

It was one of the scariest things Sidney had ever seen in her life.

Then dogs showed up.

CHAPTER TWENTY-NINE

Gregory Sayid huddled in a darkened corner of his office talking into his cell phone.

"I'm not sure how long I'll be," he said. "Hopefully, not much longer." The scientist paused before saying anything else, thinking about the events that had already occurred and what was likely occurring on an island in Massachusetts as he spoke to his daughter.

She then asked about his current assignment.

"You know I can't talk about that," he said. "Yes, it's top secret," he mimicked her with a fake chuckle. He hoped that she couldn't pick up on the concern and sense of impending dread in the manufactured attempt at jocularity.

"I'm fine, seriously," he told her.

His daughter was as perceptive as he feared.

"I should probably get going." Sayid turned from his darkened corner and noticed that he wasn't alone. Brenda Langridge leaned casually against the frame of his office doorway.

He turned away from the security officer's scrutinizing eyes.

"I love you too," he told his daughter. "Be good, and I'll see you soon."

He listened to her tell him good-bye and the sound of the connection being broken as she hung up before he ended the call.

"You know I could have you arrested for breaking protocol, right?" Langridge said as she pushed off the doorframe and entered his space.

"If it would mean that you'd lock me away someplace for the next twenty-four hours or so, I might be down for that," he told her as he sidestepped to his desk.

The top of the desk was a sea of files and paperwork. To anybody else it was an example of complete chaos, but to him it was actually a kind of order only he could understand.

"No such luck," she said, eyeing the wreckage of his desktop. "We'll be ready to take off within the hour."

Sayid sat down heavily in his chair. He knew that they'd need to head to Benediction as soon as humanly possible, but the idea of what they would be encountering—what they might find—was still an incredible weight on him.

"When are they estimating the storm letting up?" he asked, not looking up. He took a file from a smaller pile and opened it, wanting to check some things before they had to go.

"The National Weather Service estimates that it's got at least another ten to twelve hours before it subsides," Langridge said, stepping closer to his desk, tilting her head to see what was in the file he was working on. "That is, if the storm continues to behave like a normal storm, which we're not sure that it will."

He was reading a morning report on the child that they'd brought back from the Heaven's Breath occurrence.

"How's the survivor doing?" Langridge asked as she leaned over his desk, attempting to read upside down.

"Alexandria," he said, jotting down some notes in the file.

"Excuse me?"

"The survivor," he said, turning his gaze to the woman. "She has a name. Alexandria."

"Right," Langridge said, acknowledging the information but still not saying the child's name. "How is she?"

"Better," Sayid said. "They're weaning her off of the sleep and antianxiety meds, and she seems to be adjusting."

"And has she said anything more about the event?"

"The doctors and nurses are avoiding the topic," Sayid explained. "Letting her adjust some more before—"

"It might be beneficial to have some firsthand information before Benediction," Langridge explained.

Sayid now believed he understood why the security officer had refused to call the child by name. Just being known as the survivor, the child was simply another source of intel. Just a source of information, and not a little girl who had lost her mother and father when a mysterious storm raged over an island paradise and . . .

His mind was filled with the horrific images of the bodies that had been recovered after the storm.

"It might be," Sayid answered, "but I don't feel that she's far enough along to be able to contribute anything of use right now."

"So we're just going to go by the latest reports."

"Yeah," Sayid confirmed, closing the child's folder and leaning back in his chair. "At the moment it's the most up-to-date information that we have."

"Information that says that these mysterious storm manifestations seem to somehow affect the behavior of native animal species."

"That's right."

"Affect? I'm not even sure I understand what that means."

He stared at her for a moment, not sure how much more he should say before the next debriefing, but decided that it was inevitable she would know, so why not now.

"The storm—or something in the storm that we haven't yet quite determined—affects the behavior of local insect and animal life." He paused, seeing that she was truly listening to him now.

"It appears to make them more . . . aggressive," he explained.

"Aggressive how?" Langridge asked.

He thought about how he might say it, remembering the bodies that they had found and the shape that they were in, and decided that there really were not too many ways.

"It turns them into killers," Sayid told her.

CHAPTER **THIRTY**

The first thing that Cody noticed about the dogs was the way they moved. There wasn't that fluid, natural movement when a dog trotted or began to run. This was stiff, odd, like the animals were getting used to their legs.

The dogs came from the woods surrounding the house, from all sides, and Cody found that he even recognized some of them from the neighborhood, having seen them walking with their masters down the street or chasing a stick at the beach.

The only thing that wasn't familiar about them was the dark stains around many of their muzzles. Cody didn't even want to acknowledge the reality of what the stains could be or he just might find himself screaming at the top of his lungs and boarding the next train to Crazy Town.

The dogs stood in a formidable cluster at the left of the two-car garage, the pack of cats—*was that what it would be called, a pack?*—had collected over to the right.

"What are we waiting for?" Rich asked, his fingers nervously tapping on the dashboard.

Cody really didn't have an answer other than he was mesmerized by the weirdness, feeling relatively safe to observe the strangeness of it all from the inside of the car.

"We need to see Doc Martin," Sidney spoke up. "She needs to take a look at the dead raccoon if we're going to have any clue as to what might be going on here."

Cody said nothing as he put the car in reverse, turning his head to look behind him as he began to back down the driveway and—

"Son of a bitch!" he exclaimed, slamming his hand angrily against the back of the seat.

"What?" Sidney asked, concerned by the outburst as Snowy began to bark.

"The sailboat," he said, pointing out the back window. "The trailer is still attached."

Rich and Sidney turned around briefly and then back.

"I'm not going out there to unhook it," Rich said.

"Well don't look at me," Cody added.

A Labrador retriever landed atop the truck as if it had dropped out of the sky, its claws raking across the surface of the hood as it rammed its face viciously into the windshield.

They all screamed at the suddenness of the attack, the dog's yellow teeth scraping along the surface of the curved glass, leaving bloody smears as it attempted to bite them through the transparent obstruction.

"We'll take the sailboat with us," Rich screamed, pushing himself back in the seat as more of the dogs rushed toward the vehicle. "Just go!"

Cody put the car in reverse, turning again in his seat to watch out the back. The truck began to rock as it was struck on all sides.

"What the hell?" Cody said, staring out the driver's-side window at the nightmarish sight of four dogs throwing themselves into the side of the vehicle with enough force to dent the door.

Snowy was barking wildly at the Labrador, which continued to stare in at them, snapping at the glass, its mouth smeared with bloody foam.

In the side mirror Cody could see that the dogs were circling the vehicle, moving faster and faster, building up speed before they plowed into the truck once again on all sides.

"We really should get out of here," Sidney said, eyes wide and darting around.

Cody wanted to do what she asked, but . . .

He checked his mirrors as he began to back up, then slammed on the breaks again. The Labrador on the hood slipped and slid off to the side to join its angry brethren.

"What now?" Rich asked. He looked like he was going to jump out of his skin with each new bang, bump, and thud.

"I don't . . . ," Cody began.

"You don't what?" Sidney asked as they were hit on both sides with enough force to make the truck rock.

"I don't want . . . I don't want to hurt them!" he finally screamed, leaning on his horn, hoping that the sound maybe would drive them off.

Yeah, that *will happen.*

The dogs continued their assault, running about the car, darting in to collide against the sides and doors as well as bite at the tires.

"You just have to go," Sidney said. "Don't worry about them . . . you don't have a choice."

He could see that she was just as upset about the potential as he was, but there was no choice.

Cody stepped on the gas, and with the car still in reverse, backed up as quickly as he was able while paying close attention to the boat and trailer still attached to his truck.

He turned the wheel to the left, angling the car from the driveway onto the road that ran in front of the Stanmores' property. He then put the car in drive, the vehicle continuing to be hit from all sides as he sped up, the last sight he saw reflected in the rearview mirror being the pack of cats moving as one living mass following down the driveway before dispersing suddenly into the woods as if they had never been there.

Sidney turned in her seat to look out the back window at the boat and the road behind them. A pack of dogs ran through the pouring rain in pursuit of them, showing no signs of slowing.

"They're still chasing us," she said, turning back around. "This is so freaking insane I don't even know what to say."

"What's to say," Rich said. "Something has made all the animals and bugs and stuff go batshit crazy. How's that?"

"Sounds right," Cody said, continuing to drive.

Sidney pulled the bag containing the body of the raccoon a little closer. "Which is why getting this to Doc Martin is essential," she said.

"Here's a question," Rich suddenly blurted out. She looked over to see that he was pushing himself over against the passenger-side door as he spoke.

"If something is making all the animal life on the island go nuts . . . ," he said.

"Yeah?" she urged.

"What about Snowy?" he asked. "Why isn't Snowy trying to rip our throats out?"

She watched him eye her dog before raising a tentative hand to pat her head. Snowy accepted the affections lovingly, leaning over to lick Rich's face.

"I don't know why," she said as she put an arm around her dog. Snowy then decided that she needed a kiss as well. "Maybe whatever it is that's causing this . . . she hasn't been exposed to it."

She continued to think, going through countless scenarios, but nothing really felt right. They were all easily picked apart.

"This is why Doc Martin is our best bet," she said. "She can take a look at the specimen we have, and maybe we can learn something."

She looked through the windshield to see where they were and saw that they weren't that far from the center of town.

"We'll head by her place first," Sidney said. "If she's not there, she might still be at the hospital and—"

"There's someplace we have to go first," Cody said, staring straight ahead.

"Someplace first?" Sidney questioned. "Where?"

Rich was leaning over in the seat, waiting for the answer.

"The marina," Cody said. "We're going to pick up my dad."

Sidney was going to argue but quickly realized if she did, she'd sound like a total bitch. Of course he wanted to pick up his dad.

"Yeah, good idea," she said, nodding in agreement. "And then we'll go get mine."

CHAPTER **THIRTY-ONE**

Doc Martin pulled the clear plastic shield down over her face and picked up the rotary bone saw from the table.

She remembered how her staff, Sidney included, had laughed when she'd told them that she wanted to invest in the equipment.

"What the heck for?" Sidney had asked. "Are we going to be filming *CSI: Benediction* here?

They'd all had a good chuckle, but then Doc Martin bought it anyway. One never knew when a good necropsy might be in order. And even though she already had adequate tools for the job, an electric bone saw was just so damn sexy.

Now it would prove its weight in gold.

"*CSI: Benediction* my ass," she said, hefting the saw in her rubber-gloved hands. She flipped the switch to on, and the battery-operated motor hummed softly.

"Sorry about this, big guy," she said as she leaned over and touched the spinning blade to the side of Bear's head.

She couldn't help but remember Bear when he was alive, a gentle giant of a dog. Even as a puppy, he was huge, and she used to joke that he must have been given some sort of growth hormone or been exposed to nuclear radiation to grow the way he did. There had been talk among the office staff of charging for rides on the huge mastiff's back at the next school fair.

But the good memories were warped with the recollection of the usually gentle giant attempting to tear out her throat.

Doc Martin chose to believe that it wasn't Bear's fault at all, that something else—some unknown malady—was responsible.

A malady that she was hoping to discover and perhaps be able to cure.

The circular cuts around the dog's skull finally met end to beginning, the acrid smell of burning bone and blood filling the air of the cramped operating room space. She leaned over and flicked a switch to turn on the ceiling fan to suck out the lingering dust and odor, again grateful that the emergency gas-powered generator had kicked in as it was supposed to.

She set the bloody saw down on the metal table beside her and reached over to peel the layer of fur and skin away from the dog's head to expose the skull. Doc Martin then grabbed a thin chisel and hammer from the tools on a stainless-steel tray. Leaning over the dog's corpse again, she wedged the end of the chisel into the bloody line around Bear's skull and gently tapped it with the hammer. She did that all around the dog's skull until the bone cap lifted with a wet sucking sound.

"All right then," she muttered as she set her tools and the skull cap down upon the instrument table. "Let's have a look."

At first perusal the brain looked fine. Doc Martin touched the tips of her fingers on each of the cerebral hemispheres; they were squishy, spongelike, just as they were supposed to be. Carefully she reached down into the skull with both hands and gently lifted the brain so that she could see beneath it.

An icy cold finger of dread raced up her spine as she saw it.

"What is this?" she asked herself.

To the untrained eye it would have looked like just another part of the brain, but Doc Martin knew better.

It appeared to be some kind of growth. A tumor perhaps. She leaned in for a closer look, noticing the tendrils that spread out from the mass to other parts of the brain. Remembering the silvery sheen that covered Bear's right eye, she paid special attention to the occipital lobe and saw that it was permeated with thin, capillary-like growths that appeared to weave together to form a thicker connection that disappeared into the gray matter.

Doc Martin tugged slightly on the brain, pulling it farther back from the front of the skull to observe the optic nerve. The thick, silvery tendrils were completely wrapped around the sight nerve leading to the dog's right eye. It reminded her of an old telephone cord—before phones were cordless and could fit in your pocket.

The doctor was stumped. In her many years as a veterinarian she had never seen anything like this.

Setting the brain back down inside the skull, she turned her attention to the mastiff's right eye, still hanging from its socket. She gently lifted the orb, holding it between forefinger and thumb, and looked directly into it.

She was shocked to see the pupil suddenly dilate beneath the shiny membrane, opening and closing, reminding her of the lens of a camera as it tried to focus.

"How is this possible?" she muttered. The dog was dead; there shouldn't have been any activity in the eye, or any other part of the animal for that matter. Carefully she put the eye back on the table and lifted the brain for another look at the growth. It might have been a trick of the light, but she could have sworn that it had pulsed with life. She stared, and it did not move again.

She returned to the eye. It too showed no further signs of function, appearing as it should have, dead and lifeless.

But Doc Martin knew what she had seen.

The eye had focused.

Watching her.

CHAPTER **THIRTY-TWO**

It continued to pour as Sidney and her friends drove through the storm-wrought streets. Nightmarish scenarios, half glimpsed through the rapid passing of the wipers over the windshield, told them that all of Benediction was experiencing the same horrors.

Houses were on fire, shapes that could very easily have been bodies were lying by the sides of the road, packs of wild things—dogs, cats, raccoons, and whatever else called the island of Benediction home—were emerging from the thick of darkened woods to chase them as they drove past.

It was like a nightmare, but Sidney didn't think she'd ever had one so terrifying.

"It's gotta be the end of the world," Rich said as he gazed out through the windshield.

"Don't be ridiculous," Sidney snapped, not even wanting to

think about the possibility of such a thing. There had to be a logical explanation for what was happening, and once they figured it out, it would be fixed

"You don't think that's possible?" Rich asked. "What happened at the house, never mind what's going on out here?"

"I'm sure there's a logical explanation for all of it."

"The whole freakin' town has gone nuts, Sid." The pitch in his voice was climbing.

"I know what it looks like," she said, trying to be calm. "But it's not going to do us any good to make crazy assumptions before we know all the facts."

She saw the shape before anybody else did, a lone figure stumbling out from a swath of total black on the left and into the road.

"Cody, look out!" she cried, grabbing his arm as he pulled the wheel savagely to the right and slammed on the brakes.

The tires squealed as the truck skidded sideways across the wet road, whipping around the trailer with the sailboat. The trailer disconnected with a wrenching snap, and both trailer and sailboat flipped over, sliding several feet before coming to a stop, blocking the road.

It was silent in the truck except for the *swish-thunk* of the wiper blades moving across the windshield, as they waited for the next horrible thing to happen.

"Is . . . is everybody okay?" Sidney finally asked, quickly checking out Snowy, who appeared to be fine.

"Yeah, I'm good," Rich said, looking around. "What the hell was that in the road?"

Without a word, Cody opened the driver's-side door.

"What are you doing?" Sidney asked, grabbing his arm again. "You can't—"

"That was a person we almost hit," he yelled, then yanked his arm from her hand and got out of the truck.

"Be careful," she called, already sliding across the seat to follow.

"Sid!" Rich exclaimed.

"I've got to make sure he's all right," she said, turning toward her friend, who rolled his eyes with exasperation but reached for the handle of the passenger door.

Snowy jumped down beside Sidney, who placed a hand on her back, signaling for the dog to stay by her side. She stood in the pouring rain for a moment, eyes scanning the darkness for Cody and for any animals that might be coming to attack them. She spotted him a short distance away, walking down the center of the road.

"Look at my friggin' boat!" she heard Rich cry out. Glancing over her shoulder, she watched her friend as he approached the sailboat resting on its side, then she turned and ran after Cody, Snowy at her heels.

"Cody, wait up!" she hollered.

Up ahead, lying in the road, was a body.

"Oh my God," Sidney said, immediately taking the phone from her pocket and dialing 911. As with the other calls that they'd attempted, it didn't go through. Whatever was happening on the island was wreaking havoc with cell phone signals. "There's still no signal," she said, looking at the phone's illuminated face.

Snowy whined as they grew closer to the figure lying so very still in the dampness of the road.

"Hello?" Cody called out. "Are you all right?"

He knelt down on the road beside the figure, a man lying on his stomach. Cautiously Cody reached out to turn him over, but something didn't feel right to Sidney and she reacted.

"Don't," she ordered.

Cody's hand stopped mere inches from the man. He looked at her, a glimmer of annoyance in his eyes.

"I just want to see if . . ."

She was about to explain herself when the figure began to move, but not in a way that was at all natural. "Cody" was all she could manage, her eyes locked on the body.

"What?" he asked, looking from her terrified expression to the man.

The man's clothing was moving—*no*—something was moving under the man's clothes.

Cody fell backward, startled by the writhing layers of cloth. Sidney grabbed him beneath the arms and tried to haul him to his feet, just as multiple rats emerged from the back of the man's collar.

The rats paused and looked around, noses twitching as they sniffed the wet air, until their gazes fell on Sidney and Cody.

Then they opened their bloodstained mouths together and bared their nasty teeth.

Nearby, Rich stood before the wrecked sailboat and wanted to cry.

Scenes from summers past played out before the theater of his mind, followed by what was sure to be the echoing voice of his father in the not too distant future: *What the hell did you do to the boat?*

Yeah, this'll be fun to explain, if I ever get the chance, he thought.

The trailer was trashed, and the sailboat was lying on its side in the middle of the road. If a car was to come along in the gloom . . . He didn't even want to think of the repercussions.

Rich remembered the emergency equipment in a white metal box on the deck of the boat and went to look for it. It was slippery in the driving rain, but he managed to climb over the side and up to the deck of the steeply pitched boat. He found the box, still intact, near the wheelhouse. It was held closed by clips that he quickly undid, causing the lid to drop open, spilling the contents out over the side of the deck and onto the road below. Thankfully, the green plastic lantern he was looking for was secured inside the case, and he reached in to remove it. Taking his prize, Rich clambered down awkwardly from his perch and back onto the road. His fingers searched the buttons, and he managed to first turn on the lantern and then the flashing safety beacon.

The beacon pulsed brightly in his hand as he began to walk around the wreckage of his boat to place it in the road.

Sidney's scream cut through the wind and hissing rain like screeching brakes. Rich spun around, eyes searching through the gloom for his friends. Down past the truck he saw Sidney, Cody, and Snowy reacting to something that at first he could not see, but then he did.

Rats.

And lots of them.

Still holding on to the safety lantern, he started toward them and nearly lost his balance as his foot slid across something on the ground—a road flare that he remembered putting in the emergency box a few summers before.

And as he looked at the flare, he got an idea.

The number of rats that were flowing out from beneath the man's clothing was obscene.

How is it even possible?

It reminded Sidney of the clown car from the circus that her dad had taken her to see in Boston when she was little. She remembered how hard she had laughed when the little doors opened on the tiny yellow car and the clowns had just kept coming and coming.

But she wasn't laughing now as the rats kept coming and coming.

"Get back to the truck," she found herself saying as she started to back away. Snowy was already on the move, romping forward to snatch one of the gray-furred rodents up from the ground and giving it a shake so quick and savage that its neck was broken at once.

Cody was closer to the man's body, and a few had managed to crawl up onto his legs, even as he furiously backpedaled away. He yelled like a wild man as he reached down to tear the fat-bodied rodents off of him, throwing them into the road, where they simply rejoined the writhing mass of furry bodies that was on its way toward him.

"Cody, c'mon!" Sidney screamed, stamping down on one of the four rats that surged at her, the remaining three darting back before attempting to come at her from another angle.

The thought of how many rats had been on the poor guy made

her sick to her stomach. Getting hit by Cody's truck would have been a blessing.

Cody ran away from the body, a line of gray-bodied vermin trailing after him as if attached by some invisible wire. Snowy wanted to go after more of them, her hunter's instinct in full view, but Sidney was afraid that even the shepherd would have become overwhelmed by the crazy number.

Mere inches from reaching them, Cody went down. He cried out in pain as he pitched forward, falling hard upon his chest. There was a cluster of rats on his legs, scurrying up his back to reach his head and neck. Sidney saw no other choice and let Snowy free, the dog instinctively reacting, bounding to Cody's aid. The rats attempted to defend themselves against the dog, but Snowy was just too fast, savaging the rodents as they swarmed.

But the rats' numbers were growing, now coming out from the woods on either side of the road.

Sidney helped Cody up from the ground. "All right?" she asked as she pulled him by the arm. He lurched and stumbled.

"Twisted something," he said, face contorted in discomfort as he struggled to his feet.

Cody was standing, and while she helped him to remain upright, she looked toward her dog, signaling Snowy to come. But Snowy wasn't looking; instead she was facing off against the continuous advance of rats, ripped and broken bodies—trophies—piled at her paws.

"Can you stand by yourself?" she asked Cody, slipping out from beneath his arm. He acknowledged that he could, and she ran to the side of the road, looking for something that she could use as a weapon. Prepared to do whatever she had to in order to ensure the safety of her friends and dog, she found a thick piece of broken tree limb and went to join her dog. Hoping to buy them some time to get back to the truck, she screamed like a maniac, throwing the piece of tree into the midst of the gathering rodents, dispersing them.

"C'mon, girl!" she yelled, grabbing hold of the dog's collar and giving it a solid yank, but Snowy did not want to go. The dog planted her feet, ready to protect those she loved from the potential onslaught.

Sidney hadn't even heard Rich as he ran up from behind, throwing the fiery, hissing end of a road flare into the path of the advancing rat swarm.

The heat and flame seemed to confuse them, driving them back.

But the moment was only temporary.

"The truck!" Rich screamed as he turned away from the rats and started to run.

Sidney gave Snowy's collar a solid yank, and this time she obeyed, trotting alongside her master as they all ran back to the truck. She attempted to help Cody, but he assured her that he was fine, limping slightly in front of them to haul open the driver's-side door.

Sidney watched with a mixture of complete fascination and horror as the rats converged upon the flare, multiple plump rat bodies swarming upon its burning end, extinguishing the fire before turning their full attention to them once again.

"Get in!" Cody urged, and she listened, allowing Snowy to hop in first, with she and Rich climbing in behind her. Cody returned to the driver's seat, slamming the door closed just as the first wave of rats reached the truck.

They looked out through the driver's-side window at the rats and were struck by the insanity of what they saw. The rats were all perfectly still, watching them through the truck's windows.

"Look at their right eyes," Rich said.

In what little light there was they could still see it—a shiny covering glistening over the right eyes of every single one of the rodents. It was just like the raccoon and the other animals that had attacked them.

"What are they waiting for?" Cody asked.

Sidney could feel their beady eyes, like bugs on her skin.

"I don't know and I don't want to know," she said. "Let's get the hell out of—"

There were noises, soft dinging sounds reminiscent of a cooling engine.

"They're underneath the truck," Cody suddenly announced, turning the key in the ignition and slamming the car into drive. "I know what they're doing. They're trying to figure out how to get inside," he said, gunning the engine and heading down the road, leaving the swarm, and Rich's boat, behind. "But I'm not about to give them a chance."

CHAPTER **THIRTY-THREE**

Doc Martin sat smoking a cigarette, surrounded by the dead.

She'd been back to the kennels four times, carefully taking potentially affected animals from their cages, euthanizing them, and cutting open their skulls, looking for a pattern.

With each case, she found the same thing: a strange growth affecting the entire brain but connecting directly to the optic nerve and seemingly altering the function of the right eye.

She brought the cigarette to her mouth and took a puff, blowing the smoke into the air above her head, wallowing in the implications of what she had found.

What could possibly be responsible for this mutation—that was what she believed it to be—and how had it affected all the animals at her hospital?

Her thoughts began to creep outside the self-contained universe of the hospital, and she felt the cold fingers of icy dread grip her heart. If what she had witnessed in here was happening out there, in the town . . .

Doc Martin dropped the cigarette to the floor and stomped out its still-burning tip as she stood. Going to the box on the counter, she found herself a new syringe and retrieved the bottle of pentobarbital used for euthanasia, slipping it into the pocket of her lab coat. She grabbed the heavy towel that she'd used to remove the insanely violent animals from their cages and headed back through her office to the kennels.

She needed to be sure before she allowed herself to panic.

Doc Martin wondered how many more would need to be put down and necropsied before she was absolutely convinced of her findings.

As many as there were left in the kennel was the sad answer.

CHAPTER **THIRTY-FOUR**

Cody took the corner leading down into the marina parking lot a little too fast, and the back end of the truck skidded across the wet surface of the road as he gunned the engine.

"Take it easy, Code," Sidney said. "All we need is to crack up the truck. Then where would we be."

"Yeah," Cody responded flatly.

He drove down into the parking lot, taking a side road that went along the back of the property leading to his house. Pulling into the driveway, he then backed the truck up, putting it parallel to the steps before the front door.

"You guys stay here," he said, putting the car in park but leaving the engine running.

"Wait a sec," Sidney said, grabbing his arm. "We're going with you."

"I think it would be better if you stay here," he reasoned.

"I'm just going to run in, find him, and drag him back out."

Rich pressed his head against the passenger-side widow, attempting to look out through the torrential rain. "What if you run into trouble?" he asked.

"Good question, Rich," Sidney replied. She noticed that she was still holding on to Cody's biceps and slowly released her hold on him.

"That's why I think you should stay here," he told them. "If there's trouble, I'm going to need somebody to save my ass."

She wasn't crazy about his plan, but he reassured her.

"Seriously, I'll be in and out," he said, opening the door to a rush of cool, salty air. "And besides, there shouldn't be any problem—I don't have any pets."

He gave her a hint of a reassuring smile as he slipped from the driver's seat and slammed the door closed. Sidney watched him as he crossed in front of the truck, climbing the stairs two at a time before reaching the door and going inside.

It seemed as though he was in there forever.

"Do you think we should go in?" Sidney asked, petting Snowy nervously, her eyes never leaving the slightly open front door.

"No, give him a little while," Rich said. "He probably has to fill his dad in as to what's going on before coming out."

"Never mind the fact that his father will probably think he's on crack or something," Sidney offered.

"There is that," Rich said with an agreeing nod. He then looked away from the view of the front door, across the driveway, and down into the marina parking lot.

"What's going on over there?" Rich asked.

Sidney looked in the general direction and saw that there was a light inside the office flashing off and on.

"Is the power back on?" she asked, looking around for more signs that this was the case, but not seeing anything.

"The marina probably has a generator," Rich said, watching the light go on and off. "I think somebody might be trying to signal us."

Rich leaned over Snowy and Sidney and tapped the horn three times.

"What are you doing?" she asked him, not sure if it was a smart thing to draw attention to themselves.

"I think Cody should know about the light in the office," Rich said, watching the door for signs of their friend. He was going to beep the horn again when Cody came out the front and down the steps.

Rich rolled down the window. "Somebody's flashing the light in the marina office."

Cody looked in the direction, seeing the light being turned on and then off and then on again. Sidney was surprised when he started across the slightly wooded area and down the hill into the parking lot.

"What the hell is he doing?" she asked. "Is he freaking insane?"

Quickly she slid over in the seat, getting behind the wheel of the truck and putting it in drive.

Halfway down the hill to the marina parking lot Cody realized that what he was doing probably wasn't the smartest of things, especially given the current situation.

His father hadn't been in the house. He'd thought maybe he had gone up to bed early, but the second floor was as empty as the first. It didn't look as though his father had been home.

The relief he'd experienced when Rich pointed out the flashing light in the marina office was huge, momentarily canceling out his common sense.

Cody sped up his pace as he reached the lot. He kept his eyes on the front door to the office, and how the lights continued to flash off and on, and was startled—coming to a sudden stop—as the door came flying open and his father appeared in the doorway.

Cody raised his hand in greeting and was about to call out to the man when he saw that his father was yelling something to him that he couldn't quite hear over the storm.

Then he noticed the blood on his father's hands and the cuts that now adorned his face.

And was finally able to understand what it was that his father was yelling.

He was telling him to run.

Panic gripped him, and Cody started to look around the parking lot for any signs of trouble, while continuing toward the office. He started to run across the rain-swept parking lot, then felt his blood temporarily freeze in his veins, stopping him cold, as he saw something moving out from beneath a parked car. It turned out to be an empty potato chip bag caught in the stream of rainwater, and he breathed a sigh of relief as he continued toward his father.

His dad still stood frozen in the doorway, and the closer he got, the more he saw the look of absolute horror on the older man's face.

Cody wanted to tell him that everything was all right, that he and his friends were here to take him with them, but then he realized that his father wasn't looking *at* him—

He was looking above him.

He heard the sound coming closer and looked up just in time to see the huge seagull as it descended, sharp yellow beak pecking at his scalp. Cody cried out at the sudden pain from his head, arms thrashing above him to drive away the attacking bird. And where there had only been one before, now there were many, their powerful wings beating the air as they dove to attack.

It was like being in the center of a tornado, the flock of seabirds swirling around, pecking and slapping him with their powerful wings.

Cody could feel the warmth of his own blood as it ran down his neck and back. He raised his hands above his head in an attempt to ward off the birds' assault, but those too became objects of their attacks.

Blinking the blood from his eyes, he saw his father about to move from the front door. Gulls were swooping to attack him as well, and Cody screamed for him to get back inside the office.

The birds seemed to be making a conscious effort to take his own eyes, pulling at the soft flesh of his cheeks as he tried to get to cover. The pain was beyond words, and Cody felt his frustration and rage blossom. He reached up, blindly grabbing hold of anything he could—a wing, leg, or neck—to squeeze and twist before tossing the broken animal to the ground.

But for each one he took out, six more swooped in to take its place.

Cody kept his eyes tightly closed, wanting to hold on to his sight for as long as possible. He hoped that he was traveling in the right direction.

His father called out, and he tried to respond, to tell the man to protect himself, but a gull was suddenly at his face, a sharp yellow beak darting between his lips, attempting to snatch his tongue away like a fat worm. Cody went wild, swinging his arms, but with his eyes closed, he lost his balance, falling to the wet pavement on all fours.

The gulls did not let up, touching down upon his back and pecking at the soft, exposed flesh of his neck.

Cody was unable to rise, the multiple feathered bodies attacking relentlessly, but he knew that he had to keep moving. He started to crawl across the lot, hoping that he was heading in the direction of his father's office. The gulls' numbers were so great that he could no longer move, and he curled himself into a tight ball, wrapping his arms about his head in an attempt to protect his eyes and face.

He'd all but given up when he heard it—the blaring of his truck horn—and he actually found himself breaking into a smile as he listened to the sound of the truck coming closer.

Just like in the movies, the cavalry had arrived.

"Holy shit, do you see that?" Rich screamed from his seat.

Sidney saw, even though she didn't want to.

A flock of gulls had driven Cody to the ground of the parking lot and were attacking him as if he were a pile of fresh bait.

She leaned on the horn as she drove across the lot, careful not to hit the random cars that were parked here and there. Bringing the truck to a screeching stop mere inches from where her former boyfriend crawled, she began to open the door.

"What are you doing?" Rich screeched, throwing himself across her lap and pulling the door closed. "You can't."

"We can't leave him out there," she said. He had no answer, since he knew that she was right. "Hold on to Snowy; I'm going to get him back into the car."

She threw open the door and jumped out, slamming the door closed again behind her.

"Cody!" she called out, and saw him begin to angle himself toward the sound of her voice.

In seconds she was the object of attack as well.

The gulls flew at her, strangely silent, the only sound coming from them was the heavy flapping of their white and gray wings.

She didn't hesitate, running from the car, swiping her arms above her head, batting the birds away from her.

"Sid?" Cody called out. She knelt down beside him, taking him beneath the arm and attempting to haul him to his feet.

The gulls would have none of it, throwing their weighty, feathered bodies at them, attempting to drive them to the ground.

"The truck's right here," she said, crying out with each peck, pinch, and bite from the sharp beaks of the birds swarming about them.

"I'm sorry," she heard him grunt.

She could see that he was bleeding, the blood from wounds about his head streaming down to color his face crimson.

"No apologies," she said from between gritted teeth, still helping him as they tried to get to the truck.

A gull landed atop her head, the claws on its webbed feet raking across her scalp. She cried out, and Cody reacted, reaching up to grab one of the bird's legs and yank it from the air to the ground where he stomped on its puffy white chest, breaking the bird's insides in an explosion of gore.

She knew they had to be close, but the relentlessness of the storm and the flapping of the gulls had taken her off course. The bray of the truck's horn was exactly what she needed as they moved toward the sound, and hopefully, safety.

"Over here!" she heard Rich yelling over Snowy's excited barks. He continued to lean on the horn.

It was as if the seabirds knew that Cody and Sidney were close to escaping them, and their attacks grew even more aggressive, whipping wings and pecking beaks trying to keep them away from the sanctuary of the truck. She felt Cody move closer to her, pulling her head into the protection his arms.

"What are you doing?" she yelled, now fighting against him as well as the birds.

"Protecting you," he said.

"Protect yourself," she told him, grabbing his shirt and giving it a tug. "We're going to get to the truck."

The blast of water hit them with enough force to cause them to stumble back, almost knocking them from their feet. Sidney wasn't sure what happened, at first thinking that the storm had somehow intensified, but then she realized that the birds were no longer attacking. She opened her eyes to see Cody's father standing in front of the marina office, aiming a high-pressure fire hose.

"Get to the truck!" the harbormaster screamed as he directed the intense flow of water at the angry flock circling above the parking lot. The gulls turned their attention to him, and he returned that aggression, blasting them from the sky.

"We're not going without you," Cody cried, going to his father.

Sidney followed him, and the two of them stood behind the man with the hose as he doused the angry seabirds. They advanced into the lot as far as the hose was long, but it eventually went taut and they had to make their move.

Sidney studied the distance between them and Cody's truck and decided that now was as good a time as any.

"C'mon!" she called. "Run for it!"

Cody took the metal nozzle of the fire hose from his father, continuing to spray the attacking flock, giving the older man a firm shove toward Sidney. She grabbed hold of his arm, and they both began to run. Moments later Cody dropped the hose and began to run as well.

With no high-pressure stream of water to hold them at bay, the birds resumed their attack, swooping from the sky as Sidney, Cody, and his father made their way across the lot toward the truck. Rich maneuvered it around, pulling up in front of them.

"Get ready," Sidney said, swatting at the new onslaught as she turned to grip the back door handle, flinging open the door and diving in. She spun in the seat, reaching out to grab at whomever would be next. Cody was ushering his father in as the birds' attack intensified. Sidney reached for the man, her hands on the sleeve of his jacket, when he suddenly pulled away, grabbed his son, and pushed him toward the open door. Cody, shocked by his father's actions, actually fell backward onto the seat.

"Dad, what are you—"

Sidney could see the intention in Cody's father's expression, wanting his son to be safe before him. He was swinging his arms wildly at the attacking birds and was just about to duck his head to climb in when it happened.

For a split second the gulls had gone, almost as if Cody's dad had actually managed to scare them away. He was coming forward to climb inside beside them when the hawks attacked.

The birds' razor-sharp talons seemed to magically appear on Cody's father's scalp, digging into the already lacerated flesh and taking hold.

Cody's dad screamed as he was pulled backward, away from the car door. Sidney cried out, as did Cody, who frantically reached for the man. Through the doorway she saw the multiple hawks using their talons and beaks to savage the man's face and throat.

Their attack was devastating, the damage so severe that there was little the man could do to fight back. Sidney saw the horror in his expression, beneath the flow of bright red blood.

"Dad, no!" Cody cried as he actually tried to leave the car.

Sidney grabbed hold, using all her strength to pull him back into the car. Cody fought her crazily, trying to push her away, but Sidney held on with everything she had, knowing that if he got out of the car, he would not be getting back in. Rich leaned over as well, trying to help her as Snowy barked and howled, pacing back and forth nervously in the front seat.

Wrapping her arms tightly about Cody, she used her weight to pull him back away from the still-open door. The birds had begun to collect around the opening, their powerful wings flapping crazily as they tested the zone to see if it was safe to enter and attack.

Cody's dad had collapsed to the ground outside, five hawks perched upon his failing body. He tried to fight back, to bat them away, but they snapped at his hands, strong beaks severing the tips of his fingers until all he had to work with were bloody nubs. He had started to crawl toward the truck as Cody continued to scream.

"We have to do something! We have to help him!"

The presence of birds had grown, and every single size and kind of bird imaginable had come to try and kill them.

"If you leave this car . . . if we leave this car, we're dead," Sidney said, fighting back her tears, repeating the harsh-sounding words over and over again as he continued to struggle with her.

His father was a mere foot away from the car now, crawling on his hands and knees as the hawks continued their assault. Sidney, Cody, and Rich watched as he raised himself up from the ground, revealing the horrible damage done to him. One of his eyes was missing, and the entire right side of his face had been torn away to reveal the bloody skull beneath. Sidney thought that he just might make it, that he was going to try to climb into the backseat, but instead the man took hold of the truck door in his mutilated hand and slammed it closed.

Cody's dad then turned from the truck, pitched forward, and lay deathly still upon the rain-drenched parking lot, blood pooling around him.

Cody screamed as he managed to get away from Sidney, throwing her back as he slid across the seat toward the door.

"Cody, you can't," she said, watching to see what he would do. He pressed himself against the window, slapping at the glass as he sobbed.

"Get us out of here!" Sidney shouted to Rich, who still sat in the driver's seat.

Rich did as he was told, putting the car in drive and starting from the parking lot.

The gulls were back now, diving at the truck, striking the roof and windshield, leaving bloody marks and streaks as they hit. The wipers did nothing but create crimson smears across the glass, and then the windshield began to give way, spiderweb cracks exploding across its curved surface.

Snowy barked savagely and Rich swore. "I can't see!" he yelled, attempting to steer the truck through the blood and bodily fluids coating the windshield.

Sidney let go of Cody, who had gone strangely still, and leaned over the front seat, hoping to help guide their escape. The gulls' attack had broken the driver's-side wiper, leaving them nearly blind as the truck careened through the torrential rain.

She was reaching across for the steering wheel when the impact came, bringing the truck to an abrupt stop. Sidney fell over the seat, her face striking the dashboard. Through a haze she heard the blare of a horn from someplace very close by before realizing that the sound belonged to their car.

Then everything went quiet, swallowed up by the dark.

She wished it could stay like that forever.

CHAPTER **THIRTY-FIVE**

Her father appears in the doorway to her room.

In his arms he is holding a squirming bundle of white, the cutest puppy Sidney has ever seen in her life.

Snowy.

Sidney is struck by an immediate sense of familiarity, knowing that this is a memory from the past, but it does not stop her from going through the motions like she had all those years ago.

She bounds from her bed, approaching her smiling father, and she is at once aware of how good he looks, how healthy and young. Something niggles at the back of her mind; this isn't right—this isn't how it is anymore—but the closer she gets to this new realization, the deeper it recedes into the background.

The puppy is all she can think about, all she can focus on, and she holds out her arms excitedly, begging her dad to let her hold it.

Her father clings to the wriggling white pup, the shepherd burying her face in the crook of his neck. He tells her that this is a very special pup and that she is going to have to take very good care of her.

Sidney tells him that she will, still holding out her beckoning arms.

He pulls the shepherd puppy from his chest and presents the dog to her.

She takes the puppy from him and sees something strange about her. Her eyes.

They're unusually large, one of them as black as a marble, while the other—the right eye—is covered in a glistening metallic sheen.

She wants to ask her father what is wrong with the puppy's eye, but her father has changed into Cody's dad, his face torn and shredded. Blood pours from the wounds on his head and face, making puddles of red that expand on the ground around him.

He is standing in the center of a crimson island—an island of blood.

That island is Benediction.

This recognition kicks in as she pulls the puppy closer, laying the dog's head upon her shoulder. She tells the puppy that she will always be taken care of and that she will always be loved.

The puppy responds by opening her mouth far wider than she should be able, sinking incredibly large teeth for a puppy into Sidney's neck, and tearing the flesh away with a violent tug.

Sidney returned to consciousness with the taste of blood in her mouth.

It took a moment to collect herself, separating her nightmare from reality. She was crammed into a tight space and soon realized that she was lying on the floor in the front of Cody's truck.

"Everybody . . . ," she started, attempting to extract herself. "Everybody all right?"

She heard the sound of something thumping and quickly recognized it as the sound of Snowy's tail hitting the front seat.

Sidney emerged from the floor to the excited greetings of her dog, wincing in pain where Snowy's tongue licked. She believed there was a good chance that she'd broken her nose and been cut in a few places by flying glass—never mind the beak bites.

"Hello, girl," she said, climbing up into the seat.

Rich still sat behind the wheel, staring straight ahead at the shattered windshield. He had a cut above his left eye and a trickle of blood oozing from his nose. He looked to be in shock.

"Hey," she said, reaching over to give his leg a shake.

He screamed as she touched him, instantly recoiling as if under attack. His eyes were wide and wild, and for a minute she wasn't sure he recognized her.

"Rich, it's okay," she said. "It's me."

"Sid," he said, blinking rapidly, then he looked around the inside of the truck. "We hit something . . . we gotta get outta here before . . ."

There was a ghostly moan from the backseat.

"Cody?" Sidney called out, getting on her knees and peering over the front seat.

He was on the floor, curled into a tight ball. She reached down, poking him with her fingers.

"Cody, you okay?" she asked in between jabs. "Wake up."

His eyes flew open and he gasped.

"You all right?" she asked, knowing how stupid it sounded after what he'd just been through.

"Yeah," he grunted. "What . . . ?"

"We hit something," she said.

The sounds of the birds outside were steady—thumps, bangs, and scratches upon the metal roof and doors. The birds knew that they were still inside and wanted them.

Cody sat up with a groan, climbing onto the backseat.

"We can't stay here," he said, leaning over to look out a side window between the cracks and smears of blood.

Sidney was about to agree when she heard gunshots.

They all jumped, except for Snowy, and looked at each other expectantly.

"Was that . . . ," Rich began as more shots were fired.

Cody slid over in his seat, trying to see out the windows.

"Anything?" Sidney asked, looking through the windows on her side.

Her question was answered by the crackling of a radio as the strobe of a blue-and-red light illuminated the inside of the truck.

"It's the cops," Rich said excitedly. He began to beep the horn. It sounded kind of sick, but it still worked.

"You in the truck," came an announcement from the police car. "Get ready to exit the vehicle on my word."

They all looked at each other, Cody and Rich both taking hold of the door handles. Sidney grabbed Snowy's collar.

The gun shots increased, and for a few moments it sounded like a small war had erupted outside the truck.

"Now!" boomed the echoing voice of authority from a loudspeaker.

Cody and Rich both threw open their doors and rushed out into the driving rain. Sidney began to slide across the seat, pushing Snowy in front of her, then remembered the raccoon.

"Rich, take Snowy!" she called out as she twisted herself around to look on the floor of the car for the trash bag.

She found it wedged beneath the front seat and yanked it out. A rotting stink wafted out from the bag, and she stifled the urge to barf. Cinching the top of the bag tightly to try and keep the stink in, she slid across the seat and jumped out of the truck into a nightmare in progress.

The ground was littered with bodies of dead birds—gulls, hawks, and even some sparrows—and the shapes of more still swirled above them in the whipping wind and driving rain. But it was the sight of a police officer pointing his pistol at Rich and Snowy that truly frightened her.

The dog was barking at the man as Rich held tightly to her collar, preventing her from moving any closer.

"What are you doing?" Sidney screamed, leaving the truck. "No!"

The cop briefly turned, pointing his weapon toward her, before returning the gun to Snowy. "Get in the cruiser, miss," he ordered.

"Why are you pointing your gun at my dog?" Sidney asked as she moved toward Rich and Snowy, ignoring the officer's instruction. "She's no danger to you, or anybody," she said, taking hold of Snowy's collar from Rich. The shepherd immediately stopped barking.

"I tried to tell them that," Cody called out. He was standing beside the SUV with another officer whom Sidney recognized as Officer Isabel, a young woman only a few years older than herself. She was trying to force Cody into the backseat of the police SUV.

"The dog is fine . . . she hasn't been affected," Rich said.

Sidney saw the fear in each of the police officers' eyes as Isabel and her partner exchanged glances.

"Please," Sidney begged. "She's fine."

The gulls were getting brave again, flying down out of the stormy sky to circle their party.

"How do we know that?" the officer with the gun asked, his eyes focused on the dog.

"She would have attacked by now, but she hasn't. She's calm and quiet," Sidney responded.

The cop lowered his gun but didn't appear happy about it.

"Get in the car," he said, sneering.

"She's fine, really." Sidney tried to reassure Officer Isabel, who looked at Snowy with a cautious eye as they passed her. Snowy sniffed at the woman's leg, and she actually reached down to give the dog a scratch behind the ears, eliciting a friendly tail wag.

"Get in," Officer Isabel told Sidney, motioning both her and Snowy into the vehicle.

Sidney directed Snowy in first, and the shepherd took a spot beside a dazed-looking Cody. A woman holding a little girl of five or six sat on the other side of Cody. Both eyed Snowy with genuine fear.

"She's fine," Sidney said yet again, but the woman just pulled her daughter closer.

Sidney moved over on the seat as Rich got in next, the door slamming closed behind him.

"Are you all right?" she asked. Rich nodded. She then looked to Cody. "You?"

He said nothing, gazing straight ahead through the rain-swept windshield.

There were more gunshots, and the child whimpered as her mother held her tightly. Then the two officers jumped into the cruiser, breathless and shaking.

"Go, Kole," Isabel snapped as meaty bodies began to slam into the cruiser roof.

Kole put the SUV in drive and started from the lot. It was like they were in the eye of a hurricane as a storm of birds of every conceivable kind, size, and shape, swirled angrily around the SUV.

Sidney glanced outside the window and saw the body of Cody's father still lying there. She knew that Cody could see him out there as well and instinctively reached over to touch his hand. He pulled away without a word.

"Sorry about your dad, Cody," Officer Kole said. "Wish we could have been here sooner."

"We tried, but . . . ," Cody began, but his voice trailed off.

No one spoke as they drove out of the marina parking lot and onto the main road. The silence was unbearable. Sidney would have preferred the sound of birds pummeling the vehicle. The silence made her think about what was actually happening . . . and how bad it was.

It made her feel totally helpless. The last time she'd felt like this was when she'd seen her father in the hospital.

"My father," she suddenly blurted out.

Officer Isabel turned her head.

"We were going to get my father after . . ." The images of Cody's dad as he'd been taken by the birds filled her head, and she quickly pushed them away. "We were heading to get him next."

"Okay," Officer Isabel said. "We'll drop you guys, Mrs. Levesque, and Amy at the station, and then—"

"We have to get to Doc Martin," Sidney interrupted. "I have to let her know what I've found."

Officer Kole looked at her in the rearview mirror. "What've you found? Do you have any idea what's going on?"

"It might be some sort of virus, but I'm not sure. I have a specimen for Doc Martin to look at."

"A virus," Officer Isabel repeated. "Do you actually think that's possible?"

Sidney shrugged. "It's as good a reason as anything," she said. "And it only seems to be affecting animals, as far as I can tell."

"If it's only affecting animals, what about your pooch?" Kole asked, his hard eyes again reflecting his suspicious gaze on Snowy.

"Haven't figured that out yet either," Sidney said. "Hoping that Doc Martin can fill in all the blanks."

Mrs. Levesque spoke up. "We're going to the police station. You said you would take me and my daughter someplace safe." There was a nasty tension in the woman's face as her child continued to whimper pitifully.

"That's right, Mrs. Levesque," Kole said. "We'll drop you all off at the station, and then we'll head out again and—"

"We really should go to Doc Martin's first," Sidney interrupted again. "The more time we spend not trying to figure this out . . ." She paused a moment, considering her words. "The more time we waste, the more people could die," she finished with a deep breath.

Amy Levesque began to cry even louder now.

"Would you please stop?" the child's mother said angrily. "You're frightening my daughter with that talk."

"I'm sorry," Sidney said, "but it's true. Whatever is happening here is spreading like wildfire, and the quicker we figure it out, the quicker we can fix it."

"Maybe we should go get Doc Martin and . . . ," Officer Isabel began, but was quickly shot down by her partner.

"We head to the station, drop everybody off, then we go out again," Kole said. "We can't risk—"

"Exactly," Sidney piped up, annoyed by where this was going.

"Sid, c'mon," Rich said. "They're doing what they think is right."

"I get that, but they're wrong. I need to get to Doc Martin with this sample right away."

"We'll take it from here," Officer Kole said with finality. "Once we get to the station, you'll hand over that sample, and we'll take it to the doc."

Sidney was going to argue further, but the look Kole gave her in the rearview mirror told her it would be best to just keep her mouth shut. She turned her eyes away and focused on her town outside the windows.

A town that, in a very short amount of time, had gone to hell.

CHAPTER **THIRTY-SIX**

"Isaac, do you want a soda?" Dale Moore asked.

The young man stood in the center of the kitchen, rocking ever so slightly from side to side.

"Isaac?"

"Can't have soda," Isaac stated flatly. "Can't have sugar."

"Okay," Dale said, holding on to the refrigerator door and peering into the darkness inside. "How about some juice?"

"Tea," Isaac said.

"Tea?"

"Yeah, I would like some tea, please."

"Okay." Dale quickly shut the refrigerator door to preserve at least a little of the cool. "I'll make you a cup of tea."

Using his cane, Dale made his way over to one of the kitchen cabinets and opened it. "I know I saw some tea around here recently," he said, scanning the shelves. "Here we go." He grabbed the box of Red Rose and showed it to the youth. "Is this good?"

"Red Rose." Isaac read the label aloud. "My mother always buys Red Rose."

Dale set the box down on the counter, using his left hand to open it and remove a tea bag. He retrieved a mug from the drying rack and placed the bag inside.

"So, where is your mother, Isaac?" Dale asked, trying to sound casual as he filled the teakettle with water.

"Red Rose," Isaac repeated quietly. "My mother always buys Red Rose."

Dale turned the gas on ever so slightly and used the fireplace lighter to ignite the blue flame with a whoosh. He set the kettle down over the flame. "We'll let that boil, and then we'll make you a nice cup of tea."

"Red Rose," Isaac said. "A nice cup of Red Rose."

"That's right," Dale agreed. He made his way to the kitchen table, where he pulled out a chair. "Why don't you come over here and have a seat."

Isaac looked at him, and then gazed at the sliding glass doors that led outside to the yard. "I don't think so."

Dale followed the young man's eyes and saw movement in the darkness. Above the howling wind and the ferocious pattering of rain, he could just about make out the sound of clawed feet upon the wooden deck.

Instead of sitting down himself, Dale went to the glass doors and pulled the heavy curtain across their length, blocking not only the view from the inside out, but that from the outside in as well.

"How's that?" he asked the young man.

Isaac studied the curtain for a few moments. "Better," he said finally.

Dale motioned him toward the table. "Please, take a seat."

Isaac hesitated, but then slowly walked toward the table. Dale pulled out another chair for the young man.

"I'll have a nice cup of Red Rose," Isaac said.

"Yep, as soon as the water boils, I'll make you that tea," Dale told him as he lowered himself down into the chair.

Isaac followed suit.

"Where's Sidney?" Isaac blurted out, looking around. "Is Sidney home?"

"She's out," Dale said, feeling that nervous knot tighten in his stomach.

Isaac frowned, looking out of the kitchen down the hallway that led to the front door. "It's not good out there. Not good at all."

"No, it isn't." Dale shook his head. "I'm hoping that she's safe, and that she'll be home soon."

Isaac stared at the door again. "It's not good out there," he repeated.

Dale found himself attuned to the sounds out in the storm, outside the sliding doors, but the shrill whistle of the teakettle interrupted his troubled thoughts. "Let's get you that cup of tea," he said, using the cane to help push himself up from the seat.

"Red Rose tea," Isaac told him. "My mother always buys Red Rose."

"You don't say," Dale said, heading for the stove. He turned off the flame, picked up the kettle, and poured the hot water into the mug over the tea bag.

"My mother is dead, I think."

Dale almost dropped the kettle as he turned toward Isaac.

"What did you say, Isaac?"

"My mother," he repeated, looking everywhere but at Dale. "I think my mother is dead. The cats got her . . . the cats and the mice and . . . and the bugs . . . there were bugs, too. They got her."

Dale approached the table, steaming cup of tea in hand.

"Are . . . are you sure, Isaac?" Dale asked, stunned by the revelation and feeling even more afraid. "Are you sure that your mother is dead?"

He set the tea down in front of the young man as he waited for an answer.

Isaac pulled the cup toward him, peering down into the darkening hot water. "Yeah," he said as he picked up the tab and began to dunk the bag in the water. "Yeah, I'm sure she's dead."

Dale leaned upon the table. "I'm so sorry, Isaac. Is there anything I can do to . . . ?"

"Milk," Isaac said.

Dale stared, confused. "Excuse me?"

"Milk," Isaac said again, looking up from the tea. "I would like some milk with my tea, please."

Not knowing what else to do, Dale went to the fridge to get Isaac his milk.

CHAPTER **THIRTY-SEVEN**

They were all affected.

Doc Martin felt the abyss of fear open all the wider and threaten to swallow her whole.

The last of the boarders in the kennels had been euthanized and examined to reveal that each and every one, dogs and cats, had been affected.

The latest necropsies lay upon the operating table, their skulls opened to reveal a nightmare. She'd removed the brain of a cat, slicing it open for a look, and what she found had nearly made her sick. The strange growth had permeated the brain, rootlike tendrils spreading throughout the animal's gray matter and somehow turning it dangerously aggressive.

She leaned over the table, picked up a scalpel, and poked at the growth. *What are you there for?* she wondered as she sliced into the tissue mass to reveal something far more complex than a mere fatty tumor or cancerous growth.

What are you doing?

The memory of the ferocity she had encountered with all of the animals made her feel all the more queasy. She set the scalpel down with a clatter.

"It turns them savage," she said as the twisted realization began to sink in. "It turns them against us."

Stumbling back from the operating table, she sought out a chair and sat down heavily. The idea that was being conceived was totally insane, but the more she thought about it, the more she became convinced that there might be some truth to the madness.

She then thought of the myriad animal life on the island of Benediction.

If it had all been affected . . .

"Dear God," she said, springing up from her chair. "Somebody needs to be told."

She stripped off her bloody rubber gloves, dropping them on the floor as she left the operating room. She went to her desk and reached for the phone, hearing nothing when she picked it up.

What was she doing? She knew the phones were down. She pulled her cell phone from her pocket and checked it, holding it aloft just to be sure. Still no signal.

Doc Martin ran through a mental list of people she should try to talk with, deciding to start with Charlotte Gaeta, the town manager. She grabbed her car keys from the top drawer of her desk and moved to the back door. A powerful gust of warm, moisture-saturated wind rushed in to greet her as she opened the door and stepped out into the parking lot.

"Shit," Doc Martin said, lowering her face to the wicked breeze that spattered her glasses with water. The door closed behind her with finality, and she began her trek across the lot, moving toward the blue Subaru Outback parked at the far end.

She wasn't necessarily sure why she stopped. Maybe some sixth sense warned her to lift her face and check out her surroundings.

Four red foxes stood before the back of her car, watching her with unblinking eyes.

What the hell are they doing out in this? was her first thought, before the terrible realization struck home. Of course. They were probably affected as well.

"Shit," she said again as the four animals began to slowly pad across the parking lot, their attention never leaving her.

The glint of something shiny in one of the fox's eyes was all she needed to see, and without another thought, she spun around, making a run back to the hospital door. Her heart hammered in her chest, years of cigarette smoking and an unnatural love of Ben & Jerry's Chunky Monkey not doing her any favors. Her breath was like fire in her lungs as the door loomed temptingly closer. From the corner of her eyes she caught more movement, multiple shapes skulking from the darkness of the woods surrounding the parking lot.

She reached the door, grabbed the handle, and pulled.

Locked.

"Son of a . . . ," she hissed, reaching into her pocket for her key ring, fingers fumbling over multiple things before finding what she was looking for. The keys came out of her pocket but dropped from her hands, clattering to the ground. As she bent to retrieve them, she caught sight of the multiple horrors that were coming her way.

The foxes were the least of her problems now.

It was like something out of a Disney movie filtered through Stephen King. Every kind of forest animal that called Benediction its home appeared to be coming toward her as one, like they were all friends—one big, happy family out for a stroll in the hurricane.

And as they came closer, she saw their eyes, their right eyes glinting with a metallic sheen.

Keys firmly in hand, she turned back to the door, searching for and finding the right key and sticking it into the lock. She turned the key and pulled upon the door, just as her lower calf exploded in pain.

Doc Martin cried out as her leg was yanked savagely back. Managing to hold on to the door, she looked down into the face of one of the foxes, its teeth buried in her calf, eyes eerily fixed on hers.

"Let—go!" she screamed, kicking with all her might. The fox held fast, jaws clamped, teeth embedded in the muscular flesh. As she pulled back, she felt the sickening sensation of her flesh and muscle starting to tear; the pain was excruciating.

Keeping her body wedged in the doorway and one hand on the doorknob, she reached down with the other to slam her fist against the animal's snout, which caused even more agony as the fox's teeth were driven farther into the meat of her lower leg. The other animals stood watching her struggles, almost as if they'd come to some sort of consensus that the animal attacking her was doing just fine on its own.

The fox planted its feet and began to tug.

A combination of the animal's strength and her own excruciating pain almost took her from the doorway, but she managed to hold on.

Another of the foxes came forward, but she drove it back with her flailing arm and free leg.

The fox that had her leg continued to tug, but she still held on to her place in the doorway, the hope of getting inside giving her the strength to continue to fight. It was then that she noticed the insects. At first she thought they were merely reflections in the rainwater that puddled in the parking lot, but that assumption was quickly washed away as she saw what they actually were—swarms of ants and spiders traversing the puddles to get to her.

Bugs as well? she questioned. This was all getting to be way, way too much.

The second fox must have decided that this was taking too long and darted in, followed by the third, to take hold of her leg, and she began to scream. She could barely fight back against one, never mind three pulling at her.

A red haze of panic flooded through her as she began to realize that now she was indeed fighting for her life. Doc Martin reached upward toward the top of the door, ripping the keys from where they hung from the lock. She then bent forward toward the animals' heads and jammed the longest of the keys into the animal's strange right eye. For a moment the pressure from the fox's bite let up, and Doc Martin attacked the others, stabbing the key into their eyes as well.

One of the foxes released its hold, savagely shaking its head. She was able to pull her leg back and kick out, driving two of the animals away. The foxes stepped back, their heads moving strangely in the air as if trying to sense where she was. Doc Martin didn't waste a moment before hauling herself up from the ground by the doorknob, practically throwing herself inside the building. The heavy back door swung closed against her attackers.

She sat there, her back pressed against the wall, trying to catch her breath. Her leg was bleeding through her slacks from multiple bites, and she knew that she needed to clean the wounds and dress them right away.

But for the moment she decided that she would just sit there and appreciate that fact that she was still alive.

CHAPTER **THIRTY-EIGHT**

Officer Kole turned the corner onto Blake Street, driving the police SUV past Henderson Insurance and Fernando Drug before taking a sharp right into the Benediction Police Department parking lot.

Sidney was leaning forward in her seat, looking out the front windshield cleared of water by the passing wiper blades. She couldn't help but think of the beginning of some scary movie, as the unwitting main characters arrive at the haunted house/haunted amusement park/haunted hotel/haunted insane asylum—take your pick.

The Benediction Police Department building could have been on that list for sure. The building was constructed in the early 1900s as the official town hall but was converted into the police station sometime in the 1920s when the new town hall was built. It was a castlelike building of dark brick and granite, with copper-covered turrets oxidized a dirty emerald green. Her eyes immediately went to the multiple gargoyle downspouts protruding from around the roof, rainwater pouring from their open mouths. One of Benediction's founding fathers had been a very religious man and had paid to have the stone creatures brought over from Rome and placed upon the building to ward off evil and bring good luck and prosperity.

Considering what was going on, their abilities must've worn off.

Officer Kole drove around to the back of the old building and brought the vehicle to a stop at the end of a concrete ramp leading up to a metal back door. There was a sedan cruiser parked in front of them and another SUV in a space in front of a closed garage door. He put the car in park and grabbed his walkie-talkie from his belt, turning it on to a high-pitched whine and crackle.

"Does that actually work?" Sidney asked him.

"We were able to get some signal at first, but now . . ."

The whine grew louder, earsplittingly so. He spoke into the device, calling for his fellow officers inside the building, but there was no response.

"Forget it, John," Isabel said. "We'll just take them in ourselves."

She pulled a ring of keys from her belt, and Officer Kole turned to the backseat.

"All right, listen up," he said, his intense stare fixing upon each of them. "When I say so, you will all exit this vehicle and walk calmly and quickly up the ramp to the door. We will be doing nothing else except getting to the door—do you all understand?"

They all nodded, even little Amy. Sidney was going to ask about her father and Doc Martin but decided against it. She'd ask to speak to a supervisor once they got inside.

"Ready?" Kole asked Officer Isabel. She grabbed the shotgun from the floor at her feet and nodded.

The two officers sprang from the cruiser, then Isabel stood searching for trouble as Kole swiftly walked around the vehicle. He opened the rear door of the SUV.

"Let's go," he ordered brusquely.

One by one they slid out of the vehicle, Sidney pulling Snowy behind her, Mrs. Levesque carrying her daughter.

"Finally," the woman muttered as she rudely pushed past Sidney on her way up the ramp.

Sidney glanced at Officer Kole, who was eyeing her with a cold, judgmental stare. His gaze dropped to Snowy. "I'm trusting that you know what you're talking about," he said, squeezing the butt of his gun as he studied the dog.

"I know," she said just as Snowy surged in the direction of Officer Kole, barking and snarling.

"I warned you!" the cop yelled, pulling his gun and aiming.

"Stop!" Sidney screamed, getting between the man's weapon and her dog. "She's not reacting to you—she sees something."

Sidney looked to the far reaches of the parking lot and for a minute thought that the pouring rain might have been playing tricks on her eyes.

If only.

"We need to get inside," Sidney said urgently, tugging her dog toward the concrete ramp. She reached out and grabbed the officer's shirtsleeve to pull him along as well.

"What does she see?" he asked, looking off across the lot.

One could mistake it for a combination of shadows and water flowing across the slightly uneven surfaces of the parking area, but that wasn't it at all.

"What is that?" Kole actually began to walk toward the shadows, only stopping when he realized that Sidney was still holding on to his arm.

He looked at her.

"I don't think you want to go any closer," she said, beginning to pull him toward the others.

The moving shadow was flowing closer, and they could see that the solid, dark mass was made up of thousands of bodies—thousands of squirming, crawling, skittering bodies.

He looked back, hesitating.

"Kole, let's go," Isabel called out as she walked up the ramp to join the others at the metal door.

"Do you see this?" he asked her, pointing to the advancing mass of insect life.

"I see," she said, putting her key in the door. "Let's get inside."

Sidney, Snowy, and Kole quickly made their way up the ramp, Kole passing the others to join Isabel at the door.

She held the door open for them, watching the parking lot beyond.

"C'mon, guys, quick," she said, motioning them up.

Mrs. Levesque had put Amy down but held her hand tightly as they made their way toward the open door and safety.

Sidney still held on to Snowy's collar, guiding the shepherd behind Rich and Cody. She stopped for a moment and looked back over shoulder at the parking lot and the mass moving inexorably closer. Stenciling on the SUV parked by the garage briefly caught her attention, but Officer Isabel's voice distracted her.

"Let's speed it up," she commanded.

"Sorry," Sidney said as she rushed up behind her friends and into the building. Subconsciously little warning bells had begun to sound but were silenced as Isabel slammed the metal door closed and locked it behind them.

CHAPTER **THIRTY-NINE**

The specimens had started to decay.

In the tiny makeshift lab aboard the C-130 Hercules military transport plane en route to Benediction's airport, Dr. Gregory Sayid felt his frustrations intensify.

They'd done everything they could to preserve the remains from the two previous event scenes, but still the specimens degenerated. There was just enough left to give him a taste of the mystery, and it was leaving him voracious.

The plane shook with turbulence, and the closer they got to Massachusetts, to the storm, the worse it got. This one was a monster, the enormity of its spiral touching most of the state, but it was what was going on in the center of the storm that concerned him most.

"ETA about twenty minutes, Doc," Brenda Langridge announced as she peeked around the corner of the privacy partition.

"Thanks," he said, carefully taking a specimen bottle from the padded holder on the table to the left of him. He stared at the contents that were practically jelly now.

"It amazes me that that little piece of snot could be causing us so much trouble," she said, coming to stand beside him as he opened the container, tipping the bottle so that the contents slid out onto the pad in front of him.

"This little piece of snot, as well as multiple other pieces of snot in various sizes and states of decay," Dr. Sayid said.

He leaned closer to the gelatinous object, scrutinizing it yet again.

"Why do you exist?" he asked the growth that he had taken from the brain of a monitor lizard.

"That's easy," Langridge said, picking up one of his dissecting tools and proceeding to pare away the nail on one of her fingers. "To make us crazy and to give our specialized research division something to do."

He rested his chin on top of a closed fist.

"What's its purpose, though?" Sayid said. "We've found zero evidence of a viral component, but something has caused—this. What's doing it, and why?"

"Ouch!" Langridge yelped, and tossed the scalpel back onto his workstation as she stuck her bleeding finger into her mouth. "I guess that it's just nature throwing us another curveball," she said, taking her finger from her mouth and looking at it. "Wouldn't be the first time we've encountered some naturally occurring bizarreness in this ever-changing world of ours."

Sayid continued to watch the extracted growth as it sat there on the tray, decaying even though it had been kept in a series of special chemicals to prevent that very thing. All they had done was slow the process down a bit.

"The funny thing is, and it really isn't at all humorous, but I'm hoping that you're right."

He could feel her looking at him.

"Why? What else could it possibly be?"

He didn't answer her because he wasn't at all sure and didn't feel comfortable airing his suspicions.

A message came over the PA that it was time for them to take their seats and to buckle up for landing.

Sayid started to put away his supplies and specimens. He hoped to have more answers very soon, either putting to bed his crazy suspicions or dragging them from the shadows into the light of day.

CHAPTER **FORTY**

There was light in the police station, an emergency generator having kicked on as soon as the power went out.

"Hey, Kennedy!" Officer Kole bellowed as he climbed the concrete stairs to the main level, Isabel and the Levesques right behind him. "We've found a couple more!"

Sidney, Rich, and Cody began to follow.

"I wonder if the power outage erased their computer records," Rich mused aloud. He caught Cody's and Sidney's confused looks and explained further. "I've got a few parking tickets that I haven't gotten around to paying and, y'know, if the system got wiped . . ."

Sidney rolled her eyes, amazed that Rich could even think about parking tickets after what they had been through. She realized then that Snowy wasn't with them and turned to see her sniffing wildly around the base of the door.

"C'mon, girl," she said aloud even though the dog could not hear.

She descended the steps and stood beside the dog, not wanting to startle her, then leaned into her line of vision.

"Let's go; we can't lag behind," she said, making hand gestures that the dog understood. "Don't want Officer Kole to be any more suspicious of you than he already is."

The dog obeyed, following her to the stairs and staying by her side as they climbed up to join Cody and Rich, who waited on the first-floor landing.

"Did you get lost?" Rich asked.

"Snowy took a detour," she explained, thumping the dog's side with the flat of her hand.

They saw the police officers with Mrs. Levesque and Amy turn a corner up ahead and moved to catch up. But Snowy stopped short, head tilting to one side.

"What is it, Snow?" Sidney asked her.

The dog sniffed the air, whined, and then began to bark.

"She smells something," Cody said, looking down the corridor where the others had gone.

Sidney recalled what she had seen stenciled on the SUV near the garage in the lot—K-9 UNIT—and that niggling sense of unease returned.

"Maybe she smells the other dogs," Sidney said.

"What other dogs?" Cody asked.

"The dogs used by the K-9 unit," Sidney said just before the sounds of multiple gunshots echoed down the corridor.

They all looked at each other, that horrible fear back again.

Sidney considered turning and running back the way they had come when screams joined the gunshots, and before she even realized what she was doing, she began to run toward the sounds of danger.

Toward the sounds of chaos, with Snowy close by her side.

"Sid, where the hell are you . . . ?" Rich began, but let his question fade away as he too ran down the hallway, followed closely by Cody.

Sidney rounded the corner at the end of the corridor and stopped, facing a shorter length of hallway with what looked to be the main office at its end. Officers Kole and Isabel were nowhere to be found. The smell of gunfire hung heavily in the air.

"Where is everybody?" Rich asked as he and Cody came up alongside her.

"I don't know," she said. "Probably in there."

"I don't think we should—" Cody began.

"What choice do we have?" Sidney cut him off, knowing that he was probably right, but the alternative left them standing around with their thumbs up their butts waiting for something to happen.

"We go in, check it, and . . ." She stopped, starting to head down the hall.

"And what?" Cody asked.

"I don't know," she answered. "But I can't just stand here."

"I have no problem standing here," Rich said. "But if it means I'll be here by myself, then I guess I'm going with you." He looked at Cody. "What about you?"

Without a word, Cody began walking toward the office.

Sidney was first through the doorway. There was a large desk in front of her, its chair empty but stained with something dark.

She held back a gasp as she slowly approached the desk and peered around it.

The police officer lying on the floor was very dead, his eyes wide open, mouth twisted in a grotesque grimace. His throat looked as though it had been torn out.

"What is it?" Cody asked.

She turned to meet his gaze, and something in her face must have registered her shock. He rushed to her side and peered around the desk himself.

"Oh my God," he said. "We have to do something."

She agreed but had no idea what. They could run from the building, but they certainly wouldn't be any safer out there in that storm. Instead, she moved past the desk. Snowy started to go ahead of her, and she reached down, placing the tips of her fingers on the dog's back, stopping her instantly.

"Good girl," Sidney whispered, eyes scanning the spaces before them. Papers had been knocked from desks, chairs and trash cans tipped over, but she didn't see any other signs of death.

No other bodies . . . yet.

She moved farther in, but a rustle made her freeze. Snowy stopped as well, taking cues from her master, who now raised a hand, signaling Cody and Rich to stop. Sidney listened for the sound again, eyes scanning the darkened room, trying to discern any new sounds from the sounds of the raging storm outside the building.

There it was again.

She cautiously moved toward it, weaving among the desks,

trying not to step on any of the objects that littered the floor. She stopped again and heard the sound. A soft, yet very brief hissing—no, it was something rubbing against metal. Sidney moved a little bit farther into the office, standing in a short aisle between four metal desks.

The sound was close now.

She tilted to the left and looked down into the wide, terror-filled eyes of Mrs. Levesque and Amy, who were crammed beneath a desk. The mother's ragged and bloody hand was clamped over her daughter's mouth.

Sidney squatted down and was about to offer them her hand when the attack came.

The animal sprang from the shadows, clipping her and knocking her backward as it disappeared back into the gloom.

"There's something in here!" Sidney screamed, scrambling to her feet. Her gaze found Mrs. Levesque, who was crying harder now and was mouthing something that could have been *Help us.*

The animal leaped up on top of a desk in the far corner of the room. In any other situation, Sidney would have thought the German shepherd was beautiful, its golden brown-and-black fur almost shiny in the emergency lighting.

But now it was simply terrifying.

It flew from the desk, silently charging toward her, hurdling over obstacles in its path. She knew it would be on her in an instant and instinctively raised her arm to protect herself from its snapping jaws.

Snowy got there first, intercepting the dog, using her own force to crash into its side and send it sliding across a desk onto the floor behind it. Sidney heard the sounds of snapping jaws, snarls, and scrabbling claws, and instincts at once kicked in—something akin to a mother protecting her child.

Against the wall across from her she saw a coatrack—a metal pole with caps, some coats, and a sweater hanging from it. Sidney practically flew to it, grabbing the cold metal and shaking off the clothes that hung there.

She had her weapon.

Cody watched in horror as the shepherd charged his girlfriend, his *ex*-girlfriend.

Images of his father exploded in his brain. Terrifying, bloody images reminding him of what kind of night the day had become.

The memories froze him in place. Froze him with absolute fear.

Then Cody caught sight of Rich racing toward Sidney. He was willing himself to run, to rise above his terror, and was actually beginning to move, when Snowy came to the rescue. Good ol' Snowy.

He'd never seen the white German shepherd look so ferocious. She was like some sort of missile, flying through the air to intercept enemy fire. She slammed into the attacking dog, knocking it away from her master. If things weren't so freakin' terrifying, it would have been spectacular.

He saw that Rich had stopped to help Mrs. Levesque and her daughter climb out from under the desk. Sidney had grabbed an old coatrack and was heading toward the fighting dogs. Cody was about to help her separate the dogs when he sensed it. Like a cold breeze down the back of his neck.

He spun around to see another dog in mid-leap, silently bearing down on him, white teeth glistening in the faint glow of the emergency lights.

There was a part of Sidney deep inside—the civilized part, she guessed—that screamed for her to stop as she smashed the coatrack down upon the attacking dog's head. The animal didn't make a sound as the metal connected, opening up a bloody gash just above its right eye.

Its right eye.

The dog stopped fighting for a brief instant, and as it turned its gaze on her, she saw what she had seen in the other affected animals.

Or was it infected animals?

A silvery covering over the right eye.

Snowy took full advantage of the other dog's pause, snapping her powerful jaws around the animal's throat and thrashing savagely as she growled.

Sidney continued to bash the dog—probably one of the drug-sniffing dogs that loyally worked with the island's police force. But she couldn't consider that now. Instead, she forced herself to tap into the rage and fury caused by the horrors of the past several hours and beat the dog that was attempting to harm her friend—her Snowy.

The police dog didn't make a sound as Sidney and Snowy savagely turned the tables on the attacking animal. Its jaw was broken and askew, its eyes—especially the right one—damaged and swollen, and finally the police dog appeared unable to continue its fight.

Sidney grabbed for Snowy, pulling her back and away from the injured police dog, watching as it swayed from side to side, moving its head as if attempting to see with its damaged right eye. She couldn't stand the sight of its struggle. It was time to be human again, she decided, taking the pointed end of the metal shaft and driving it down into the pathetic creature's neck.

The dog attempted to surge forward, its legs scrabbling against the hardwood floor, but its movements soon grew slower, more feeble, until finally it went still.

Sidney actually screamed as the sound of gunfire boomed through the office space. She spun around, heart pounding in her chest, adrenaline surging through her veins, and she wondered what more horrible things she would be forced to do tonight.

Across the office she saw Cody thrashing on the floor, the large body of another German shepherd sprawled atop him. She was just about ready to retrieve her makeshift spear and go to his aid when he pushed the limp body of the dog off of himself. Movement from the corridor at the far end of the office caught her attention next, and she realized it was Officer Isabel slowly lowering her weapon. Officer Kole, who looked as though he might have been injured, and some other very scared-looking people were crowding up behind her.

"You guys all right?" Isabel asked.

"Yeah, yeah, we're good," Rich said. He was by the entrance to the office with Mrs. Levesque and her daughter.

Sidney and Snowy walked over to Cody. Her ex looked a little shaken as she offered him a hand up. He hesitated for just a moment but took it, allowing her to help him. Snowy was sniffing the bleeding corpse of the other dog.

"Get away from that, girl," Sidney said, reaching to pull the dog away. She still didn't know the reason for the strange animal behavior and didn't want to take any chances.

Another police officer, an older, bald-headed man, left the group to approach them. Sidney had no idea who he was but noticed a K-9 patch on the sleeve of his uniform. He passed them to stand above the dead shepherd. Slowly he dropped to his knees and pulled the animal up into his arms.

"They were fine all day," the officer said, just as much to convince himself as anybody. "And even when things started to . . . to go crazy, they seemed all right so I brought them back here."

He stroked the dog's blood-speckled fur lovingly, and Sidney could not help but feel her heart break for his loss.

"I was going to put them in their kennels. They liked their kennels, they felt safe there, but then . . ." He paused, and then slowly turned tear-filled eyes toward Sidney. "They weren't themselves," the policeman said. "They were something else entirely."

It seemed as though he was looking for some kind of answer, something that would make sense out of the insanity he was—they all were—experiencing.

"I've seen it with other animals today," Sidney said. "Cats, dogs, raccoons . . . even insects."

She could see that he was now looking at Snowy.

"Why isn't she . . . ?" he started to ask.

"We don't know," Sidney said, her protectiveness coming through again. She reached down to pull the dog closer to her. "There has to be a reason, but we just haven't thought of it yet."

She could sense that the others had joined them, milling about the dead animals, muttering among themselves.

"We thought we'd lost you guys," Officer Isabel said. "When we came into the office, we found Kennedy dead." She briefly looked over to the front desk. "And then the dogs attacked. If it wasn't for Donovan here getting us all down to the holding cells, it would have been a massacre."

"Sidney?" a voice called out, and Sidney turned to see a pajama-clad Pam stagger over.

"Oh my God, Pam . . . are you all right?"

Her coworker seemed to consider the question for a moment, then rushed to Sidney, throwing her arms around the girl. "No, no, I'm not all right at all . . . nothing is all right." She sobbed into Sidney's shoulder, then sniffled loudly and pulled away.

"Sorry," she said, wiping a hand over her face. "Been holding it together most of the night, and just couldn't do it anymore."

"It's okay," Sidney said, rubbing her arm.

"No, it's not, Sid," Pam said, shaking her head. "It's horrible . . . from what I've seen, all the animals have lost their shit. I barely got out of my house alive. Fribble . . ." She stopped, and her eyes began to fill with tears again.

"I know," Sidney said. "It's bad . . . I know."

"He attacked me," Pam continued in a trembling voice. "I think . . . I think that he . . ." She fell silent, obviously remembering the horror that she'd experienced. "I think he was actually trying to kill me."

She pulled the collar of her pajama top down to reveal the

deep scratches and bite marks in her neck and shoulder.

"We should clean those before they get infected," Sidney said, stepping closer for a look.

"Yeah." Pam shrugged, pulling the collar of her pajamas back over the wounds. "What's going on out there, Sid?" she asked. "What could possibly be doing this?"

Sidney looked around to where she'd dropped the trash bag with the raccoon inside. It was over by the wall, just inside the office space.

"I don't know," she answered her friend. "But if anybody can figure it out—"

"Listen up, people," Officer Kole suddenly spoke up. The man was favoring his arm, and Sidney could see where blood had dripped down beneath his shirt to the back of his hand. "I think the situation here is pretty much safe," he said with authority. "We'll hole up here until we can find out what the hell is going on, and what to do about it."

"Officer," Sidney said. "I need to get to Doc Martin."

"I don't think it's wise for anybody to be out there and to—"

"No," she interrupted as she strode across the room and picked up the green trash bag, holding it up. "I need to get this specimen to Doc Martin. If there's anyone on this island who can figure out what's happening, it's her."

The room was silent, and Sidney could feel everyone's eyes on her, waiting to see how this would play out.

"I understand where you're coming from with this," Officer Kole said, walking slowly toward her. "But I can't allow any of my officers—"

"I don't need any of your officers," she blurted out, not really thinking through her answer, but now that it had left her mouth she was fine with it—a little scared, but fine with it.

The man made a face that said he was either in pain or very, very annoyed with her.

"I can't in all good conscience allow you to go out in . . . that alone." He pointed to the window, where rain spattered the glass as if someone was holding a hose on the panes.

"She wouldn't be going alone," Cody said, moving closer to her.

Rich cleared his voice nervously and stepped forward as well. "Yeah, she wouldn't be alone," he agreed.

Officer Kole studied them intently. "You've seen what it's like out there," he said. "You three will be risking your lives."

"Four," Officer Isabel corrected.

"Excuse me?" Kole said, gazing at her incredulously.

"Four of us will be going," she said firmly.

"I need you here."

"And I understand where you're coming from, but if Doc Martin can help figure this out, someone has to get to her."

Kole continued to stare at his partner as if searching for some crack in her logic. "I trust your judgment," he finally said. "Don't necessarily agree with it, but I trust it." Kole turned his eyes toward Sidney and her friends. "Let's just hope Doc Martin is worth the effort.

The silence that followed was broken by the noise from Sidney's stomach. She placed a hand upon her empty belly and tried to ignore it.

"Maybe you should all have something to eat before you head

out," Kole said. "I've got the keys to the vending machines. Won't be all that nutritious, but at least it'll take the edge off."

"Thanks," Sidney said, still feeling a bit embarrassed.

"Can't go out into the end of the world on an empty stomach," Rich said, and all eyes turned to him.

"Oh, did I say that out loud?"

Sidney smiled weakly at that, as did Cody, a scared part of her now wondering if he just might be right.

CHAPTER **FORTY-ONE**

The vessel that had once been Ronald Berthold—man, husband, certified public accountant—stumbled down the rain-swept streets of Benediction as more vessels of varying sizes and shapes swarmed around him.

Searching.

He—*they*—had a purpose, and they would carry out that purpose no matter the cost.

The former Ronald Berthold paused in the center of the street, craning his neck, seeking out the sound that had drawn it and the others in this direction.

There, above the noise of the storm—the hum of a machine.

Focusing its senses upon the sound, the human vessel began to walk again. The other multitude of vessels, hearing it now as well, followed.

Drawn toward the sound.

Where there was sound, there would be life.

CHAPTER **FORTY-TWO**

After cleaning up a bit in the restroom, Cody sat as far away from the others as he could, gnawing on a stale granola bar.

Have to keep the strength up, he thought with sarcasm as he washed the dry snack down with a gulp of bottled water.

He couldn't get his father out of his head.

Over and over the scene in the marina parking lot played out in his head, his dad sacrificing himself to make sure that everyone else lived.

The image of his father's face, blood from the deep wounds in his scalp cascading over his shocked features, had burned itself onto Cody's brain, and no matter how hard he tried to forget, it always was there.

With the sickening vision came the guilt. His father had died before his eyes, and he hadn't done anything to stop it.

"Hey," said a voice softly. He knew who it was and didn't want to look.

"Hey," he answered.

"You okay?" Sidney asked.

He wanted to tell her to leave him alone, to go away, remembering that she was the one who had held him back. If it wasn't for her . . .

"Yeah, I'm fine. Just really tired. Trying to get some rest before . . ."

She took a seat on the floor beside him, and he heard the rustling of a wrapper as she prepared to eat something. He ignored her, taking another bite of his granola bar.

"Granola," she said. "Probably a better idea than chocolate, but I've always been weak."

He didn't respond, just chewed slowly, like a cow chewing its cud. He wanted to be mad at her. Not only had she broken his heart, she'd kept him from saving his father's life. He wanted to bundle it all together into one great big seething ball of hurt and rage, but . . .

He couldn't do it.

Deep down, he knew that Sidney had saved *his* life. If he'd gone out there to help his father, he would have died as well.

Cody took a long swig of water and looked at her. She had cleaned the dried blood from her face too.

"What?" she asked, a piece of chocolate in her mouth. "I've already told you I'm weak."

"You're not weak," he said, shaking his head. "Well, maybe a little."

She looked at him, surprised by his attempt at a joke. Then she leaned into his shoulder. "I'm really sorry about your dad," she said.

"Me too," he answered, trying to keep his emotions in check.

They continued to eat in silence.

"He didn't hate you, you know," Cody said after a moment.

Sidney looked at him. "Really? Could have fooled me."

"It wasn't hate at all," Cody explained. "I think it was more like . . . jealousy."

"He was jealous of me? How?"

Cody shrugged as he munched on another square of granola.

"I think he knew how smart you are, and how much I admired that about you. How I would listen to you"—Cody shrugged—"and not really listen to him all that much."

"I would never have guessed that," she said, breaking off a piece of chocolate and putting it in her mouth.

"It's not like you could have," Cody told her. "He kept a lot of stuff to himself, but I could see it, how he acted whenever I talked about you."

She unscrewed the cap on her own bottle of water and took a long swallow. "Now I feel really bad."

"Why?" Cody asked. "I just thought you'd like to know he didn't hate you."

"I guess it is good to know," Sidney agreed.

"Anyway, it's all good," Cody said with finality, finishing his granola bar and crinkling up the wrapper, wishing he could believe his own words.

CHAPTER **FORTY-THREE**

Officer Riley Donovan stroked the head of his dog Scarlett and then of her brother, Samson.

He had carried their bodies down to the station garage and was kneeling between the two.

He told himself that he wouldn't cry, but he felt the barriers he'd erected start to crumble as emotion welled up inside of him and the tears began.

He'd loved these dogs, and he was certain that they'd loved him. He knew that they'd had no control over their actions. What he'd seen in the office were not his dedicated, loving, and hardworking partners. They had been replaced by something else.

Something cold, calculating, and monstrous.

Donovan couldn't take his eyes from the pair of German shepherds. He could tell himself that they were only sleeping, but he knew the truth, and it was like a knife to the heart. Finally he stood and threw an old comforter he'd found in a supply closet over them, watching as it settled across their unmoving bodies.

He sniffled once, then took a deep breath and turned away from the dogs. *Might as well check the generator before I go back up,* he thought, walking toward the chain-link enclosure where the generator rumbled.

Stepping inside the enclosure, he checked the gas gauge and saw that the tank was half full. They still had a few hours left. Satisfied, Donovan left the enclosure, shut the gate, and was ready to leave the garage area when he heard a faint bump. He turned toward the closed garage door, where he saw the profile of a man walk past the long horizontal window.

He quickly walked toward the door.

"Hello?" he called out.

The man's face appeared in the window again, followed by a single bang.

"Holy crap," Donovan said. "Hold on! I'll raise the door enough for you to crawl under," he hollered to the stranger.

Again there was the single thump of a fist hitting the metal door.

"Get ready." Donovan hit the button on the side of the garage door, and it began to rise with a whine and the clanking of gears.

A flow of insects immediately scuttled inside.

"Jesus!" Donovan cried, frantically stomping on the spiders, centipedes, and beetles that washed in like water. "Hey, buddy, hurry it up!" he shouted.

The man suddenly appeared, trying to duck beneath the door.

Donovan grabbed his arm and pulled him in. The man stumbled to the floor, and the officer left him there while he darted over to the controls and hit the button to shut the door.

"Are you okay?" Donovan asked over his shoulder as he stamped on the remaining bugs. The man didn't reply, so the officer turned, only to look directly into the face of the man he'd saved.

It was then that he could see the man wasn't okay at all. There was something seriously wrong with him. It looked as if his skull had been bashed in, and there was a glistening covering, like a cataract, over his right eye. And his mouth—his mouth was stained red as if he'd just taken the biggest bite from a blood pie.

And before Donovan could react, the man rushed toward him with incredible speed, mouth open, and sank his teeth into the officer's throat.

It happened so fast, Donovan didn't even have a chance to scream.

CHAPTER **FORTY-FOUR**

Sidney watched as Officer Isabel spoke softly with Officer Kole in a corner of the room. The older officer handed the young woman another firearm in a holster, which she secured to her belt as they spoke.

Finally Officer Isabel approached Sidney, shotgun slung over her shoulder. "Are we ready?"

"Yeah," Sidney said, leaning down to retrieve the trash bag. A nasty odor wafted from it, and she tried to cinch the top tighter.

"Are your two friends coming?" Isabel asked, looking around for them.

"Yeah, I think so," Sidney said. She looked up to find Cody talking with Officer Kole. The officer handed him a gun as well, and the two shook hands. Cody stuck the gun in the front of his pants and walked over to Sidney and Officer Isabel.

"Do you know how to use that?" Sidney asked, nodding toward the gun.

"Well enough," he said.

In all the years they'd been together she had never known him to have any interest in guns.

"When did you ever learn to fire a gun?" she asked incredulously.

"You weren't always in my life," he said petulantly. "My dad taught me how to shoot when I was little."

"You never mentioned that."

"I'm sure there's a lot I never mentioned," Cody said, and looked away from her to Officer Isabel.

Ouch! Sidney thought. *So much for still being friends.*

"Where's the other one?" Isabel asked. "We need to get rolling."

Sidney looked around at the various groupings of people and found Rich with Amy Levesque, surprised by what she saw.

What would Rich be saying to a preschooler?

"But the ponies are animals, right?" Amy asked. She sat atop a desk, watching as Rich drew a picture.

"Yeah, they're animals, but they're nice."

"But the animals want to bite us," Amy said. "That means the ponies would want to bite us too."

"No, not the ponies," Rich reassured her, looking up from his drawing and shaking his head. "The ponies are magic, and smart, and nice—"

"Not Nightmare Moon!" The little girl shook her head vigorously.

"Well, she starts off bad, but I'll let you in on a little secret." Rich looked around, then leaned close to the little girl and in an exaggerated whisper said, "Remember the name Princess Luna, okay?"

The little girl nodded. "Princess Luna, got it."

"Good." He went back to drawing. "So I want you to keep this drawing with you all the time, and when you get scared, you look at it."

"Okay," Amy said, tilting her head to see his work. "Which pony is that?" she asked him.

"Which one is your favorite?"

"I like Twilight Sparkle, but Rainbow Dash is my favorite too."

"This is Rainbow Dash," he said, trying to remember some of the cartoon pony's details.

"No, that's not," Amy told him. "That doesn't look like Rainbow Dash at all. That looks more like Pinkie Pie."

"Okay, it's Pinkie Pie."

"I hate Pinkie Pie."

Rich couldn't help but laugh, putting his head down on top of the drawing.

"Hey, Rich?"

He turned to see Sidney standing behind him.

"You coming?"

"Yeah," he said. "Yeah, sure." He picked up the paper and gave it to the little girl. "Here ya go. Since it doesn't look like Rainbow Dash, and you hate Pinkie Pie, maybe you can make this your very own pony," he said as she studied the drawing very carefully.

"I'll name her Richacorn!" Amy proclaimed. She took the pencil from Rich's hand and began to add to his drawing. "But I'll have to give her a horn on her head."

"Her?" he asked.

The little girl nodded.

"All right then. I've gotta run some errands while you do that."

The little girl continued to draw, singing to herself as she did. Rich watched her for minute, then stood and joined Sidney.

"Ready," he said.

"Rainbow Dash?" Sidney asked.

Rich shrugged.

"Pinkie Pie?"

He shrugged again.

"I don't know you." Sidney slowly shook her head.

"I'm a mystery wrapped in an enigma."

"Yeah, you're something," she said, smiling slightly, and he felt his heart do that stupid thing it often did when he was around her.

He hated that.

"Are we going or what?" Rich asked, feigning annoyance.

"Yeah, c'mon, Richacorn," Sidney said, walking away. "Cody and Officer Isabel are waiting by the door."

"I'll never live this down, will I?"

"Absolutely not," she said with a smile.

It was the last thing Rich saw before it all went dark.

There was a collective gasp as the lights went out.

"It's all right, everybody." Officer Kole's voice boomed in the darkness. "The generator probably ran out of gas. Give me a minute and—"

He never finished.

Snowy began barking just as Sidney heard the clicking. The unmistakable sounds of animal toenails upon hard wood.

"We've got to get out of here," she said, hoping that Officer Isabel was close enough to hear. "We've got to get everybody out of—"

Multiple cell phone screens lit, illuminating the darkness, revealing the darting shapes of animals that had somehow found their way into the building.

"They're inside," Sidney hissed, searching the darkness for her friends. She could feel Snowy protectively at her side and put out her hands for Rich.

"Rich!" she called out.

"I'm here," he answered just as screams erupted through the room.

It was madness. A sensory nightmare of the highest order. The sounds of panic reverberated through the office, footfalls as people ran, furniture toppling over, objects crashing to the floor, and other sounds . . .

Sounds that Sidney did not want to hear.

Screams—screams so filled with fear that they were almost contagious, screams that were savagely cut short, one after another after another. She wanted to shut her brain off, curl into a ball, and wait to die.

But she wouldn't do that—couldn't do that.

She needed to get out of there, to escape the beasts. That's what they were now. They weren't really dogs and cats and raccoons and squirrels anymore; they were something else, and "beasts" seemed quite appropriate.

Sidney reached out and felt Snowy quivering by her side. The poor animal could not hear the chaos—the screams of the dying—but she could sense what was happening.

See what was happening.

Smell what was happening.

"Sid!" she heard Cody call out, and she turned toward the sound.

He stood no more than six feet away, near the entrance to the office, holding up the illuminated screen of his cell phone.

But the light attracted more than just Sidney.

"Cody, behind you!" she screamed as she watched three large dogs emerge from the darkness to his right.

Cody began to turn, just as the deafening blast of a shotgun sounded. Cody jumped back, dropping his cell, and the dogs scattered as a portion of the wall behind them tore away.

"Let's go!" Officer Isabel cried out. The beam of a flashlight lit up the area around her near the back of the office.

It was still chaos, the screams and sounds of people trying to escape. Sidney moved toward the light, making sure that Snowy was by her side. She looked to where Cody had been and saw hints of frantic movement before her ex appeared. At first she thought he'd been hurt, his face spattered red.

"I'm all right," he said, reading the panic in her eyes. "The blood's not mine this time."

Rich was suddenly with them, little Amy in his arms. She was crying but clutched the drawing tightly in her small hand. The child's mother followed closely behind. More people joined them, drawn to the moving light of the flashlight.

"C'mon," Sidney said, trying to push people toward Officer Isabel.

The screams were suddenly close as people behind her were pulled back into the darkness. They didn't last long though, ending in wet ripping sounds and gurgling.

She could only imagine what was happening.

She was turning away to follow the light when something snagged the leg of her pants and she fell forward, chest and hands hitting the floor with a loud slap. The trash bag flew from her grasp as she felt herself dragged back, away from the light.

She watched as Cody, Snowy, and Rich continued toward Officer Isabel, unaware of her plight. She tried to cry out, but the air had been punched from her lungs when she hit the floor.

Tamping down the fear and panic, she dug her nails into the hard wood and flipped herself onto her back. Hauling back her free leg, she drove the heel of her foot into the snout of the dog—*the beast*—that held her, a chocolate Labrador with a head as square as a box. It did not yelp or cry out, even though blood poured from its nose, as it continued to tug on her leg. She raised her leg and was ready to kick again, when a Saint Bernard appeared beside the Lab. She knew this dog. His name was Tiny, and he was, to quote Doc Martin, a gentle soul.

Her brain quickly corrected that bit of info as the animal took her entire foot into his mouth.

She managed to cry out as the massive maw closed upon her ankle. The pressure was incredible as the dogs pulled her farther into the shadows. She thrashed wildly, screaming now, knowing it was only a matter of time before her bones snapped and the dogs came for her throat.

Suddenly the darkness exploded in a deafening burst of light and fire. The great beast that held her grunted, then fell into the Lab, blood spurting from his neck in a geyser of crimson. The Lab lost its grip on her pants, and she managed to wrench her foot, soaking wet but intact, from the mouth of the once-gentle Saint Bernard.

Sidney scrabbled backward, eyes frantically searching for her savior.

Officer Kole leaned against a file cabinet, one hand clutching his revolver, the other holding on to a bleeding wound torn in his throat.

"Go," he croaked.

She jumped to her feet and started toward him, but he raised his weapon and she froze. The gun fired, and Sidney spun around to see something dark and muscular thud to the floor.

"Didn't . . . you . . . hear me?" he asked, firing his weapon again. "I said go . . . I'm done. . . ."

She wanted to help, but that awful sense of being too late overrode the desire, and she turned away. The officer continued to fire at the beasts that converged on him, covering her escape, until his gun went silent.

And the beasts took him.

Sidney raced through the doorway at the back of the office and into another hall. It was dark, and she couldn't see the others ahead of her.

She removed her phone from her pocket and illuminated the

screen. In the dim light she could see that she was in a short passage with a stairway at the end. She also saw the body of a man lying on the floor, eyes wide open in horrific death, his belly torn open, his insides strewn about like a discarded piece of rope. She remembered seeing him earlier near the coffee machine and had watched him pull a liquor bottle from his coat pocket and pour its contents into his coffee.

I could use a little of that right now, she thought.

Carefully she stepped over him, then put her phone back in her pocket. Running her fingers along the wall, she cautiously made her way to the stairs, stopping at the top until her hand found the metal railing.

She made her way down, counting the steps as did.

Twenty-four.

She reached a small landing where the air smelled of oil and gasoline, and she remembered the closed garage door that she'd seen at the end of the driveway when they'd first driven into the station lot.

Five. Five more steps.

And then she remembered the trash bag.

"Shit," she hissed, feeling that sense of nearly overwhelming panic.

She turned and considered going back up the stairs. The twenty-nine steps.

No, a voice inside her head ordered. Hell, knowing the doc, she probably already had her own damn specimen.

She took the phone from her pocket again and used it to illuminate her path as she turned and slowly walked forward into the darkness of the garage. The cement floor was slick beneath her sneakered feet, and she almost fell as she stepped in a dark puddle.

Oil, she guessed, based on the smell of the place.

Ahead of her, she could make out the metal garage door, half open. Officer Donovan was slumped against the wall next to it, his head lolling oddly to the side.

Not oil.

And now, sadly, she knew how the beasts had gotten into the station.

She continued to move slowly toward the open garage door, listening intently for sounds of animals. It was still pouring outside, and the smell of the ocean carried on the wind reminded her of how much she loved the summer rain—correction, *used* to love the summer rain.

Her foot touched Officer Donovan's leg, and she turned the light of her phone on him. His head looked as though it was merely hanging on by a thread of skin. She was about to turn her phone off when she noticed the gun, still holstered at his hip.

She hesitated for only a moment before bending down, unsnapping the holster, and retrieving the weapon. It felt fake in her hand, far lighter than she would have imagined, but as she hefted the weapon, she suddenly found herself feeling a little bit better—safer—and more confident in her survival.

Yeah, we'll see how safe I feel when it comes time to use it, she thought as she slid her phone back into her pocket and moved to the half-open garage door.

Sidney flinched as she leaned out into the downpour, the rain still coming down so hard that it felt like tiny needles on her exposed skin. Holding the gun at her side, she started up the driveway, noticing that the SUV that had been parked there was gone. *How could they have left me behind?*

Shrugging off a wave of anger and despair, Sidney crept up the driveway, staying low to the ground, making it harder to be seen. At the top of the drive she looked out over the parking lot and at the few vehicles that remained there. *All these cars and no way to drive them,* she thought, frustrated that she'd spent all her time learning about animal physiology instead of how to jack a car.

Through the pouring rain, she scanned her surroundings for animal life, only slightly relieved that she could see no signs. But still, she couldn't stay in the driveway. She hugged the wall of the building, using the shadows for cover as she cautiously made her way to the front of the police station. Depending on how bad it actually was on the island, maybe she'd get lucky and be able to flag down a passing car.

She reached the corner of the building and stopped, suddenly fearful of what she might find around it. She gripped the gun tightly and pressed herself to the brick wall. Then, taking a deep breath, she carefully rounded the corner.

A lone figure stood at the bottom of the front steps, the doors to the police station yawning open behind him. A jolt of excitement shot through her. She wasn't alone. But as she began to step from the shadows, there was a flurry of movement from inside the doors, and a pack of dogs spilled out onto the stoop, surveying the area with cold, unfeeling eyes.

Sidney knew that she shouldn't, that she should remain in hiding, but she just couldn't do it. She came out from alongside the building, waving her arms so that he would see her. Maybe he had a chance, maybe if he ran toward her, the two of them could . . .

She was certain that he saw her, but he continued to stand stiffly, watching—possibly too afraid to move. She knew that feeling. The dogs had begun to descend the stairs behind him.

"C'mon!" she shouted as she ran toward him.

But he remained silent and still.

Then the dogs did an odd thing. They completely ignored the man, walking around him and heading inexorably toward her. She wanted to run but knew that they would take her down in an instant. There was only one chance for her, even though it would nearly kill her to do it.

Slowly, sadly, Sidney raised the gun and fired at the dog closest to her. The first shot missed, striking off the curb. She tried again. The gun roared when she pulled the trigger, and this time the lead dog went down, its front leg shattered by the impact of the bullet. She forced herself to remember the attacks in the station, the horrors that she'd seen, and fired again. Another dog went down.

Then the stranger began moving toward her, arms outstretched.

He had almost reached her when she noticed all the blood—on his face, the front of his clothes, his hands. He walked so stiffly, like a zombie, and his skull was severely misshapen.

And then she saw his right eye.

Panicking, she stepped backward, but her foot caught on the curb at the end of the walk, and she went down, hitting her head on the slick pavement. She tried to aim her gun at the advancing stranger, but her vision was askew. She fired anyway, missing by a mile, and tried like hell to get to her feet before—

The man rushed at her, moving like some sort of predatory animal. His cold hand wrapped around her wrist, and he yanked her toward him with such force that she lost her hold on the pistol and it clattered to the ground. He leaned forward toward her, mouth agape. She saw bits of what could have been strings of meat trailing from between bloodstained teeth and suddenly understood the horrors of what this stranger had done.

That he was like the animals.

She tried to fight him, but he was incredibly strong, coming closer, the stink of him in her nostrils, the warmth of his breath on her exposed neck.

Sidney imagined what it would be like, the feeling of human teeth plunging into her throat, breaking the skin, tearing away the flesh as gouts of blood bubbled up from the gaping wound. And then she heard the screeching of brakes behind her and the sound of someone shouting her name.

There was a sudden rush of something white, followed by a grunt, and then her attacker was lying on the street, something of equal savagery perched upon his chest.

It took her a moment to realize what had happened.

"Snowy!"

Arms grabbed her around the waist from behind and she screamed, fists flying.

"Hey!" a familiar voice yelled. "It's me, Sid!"

And she turned into Cody's arms, staring at him in shock as her mind tried to catch up with what was happening. He began to pull her toward the SUV where Rich and Officer Isabel waited.

"Snowy," she said, wrenching herself away from Cody and turning back toward her dog.

She was desperate for the dog to look at her so she could signal that it was time to go, but the white German shepherd was still perched atop the man, biting at his flailing arms.

Another dog barreled seemingly out of nowhere and plowed into Snowy's side, knocking her over. Snowy rolled to the ground with a yelp but quickly got back to her feet.

Sidney recognized her dog's attacker, and she bet Snowy did as well.

There was no mistaking Alfred, the nasty French bulldog, in all his squat, muscled glory.

Snowy bared her fangs and snarled as the Frenchie slowly plodded toward her. Other dogs were following Alfred, and more animals were beginning to slink from the surrounding area. The shepherd was favoring her front paw, and Sidney knew she wouldn't be able to fight the pack coming for her.

Frantically Sidney's eyes scanned the rain-swept street and finally stopped on the gun lying there, not far from the curb where she'd fallen. She raced over, grabbed it up, and aimed. The shots went wild but were enough to distract the advancing animals, which was good because she was all out of bullets.

All eyes were suddenly on Sidney, including Snowy's. She tossed the empty gun in their direction, hoping that she would take out at least one of them.

"C'mon, girl!" Sidney yelled, waving her arms and starting to run.

Snowy followed, plowing through the pack of dogs. Even with an injured leg, she was able to outrun them.

The SUV pulled up closer beside Sidney, and she opened the back door, turning around just as Snowy leaped up, paws on her shoulders, licking her face.

Between licks, Sidney could see the man now standing in the middle of the street, Alfred by his side, the other beasts all around them.

"Not now, girl," she said, pushing Snowy down and motioning toward the backseat of the SUV.

As Snowy jumped into the vehicle, the animals started toward them, one by one, from a trot to a gallop.

"Let's get out of here," she shouted to her friends as she practically fell into the SUV behind Snowy, slamming the door shut.

The SUV lurched forward into the night.

And the beasts followed.

CHAPTER **FORTY-FIVE**

The rules had shifted again.

As the SUV barreled down the rain-swept deserted streets of Benediction, Sidney could not help but think of how this latest wrinkle could be a game changer.

"Who was that guy?" Rich asked. He was staring out the back window, even though they could no longer see the man or his pack of animals. "And why was he attacking you?"

"I don't know," Sidney said. She was still running her hands over Snowy's filthy body, looking for signs of injury. "But . . . but I think he was affected."

Cody sat in the front seat beside Officer Isabel, who was driving. He turned to look at Sidney. "What do you mean?"

"I mean that I think he was changed . . . like the animals have been changed."

"But it hasn't been affecting people, right?" Officer Isabel asked. Sidney could see her frantic eyes in the rearview mirror.

"No." Sidney was trying to put the pieces together. "Not so far that I've seen. It's only been the animals."

Rich had taken his eyes from the rear window and was patting Snowy.

"Are you sure he was affected?" he asked. "Maybe he was just a crazy person or something."

"No." Sidney shook her head, remembering how he moved—how he looked. "His right eye," she said.

"What about it?" Officer Isabel asked.

"So far the animals I've seen changed by this have this weird shiny covering over their right eye."

"What, like a cataract?"

"Yeah, kinda," Sidney answered. "But that guy had it too."

It was quiet in the car except for the hissing of the rain outside.

"So, what are you saying?" Rich finally asked. "That people are going to start going crazy and trying to bite our faces off?"

She looked at him. "I don't know. I guess I could be saying that."

"But wouldn't we have seen more people changed by now?" Officer Isabel asked. "Back at the station there had to be what, twenty-five, thirty people in there. No one showed any signs of wanting to hurt anybody else."

"True," Sidney said. "But if this is some sort of disease—a virus or something—maybe it's changing . . . mutating. Maybe that guy was just the first."

Cody laid his head back against the seat. "Great. Like things don't suck enough already."

"Or maybe it's something else entirely," she said, her mind drifting over the events of the past hours.

"What the hell is that supposed to mean?" Rich asked.

Sidney shrugged. "Something is telling me this isn't a disease."

"So we're still left with the big question then," Officer Isabel said.

"Yeah—what the hell is it?" Sidney looked out her window as the images of the place she'd spent her entire life swiftly passed by. A place that had gone to hell in the space of hours.

She caught glimpses of things she would have rather not seen: burning homes and stores, bodies lying in the street. And when she realized they were in the vicinity of her home, she dared to ask the question.

"My father?"

She caught Officer Isabel's eyes in the rearview mirror.

"We'll stop and get him," Isabel said.

"Thanks," Sidney said, feeling the tiniest bit of relief. Now the chore would be to hold on to that positive sensation and not let it become swallowed up by the darkness closing in all around them.

But it was getting harder and harder to do.

CHAPTER **FORTY-SIX**

It was as if a giant's hand had closed around the C-130 Hercules military transport and was intent on shaking it to pieces.

Dr. Sayid gripped the sides of his seat so tightly that he thought he might rip through the cushioning as the great aircraft was pummeled by the storm.

"How are you doing there, Doc?" Brenda Langridge asked from the seat across from him.

He opened his eyes enough to see that she was smiling, obviously amused by his discomfort. "How do you think?" he snapped, feeling as though the workings of his stomach were going to shoot up his throat and onto the floor as the craft plummeted, only to rapidly ascend again. "Are we going to make it?"

"Probably." She shrugged nonchalantly, raising her voice to be heard over the sounds of the craft's four propellers. She leaned forward to glance out a nearby window. "The C-130 is the workhorse of military transport. Plus this bad boy has been souped up special for us so we can travel in comfort."

"Seriously?" Sayid asked, feeling as though he were sitting in some sort of medieval torture device.

"What, you don't like the seats?" she asked.

He didn't respond, certain that just by looking at him, she'd know his feelings. Instead, he looked at the other six members of his science team and security crew seated at the opposite end of the transport. It made him feel a little better to see that most appeared to be enjoying the experience as much as he was.

The plane began to shake so violently that Sayid was sure they were going to crash. *This is it,* he thought, glad that he'd had the opportunity to speak to his daughter one last time before . . .

Then the shaking seemed to calm a bit, and he got that hollow, dropping feeling in his belly, like coming down from a great height in an elevator.

He glanced at Langridge to find her smiling at him.

"I'd say we'll be touching down shortly," she said. "That wasn't so bad."

The doctor just nodded, desperately wanting to be off the transport, with his feet planted firmly on solid ground. But then he remembered where it was they were landing.

And what they would be encountering.

CHAPTER **FORTY-SEVEN**

Raccoons were trying to get into the house.

If it wasn't so unbelievable and kind of disturbing, Dale thought, it might have been funny.

He and Isaac had been sitting in the kitchen when they'd heard the sounds of somebody trying to open the latch on the sliding doors. When Dale had pulled the curtains aside to see who was on the deck, his blood had run cold.

It wasn't someone at all. Multiple raccoons were standing on his deck, eerily—patiently—watching as one attempted to work the handle and slide the door across. Quickly Dale had checked to be sure it was locked as the raccoons watched him through the glass with an intelligence that he'd never witnessed before in the animals.

It was then that he'd decided they should do something more than just sit and have tea.

"It's kind of a mess," Dale said as he pushed open the door to the garage. He moved the beam of a flashlight over the multitude of boxes, stacks, and piles of items he'd accumulated over the years in his contracting job. "I've got a battery-powered lantern somewhere over here," he said, playing the light along the side of the three steps that led from the kitchen doorway to the garage floor.

"There's a lot of stuff," Isaac said from the darkness behind Dale.

"Yeah," Dale agreed, finding the lantern on a shelf to the left of the door. He turned the knob on, hoping that the battery still had some juice left in it. The light came on, chasing the shadows to the four corners of the vast and cluttered space.

"There we go," he said, placing the lantern on top of a stack of boxes that contained floor tiles left over from a kitchen job a few years back. He'd always meant to sell those tiles, but had never managed to get around to it.

"Yeah," Dale said again, looking around at the representation of the life he'd once had, before the stroke. He had a habit of holding on to anything that could be used again on a future job, and it was all here, stacked inside the garage that hadn't seen a car in well over ten years. It was like a yearbook of his job life. Every item reminded him of the work he had put his heart and soul into—every tool or box of supplies, the cans of paint, and boxes of ceiling tiles. Hell, he even had dynamite that he'd used to clear away some old tree stumps when he'd been hired to add a solarium to a property. "There is a lot of stuff."

Isaac started carefully down the steps. "Reminds me of my house," he said, eyes darting around, taking it all in.

"You have a lot of stuff, too?" Dale asked. He and Sidney had always suspected that Isaac's mother was a hoarder.

"Lots of stuff," Isaac said, as he continued to look around. "Never know when you're going to need something," he added. Dale wondered if he wasn't parroting his mother.

"That's true," Dale said. "Probably why I saved all this myself."

"Yeah," Isaac agreed, peering into some of the boxes.

Dale was careful as he made his way along the stacks of project leftovers, taking it slow and easy so that he didn't lose his balance. Sidney had forbade him from coming in here alone.

"Hey, Isaac," he called out. "I could use your help over here."

He could hear the youth making his way over to where he stood beside piles of extra wood leaning up against the garage wall.

"Yes?"

"See all this wood here?" Dale asked.

The young man nodded.

"We're going take it into the house."

"Why?" Isaac asked.

"We'll use the wood to cover up the windows, and reinforce the entrances to the house."

Dale watched the youth to see if his explanation was sinking in.

"We'll use the wood to cover up the windows and doors so things can't get in," Isaac said, showing that he did indeed understand.

"You've got it," Dale said.

Isaac approached the pile and began to pick up the smaller pieces first, collecting them in his arms.

"If you don't mind, you can handle the wood, and I'll take the tools," Dale said as he maneuvered around the young man to a dusty old duffel bag filled with equally filthy tools. These were his emergency tools, the ones that should have been tossed out once he got new ones but hadn't been. Just like everything else in the garage.

Without thinking, Dale reached down with his bad arm and tried to pick up the heavy bag. It clattered back to the concrete floor. "Damn it," he hissed, cursing his infirmity. He changed hands, picking up the bag while trying to maintain his balance.

He saw that Isaac was watching him, his arms loaded with wood.

"What's wrong with your arm?" the young man asked.

The tool bag was heavier than Dale remembered it being, and he placed it on the floor again at his feet. "I had a stroke a few years ago," he said, feeling a flush of anger go through his body. "Not quite back to where I should be yet."

Yet. That made him angry too since he knew that there was no chance he'd ever be back to what he was.

He picked up the tool bag again, his frustration lending him some strength. "Let's get this stuff into the house and—"

"I got hit by a car when I was just a little boy," Isaac blurted out. "The tire ran over my head." He wasn't looking at Dale as he spoke, his hand going up to touch a scar on the side of his head. "That's why I'm . . . different."

He then looked at Dale, pulled the wood up tighter in his arms, and turned to leave the garage. "Gotta get this stuff into the house," he said, turning and heading for the kitchen.

Without a word, Dale followed, dragging the tool bag behind him.

Dale was much slower at navigating the stacks, and Isaac was

SAVAGE / 291

already out of sight when he heard a tremendous crash from the direction of the kitchen door.

"That's okay, Isaac," Dale said, trying to quicken his pace, thinking the young man had dropped his armload of wood. But as he maneuvered around an old washer and dryer he'd been hoping to get up on Craigslist, he didn't like what he saw.

Isaac was on his back at the foot of the stairs, pieces of wood scattered about him. The young man's body had gone completely rigid, his hands like claws moving up toward the sides of his face—to his ears—but hesitating.

"Isaac," Dale said, dropping the tools and lurching toward the youth. He had no idea what he could do, but he had to at least try. "It's okay, buddy, everything is going to be okay."

Isaac's mouth was moving; he was trying to speak, but he couldn't seem to get the words out.

"What's wrong? What did you do? Did you fall and hit your head? What . . . ?"

He was convulsing now, as if he was having some sort of seizure.

On a small workstation table covered with cans of paint, Dale saw a stack of old towels that he used as rags and drop cloths and made his way toward them. Grabbing a handful, he returned to where Isaac still thrashed and twitched and managed to lower himself to his knees beside the boy using his cane and the stair rail. Then he placed the towels beneath Isaac's head.

"It's all right," he said, trying to reassure the youth. "Everything is going to be okay."

Dale had no idea if the kid was prone to seizures, but without phones to call for help, there was nothing to do but sit with him and wait it out. He patted Isaac's chest with a comforting hand. "You just lie there for a bit, and we'll see if you feel any better in a while."

Isaac's hand shot out, wrapping painfully around Dale's wrist, pulling him closer as he looked into Dale's eyes.

"The bad radio," Isaac gasped. "It's getting... louder." His hand hovered clawlike and horrible around the hearing aid in his right ear and the scar on the side of his head.

Dale had no idea what the young man was experiencing, but the look on his face told him it was something awful.

The bad radio in Isaac's Steve ear was telling him to do things... horrible things.

He couldn't understand what was happening as the static crackled, and the sound tried to worm its way inside his head—inside his brain.

The bad radio wanted to take over, to push him so far down that he—*Isaac*—wouldn't exist anymore.

He didn't want to go away... didn't want to listen to the bad radio and the horrible, horrible things it was telling him to do.

But the bad radio was loud—strong—filling his head with a powerful message of violence and terrible images of what it was doing out there in the storm.

It forced him to look through its eyes... its many, many eyes... so many eyes.

It forced him to see—

Everything.

CHAPTER **FORTY-EIGHT**

"Where again?" Officer Isabel asked as she turned the corner onto Bennett Street, the driving wind and rain pummeling the police vehicle.

"It's off of Lansdale," Sidney said, trying to see through the deluge of water.

"Got it," Isabel said over the hissing rain and the rhythmic back and forth of the wiper blades.

A gnawing nervousness was growing in Sidney's belly. She wanted to tell the officer to hurry up, but she knew they were going as fast as they could in the dangerous conditions.

"Hey, slow down," Rich suddenly spoke up, his face practically pushed into his window as he struggled to see in the storm-swept night. "Do you see that?"

Officer Isabel brought the car to a halt and stared through her own window. "Where are we looking?"

Sidney slid across the seat and tried to follow Rich's gaze.

"What are we looking for, Rich?" Cody asked as he leaned toward Isabel, attempting to look past her shoulder into the darkness.

"I . . . ," Rich began, still searching. "I thought I saw . . ."

And then.

"There!" he said, tapping his index finger on the glass. "It looks like a truck . . . or maybe an SUV. Oh God, please don't let it be the K-9 truck."

A sudden, solemn silence descended on the group. Two other groups from the police station had escaped just ahead of them in two more department rides. Sidney guessed that the little girl Amy and her mom were in the K-9 vehicle.

"Where?" Cody asked, looking all the harder. "I still don't—"

"Shit," Officer Isabel cursed, and that was when Sidney saw it. It was indeed the police SUV, and it was lying about ten feet into the woods, on its roof.

Isabel was trying to bring their vehicle closer to the wreck when something surged up from the road in front of them. The police officer let out a shrill scream as the headlights illuminated what was in the road ahead.

It looked almost like a wave of water about to flow over them, but where would a wave of water come from on an old backwoods road?

But as it flowed closer, Sidney recognized it for what it really was.

She wanted to scream too, but it was too late.

The wave—yes, it was a wave, but not comprised of water—was

alive, made up of thousands, if not hundreds of thousands, of living things, warm-blooded and cold—insect, reptile, amphibian, and mammal.

Life, large and small, merged together into an undulating wall, surging toward the vehicle as if it was one single entity. If it wasn't so damn horrifying, it would have been fascinating.

"Hold on," Isabel shouted, swiftly putting the car in reverse and flooring the gas. The tires screeched and smoked as they spun upon the wet road, finally gripping enough of the tarmac to send them racing backward.

They were all screaming, and Snowy barked viciously, aware again that they were under attack.

Cody pounded the dashboard, screaming a single word over and over again as if it could somehow make them move faster. "Go! Go! Go! Go! Go! Go!"

And for a moment Sidney thought they had managed to outrun the wave, that it was going to fall like real waves upon the beach, but the wave defied all logic as it surged up, growing impossibly larger, towering over the vehicle, before crashing down upon the road and flowing beneath the SUV. They could feel it through the floor of the police vehicle, striking against the truck's underside, before flexing its terrible, singular self, pushing off from the ground and lifting the truck from the road.

They screamed together as the SUV flipped, the windows exploding inward as the vehicle came to rest in the road upon its side. Sidney and Snowy fell in a heap atop Rich, pressed against the car door.

"Sorry," she said, trying to reposition her eighty-pound dog and get herself off of her friend.

"It's okay," Rich said, lending her a hand. They all carefully righted themselves, amid sounds of the living wave sliding across the SUV, probing, seeking a way inside.

Seeking the life within.

Rich peered over his seat as Officer Isabel frantically searched for her shotgun, and Cody struggled to stay out of her way.

Sidney attempted to find the proper handhold to haul herself up through the shattered window now above her. She planted her feet against the back of the front seat and started to push herself up toward the opening when a shape moved across the window.

The wave probed at the edges of the shattered window frame, fingers made up from what appeared to be the pink, hairless bodies of moles and baby mice about to spill over inside the vehicle.

Sidney dropped back down as Snowy began to furiously bark. She searched the inside of the car for some place that they could go, believing that it was only a matter of seconds before the mass of life flooded the vehicle to get at them.

"Can we crawl out the back window?" Sidney asked as Rich tried to maneuver himself over the seat.

But it was too late.

The living mass started to extend down into the overturned SUV, and Sidney came to the sickening realization that she might not survive the night after all.

The blast from the shotgun was deafening within the enclosed space, and the tendril comprised of insects, mice, moles, and hundreds of earthworms exploded spectacularly to spatter them and everyone inside the SUV.

"Get out, get out now!" Officer Isabel screamed.

Sidney didn't need to be told twice. She climbed up the back of the front seats, grabbing hold of the window frame to haul herself outside. Isabel was already out, sitting atop the front passenger door, shotgun aimed.

"Move it, Sidney," she commanded.

Sidney spun around on her knees and leaned back in through the broken window. "Push Snowy up to me!"

Rich and Cody managed to get the dog up, her legs scrambling wildly for purchase as Sidney pulled her through the window, nearly falling off the SUV in the process.

The shotgun fired again, and then again.

"Move it people!" Officer Isabel screamed, and it was then that Sidney noticed her voice sounded strange. She looked at Isabel and saw the small puddles of blood forming on the door of the SUV where the officer knelt with the gun.

"You're hurt," Sidney said, moving toward her as Rich leveraged himself out of the window. Something must have cut her when the SUV flipped.

"We don't have time for this," Isabel said, firing again. Her shots hit their targets, but the undulating mass of life slowly reformed each time it was hit. "We've got to make a run for it."

Cody crawled up and out of the window next to Isabel, giving her a handful of shotgun shells. "Here, thought you could use these. I picked them up from the floor."

Isabel reloaded the gun methodically and shoved the extras in her pockets. "How far to your dad's place?" she asked.

Sidney looked down the length of road. "Not that far," she said. "Maybe a five-minute walk—less if we're running like hell."

"Then you three need to run like hell." The police officer fired the shotgun again at the advancing mass.

The wave had pulled back into the darkness of the forest beside the road, and Sidney thought maybe they actually had a chance, but she was quickly proven wrong when it exploded from the woods, bigger and nastier than before.

"Watch it!" Officer Isabel roared, managing to get off another shot before the living wave crashed into the back of the SUV. The impact spun the vehicle and sent its passengers flying from their perches atop it.

Sidney landed in the center of the road, rolling to her feet, trying not to think about how badly her body ached. She quickly looked around, finding Cody and then Rich. Snowy was beside Officer Isabel, who looked as though she was having some difficulty standing.

The living mass lifted itself up from the ground, swaying like some gigantic poisonous snake, readying to strike.

Isabel got to her feet, using the shotgun as a crutch. She petted Snowy's head vigorously, and then motioned for the dog to go as she raised her weapon.

"C'mon!" Sidney yelled to Officer Isabel as Snowy and the guys joined her in the road.

Isabel turned toward them, swaying slightly, and Sidney was

shocked by the amount of blood she saw on the front of the officer's uniform.

"Go . . . ," the police officer said, waving them away. "Get out of here!"

She spun around to the organism as it seemed to notice her, what could have been millions of eyes all zeroing in on the woman who stood defiantly before it.

"Officer Isabel, please!" Sidney called out frantically.

"You heard me! Get the hell out of here!"

Rich took Sidney's arm, trying to pull her along, but Sidney tore it away. The living mass seemed to sense their movement and turned in their direction.

"Hey!" Officer Isabel screamed, moving closer to its writhing body. "Hey, right here!"

The thick tendril of life spun toward the police officer, rearing back and studying her as she brandished her weapon.

"Yeah, that's it—right here—you ugly freak of nature."

"No!" Sidney cried. "You can't do this!"

"Get out of here! Save this island!" Isabel shouted as she turned and made for the back of the overturned SUV.

Cody and Rich began to drag Sidney away, even as she fought them.

"You do your part," Isabel said. She aimed the shotgun at the SUV's gas tank. "And I'll do mine."

With that, she fired a single shot, setting off an explosion that consumed her whole and engulfed the monstrous organism in hungry fire.

The force of the blast blew Sidney, Rich, and Cody backward.

Sidney could hear only ringing in her ears. She opened and closed her mouth and moved her jaw about painfully, hoping to return the sounds of the world. She stared at the burning wreckage of the SUV and the piles of flaming animal bodies littering the ground up ahead. Something warm and wet touched her hand, and she let out a scream that she could not hear, looking down to see a cowering Snowy. Realizing what she'd done, Sidney bent down, wrapping her arms around her dog's neck and speaking into her thick, wet fur.

"It's okay," she said, the vibration of her voice allowing her to communicate with her best friend. "Everything is going to be okay."

But as she said this, she knew the words were wrong—a lie. Rich and Cody had come to join them, and they all stared at the flaming wreckage, seeing movement from the woods beyond, Officer Isabel's sacrifice merely a pause in the night's horror.

It wasn't okay at all.

CHAPTER **FORTY-NINE**

He jumped at every sound, his imagination getting the best of him.

Was that breaking glass? Was that the door swinging open?

Dale sat uncomfortably by Isaac's side, hoping that the seizure, or whatever it was that the poor kid was going through, would pass.

"C'mon, buddy," he said, laying his hand upon Isaac's shoulder.

A noise startled him, a thumping sound that he couldn't quite place. He turned enough to peer up the stairs and through the open doorway. The sound most definitely came from somewhere up there.

He looked back to the youth. He seemed to have calmed a bit, his body no longer as rigid. Dale suddenly remembered a kid that he'd gone to elementary school with. He'd had epilepsy, and after he had a few seizures in class, they'd never seen him again. He figured the kid's parents had taken him out of school.

It was kind of sad. He didn't think that Isaac had ever gone to school, certainly not on the island. Dale's recollection was of Isaac and his mother, always together. He wondered about the life the boy had led, feeling bad that he'd never reached out in any way, even to just say hi or how are you today.

Another noise from the house interrupted his thoughts. This one was louder and more forceful.

Dale immediately imagined that it was Berthold, back to the finish the job. He couldn't just sit there. Glancing past Isaac's body, he focused on the bag of tools that he'd dropped.

Using his cane, he managed to push himself up far enough to grab hold of the stair rail, then used that to haul himself to his feet. The exertion left him winded and disgusted. He leaned against the railing, catching his breath and listening to the sounds of the house. He heard everything now, every bump, tick, patter—

And crash.

It was the front door; he was sure of it. He grasped his cane, and using it to steady himself, lurched toward the tool bag, managing to avoid Isaac's body and the boxes piled all around them.

Using the end of his cane, he parted the opening in the bag, relieved to find what he sought right on top. The banging sound came again, only this time it was louder, as if someone—something—was trying to force its way inside. Bracing himself, Dale attempted to bend his knees, but only one obeyed. Thankfully, it was just enough to let him grab hold of the claw hammer and pull it from the bag.

Hefting the hammer in his stronger hand, he hobbled back toward the steps, remembering the days when he hadn't needed a weapon, when no one was stupid enough to break into *his* home.

But now . . .

He squeezed the handle of the hammer with all his might, attempting to will some of that long-lost strength back into his beleaguered body, as he made his way toward the stairs. *Wishful thinking,* he thought, unsure of how much of a threat he would be, but he had to do something. He wasn't about to cower in the dark as somebody attempted to break into his home.

He was pathetic, but he wasn't a coward.

It seemed to take forever, and most of his strength, to make it up the three stairs and through the kitchen to the front door. It was still closed. Cautiously approaching, he leaned against it, listening, but all he could hear were the sounds of the storm still going on outside.

The doorknob rattled, and he gasped, jumping back, almost tripping over his own feet. He managed to stop himself with his cane and hold on to the hammer.

The doorknob rattled again, followed by the nearly deafening sound of the lock sliding back, and then the door began to open.

Dale was wild with fear and anger. If he was going to strike, he had to strike first—and hard. He doubted he would have much of a second chance. He raised the hammer.

"It's Sidney," said an unexpected voice, so close that Dale nearly screamed.

With the hammer still raised, he turned to see Isaac, looking pale and weak, standing in the doorway to the kitchen.

"It's Sidney," the young man said again as the door pushed open and Dale's daughter rushed into the house.

"Sid," Dale exclaimed, letting the hammer fall to the floor with a thud.

"Dad," she said, throwing her arms around him.

"Where have you been?" he asked, holding her tightly. She was wet and cold and dirty, but he never wanted to let her go. "Where have you been?" he asked again, choking back tears.

Snowy bounded into the hall, barking and wagging her tail, with Sidney's friends Rich and Cody close behind her. At least she hadn't been alone.

"Something's going on, Dad," she said, pulling back from him. He could see the fear in her eyes.

"Yeah, I know," he said, grabbing her for another hug. "I know."

CHAPTER **FIFTY**

The thing that used to be Ronald Berthold walked through the dwindling fire with little concern of being burned. It stared at the blackened wreckage of the SUV and the human remains tossed to the side of the road, although only its right eye seemed to function. It tilted its head and turned its attention to the wooded area where another vehicle lay on its back.

The other vessels gathered around him, their right eyes scanning the wreck and the woods beyond as well.

Something moved not far from the vehicle, and all eyes turned in its direction. Leaves rustled, twigs snapped, and thousands of silvery eyes watched.

A lone figure—a human male—rose from the foliage, crawling on his hands and knees, begging for help. His clothing was covered with blood, and he seemed dazed and confused.

The things by the side of the road watched the survivor as he crawled toward them. "Please, help me."

The dog that had been owned by the former Ronald Berthold stepped from the gathering of animal life and slowly padded toward the man. He saw the dog as it came toward him and tried to flee, but he was too weak.

The dog pounced, knocking the man onto his back, and sank its teeth into the man's neck, ripping out his throat in one savage bite.

The dog shook once, then turned and rejoined the other vessels.

As one, they began to walk away, down the center of the road.

In search of further human life to eliminate.

CHAPTER **FIFTY-ONE**

Sidney had to keep moving or she'd fall down.

She paced about the living room, then went to the window, pulling back the curtain to peer outside. There were things in the darkness of the storm. Things that scratched at the doors and windows. Things that wanted to get in.

"We've got to get you out of here," she said, letting the curtain fall back into place as she turned to address her father.

Dale was sitting in his chair, Snowy by his side. Cody and Rich were on the loveseat, looking as though they might fall asleep, and Isaac stood just inside the doorway to the kitchen, playing with the hearing aids in his ears.

"I don't think that's necessary," Dale began. "Isaac and I were just about to start boarding up the windows and—"

"I don't think you understand how bad it is," Sidney interrupted, trying to keep the intensity in her voice from climbing. "Benediction is experiencing some sort of..." She had to think again about how to describe what was going on. "Epidemic or something," she finished.

"You think a disease is doing this?" Dale asked.

"Kinda sorta," Sidney answered with a shrug. "It's the best I've got right now. Something is making the animals incredibly aggressive, and they all seem to have the same shiny film over their right eyes as a symptom. Only the right eyes." She pointed to her own. "Is it some kind of disease like rabies? A virus? I don't know, but it seems—"

"We still don't know why Snowy hasn't got whatever it is," Rich said, leaning forward, his elbows resting on his knees. Snowy saw that he was looking in her direction and wagged her tail.

"Another part of the mystery," Sidney said, not even wanting to think about what she would do if Snowy ever were to succumb.

"It's not just animals," her father said.

All eyes in the living room turned to him.

"I was attacked here," he said. "By a guy . . . Berthold is his name, I think."

"Who?" Sidney demanded. "Mr. Berthold attacked you? Are you all right? Why didn't you say—"

"I'm fine. Isaac got here just in time."

Sidney looked to the doorway to see that Isaac was listening.

"Thank you, Isaac," she said, and he quickly looked away.

"I didn't recognize him at first," Dale explained, "but he broke in and attacked me. There was something wrong with his right eye, just like you said."

Sidney felt a familiar chill run down her spine.

"Is this another one, Sid?" Cody asked.

"There was a weird-looking dog with him," her father then said.

Sidney knew exactly who it was that had attacked her father—and her, not long ago.

"No," she said, "this is the same guy. Mr. Berthold. He has a French bulldog, right?"

"Yeah," her father said. "A French bulldog. That's what it was."

"Holy crap," Rich said. "That's the same guy that went after you back at the police station."

"So it means that there's still only one human that has been affected," Sidney said.

"So far," Cody added.

"So far," she agreed. "I have no idea why, but it makes me feel a little better."

Rich laughed, although there wasn't much humor in his expression. "Seriously? Something can actually make you feel better about all this?" He spread his arms, which drew attention to the sounds outside the house.

They seemed to be getting louder.

"Hey, you take what you can get," Sidney said, moving back to the window and reaching for the curtain. "We need to figure out how we're getting—"

A window exploded in a shower of glass, wind, and rain.

Sidney yelped in surprise, throwing herself back against the wall as the animal that had forced itself inside raised itself up from the ground to glare at her, pieces of glass dropping off its sopping-wet body to tinkle to the floor.

The fox was large, probably the biggest she'd ever seen, and she watched with growing horror as ticks and fleas leaped from its orangey red fur to the hardwood floor and began to make their way toward her.

"Sid, get out of there!" Cody yelled, and she was torn from the nightmarish sight to see her ex-boyfriend crossing the room, pistol in hand, firing at the tensing animal.

The beast spun away from her as Cody's first shot nicked its shoulder. He fired again as the fox rushed him, a headshot ending its progress.

"The window!" Rich screamed, already moving.

Sidney glanced over to the billowing curtain and saw movement at the ledge, furry things attempting to haul their bodies up onto the windowsill and through the opening.

Rich grabbed the wooden coffee table, lifted it from the floor, and shoved it against the broken pane, blocking the opening. "Anybody got a hammer and nails?" he yelled, the sounds of things thumping angrily at the table filling the room.

Sidney saw her father struggling to stand and ran toward him.

"I've got this, Dad," she said, motioning for him to sit back down.

"In the garage there's—"

"Got it," she said, disappearing from the room and running down the hallway to the garage.

She knew right where to look, picking up a hammer with a box of nails and heading back into the house, nearly colliding with Isaac.

"Isaac," she said, stepping back away from her neighbor.

The young man looked out, twitchy, his right hand shooting up to the side of his head, and then began playing with the hearing aid in his ear.

"The bad radio," he said, his expression pinched.

"The bad radio?" she asked, confused. "What's that mean, Isaac?"

He looked as though he might start crying, moving his legs up and down, like he was marching in place.

"The bad radio is bad," he said, closing his eyes as if in pain. "Inside my head, playing in the Steve ear. Very bad."

"I don't understand, Isaac," she said. "What does that mean?"

"Sidney!" Rich screamed from the living room.

She started to go around Isaac to help the others.

"The bad radio wants me to do things!" Isaac screamed, slapping one of his hands against the wall. "And I won't . . . I won't do it . . . I won't . . ."

Sidney was suddenly afraid of him. His hand was back up to the hearing aid, fussing with it, playing with the controls, taking it from his ear, and then putting it back.

She left him there in the hallway, his words echoing in her mind as she bounded into the living room.

"Did you have to run out to Home Depot?" Rich asked, clearly annoyed that it had taken her so long. She could hear something outside scratching at the bottom of the table.

"Sorry," she said, grabbing a handful of nails and the hammer and beginning to nail the table to the window frame.

"We've been hearing stuff," Cody said, eyes darting around. He was still holding the pistol, ready to use it if necessary. "It sounds as though it might be getting worse out there."

With the broken window secure, Sidney stepped back.

"That should be good," she said, staring at her work, but her thoughts were elsewhere. She was thinking of the man who had attacked her and supposedly her father: Berthold, the only human who seemed to be affected by what was going on with the animals on the island.

She slowly turned toward her friends and father and caught a glimpse of Isaac as he paced on the outskirts of the kitchen. He still looked as though he was having issues, struggling with something he was calling the bad radio.

She watched his hand go up to his head again, and he winced in pain. Obviously fighting something. Fighting the bad radio.

"Sid, you okay?" her father asked.

She didn't answer him right away. There was something going on here—something that she wasn't putting together.

"Yeah," she said, walking slowly across the living room, keeping an eye on Isaac as he paced. She could hear him muttering. She knew that he was mentally handicapped, but she'd never seen him acting this way before.

Something was wrong with him, as was with the animal life on the island. . . .

Sidney looked down into the smiling face of her dog. Eye contact made, Snowy immediately sat down and wagged her tail.

Animal life except for Snowy.

"Sidney?" Cody called to her. "We should probably think about . . ."

She ignored him. There were answers here, she could feel them—see them, dancing just beyond the periphery of her sight.

"Wait," she said, holding up the hammer.

What made Snowy different?

Isaac came farther into the room from the kitchen, his hand fixed upon his ear, fingers playing with his hearing aid.

Snowy couldn't hear . . . Snowy was deaf.

Isaac pulled the hearing aid from his right ear and looked at it furiously before putting it back. She heard him mumbling about it again—the bad radio.

Two facts suddenly collided, igniting sparks inside her brain.

"Sidney, we really should be figuring out what we're doing here," Rich said.

She looked at him, a self-satisfied smirk tugging at the corners of her mouth.

"What?" Rich asked, confused by her expression.

She ignored him as well, continuing to run through the facts in her head, picking them up, looking at them from every angle.

"What's going on, Sid?" Cody urged. "You're kinda starting to freak me out here."

"Did you figure something out?" Her dad wanted to know.

"Isaac," she said, pointing toward the doorway where the young man had been standing. "He's having some sort of problem with his hearing."

"Yeah, he's been like that since he got here. I think he's hearing things or something," Dale offered.

"Right," Sidney said. "He's hard of hearing," she presented to them, wondering if their thoughts would go where hers had. "He wears hearing aids . . . he says he hears the bad radio."

Rich had come to stand beside Cody.

"Yeah," Rich said. "He wears hearing aids . . . he's picking up a radio station or something."

Sidney pointed at him.

"Or something."

"I'm completely lost here," Cody said.

"Snowy," she said. "Snowy isn't affected by what's going on with the animals."

They waited expectantly for her to go on.

"She's deaf," she said.

"I don't see where you're going with—"

"Maybe she can't hear the bad radio," Sidney suggested, interrupting Cody.

Rich still looked confused, but she could see that Cody was on her thought path.

"You think that the reason the animals are losing it is that they might be hearing something?" Cody asked.

"Why not," she said. "It explains why Snowy isn't trying to eat us and what Isaac might be picking up through his hearing aids."

It had gotten suddenly very quiet, and they all seemed to notice.

"Why don't I think this is a good thing?" Rich asked, looking around.

"Where is he?" Sidney asked. She moved toward the kitchen doorway, Snowy springing up to be by her side. "Where's Isaac?"

She walked from the living room down the hallway to the kitchen, looking for the youth.

"Hey, Isaac?" Sidney called out, entering the kitchen. "I want to ask you a few questions about the bad . . ."

What she saw going on in the kitchen froze her in place.

Isaac was standing in front of the sliding glass doors, the curtains that had been closed now pulled apart. There were things, lots and lots of things, moving around just behind the glass.

Pacing. Waiting to get in.

"Isaac," she said in her calmest voice. "What are you doing?"

He was breathing incredibly hard, as if he'd been exerting himself.

"I'm trying," he said, his voice strained with emotion.

"What are you trying to—"

"I can't . . . I can't do it," he moaned, reaching for the handles on the sliding door.

"Isaac, don't," she said, starting across the kitchen.

"I can't fight it anymore," he said, his voice flat—emotionless. He undid the lock and began to slide the doors open. "Can't fight the bad radio."

Sidney dove across the kitchen, slamming her body into Isaac's and knocking him away from the glass doors. Then, grabbing the door handles, she desperately tried to slide the door back, but it wouldn't move—multiple sets of clawed limbs were jamming its track, clamoring to get into the house.

Sidney leaned into the door, using all her strength to force the heavy glass door closed. At first she didn't think she'd be able to do it, but she remembered the experiences of the past hours and the horror that the transformed animals could heap upon them. The door was going to close—no matter what.

Screaming with exertion, Sidney managed to slide the door closed, crushing limbs, grinding bugs, and severing paws as she forced the door over its track. She peered through the glass and felt the adrenaline rush out of her as her heart sank. She'd won this battle, but judging by the growing numbers outside, it would be only a matter of time before the animals and insects had their way and forced themselves inside. She clicked the lock in place and pulled the heavy curtains over the scene on the deck.

The others were piling into the kitchen, demanding to know what was going on. She stood over Isaac, who now cowered on the floor, muttering things over and over again about the bad radio. She wanted to tell them what he had done, to turn their rage on him, but she knew that it wasn't his fault.

The bad radio, she thought.

"They almost got the door opened," she said, feeling as though she'd just run a full marathon.

Cody went at once to the curtains, sliding them open to inspect the door. He saw what she had seen, as well as the bloody parts left there.

"Jesus," he said, stunned by the growing presence.

"Yeah," she said.

Sidney went to Isaac and bent down beside him. "C'mon," she said. "Let's get you up." She took his arm and began to pull, and he turned to look at her.

"I'm sorry," he said, eyes filled with tears. "The bad radio . . . it was so loud . . . so loud . . .

"It's okay," she said as she helped him up.

"I didn't want to listen." His hands fluttered toward the hearing aid in his right ear. "I didn't want to listen . . . I didn't want to see . . ."

His last words stopped her.

"What does that mean, Isaac?" she asked. "What didn't you want to see?"

He was rocking back and forth now, humming some unrecognizable tune.

"Isaac, please." She gently urged him to continue. "What didn't you want to see?"

"The bad radio puts pictures inside," he said, placing the ends of his fingers against his skull. "It wants me to see what it's doing."

He looked to be in pain again, his face scrunched up.

The kitchen became filled with the sound of pounding, as if it had started to rain rocks outside. But Sidney knew better.

Snowy had begun to pace, whining pitifully as she looked about. She might have been deaf, but she could sense what was happening.

"Sid," Rich said, eyes darting about.

"It is getting worse," she said. "They're getting desperate, and they're not going to stop until they're in."

"We can board up more of the windows and . . . ," Cody began.

She shook her head and motioned for the nervous Snowy to come to her. "No, we have to get out of here."

"And go where?" Rich demanded. "Wouldn't it be safer to just hole up here?"

"Maybe," she said. The sounds outside were louder now, and she swore she could feel the floor beneath her feet vibrating from the intensity of the assault. "But I doubt it."

"Then where?" Cody asked.

"I think we need to stick to our original plan," she said. "I think we need to go to Doc Martin and let her know what we've found out."

"And what is that?" Rich asked.

Sidney didn't know if she'd ever seen her friend so serious.

Isaac was rocking more heavily now, his arms clamped around his head.

"That this isn't a disease, or some sort of poisoning."

She looked away from Isaac's torment, to her friends.

"We have to let people know that something is causing this . . . the bad radio or whatever you want to call it. We have to let people know so that it can be shut down."

CHAPTER **FIFTY-TWO**

Dale Moore had been heading toward the kitchen, drawn to the sounds of panic but nearly falling on the way. *What exactly am I going to do anyway?* he thought as he regained his footing and stopped just outside the kitchen doorway.

He listened to his daughter, proud of the girl he'd raised, impressed by the woman she'd become. He could only imagine what the future held for her.

If there was to be a future.

The sounds from outside were growing louder, more forceful, and he knew it was only a matter of time before whatever was out there got into the house.

He wasn't sure if he really agreed with their plan to leave the relative safety of the house, but he knew the options were limited. And that's when he decided on a plan of his own.

He managed to slip into the garage unnoticed, feeling really positive about something for the first time since his stroke.

It felt strangely reassuring to finally know what his future would be.

CHAPTER **FIFTY-THREE**

"Weapons," Sidney said, opening up the kitchen drawers and pulling out a tray of silverware and handfuls of cooking tools. "We need weapons if we're going to make it to Dad's truck in one piece."

Rich joined her at the kitchen counter, helping her sort through the various pieces of kitchenware. "Knives are probably the best bet," he said.

"Knives, forks, anything we can use to poke or stab," she said as she picked up a particularly long carving knife, its blade sheathed with cardboard.

She pulled the cardboard away and brandished the blade. "I think I could do some damage with this," she said.

Cody was back at the glass doors and had pulled the curtains slightly apart. "We're still going to have to get through them," he said grimly. "They'll be swarming us whether we have a sharp knife or not."

Sidney knew he was right. "We have to at least try to protect ourselves," she said. "Maybe keep the bites to a minimum."

"A suit of armor would be good," Rich said, trying to find an appropriate weapon for himself. He seemed to be particularly enjoying a metal meat tenderizer, smashing invisible skulls in front of him.

His joke made a weird kind of sense.

"No armor," she said, suddenly taking off down the hallway toward her bedroom. Just inside her closet door she found a large plastic bag and hauled it from the room. "But maybe these will help."

She dumped the plastic bag on the floor in the kitchen and untied its top as Snowy gave it a good sniff. "We were going to donate these to Goodwill but never got around to making the call for pickup," she said, pulling the bag open.

Cody and Rich approached to peer inside the open bag.

"Old clothes?" Cody asked.

"Yeah," Sidney answered, reaching inside. "Mostly winter stuff. Heavy winter stuff."

Rich bent over and pulled out a flowered shirt. "I think the color might clash with my eyes," he said.

"Don't be a jackass," she said, ripping it from his hands. "We can layer," she explained, fishing around and finding a heavy plaid shirt that had belonged to her father. "Put this on over your shirt and whatever's biting hopefully won't be able to get through."

"That's not a bad idea," Cody said, bending down and fishing through the bag. He pulled out a heavy blue sweatshirt. "You were getting rid of this stuff?" he asked, looking at the New England Patriots hooded sweatshirt and then to her. "I gave you this."

He sounded hurt, but she didn't look at him.

"I don't wear it anymore and will only have so much closet space at school," she said.

"Nice," Rich said, snatching it from Cody's clutches. "I'll take that."

Sidney found some old winter hats and gloves and put them on the counter. "We layer up, and with the weapons we put together I think we have a chance."

Cody grunted in agreement, finding a heavy flannel shirt, checking the size, and putting it aside.

She found a large fleece jacket. "This will fit you, Isaac," she said, tossing it over to him.

The jacket landed at his feet and he looked at it. "Too warm for a jacket," he said.

"Yeah, I know," she told him, "but if you put it on, it might keep you from getting bit."

He considered that, then leaned over from the chair, pulling the jacket toward him.

"We only have to make it from here to the driveway," she said, the useful contents of the donation bag exhausted.

"And your dad is okay with this?" Cody asked.

"Can't imagine he wouldn't be," she said, and then she paused. "Where is he, anyway?" she asked.

"He was in the living room last time I saw him," Rich said, attempting to pull the Patriots sweatshirt on. It was a little snug, but he managed.

"Mr. Moore went to the garage," Isaac said. He was playing with the zipper on the fleece. "I saw him when you were talking. He went to the garage."

Sidney headed for the garage door. "Dad?" she called out. She grabbed the doorknob and turned it. "Dad, we've got to leave soon, and I want . . . "

What she saw as she opened the door stole her words away.

"Hey, kiddo," her father said.

She stood at the top of the steps in shock.

"What . . . ?" she began but again couldn't finish.

He sat on an old folding chair close to the garage door—with a stick of dynamite in his hand.

"What the hell are you doing?" she finally managed to ask.

"Getting the dynamite ready," he told her matter-of-factly.

"Ready for what?" she asked, rushing down the steps to join him.

"You're a smart kid, Sid," he said. "What do you think?"

"You're going to blow something up?" She had slowed her pace and was cautiously moving closer.

"There's the smarty-pants I know and love," he joked, but there was something in his tone that told her things weren't right.

"What are you going to blow up, Dad?"

He was checking the sticks of dynamite, prepping them, then setting them down on top of a box on the floor in front of him.

"Did you know that dynamite goes bad?" he asked instead of answering her question.

"Yeah," she said, nervously watching him.

"You can tell that it isn't any good when it sweats," he continued, and then laughed. "And do you know what the sweat is?"

"Besides dynamite sweat?" she asked him.

He chuckled some more. "Nitroglycerine."

"Seriously?" she asked, actually finding the bit of information strangely interesting.

"Would I lie to you?" he asked, looking up and into her eyes.

"What's going on, Dad?" she asked him again.

"I heard you in the kitchen, talking with your friends about getting out to find Doc Martin."

"Yeah," she agreed slowly. "I think what's going on has some biological connection, and she's probably the best one to help us figure it out," she explained.

Her father nodded as he gently placed another stick of dynamite on top of the box. "Sounds as good a plan as any. When are you leaving?"

"Soon," she said. "We're getting some stuff together, you know, things we can use as weapons."

"You taking my truck?"

She nodded. "If it's okay with you."

"Sure you can."

"We're layering up with those old clothes we were going to donate," she explained. "Might help us get through whatever's waiting outside. There's plenty left for you—"

"I'm not going," he interrupted flatly.

"What?"

"I'm not going," he said again, looking at her and shaking his head.

"Bullshit!" she exclaimed, feeling her anger spike.

"Listen to me," he said.

"No." She could hear her voice rising. "I'm not going to listen to crazy shit like that. I'm not. You're coming with us."

"Sid, I can barely get across the room without falling down. You know that."

"That's no excuse," she countered. "We can help you."

"I'll do nothing but slow you down," he said with finality. "You have no idea what you're going to encounter out there. You can't be worrying about me. I won't allow it."

She immediately thought of Cody's father. She wasn't the least bit religious, but suddenly she felt as though she were somehow being punished by a higher power.

"You're crazy if you think—"

"I've made up my mind, Sid," he said.

She felt scalding tears well in her eyes, and suddenly she couldn't stop the words. "You want to die, don't you? You've wanted to die ever since the stroke."

He continued to check the dynamite sticks in silence.

"You're not saying anything because you know I'm right."

Slowly he raised his eyes to meet hers. "Yes, you're right," he said simply.

Sidney felt as though she'd been punched in the gut. She'd never expected him to admit something that she found so horrible.

"Maybe not right away," he said. "I was terrified to die when it first happened and I didn't think I was going to make it. I would have given anything to live then."

"So what happened?"

He seemed to consider his words before he spoke. "This isn't living, Sid," he said after a moment. "I'm nothing but a burden . . . to you, and to myself."

"That's bullshit and you know it."

"It's not. The medication and physical therapy are only going to go so far. And when I get to the end, what will I get for my troubles? I'll have regained what? Maybe sixty percent of what I used to be?"

"You'll be alive."

"This isn't being alive," he snapped. "And it took the island going to shit for me to finally know it."

She was furious with herself for not realizing this sooner. Here was an active man, once filled with nearly boundless energy, reduced to a shell of his former self. She could only imagine how she would have felt in his shoes.

But would she want to die?

"Dad," she begged, "you're not thinking clearly."

He smiled at her, but it was a sad smile. "I am. In fact, I haven't been this clear in months."

She felt some tears let go and quickly wiped them from her cheeks.

"Do you really think I'll let you do this?" she asked.

"You know it's what I want."

"But it's not what I want."

"It's not about what you want, Sid."

She glared at him.

"I'm sorry," he said. "I'm so very sorry, but I can't risk slowing you down. I won't have you risking your life to save my broken one."

The sounds of things outside were louder now, and Sidney looked at the garage door, imagining the twisted forms trying to get in.

"And I'm not about to let them have me either," he said, following her gaze.

She thought about all the ways she would drag him from the house, but he was stubborn and she knew he'd fight her. If that was the case, they'd never make it to the truck, and not only would he be dead, all of her friends would be too.

But how could she leave him here to die? To blow himself up? Would she even be able to live with herself?

"What if I told you that I need you?" she said. "That even if I manage to survive all this, living just wouldn't be worth it without you in my life."

"I'd be flattered."

"It's true." Sidney knelt down in front of his chair and took his right hand, the one damaged by the stroke, in hers. "You're my dad. What would I be without you?"

She could feel his attempt at squeezing her hand, but it was so very weak.

"I've been lucky enough to see the woman you've become," he told her. "I can only imagine what's ahead for you."

"Please?" she begged, no longer fighting the tears.

"Go on, get out of here," he said, pulling his hand roughly from hers. "I have things to do." He leaned over to pull a battery and what looked like a detonator from inside another nearby box.

She couldn't move, her feet suddenly feeling as though they weighed thousands of pounds.

"What are you waiting for?" he asked, not looking at her. "Go," he said firmly, but she still didn't—*couldn't*—move.

"God damn it, I told you to go!" he shouted, and she could see it all there in his eyes. All the anger and sadness that had collected inside of him since his debilitating stroke.

She found herself stepping back toward the stairs, knowing there was nothing more she could say. But as she set her foot on the first step, she realized there *was* one last thing to be said. She knew it wouldn't change anything, that his mind was made up, but she had to say it.

"I love you, Dad," she said, turning back to face him, trying to keep her voice from cracking.

"I love you too, Sid," he said as he twisted some wire around a terminal on top of the detonator.

And that was it. She turned and climbed the steps, leaving him there to his own devices.

Leaving him there to his fate.

Sidney had just entered the kitchen when all hell seemed to break loose outside.

It sounded as though the house was going to fall down around her. She stopped, almost going back to the garage, but didn't.

As much as it pained her, she had to leave her dad there.

It was his choice.

Cody turned toward her wearing a very serious expression. "We've got to get out of here now," he said before she could even ask what was happening. "The glass in those doors isn't going to hold for much longer."

Sidney saw that he was already wearing multiple layers, the

shirts and jacket buttoned and zipped up to his throat. She needed to get her own layers on, and fast.

Rich and Isaac were in the midst of their own preparations, Snowy watching them intently. Rich was taping a steak knife to the stick end of a plunger. A broom handle with a carving fork attached to its end was leaning against the counter. Isaac was slowly pulling on a heavy sweatshirt.

Sidney grabbed an old sweatshirt covered in different colors of paint and slipped it on as quickly as she could.

"Where's your dad?" Cody asked.

"He's not coming with us," she said, not wanting to elaborate.

"What do you mean he's not coming?"

"Your dad's not coming?" Rich asked, looking up as he finished taping the knife to the wooden plunger.

"No," she snapped, feeling her emotions start to rise. "He's not coming. How many other ways can I say it?"

Cody was stunned. "Sid, you can't be serious," he said, and started toward the door to the garage.

"Cody, no!"

Cody stopped and turned. "I'm not going to—"

"Yes, you are," Sidney said. "There's nothing you can do, nothing any of us can do."

"We can force him."

She shook her head, the tears flowing again. "I tried, I really did. But he wants to do this."

Cody seemed to struggle with continuing on to the garage or staying with them. "Sid, I . . ."

"Forget it; we have to go," she said, and turned her back on him, grabbing a carving knife from the table and sliding it through her belt loop. "The fastest way to my father's truck is out the front door," she said, taking the keys from a row of hooks hanging from a bulletin board next to an old wall phone. Then she started from the kitchen to the hall leading to the front door.

"What's going to keep them from swarming us when we open the door?" Cody asked from behind her.

Part of her was glad that Cody hadn't attempted to change her father's mind, but part was also disappointed that he hadn't.

Sidney peeked through the peephole in the door to see the front yard swarming with life. The animals and insects knew they were inside and were just waiting for them to come out.

"There's a lot of them out there," she said, pulling away from the door. "How do we drive them back?"

Cody, the spear in his hand, stepped closer. She noticed he still had the gun that was given to him at the police station stuck into the waistband of his jeans.

"I don't think our weapons will do much," Cody said, taking a look for himself. "They'll be all over as us as soon as we open the door.

She nodded as Snowy padded down the hall with Isaac behind her.

"Hey, guys," Rich called out from the kitchen.

They all turned toward the kitchen doorway as Rich appeared there holding a red fire extinguisher that Sidney's dad kept on the counter beside the stove. He'd put it there after a nasty grease fire she'd caused while cooking a hamburger when she was twelve.

"What about this?" Rich asked.

Sidney's gears were turning. CO_2, flame-suffocating chemicals—it could be just the thing to help them clear a path from the house to the truck.

"Give it," she ordered, moving her fingers in Rich's direction. Her friend came down the hall and handed the tank to her.

"I think this might do it," she said, hefting the extinguisher. "We spray to drive them back, and keep spraying until everybody gets to the truck."

"Will that work?" Rich asked.

"Better than anything I can think of right now," Sidney said.

"I'll do it," Cody said, moving to take it from her.

"Like hell you will," she said, stepping away from his reach.

The sounds from outside were becoming more raucous, and she could have sworn that she heard glass tinkling to the floor.

"Are we ready?" she asked.

"Keys," Cody demanded, holding out his hand.

Sidney reached into the pocket of her sweatshirt and removed the keys, handing them to him. "I'll give you that."

"What's my job?" Rich asked.

"Make sure Snowy and Isaac get safely to the truck," she said.

Rich nodded, patting Isaac on the shoulder. He had his meat tenderizer in one hand and his long-reach knife in the other.

They stood there for a few moments, no one really wanting to give the go-ahead. And then Sidney heard her father calling out from the garage.

"Go on," Rich said. He put out his hands for the extinguisher.

She handed it over and trotted down the hallway, Snowy by her side. She threw open the door, certain that her father had changed his mind. Instead, she saw him still in his chair, surrounded by dynamite, wires running from the ends of the explosive sticks to the detonator he held in his hands.

Her heart sank. "I thought you had changed your mind," she said dully.

"No," he said firmly. "I wanted to let you know I'm ready. It's time for you to go."

"Dad, please reconsider," she started.

"Clock's ticking, Sidney," he said. "Go. I love you." Then he pressed the button to open the garage door. "Come and get me, you filthy bastards!" he cried.

The insects were first, flowing under the door as it rose, crawling onto his body.

Sidney knew she had to leave before she couldn't but chanced one final look over her shoulder as she passed into the kitchen.

Bugs were crawling up onto his neck and face. He caught her look and nodded. "Beep the horn when you're safe."

Sidney ran through the kitchen and down the hall to her friends. "Get ready," she said, stopping short and wrenching the fire extinguisher from Rich's hands.

"Where's your father?"

"Where he wants to be," she said as she pulled the pin. "Open the door. We're leaving."

CHAPTER **FIFTY-FOUR**

Dale Moore would have been lying if he said he wasn't having second thoughts.

Nobody really ever wanted to die.

Even as he was, less than half of what he used to be, a part of him still struggled to remain. He guessed it was some primitive part of the brain that had existed to keep the species alive ever since mankind dropped down from the trees.

What if there really was nothing after this? Was that actually better than a life plagued by handicap?

Had he been wrong? Did he really want to stay alive?

Maybe he had, but now . . .

The insects were crawling under his clothes, biting and stinging his flesh. No matter how many he swatted away or crushed against his body, they were still there, an endless swarm of bugs and spiders.

He had to force himself to remain in the chair, knowing that he'd probably make it only a few feet before landing on the floor, rolling around like a turtle on its back.

No, he would hold out as long as he could for Sidney and her friends.

His grip tightened on the detonator in his lap. As soon as she beeped the horn . . .

The insects were just the first wave. He could see the cats jumping over the fence, skulking through the front yard, many wearing pretty collars, some with bells on them. If the insects failed, they'd be there to take him out. He'd never really cared for cats. He'd always been a dog person. Dale found his memory going back to a day in his childhood, his grandmother having come to stay with them for the weekend. He remembered her telling him a story of when she was a young girl in Ireland, and how new mothers were always afraid of the wild cats that were about. He had asked her why, and she had told him the cats would come into the baby's crib, perch upon the sleeping child's chest, and steal away their breath.

Dale heard the ringing of a bell as the first of the cats pounced upon his chest, its claws piercing his shirt to hook into the tender flesh beneath. He cried out in pain, swatting the silent beast away, before the others leaped upon him, scrambling up his body to get to his face.

To steal his breath away.

CHAPTER **FIFTY-FIVE**

Cody threw open the door, and Sidney stepped out, spraying a cloud of choking CO_2 at the animals swarming upon the porch.

"Run!" she screamed, relieved to see that she had been right, the cold blast from the fire extinguisher actually driving the animals back. She fired more of the chilling CO_2 and chanced a quick look over her shoulder to see Rich, Snowy, and Isaac following Cody to the driveway and the waiting truck. She sprayed one more arc of the choking white chemical, then darted off the porch to the left.

And slammed into somebody standing in the cold, swirling mist.

Sidney let out a yelp, falling backward and dropping the red canister. It took a moment for her brain to process what she was seeing: the man who had tried to kill her. He glared at her with horrible mismatched eyes, a bloody smile upon his face. Alfred the nasty French bulldog stood by his side.

She frantically reached for the extinguisher while keeping an eye on the man as he lumbered toward her.

Multiple stings of burning pain caused her to cry out, and she yanked her hand back as a cloud of wasps swarmed around her salvation. She scrambled to her feet, ducking beneath Berthold's filthy hands as they reached for her. Alfred decided to help then, lunging forward and sinking his nasty, bulldog teeth into the meat of her thigh.

She pitched forward, landing hard on her side. Then quickly rolling over onto her back, she managed to wrench the dog off of her, losing a chunk of her leg in the process and flipping him backward. The pain was intense, her vision swimming as she struggled to get to her feet.

Remembering her weapon, she reached to her side, found the carving knife's wooden handle, and yanked it from her belt.

Alfred was back, and all she could see was his open, slavering maw as it came at her. She stabbed at the French bulldog's face, the point of the knife entering his jowls and scraping across his gums and teeth. There was suddenly blood, lots of blood, as she pulled back on the blade, ready to stab at the dog again.

But now Berthold was crawling on all fours toward her like some kind of animal. He reached out and grabbed her ankle, dragging her back down to the waterlogged lawn. She dropped her knife and found herself staring up into the man's leering face as he bore down upon her, his filthy hands closing around her throat.

And starting to squeeze.

Isaac had started to slow down, his hands again going up to his head.

That's all I need, Rich thought, turning and grabbing the kid. "C'mon, Isaac! We have to get in the truck."

"It's getting loud again," Isaac whined. "The bad radio is getting loud again."

"Maybe it won't be so loud in the truck," Rich said as Cody reached around from the driver's seat to open the back passenger door.

Rich pushed Isaac inside, then turned and gestured for Snowy to climb in as well.

The German shepherd looked at him, and then turned around to stare in the direction they'd just come from. Exasperated, Rich ran to her and picked her up.

"She'll be right here, girl," he said, even though he knew she couldn't hear. He hefted Snowy onto the backseat beside Isaac and slammed the door closed. Then he raced around the truck to the front passenger door. He stopped, hand on the door handle, staring off in the direction of the house. Animals were coming across the side lawn toward them, probably drawn to their movement, their life. Some were still coated in powdery white from the fire extinguisher.

Where is she? he wondered, staring ahead, hoping to see her coming around the corner.

But Sidney didn't come.

"Get in the truck!" Cody yelled, and Rich ignored him, waiting.

"Rich, get in the truck, you stupid—"

"Where is she?" Rich asked, opening the door and leaning in toward Cody.

SAVAGE / 339

Cody looked nervous, antsy, his hands clenching and unclenching on the steering wheel. "I don't know. Get in the truck before—"

"Something's wrong," Rich said, standing up to look toward the front of the house again.

Isaac was grabbing at his head and moaning, rocking back and forth, muttering beneath his breath, and Snowy whined pitifully.

A rottweiler the size of a hippopotamus suddenly lunged around the truck at Rich. Rich managed to duck into the truck and slam the door closed just as the dog hit it.

Furious, it leaped against the truck, its slathering jaws biting at the window.

"Where is she?" Rich asked again.

Cody looked like he was going to jump out of his skin.

"She's coming," he said, looking out his window that was now being assaulted by stinging insects slamming against the glass. "She's coming."

The rottweiler leaped against the door, scratching with its large paws, trying to get in.

Rich looked at Cody. He could see that he was scared as well. Terrified that something had happened.

Where is she?

Rich suddenly slid across the seat, slamming his hand down in the center of the steering wheel and leaving it there.

Beeeeeeeeeeeeeeeeeeeeeeeeeeeeeep.

CHAPTER **FIFTY-SIX**

Dale Moore was waiting to die.

He was definitely ready, but he had to wait . . . he had to hold on until it was time.

The animals were all over him, the cats doing the most damage as a pack of dogs sat passively on the sidelines, waiting to see if they would be needed.

The pain really wasn't quite so bad anymore, most of his body having gone coldly numb. It wasn't too different than after the stroke.

He kept his eyes shut, feeling the insects on his lids, biting—gnawing.

He wasn't sure how much time he had left. He was losing a lot of blood for sure and could feel his hold on his poor tortured body beginning to slip away.

But he could not go yet; he had to fight the pull of the end.

He had to be sure that she was safe. He needed to be sure that she had reached the safety of the truck before . . .

Something large, and far heavier than bugs or cats, leaped up onto his lap and sank its teeth into his neck. Dale's eyes shot open as his throat was at first crushed and then torn open. He could see his own dying reflection in the silvery coating that covered the dog's right eye.

It must be time for the second shift, he thought, feeling the blood pump from the gaping wound in his neck and down the front of his shirt, the pull of death even more forceful now.

Then thankfully, he heard the blare of his truck's horn. Sidney was safe, and it was time for him to go.

And to take as many of these nasty sons of bitches with him as he could.

Dale Moore had always said that he'd want to die with his family and friends surrounding him, leaving the world with the knowledge that he'd done good and he was loved.

Two out of the three would have to do, he thought as his ragged and bloody fingers twitched upon the detonator, applying just enough pressure to—

The garage, and everything inside it, was consumed in fire.

Berthold's twisted face started to blur, obscured by blobs of writhing color that appeared before Sidney's oxygen-starved eyes.

She was trying to fight him, thrashing and bucking, but he easily outweighed her by forty pounds.

Sidney found herself transfixed, nearly hypnotized by the single glistening eye inside the right socket of his skull, the way it moved, dilating and contracting, reminding her strangely of a camera lens attempting to focus.

In and out, drawing her in, pulling her within the solid blackness of the strange eye's center as her strength began to ebb.

The blaring horn snapped her from her trance, sending an adrenaline surge shooting through her body like lightning. One last chance to survive—one last chance to live.

It took all she had left. She drew her legs up underneath her attacker while placing both hands upon his shoulders. Then she wrenched her body to the side, rolling the man from atop her. He grunted as he landed on his back.

Sidney gasped for breath as she scrambled away from the man. Her hand fell on her knife as she went, and she gripped it tightly.

Alfred had come to the man's side, the dog's face a mask of torn skin and blood. She watched the man rise to his feet even as she struggled to stand, the wound in her leg throbbing painfully.

She was barely to her feet, and Berthold and the dog were slowly stalking toward her, when the explosion came.

A roaring, fire-spewing dragon that picked her up and threw her across the yard.

"I'm going to look for her," Rich said just as the house exploded.

The truck rocked, licked by tongues of flame before being pelted by burning pieces of vinyl siding and pink insulation.

Cody looked at him, the expression on his face probably very much like Rich's own.

The rottweiler was still outside the passenger-side door, surrounded by pieces of burning debris.

"It's still out there," Rich said, slamming his hand against the closed window. "We have to . . ."

Cody turned the engine over and put the truck in drive.

"Hold on," he said as he stepped on the gas.

And for perhaps one of the first times in his life, Rich did as he was told without question.

The peace of unconsciousness was calling to her in a soothing voice that she could hear just bellow the bells ringing in her ears. It was trying to tell her to give in, to come on down to Dark Town and rest a spell.

It wanted her to give up, to throw in the towel, to tap out.

But Sidney didn't feel like dying.

She forced her eyes open and looked at her childhood home in flames.

"Dad," she croaked as she watched the burning remains, knowing he was gone.

Dazed, she climbed unsteadily to her feet and began to limp toward the driveway, where she hoped the truck, her friends, were still waiting. Something clamped around her ankle, and she fell to her knees in the grass, crying out in pain as the wound in her thigh reminded her it was there.

Berthold was still alive, his body blackened and burning. He was holding tightly to her ankle, attempting to pull her closer. Not too far away, she could see Alfred, flat on his stomach, the fur on his back smoldering as he dragged himself toward her.

Why can't they just die? she thought, frantically trying to shake the man's hold on her leg. His face was a horrible mess now, a mass of lacerated flesh and weeping blisters. His left eye was swollen shut, but the right was still wide with life.

She stared at it as she struggled, the silvery orb growing larger and smaller. She hated that eye and what it represented: the end of the life she had known.

She'd had enough. It was time to end this. Sidney gripped the knife and surged toward that silvery eye, plunging the blade into its center, hearing an oddly satisfying pop. She twisted the knife for good measure, then pulled back.

Berthold froze, strange silver liquid—like mercury—running down his burned and blistered face before he pitched forward to the ground, dead. Sidney yanked her foot from his blackened grasp and turned, horrified to find Alfred almost upon her.

She pushed herself back, ready to fight if she had to, when the truck appeared with the roar of its engine, barreling across the grass, the front tires running over the French bulldog's head as the vehicle came to a stop.

All she could do was stare as the door to the truck swung open and Cody reached for her.

"You really do need to keep up," Rich screamed from the passenger seat.

Sidney scrambled up and into the truck.

Before something else tried to kill her.

CHAPTER **FIFTY-SEVEN**

Doc Martin hissed and gritted her teeth as she cleaned her wound. She thought of the shots she would have to get, tetanus for sure, and probably rabies.

She thought about rabies for a moment but knew in her gut that it wasn't that at all. *Rabies would be easy,* she thought.

What they were dealing with here and now was something altogether different and quite terrible.

She got some gauze pads and tape and bandaged her leg, then sat back to check her work. Deeming it satisfactory, Doc Martin tugged the leg of her torn and bloodied slacks down and cautiously stood. There was some pain, but she felt like she could walk—and maybe even run—if she had to. She stomped her feet for good measure and winced from the pain, but it was manageable.

The sound of the storm outside, as well as the scratches and rustlings of animal life searching for a way inside, made her listen. Whatever it was going on out there was bad and people needed to be warned, but she wasn't doing anybody any good trapped in here.

Limping from the back area, Doc Martin went up to the front of the clinic. In the faint red glow of the emergency lights she approached the main entrance, peering through the glass at the darkness outside. It was as if they were drawn to her presence, a veritable menagerie of dogs, cats, and rodents flowing from around the parking lot toward the front door. A Labrador–pit bull mix that she recognized from the neighborhood ran at the door full tilt, slamming its face into the glass, leaving a bloody stain behind as it stumbled back.

The silvery covering on its eye was evident, as she suspected it would be.

The mob of angry animal life was increasing as she stood there, hurling their bodies unmercifully against the glass that separated them from their prey.

Doc Martin stepped back, retreating into the front lobby, and was surprised to see the assault upon the door stop, the animals ceasing their attack, now that she was no longer visible. They continued to peer inside though, their heads tilted in such a way that their right eyes were the ones doing the searching.

She remembered the odd sensation she'd experienced when examining the right eyes of the animals from the kennel, like she was being watched—observed.

Returning to the back area, she was even more resolute that she needed to get out of there and get to a person of authority to explain what she had discovered. But in order to do that she needed to escape the building and get to her car without getting killed.

She had to somehow keep the animals away from her.

Remembering the number of beasts that she'd encountered out in the parking lot earlier, she wasn't feeling optimistic about her chances.

But she had to try something.

Walking around the back room, her eyes looked to every surface, every item. Her objective was to get to her car, but she had to keep the critters at bay.

On one of the shelves she saw a few plastic bottles of isopropyl alcohol. The liquid was extremely flammable and maybe just what the doctor ordered. She grabbed a bottle from the shelf, giving it a casual shake as she thought about how to use it.

"A torch," she said out loud, the sound of her own voice in the empty office actually startling her. "I'll make a torch."

She turned from the shelf, looking for what she could use to pull this off. In the far corner of the room there was a bucket and mop, and she set the alcohol bottle down on the counter as she went to it. As it was, the mop handle was too long, and she leaned it against the counter, lifted her good leg, and brought it down upon the wooden body with a loud snap.

"This should do it," she muttered beneath her breath, the mop handle now half the length. From the bottom drawer of a cabinet she found a stack of towels and pulled them out. Going for her scissors, she brought them back and proceeded to cut the towels into strips, and when she felt there were enough, started to wrap the end of the mop handle, layering the thickness. When she was satisfied with what would be the torch head, she grabbed the bottles of alcohol and proceeded to fill the mop bucket, placing the rag-covered head down into the strong-smelling liquid. The fumes were nearly overwhelming, and she stepped back from the bucket. She wanted to be sure that the torch head was completely saturated, so she left it soaking as she scoured the area for other items to help her.

In the corner was a pair of heavy work boots that had been left from the particularly rough winter. She kicked off her sneakers and slipped into the boots, tucking her pants legs into the tops before tightly lacing them.

She then retrieved a pair of thick work gloves that they'd sometimes used when dealing with uncooperative cats and slipped them on over her hands. It wasn't much, but at least there would be some parts of her that would be protected.

It was now or never, and Doc Martin decided that now was the only option. She thought about the best way to leave the building, deciding that the back would be closest to her vehicle.

The gears inside her head were clicking again, and they locked into place as she went to retrieve her torch. The wheeled plastic bucket was still partially filled with isopropyl alcohol and still incredibly flammable. Resting the torch against the counter, she found a roll of gauze and made sure that she had her lighter and proceeded to roll the mop bucket to the front lobby, being sure to stay out of sight the best she could. From what she could observe through the windows, the lot appeared partially empty. She was sure that the beasts were waiting just beyond the periphery of light, waiting for her to try and escape.

They would be right about her plans, but not from where.

Stealthily, or at least as stealthily as a sixty-one-year-old woman could be, Doc Martin made her way toward the front door, pushing the alcohol-filled bucket in front of her.

Standing at the door, she reached up to the lock and clicked it open. Looking out over the front lot, she was amazed to see that the sound had actually drawn the attention of some of the beasts. A flood of muskrats—*or were they possums?*—swarmed from the darkness toward the door.

Quickly she fished the roll of gauze from her pocket and lit it with her lighter. Then she opened the door to the howling wind, and before anything could make its way in, she dropped the burning gauze into the bucket with explosive results. The alcohol immediately caught fire with a burst of blue flame, and she kicked the wheeled bucket out the door, where it rolled, burning, into the lot.

As she quickly shut the door, she saw that the animals were drawn to the still-moving bucket. Without another look, she raced to the back of the clinic, where she retrieved her torch. She stood at the back door, lifted her lighter to the head of the torch, lighting it with a rush of high flame. She tensed, took a deep breath, and pushed the door open. The lot seemed to be clear, and she rushed out into the rain, eyes searching for signs of animals. It had been quite some time since Doc Martin had gotten this much exercise, but she gave it her best shot, legs pumping as she held the torch out in front of her, eyes fixed on her car. The bite wounds on her leg hurt like hell, but she ignored them.

She had crossed half of the lot when she chanced a quick look over her shoulder. She could see the front of the building, where the bucket had stopped burning, and the crowd of beasts surrounding it was beginning to disperse . . .

Beginning to notice her.

"Shit," she hissed as her heart thumped wildly in her chest. Wouldn't it be her luck to have a heart attack right then? She continued to push herself toward her car at the far end of the lot. She was close, but so were the sounds of animal claws clicking on the pavement behind her.

Doc Martin spun around, waving the torch at the pack of dogs that had just about reached her. "Yaaah!" she screamed at the beasts as she continued to back toward her car. The flame of the torch seemed to slow them, but it was raining heavily and she knew the torch wouldn't last much longer.

She backed right into the side of her car, nearly dropping the torch. Sliding along the side, she made her way to the driver's-side door. She shoved her free hand into her pocket, fumbling for her keys, only to have them fall from her gloved hand as she pulled them free.

"Son of a bitch," she snarled. Keys just weren't her thing today. Still holding the torch in front of her, seeing its flame in the glint of silvery right eyes, she bent to retrieve the keys. And just as her fingers closed around them, the animals surged.

It was an odd sight, and Doc Martin found herself pausing for a moment to watch. They seemed to move as one, flowing toward her very much like an ocean wave. Then she shoved the torch into the body of the mass, hoping that it would give her enough time to get into the car. The single, writhing mass broke apart as the flame touched them, but Doc Martin was already turning, pressing the button to unlock the Subaru wagon. She opened the car door and dove into the front seat, managing to pull the door closed again just as the first animal slammed into it.

Doc Martin's breathing came in labored gasps, her heart racing a million miles a second as she realized that she'd actually survived—for now.

The windshield and side windows were spattered with blood and the life stuff of insects attempting to breach the barrier that separated them from their prey. The beasts were relentless in their attack, the car rocking with their onslaught.

She put the key in the ignition and turned the engine over, stepping on the gas and revving the engine in a roar of victory. Putting the car in reverse, she hit the gas and backed up as quickly as she could. The car bumped and rolled as her tires ran over multiple obstacles attempting to thwart her progress. Doc Martin didn't want to think of what was beneath her wheels as she stepped on the brake and put the car in drive. The car shot forward but quickly shuddered to a stop. She stepped on the gas and could feel the Subaru fighting to go forward, but something was stopping it.

Something was preventing the vehicle's tires from turning. It was almost as if she was stuck in thick mud.

"Don't do this," she screamed, putting the car in reverse and attempting to go backward before trying to go forward again. "I beat you fair and square, you sons of bitches."

The tires spun and whined, furiously fighting for traction. She imagined the wheel wells jammed tightly with the bodies of crushed animals. The car made it a few feet forward but was stopped again. She could actually feel them moving beneath the wagon, the bodies of multiple animal and insect life forms thumping and banging off the undercarriage.

Again she put the car in reverse, stepping on the gas, making her tires spin across the slippery surface of the parking lot, before slamming on the brakes, putting the car in drive once more, and hitting the gas. The Subaru went farther this time, but swerved to one side as the all-wheel drive became clogged, allowing only three of the wheels to turn.

"You bastards," she hissed, putting it in reverse. "You're not going to get me—not like this." She was practically crushing the accelerator when she noticed the first of the flying insects inside the car with her. It started with something no bigger than a gnat, and then a cloud of the annoying flying insects followed. It took her a minute to realize that they were coming in through her vents. She reached down to close the openings as quickly as she could, but it was already too late. The flies were next, and then she noticed the yellow-and-black-striped bodies of the wasps.

Doc Martin swatted crazily as the bugs came at her face, flying into her mouth, eyes, and ears. The wasps were aggressive in their savagery, sinking their stingers repeatedly into the flesh of her face and neck.

She screamed but almost immediately began to cough and gag. The gnats had found their way up into her nose, coating the back of her throat, choking her on their tiny bodies. Unable to breathe, she found her vision failing and dizziness making it impossible for her to drive.

The inside of the car was filled with the buzzing of thousands of insect wings. They were in her eyes and mouth and down the front of her clothes, and she just couldn't stand it anymore.

Knowing that it was likely her end, but not wanting to die this way—stung to death while choking on the bodies of flies—the veterinarian opened the door and threw herself out onto the ground, coughing and gagging and throwing up what little her stomach contained. Her eyes were tightly closed against the insect onslaught, but she could hear the sounds of the larger animals as they approached. The insects had gotten her out of the vehicle, and now the warm-blooded beasts would finish her off.

She was sad that she hadn't gotten away, sad that she would be unable to warn the island—the world—of the strange threat besieging them, but she believed that she'd put up a good fight.

And that was going to have to do.

She felt the rush of intense heat on the flesh of her face and opened her eyes to the hellish vision of the animals that had been closing in on her to attack being eaten up and dispersed by tongues of angry fire.

Doc Martin recoiled from the flames, throwing herself back against the side of her car.

Her eyes had swollen partially shut from the yellow-jacket stings, but she managed to force the flesh apart enough to see. She climbed up from beside her car and looked across the parking lot to see a kind of transport vehicle. It looked military. And there were men—

heavily garbed men, their faces and bodies covered in protective gear—wielding flamethrowers, burning away the attacking animals.

What in the name of all that's holy is going on? the old veterinarian wondered, feeling herself growing faint as she leaned heavily against the side of her car.

The men advanced across the lot, still firing their weapons, and she found it incredibly disturbing that even as they were burned alive, the animals—the dogs and cats and foxes—did not cry out in pain.

All they did was burn.

Doc Martin pushed off from her car, avoiding the burning animal bodies. The men with the flamethrowers turned toward her defensively, and she thought that they might burn her as well. Throwing up her hands in surrender, she stared at them through swollen eyes.

"Who are you?" she croaked.

A figure emerged from the transport vehicle and carefully approached. She noticed that he was a handsome, dark-skinned man, and he looked at the carnage with a kind of grim disbelief.

"I'm Dr. Gregory Sayid," he said, still not looking at her, his gaze fixed on the burning animal corpses. "And we're here to help."

CHAPTER **FIFTY-EIGHT**

Unasked questions about Dale Moore and what he had done hung in the air like a bad smell. Sidney could feel her friends' eyes glancing at her as she silently sat between them, staring through the windshield at the road ahead.

"Sid, I . . . ," Cody began, but she didn't want to discuss it.

"Stop," she said flatly.

"Believe me, I understand what you're . . ."

"I said stop."

And he did, continuing to drive in silence down Benediction's small, winding streets. There were cars scattered here and there, doors open wide, their former occupants having fled, but in some cases . . .

She didn't want to look at them; she didn't want to see any more death. She just wanted to get to Doc Martin's place. Things would get better then.

At least that's what she hoped.

"Mr. Moore is dead," Isaac suddenly announced from the backseat, his voice flat and emotionless.

Sidney felt the muscles in her neck and back tighten up as the words hit her. The pronouncement of her father's death.

"Hey, knock it off with that!" Rich yelled, turning around in the seat.

"It's all right," she said. She felt the hot tears well up in her eyes, threatening to spill out over the edges, to cascade down her filthy face. She reached over and popped the glove box open, grabbing some napkins from inside. A flat bag slipped out and fell to the floor.

Rich bent down to get it, ready to put it back, but she was curious.

"What's that?"

"A bag," Rich said, showing it to her.

She took it and peeked inside and began to sob as the walls around her emotions collapsed.

"Sid, what is it?" Rich asked, obviously uncomfortable with her crying. She couldn't answer him, giving the bag back to him as she brought the wrinkled paper napkin up to her face to try and stem the flow of tears.

She could see him looking into the bag and partially removing the greeting card. It was a graduation card, something her father was likely planning on giving her, but then a stroke got in the way. She cried all the harder with the thought of the effort it must have taken for him to get the card. He never remembered stuff like that, and the fact that he had just went to show her how important he thought her achievement was.

Rich slid the card out and read it before putting it back into the bag and returning it to the glove box. "It's nice," he said as he closed the glove box with a snap.

She nodded. "He must've forgotten it was in there," she said through her tears. And then something through the windshield caught her attention. "What is . . . ?" she started to ask, raising her hand to point at the road ahead of them.

Cody slammed on the brakes.

The surface of the street ahead moved with life, a living blanket that just lay there, writhing as if . . .

"What's it doing?" Cody asked in a whisper.

"Waiting," Sidney replied, not knowing why she had answered in such a way, but somehow knowing that she was right.

"Waiting for what?" Rich asked.

The layer of living things suddenly surged up from the road, flowing toward the homes along the street—

Until it saw them.

The wave stopped and shifted in their direction.

Sidney could just imagine the thousands of eyes—the thousands of right eyes—fixing on their truck.

"Back it up!" Rich screamed as the wave reared up, and then threw itself toward them, flowing down the center of the road.

Cody did as he was told, putting the truck in reverse and stepping on the gas, turning and looking out the rear window as he steered the vehicle backward.

The mass of life was fast, picking up speed as it gave chase. Sidney stared through the truck's windshield, taking in all its horrific details as it flowed steadily closer. She could just about make out the individual pieces of life—dogs, rats, raccoons, cats—floating in a sea of what appeared to be insects, hundreds of thousands, maybe even millions.

The organism—there was no other thing she could think to call it—churned and moved as it propelled itself across the ground, the living bodies of animals briefly appearing before being submerged in a sea of bugs as others rose to the surface.

And then there were the bones.

At first she didn't quite understand what she was seeing. For a moment she believed that they were pieces of wood—limbs of trees picked up by the undulating mass—but when she saw the skull, its jaw hanging open in a silent scream, she understood the horror of what it was.

The remains of victims were a part of its body, flowing within the multitude that made up its mass.

It was an awful sight. She tore her gaze from the nightmare steamrolling down the street after them and quickly figured out where they were.

"Up on your right, Powell Road," she called out.

Cody slammed on the brakes and turned the wheel roughly, spinning the car around, pointing it toward what looked to be a rough section of woods.

"What the hell are you doing?" Rich screamed.

"Powell Road," Sidney said. "Cliffside Condominiums?"

Everyone in Benediction knew the story. Big-time real estate developer Travest Powell had bought up all kinds of land and was planning on building a deluxe condominium complex. Some of the land had already been cleared when the market went bust, and Powell had ended up losing his shirt to the bank. He'd committed suicide on his private yacht, just before the bank was about to take that from him as well.

Cody put the car in drive and aimed the truck toward the wooded area. The remains of the road were still there, but it was a bumpy mess.

"Hang on back there," Sid said, turning to see Snowy bouncing around as Isaac clutched the door armrest, looking as though he was about to be sick.

Or was the bad radio at it again?

The truck bounced so violently that she flew up and hit her head off the roof of the cab.

"Sorry!" Cody said through gritted teeth, doing his best to avoid the larger ruts as he steered the truck over the rocky road.

"Just stay on this road and we'll end up near the cliffs," Sidney said. She leaned backward over the seat to look out through the rear window, wondering if the mass of animals was following. Snowy enthusiastically licked her face, and she patted her dog lovingly, reassuring her.

There was some movement in the pouring rain and darkness, but it looked as though they were safe—for the moment.

Cody gunned the engine of the truck, and they bounced up out of a series of deep ruts where the dirt had been washed away by the storm's steady rainfall. Sidney placed one hand by her side on the seat and the other on the ceiling in an attempt to brace herself.

"We should come out on Pirate Road, and then we'll go around the cliffs and back onto Dobson," she said, seeing a kind of childhood map drawn inside her head.

Cody continued to drive, his gaze on the road ahead of them intense. They passed the area where the land had been cleared of trees, rocks, and brush. One foundation had been laid before the endeavor had ended.

"Keep going straight," she ordered, leaning forward in her seat and pointing through the windshield at the road ahead.

"I know," Cody growled, concentrating on the rough road beneath them. Makeshift paths, really, that hadn't seen any vehicles since construction was halted.

They continued to be bounced around by rocky and uneven terrain made even worse by the heavy rainfall. Sidney heard a sudden, plaintive moaning from the back and turned to see Isaac looking even worse.

"Hold on, Isaac," she told him. "We're almost to Pirate Road, and then things will get a little less bumpy."

"No! No! No!" he cried out, and grabbed at his head again with both hands.

"What is it, Isaac? Is it the bad radio again?"

"Yes," he answered, sounding as though he were in a great deal of pain.

Snowy's tail wagged nervously as she tried to lick Isaac's face. Sidney leaned over the seat, reaching out to place a comforting hand on the young man, but he was becoming more frantic.

"Hang on," she said, her fingertips brushing his knee. "We'll be safe soon." She tried to reassure him.

"It's loud," Isaac screamed. "It's so loud!"

"What's happening to him?" Rich asked, on the verge of panic.

"I have no idea," Sidney answered, watching as Isaac suddenly curled up in a tight ball on the backseat. "I think he may be hearing something that we can't."

"Why can't we hear it?" Rich asked. "I know why Snowy can't, but why him?"

"I don't know . . . maybe it has something to do with the accident that he had as a child that made him the way he is. . . ."

Isaac uncurled from his fetal shape with a scream, his eyes wide and bloodshot. "It's too close!" he shrieked, his bellow deafening within the confines of the truck cab. "Too close!"

He twisted toward the door and took hold of the handle.

"He's gonna open the door!" Rich shouted.

"Isaac, no!" Sidney yelled, pushing her upper body over the seat to prevent the young man from opening the door. She grabbed at his legs, pulling herself over the top of the front seat to stop him. "You can't!"

Isaac continued to cry out in torment, yanking on the handle. The door began to open. Sidney was able to reach across his squirming form and grab hold of the padded elbow rest to pull the door closed.

The car dipped, the entire front end of the truck plunging forward before heaving back up again, which sent them all tumbling about in the backseat as Isaac continued to cry out. Snowy yelped as Sidney did everything she could to keep the passenger door from opening.

Isaac knew that he shouldn't open the truck door, but the bad radio was so very loud and calling to him.

He wanted to escape, to run away as far as he could so that he did not have to hear the horrible sounds anymore.

But there was another part of him, a part that wanted to go toward that horrible, horrible sound.

As the truck bucked and rocked, Isaac had no idea what to do, the bad radio growing so loud inside his head that he thought it just might explode. He didn't want Sidney to see his head explode. That would be very embarrassing.

But the bad radio was so loud.

Sidney was trying to keep the door closed, trying to keep him in the truck, and he didn't want to make her mad at him.

The bad radio was screaming, so close, and all he could do was hold his head to keep it from exploding and hope that his cries would drown out the noise in his mind.

Cody drove the truck up the sand-and-dirt incline, gunning the engine and making the tires spin for purchase as he made his way up onto Pirate Road.

He was going fast, focusing on keeping the truck on the road, and it was almost too late before he noticed the presence spread out over the road in front of him.

"What now?" Rich suddenly yelled, pushing himself back in his seat as he pointed out the writhing mass that stretched from one side of the road to the other.

Cody almost slammed on the brakes, but he was moving too

fast. He didn't want to risk sending the truck into an uncontrolled skid and decided instead to drive straight over whatever was covering the stretch of road before him.

Leaning forward in his seat, clutching the steering wheel so tightly that he was surprised it didn't snap in his hands, Cody squinted through the rain and fog coming in off the ocean and stepped on the gas.

"Hold on."

The headlights of the truck illuminated the writhing mass, reflecting off the wet and glistening shells of thousands of crabs and lobsters that must have come up out of the ocean to participate in Benediction's night of total insanity.

The wheels of the truck drove over the multitude of spiky carapaces, sending pieces of shells, soft guts, and fluids spewing up over the front grille and hood and spattering off the windshield.

There came a loud bang, like a shot of gunfire, and Cody found himself having difficulty steering as the truck's front end leaned down and to the right.

Blowout.

He smelled the cloying, heavy odor of burning rubber wafting into the truck, riding atop the smell of the sea, and heard the *fwap! fwap! fwap!* sound of a shredded tire disintegrating as he drove.

It was hard to control the truck, steering the best he could as he pulled over to the side of the road.

"Dude, this is not good," Rich said.

"Yeah," Cody agreed.

But it was about to get worse.

The truck stopped moving, and slowly Sidney unhooked her fingers from the armrest, cautioning Isaac to remain calm.

"All right," she said, attempting to remove herself from across the young man's lap while trying to keep some semblance of her dignity. "Let's keep calm. Take deep breaths, Isaac, deep breaths."

Isaac was trying; he truly was. The young man was rocking back and forth now, his lips moving wildly as he spoke so only he could hear.

"That's it," she said, reassuring him. Snowy nudged her nervously, sticking her large head underneath Sidney's arm for attention. "Hold it together now."

She looked to the front seat.

"What's the story?"

"Don't even have to look," Cody told her. "Flat tire. Maybe more than one."

"What'd we hit?"

"Crabs," Rich answered.

"Crabs? Seriously?"

"And lobsters," Rich added. "So what's the plan now? Do we risk staying here or . . ."

Isaac let out a bloodcurdling scream, his fingers raking down the side of his face as he began to thrash. Sidney threw herself on him, trying to prevent him from hurting himself, but he was just too strong. His arms whipped around, knocking her backward into the space between the seats.

"Stop him!" Sidney cried, struggling to get back up.

Cody and Rich both turned, but it was already too late. Isaac had the door open and had fallen out onto the side of the road, moaning and carrying on about the things inside his head. Snowy had followed him and was sniffing at him nervously.

"Isaac!" Sidney cried out, pulling herself up onto the seat, reaching for him, but he was already moving, running across the road and into the woods, heading in the direction of the forest paths that led up to the hilly cliffs that looked down onto Benediction Cove.

Snowy chased after the young man, barking as she ran. They could hear him as he struggled through the heavy underbrush, grunting and muttering, the sound of him growing distant as he made his way deeper into the wooded area.

The shepherd turned to see if the others were following. Sidney jumped from the truck and was about to run when a firm hand reached out, grabbing her arm.

"What are you doing?" Cody asked, his eyes darting around for signs of danger.

"I'm going after him," she said, attempting to pull her arm away.

"Are you crazy?" he asked. Rich had joined him, as had Snowy. "You wouldn't last a minute."

Sidney could no longer hear Isaac, the sounds of his progress swallowed up by the sounds of the storm.

"But we can't just let him—"

"Yes, we can," Rich said. "I'm sorry, but Isaac is on his own now."

"Where the hell does he think he's going, anyway?" Cody asked, angry. "I know he's not right in the head, but you'd think the concept of self-preservation . . ."

Sidney had stopped hearing her ex's rant after his question of Isaac's destination. It was a good question.

Where is *he going?*

She stared off into the woods, remembering her childhood romps here, the many summer afternoons that she and her friends had spent climbing the cliffs and venturing into areas forbidden by their parents.

The pirate caves.

The cliffs were riddled with a system of caves that had supposedly been used by pirates to hide their booty in the late 1800s, even though no treasure had ever been found.

But it didn't keep Benediction's kids from trying to be the first to find some.

Isaac was being drawn toward the sound—toward the bad radio. He said it was louder, closer.

"I know where he's going," Sidney said, interrupting Cody's rant.

"I really don't care at this point," Rich said. "He's fried his own ass, as far as I'm concerned. And we might want to think about getting back into the car before something decides to make us a snack and—"

"Where?" Cody asked Sidney.

"The caves," she said. "I think he's being drawn to the pirate caves."

"By the bad radio?"

She nodded. "Whatever that is."

"So the bad radio is in one of the pirate caves?" Rich asked.

"Whatever is broadcasting the signal, or sound, or whatever it is that's doing this . . . I think Isaac is being drawn to it."

"It's not safe," Cody said, staring up toward the cliffs.

She looked as well, noticing for the first time since this nightmare began that they weren't being attacked.

"Probably not, but it seems safer now than it has all day and night."

They were all looking around now, surprised that they hadn't noticed it sooner. There was no longer any animal or insect life around them.

"Can we be sure?" Rich asked.

"About as sure as we can be about anything that has gone on tonight."

"So I'm guessing you still want to go after Isaac," Cody said.

Sidney turned back to the car, retrieving the weapons that they'd made back at her house.

"Yeah," she said, "I do. And I want to find this bad radio."

"And then what?"

"What else do you do with a radio?" she asked them. "You shut the damn thing off."

They each took their weapons, their spear and their knives, and started into the woods.

Sidney let Snowy lead the way, the white fur of the dog glowing in the early morning gloom like a ghostly apparition. She only went so far as she surged ahead, sniffing at the ground, before running back to them.

Sidney urged her on with a hand gesture, telling her to find him—to find Isaac.

She was on guard despite her exhaustion, every sense on alert, constantly looking around, eyes scanning every surface for bugs or animals, ears listening for the crack of a branch or the rustling of leaves. Cody and Rich were no better, twitchy and wary of every sound.

The rain was still falling, but Sidney dared to believe that it might have been letting up, that the storm might actually be receding. She listened to the sounds in the distance, the hiss of what seemed like a perpetual rainfall suddenly overwhelmed by the soothing roar of the ocean around them.

It was unbelievably muggy, and they found themselves shedding the extra layers that they'd put on back at her house. If they hadn't, she was sure that they would have passed out from heat exhaustion. She was becoming winded, the constant stress and lack of rest chipping away at her stamina. She was tired five hours ago, but now she was experiencing something beyond exhaustion.

Snowy's ghostly shape returned to them excitedly, and she yipped as she stomped her paws on the wet, slimy inches of leaf fall, before turning around and running off again.

"I think she's found his trail," Sidney told her friends.

Cody grunted, forging onward up the inclining terrain, using the end of his makeshift spear to help him climb. Sidney was about to follow, turning slightly to make sure that everything still appeared to be all right, and found Rich simply standing, staring off to where they'd just come from.

"It all seems so normal now," he said. "If you didn't know, you wouldn't even realize."

She could see what he meant. It was all so suddenly calm there.

But those feelings of quiet were quickly dispelled as the memories of the past hours rushed forward.

If you didn't know, but she did, and she wanted to keep moving just in case.

"C'mon," she said to him, and Rich looked at her and smiled weakly.

"So you two finally broke up," he said, walking beside her.

She looked at Cody's back as he climbed ahead of them, following Snowy. At one time she would have gotten a warm sensation, a tingle, when looking at him there, but now . . .

"Not the best time to be talking about that," she said.

"No, but I just wanted to be sure it was really true, in case a beaver ate my face, or something."

She couldn't help but be amused by his nonsense.

"Benediction doesn't have any beavers," she told him.

"Yet," he said, slipping on the muddy mixture of sand and dirt and almost sliding back down the hill. "This has all been in preparation for the beavers' arrival."

"You're such an idiot," Sidney told him.

"But I'm still alive," Rich said. "An idiot, but still kickin'. Has to count for something."

Yes, it does, she thought. It was amazing that they were all still kicking, to put it in Rich's terms. She wondered how many on the island weren't and felt a depressing heaviness that nearly forced her to sit down in the cold rotting leaves and mud as she remembered that her father was gone. She saw him inside her head, sitting in the garage, surrounded by explosives.

And then she remembered the blast and the fire, and that he was gone.

"Never underestimate an idiot," she said, feeling a burning surge of energy through her tired muscles as she pushed on ahead, attempting to catch up to Cody and her dog.

The island authorities had done all they could to make the pirate caves off limits to curious thrill seekers, putting up chain-link fencing around the openings with huge DANGER, and DO NOT ENTER signs that threatened criminal prosecution if ignored.

Fat lotta good that did.

For as long as Sidney could remember, the caves were those special forbidden places that everybody wanted to explore, their stories passed from the high school kids right down to grade school.

She didn't really remember when it was that she had gotten her first look at the caves, guessing that it was probably some time in junior high school. One of her classmates had actually planned a party inside, and she and a friend had gone but left early because it had been so darn cold. And it was a good thing too, because the police had found out about the gathering and had shown up to make an example of those in attendance.

Sidney thought of that night, probably the first time since it had happened, as she stared up at the dirt-and-rock face of the cliff and the jagged opening that she could just about make out from where they were standing.

"He's up there," Cody said, pointing.

"I hope he's careful," she said. "That whole area is pretty rocky and unstable, especially after a heavy rain."

They began to climb toward the opening, being careful themselves on the rocky incline. The rain had loosened the dirt and rocks, and it crumbled beneath their weight as they moved.

"So what are you expecting to find up here, besides Isaac?" Rich asked.

"I don't know," Sidney answered, stepping up onto a more solid ridge and reaching back to help Cody up. "Isaac appears to be drawn to the bad radio, whatever that is."

"And you think it's up here somewhere? In the caves?" Rich asked.

"Can you think of any better place to hide?"

"Do you seriously think that someone's doing this on purpose?"

Sidney was already on the move again. "I don't know what to think," she said breathlessly.

"I could wrap my brain around this being some kind of disease, but that shit is just too much," Rich said with a shake of his head.

"What I don't get is why?" Cody asked. "If what you suspect is true . . . that there's some kind of signal being broadcast to make animals go crazy . . . why? What's the purpose?"

Sidney didn't have an answer and didn't even want to risk trying to come up with one. She was certain that a lot of people had died on the island during the last several hours, and if what had caused their deaths was something intentional . . .

Maybe it was as simple as that.

Maybe it was all about death.

CHAPTER FIFTY-NINE

They found Isaac kneeling beside the chain-link fence that had been placed before one of the cave entrances. He was moaning, crying, and mumbling to himself, hands holding on to the fence, face pressed to the links, unable to go any farther.

"Isaac," Sidney said as she carefully approached him. "We were worried about you, bud."

Snowy ran over to the young man, sniffing at his face before giving him a kiss and covering his cheek with slobber. Isaac actually looked stunned, his red-rimmed eyes going wide with shock.

Sidney grabbed the dog and pulled her back, just in case.

"She kissed me," Isaac said, the glazed look in his eyes slowly seeming to dissipate.

"She certainly did," Sidney said, still holding on to the animal. "Are you okay, Isaac?"

He seemed to think about that for a minute before answering. "Yes. Right now I'm okay." He turned his attention back to the cave opening beyond the fence. "But I don't know for how long."

"Is it in there?" Rich asked as he squatted beside Isaac and tried to see into the cave. "What's causing the problems on the island, is it in there, Isaac?"

The young man seemed confused, his hand again fluttering around his ears. She could see the bloody scratches that he'd dug in the sides of his face.

"It's quiet," Isaac said. "Right now it's quiet . . . but I . . . I can still feel it . . . close . . . so very, very close." His voice had dropped to a whisper as he looked through the holes in the chain link.

"I'm not sure about this," Rich said, standing up and backing away from the fence toward Sidney.

"Aren't you the least bit curious?" Sidney asked, peering into the cave mouth.

"Yeah, but . . ."

"How do we get in?" Cody asked, walking closer to the fence to inspect it. It had been bolted to the rock on either side of the cave entrance, leaving only a small opening at the top. "I guess we could climb."

He wrapped his fingers through the holes of the chain link and started to look for a foothold for his boot when Isaac lost it.

He jumped to his feet with something that sounded more like a roar than a scream, grabbed hold of the fence in both hands, and pulled. Cody leaped out of the way, and Sidney stumbled back, nearly tumbling from the ledge as her neighbor unleashed his fury upon the fence, actually managing to rip the obstruction from where it had been bolted and tossing it into the woods below.

They were all frozen, unsure of how to react—unsure of how Isaac was going to act.

He looked at Sidney, breathing heavily, before turning and plunging into the darkness of the cave.

She immediately began to follow, both Rich and Cody reaching out to stop her.

"You can't be serious," Rich said.

"Don't you think we should have some sort of plan before—"

"How about we go in and bring Isaac out," Sidney said, shrugging off their hands. "Anything else, we'll just have to figure out as it happens."

She didn't say anything more, not wanting the courage that came with this latest adrenaline surge to pass before she was able to act.

The first thing that she noticed as she entered the cave was the temperature. Even after all this time—

It was as cold as she remembered.

The last place Sidney wanted to be was inside the pirate cave.

But something drew her forward.

She could hear breathing, the shuffling of feet upon rock, and the occasional whimper from the darkness somewhere ahead of her.

Her phone's charge was low, but she had to see where she was and turned on the light to illuminate her surroundings.

The cave was just as she remembered it: cold and damp, showing signs that civilization had stopped by for a party or two. The phrase "Shit happens" was spray-painted on a nearby wall, and at the moment she couldn't have agreed more. An empty vodka bottle and some rusting beer cans littered the floor along with some old candy wrappers. It didn't appear that anyone—*anything*—had been inside the cave recently.

Rich and Cody were suddenly beside her, holding up their phones as well. Snowy sniffed the piles of trash, making soft mewling sounds that told Sidney she had caught wind of something that made her nervous. She reached out and ran her fingers across the dog's white flank. Snowy leaned in to her, nuzzling her hand nervously.

"It's all right, girl," she said softly, wanting to reassure herself as much as her dog.

She wasn't doing that great of a job.

"Are you sure about this?" Cody asked, shining the light from his phone to the back of the cave where it curved downward into darkness.

Her free hand slipped to her belt, where her fingers found the wooden handle of her knife. "Yeah, but let's keep moving before I change my mind."

"You know, it's perfectly all right to change your mind," Rich offered. "In fact, it says you've put a lot of thought into a particular topic and—"

"Shut up, Rich," she and Cody said in unison. They looked at each other in the sickly glow from the phones and briefly smiled before turning away.

Not wanting to waste the battery, Sidney turned off her phone's light. Cautiously she approached the back of the cave, practically pulled by the mystery of what she might find. To say that she wasn't terrified would have been absolute crap; she doubted that she'd ever been so afraid, other than after learning of her dad's stroke, but this was different. This fear had substance—it had teeth—and if she wasn't careful, it would most definitely kill her.

She moved as close to the curving cave wall as she could, gradually following it around the corner, preparing for even thicker darkness as she moved away from the meager light of the cave's entrance. But there was no need.

A soft light glowed from somewhere in the distance.

She stopped. She couldn't remember if Isaac had a phone with him or not. She watched the light as it seemed to pulse, reminding her strangely of the beating of a heart.

"Where's that coming from?" Cody asked very close to her ear, making her jump.

She shook her head to let him know that she had no idea.

Rich peered around them, swallowing nervously. Snowy stood beside him, gazing at the throbbing light as if hypnotized by it.

She felt Cody's eyes on her, a silent question of whether or not they should go on. The answer was obvious, at least to her, and she headed down the tunnel passage, careful not to step on any of the loose stones that littered the descending floor. She sensed Snowy coming up alongside her and put her hand down to slow the dog's progress. She did not want her getting anywhere before them.

They were drawn toward the pulse, the gradual curve of the tunnel passage promising revelation somewhere up ahead.

Sidney hadn't known that the cave was so large and went so far back into the cliffs. No wonder town authorities wanted to keep people out. She could just imagine the danger of somebody getting lost or injured within the vast cave system.

The passage was becoming noticeably wider, and the greenish-tinged light brighter, signaling that they were close.

But to what she did not know.

The rocky floor of the passage dipped dramatically, leading into what appeared to be a cavern, and hopefully the answers to what had happened in Benediction.

And to the mystery of the bad radio.

She moved even quicker down the natural corridor, the intensity of her curiosity allowing her to shuck off the blanket of exhaustion and giving her a second wind.

The strands of cobwebs that stretched across the passage tickled her face, causing her to recoil in disgust. Sidney stepped back, bumping into Cody and Rich behind her as she wiped the gossamer threads from her hair and the front of her clothes.

Snowy started to bark crazily then.

Something quite large skittered across the ceiling toward them, lowering itself down on thick, silken strands to block their way.

"Oh God," she heard Rich say behind her.

Her own voice had been stolen away by the shocking sight.

At first glance, in the shifting gloom and eerie pulsing light, she thought it was a cat, but then she noticed the number of legs was all wrong. It hissed at them, but she still couldn't figure out what it was, even as it crawled closer across the rocks.

She took her phone out and lit up the corridor for a better look and immediately wished she hadn't. It was like nothing she'd ever seen before. It certainly had aspects of a tabby—the orange-striped fur, with large white paws—but also very noticeable characteristics of a spider. Long, spindly insect legs protruded from its side covered in thick black hairs. It also had multiple sets of green, bulging eyes, as well as a swollen, rounded abdomen from which the thick webbing that crisscrossed the cave corridor was emitted. The animal was like something out of the worst of nightmares, two completely different species crammed together to form something very unnatural.

The monster advanced on them, moving awkwardly as if it was still getting used to the horrible absurdity of its body. Sidney could do nothing but watch as it skittered over the rocks, screaming as razor-sharp pincers shot from its mouth.

Cody pushed Sidney aside and went for the hellish animal, pinning its cat-spider body to the floor of the corridor with his makeshift spear. The monster shrieked in pain, its multiple, spindly limbs clawing at the ground as it attempted to free itself. Snowy surged at the thing, her jaws snapping menacingly. The monster continued to yowl, its pincers dripping venom as they snapped, streams of liquid webbing covering the floor of the passage.

Sidney couldn't stand the sounds of its cries and removed the knife from her belt loop. She stabbed down with the blade, catching the monstrous cat's forehead and penetrating its skull. Its body trembled and thrashed all the harder, actually almost succeeding in freeing itself before it went still.

"What the hell is that thing?" Rich asked, his voice trembling with fear as Cody pulled his spear from the body with a horrible squelching sound. "That isn't right . . . that isn't right at all."

A *watchdog,* Sidney immediately thought, having no idea where the bizarre idea had originated but feeling like it might be right.

"Y'know what?" Rich continued, his words spilling from his mouth like vomit. "I draw the line at monsters. I draw the freakin' line at spider-cats or whatever the hell that is."

Sidney's mind was on fire, and she found herself wondering if this was somehow the next step. At first it was the individual life forms, and then those life forms merging to form one dangerous single organism, and now this—an amalgam of different kinds of animal life.

She squatted down next to the thing to examine it.

"Sid, I wouldn't get too close," Cody warned.

"It's dead," she said, checking out the twisted thing's body. Yes, there was most certainly spider and cat there, but on closer inspection she saw signs of other life forms as well. It had a thick shell covering parts of its body and feathers growing the length of its spine.

"What could have caused something like this?" Cody asked.

She looked up from the corpse of the impossible animal and down the length of the tunnel that still glowed with the eerie, throbbing light.

"I think we're going to find out," she said.

"Great," Rich said. "Just great."

The strange light up ahead was thrumming faster as if attuned somehow to the beating of her heart, and she found herself again proceeding down the descending stone corridor. She was careful this time, eyes scanning the walls of the passage for signs of webbing or anything that might do her and her friends harm.

But there was nothing to hold them back, and she charged to the end of the natural stone passage into the chamber of the pulsating green light. She tightly clutched her knife as she found herself standing upon a ledge, looking down into the rounded sunken chamber.

Nothing could have prepared her for what she saw. Not even the events of the last hours. Her brain always searched for the rational, but what she saw now was in no way rational. What was below her on the cavern floor was totally, inexplicably . . .

Unnatural.

Every instinct, every primitive part of her, was screaming for her to run, to turn around, grab her friends, and run as fast and as far away as they could.

It rested within a nest of rock.

Sidney searched for the proper words as she looked at it, settling on something that was merely adequate, for there had never been anything, as far as she knew, like this before.

Its flesh was pale, translucent, pulsing with an eerie inner light.

She felt herself drawn closer, moving to the edge of the rock ledge to gaze down at the sight that filled her with such horror and, she hated to admit it, fascination.

It was practically screaming, *Come look at me.*

Perhaps it was the friends at her back that gave her this courage to confront the unknown, or perhaps it was just stupidity, but Sidney squatted at the edge of the cliff and peered down into what was nestled in the bowl of the cave.

It looked like some sort of enormous internal organ. Her thoughts immediately flashed back to the countless videos of surgeries she'd watched throughout the years at the clinic. Its gelatinous surface was covered in thick, hairlike tendrils. The long black appendages reached out, swaying in the air like the tendrils of some sort of undersea life form moved by the current, what looked to be flashes of electricity crackling from the tips of each of the hairs. Electrical flashes discharged into the ether.

"I . . . I think we should go," whispered a voice that wrenched her from her current reality. She turned to look at a terrified Cody, wide eyed and sickly looking in the greenish glow emitted by the organism below. Rich furiously nodded in agreement. Snowy looked skittish as well, ready to bolt, the thick hair on the back of her neck and running along her spine standing on end.

Sidney knew they were right. This was far too much for them to comprehend, never mind deal with, but they needed to find their friend.

"We have to find Isaac," she said, turning back for one last look, her eyes taking in the secrets of the underground chamber. Thick cords of flesh, like roots, spread out from beneath the organism across the rocky floor to flow up the sides of the damp stone walls. From this network of veins, large, fleshy sacks like strange clusters of perverted fruit dangled down from the ceiling.

The sacks moved, the skin languidly stretching taut as something shifted within.

"Sidney, please," she heard Cody say. His voice was trembling. "I'm really, really scared and—"

Isaac's scream cut through the silence of the cave like a knife.

Sidney froze as her eyes searched for her friend. She found him at the far end of the cavern, wedged deeply into a corner, cowering and crying as something attacked him.

"We've got to do something," she said, looking for a way down onto the chamber floor.

"Are you nuts?" Rich asked, already moving to go. "We need to get the hell out of here and tell somebody about—"

Isaac cried out again, and she was on the move.

"Sidney, no!" Cody hissed.

She climbed over the edge of the cliff, finding enough hand- and footholds in the rock to allow her to begin to descend to the cave floor without too much trouble.

Cody watched her with absolute panic.

"She's going to get us killed—or worse," she heard Rich say, and she couldn't say that he was wrong, but she couldn't leave her friend.

She wasn't too far from the floor of the chamber when a section of the rock face crumbled away beneath her foot. She lost her hold and fell from the wall.

"Sidney!" Cody screamed.

Snowy had started to bark like crazy, the sound reverberating throughout the chamber.

So much for stealth, she thought just before landing on her back. She lay there stunned for a moment, looking up at the cave ceiling going in and out of focus, noticing the multiple fleshy sacks of varying sizes hanging above her, throbbing with life.

She managed to push herself up, rolling onto her side and crawling to her feet. Her spine felt bruised, but she didn't think she was hurt in any other way as she started across to where she'd seen her friend.

Isaac had been wedged into a corner, and one of the thick, fleshy roots that emerged from beneath the organism had attached itself to his lower half, a viscous liquid flowing from the veined appendage to cover him. Taking in the disturbing sight, she believed she now understood the origins of the sacklike objects that hung around them and found herself wondering what the others contained.

Isaac had gone eerily silent, the liquid skin solidifying as it flowed onto his body, cocooning him.

She stepped closer, and his eyes widened with recognition.

"Don't worry, Isaac," she said, trying to figure out what she would do next. "I'm going to get you out of this."

There was a noise behind her, and she turned to see Cody coming down the wall, Rich following closely. Snowy remained on the ledge, barking and pacing as she tried to figure out how she too could join them. Sidney was glad that she was up there, not wanting to see her hurt in any way.

"What's it doing to him?" Rich asked as he and Cody came to stand beside her, looking at poor Isaac.

"That," she said pointing out the hanging sacks. "We have to get him free."

She had no desire to come in contact with the vein but knew that there wasn't any other way. Reaching to her belt, she removed the knife.

"What the hell are you doing?" Cody asked, eyes darting around.

"What does it look like?" She was ready to cut into the fleshy root.

"You can't do that," he hissed, grabbing her arm.

Sidney looked at him, and he must have seen the determination in her eyes.

"But what if it . . . ," he started, turning to look at the alien organism as it pulsed and writhed within its nest of rock.

"We have no idea what it will do," she said, freeing her arm from him.

"And is that a good thing?" Rich asked.

"Well we can't leave him like this," Sidney said, looking to Isaac, his body now almost completely cocooned within the viscous fluid secreted from the puckered end of the appendage.

Without further interruption, Sidney went to work, sinking the blade of the sharp kitchen knife into the rubbery flesh of the vein. Thick, black, foul-smelling fluid spurted up from the wound as she hacked and cut. It was disgusting, and she wanted so badly to vomit, but she decided that she could throw up later when Isaac was free.

"Sid," she heard Cody say from behind her.

"I'm busy," she said, grunting as she continued to cut through the thick muscle and fat. It was like cutting into an enormous earthworm.

"Sid, something's wrong," Cody said more forcefully, and she took a moment to see what he was talking about.

Something was most definitely wrong.

The organism was throbbing and pulsating even faster now, and the greenish light it emitted had changed to an angry red. The end that she'd cut suddenly recoiled, spewing gouts of fluid as it was drawn back beneath the undulating mass.

"I think it's pissed," Rich said, and Sidney had to agree.

The organism had started to expand and then quickly contract, all the while growing darker and darker in color. It now resembled an enormous clot of blood as it quaked.

Sidney returned her attention to Isaac, tearing away the solidifying flesh that covered his body.

"You all right?" she asked him as she peeled the rubbery skin away.

Isaac stared at her blankly, his mouth moving, though no sound came out. It was as if he was in shock.

"We're going to get you out of here," she reassured him. "Can you stand up?"

She tried to help him stand with Cody's help, and then things went from bad to worse.

"Oh shit," Rich said. "Guys."

They all looked up and watched as the multiple fleshy sacks hanging from the walls and ceiling began to react, each of them splitting open, what was inside splashing to the cave floor.

From the viscous puddles on the cave floor, animals emerged, but they were animals the likes of which had never been seen before.

They were like the twisted thing that had attacked them in the tunnels—horrible mixes of pre-existing animal life that made up what was best described as monsters.

"The bad radio," Isaac said, his voice slurring as if drunk. "The bad radio is angry."

"No kidding," Sidney said, pushing the stumbling youth as gently as she could toward the end of the cave where they would, hopefully, make their escape from the cavern floor.

Hopefully.

The monsters came at them silently, their silver right eyes reflecting red in the pulsing light of the alien organism.

Something undulated across the cave floor, and Sidney was certain it had once been partially a seal. Its mouth opened wider and wider as it came at them, lobsterlike appendages erupting from its fleshy gray sides helping to move its smooth body over the rocks.

Cody was the first to react. He charged toward the twisted thing with a yell, meeting it halfway and jamming his spear into its sausage-shaped body. The thing did not even scream as the carving fork pierced its monstrous flesh.

There were others converging now.

"We're not going to make it out of here," Rich said breathlessly, standing beside her. Sidney still held the knife, which was covered in the blood of the thing that she believed was somehow responsible for all that had happened to her friends, to her family.

To her home and island.

She had hurt the thing that pulsed and jiggled and shot sparks into the air; her hand was covered with its blood. And as the swarm of monsters came toward them, she swore she would hurt it again. She would make it so this thing remembered her.

She would kill it if she could.

What might have once been a muskrat, now with multiple pairs of dragonfly-type wings, flew at them from across the cave, and she tensed, ready to fight. Holding out her knife, she watched as it circled them from above and then dropped down. The thing was awkward in flight, heavy, as it landed on her shoulder, its multiple, vein-covered, cellophane-like wings fluttering noisily like crinkling paper as it attempted to maintain its purchase upon her. She grabbed the thing in her hand, its thickness disgusting to the touch, and brought it to the ground, pinning it and stabbing it repeatedly.

"We're going to fight," Sidney said loudly and strongly enough for her friends to hear and, hopefully, be inspired. "We're going to fight for as long as we can, and then we're getting out of here."

"It's good to have goals," Rich said, hefting both his meat tenderizer and homemade knife-sword.

Cody was still out in front of them, his spear flashing in the red light of the alien mass as the twisted bodies piled up in a ring around him.

They could hear the sounds of more life forms—monsters—being birthed from the leathery sacks, the tearing noise followed by the disgusting sound of new life landing upon the cave floor with a wet plop.

And the scarlet-hued organism continued to beat and writhe, bolts of crackling energy traveling up the ends of the thick black hairs to shoot off into space. Sidney knew that meant something, and if she was able to stop it—

"Sidney, watch out!" Rich screamed as a hairless dog with the face of a snapping turtle charged her like a bull. He threw himself in front of her and Isaac, his metal meat hammer coming down hard on the side of the turtlelike head with a horrible squishing sound. The creature's head exploded as its muscular body thrashed upon the ground. Rich kicked it aside, ready for whatever was coming next.

They were making slow progress across the cave, keeping the

jagged walls of the chamber to their backs. Sidney watched her dog from a distance, the white German shepherd still crazily pacing upon the rock ledge, desperate to come down to them, but each and every time the dog would look at her, Sidney was sure to show her the hand signal to stay.

Stay. Do not come down here. She did not want to see her baby, her best friend, hurt in any way.

Stay.

The number of animals attacking them continued to grow. For every one they bludgeoned, stabbed, or speared, three more twisted things seemed to emerge to take their place.

And they killed those as well.

Even Isaac had gotten into the game, using large rocks as his weapons, throwing the stones with incredible force or slamming them down upon soft, hairless bodies.

But how long can we keep this up? Sidney wondered, feeling her exhaustion beginning to take hold. She wasn't moving as fast now; the monsters were able to get closer before she could strike them down.

Sidney pushed the thought from her mind as they got close to an area where it looked as though they might be able to climb up onto the ledge. This was where they would make their stand, she decided, where they would either escape or meet their end. It sounded like an action movie cliché, but at that moment, as they watched the malformed life forms attacking them, she was amazed, and a little bit amused, at how true it was.

The animals were becoming faster, even more aggressive, if that was possible. It was almost as if the pulsating red thing in the center of the room sensed that they might actually escape and had no intention of letting them do so.

"We've got to start climbing," Sidney said. She'd taken Rich's short spear-sword and was slashing and jabbing to keep the latest wave of creatures back. Cody darted forward, stabbing with the longer spear, then returning to where they stood before darting forward again.

"You start," he said.

"No way," Sidney answered. "You and Rich help Isaac," she said, pausing for a moment to plunge the end of Rich's short, bladed weapon into the eye of something that had once been a dog, though now she had no idea what it was.

"Help Isaac, get up onto the ledge, and then you can help me."

"I'm not doing that," Cody said, that stubborn streak that she'd once found kind of sexy coming through.

Now she just found it aggravating.

"You'll do it because we don't have the time to argue," she said, eyeing the buildup of beasts ahead. It was like a screwed-up assembly line, the twisted animals waiting to be stabbed, speared, or have their heads bashed in.

Cody still wasn't budging, his spearing getting more forceful, angry.

"Please, Code," Sidney pleaded. "Look at him—what does he weigh? One-fifty? I can't help him."

His eyes darted over to Isaac, who was having a hard time standing up, even with Rich's help. "You did this to me back at Rich's house, in the bathroom," he said. "You almost didn't make it out."

"Yeah, but almost doesn't count. I *did* make it out. Think of that when you're doing what I told you."

She grabbed hold of his spear and yanked it from his grasp, giving him her smaller, shorter weapon. "I'll use this until you're done."

Cody dispatched a few more snapping, slithering beasts, then finally turned to Rich and Isaac. "C'mon, help me get Isaac up there," Sidney heard him say.

Rich started to argue, but Cody ignored him.

"Isaac, we're going to climb up, all right?" Cody said.

Sidney continued to stand her ground, her back to the wall, her eyes attempting to take in all the nightmarish stuff before her. Something with the head of a fox snapped its jaws around the end of her spear and twisted, wrenching the pole from her grasp. The spear clattered to the ground, where it was at once swarmed upon by all manner of new and writhing insects. She needed that spear or she was finished, and she plunged her hands into the squirming mass to retrieve it. The insects began to sting and bite, and she cried out in pain, but she found the spear, wrapping bloody and swelling hands around it, and hauled it up from beneath the ocean of squirming terror.

"Sidney!" she heard Cody's voice calling to her from behind. She turned her face just enough to see that they were actually halfway to the ledge above.

"Keep going!" she ordered.

Her hands were on fire from the insect stings, and as she continued to fight—to spear and slash—she caught a glimpse of them. They were covered in blood and slime, so swollen that they didn't even resemble her hands anymore. They looked like the hands of some fat old man.

If she wasn't fighting for her life at the moment, she might have started to cry.

"Sidney, come on!"

It was Rich calling now, his voice high and almost hysterical.

She knew that she had to turn and begin her climb, but her eyes kept going to the crimson, gelatinous mass—the alien organism—as it throbbed with evil intent. She noticed that a barrier of the larger animals had taken up guard around it, protecting it. That just seemed to drive her forward, wanting to get closer, to threaten it with her presence, but she knew that this wasn't smart.

It was time to retreat, and she started to back up while still managing to fight her attackers off.

But still the organism taunted her.

How dare that horrible thing do what it did to her friends? To her island?

How dare it?

Her anger made her fight all the more fiercely as Cody and Rich screamed impatiently for her to climb. Even Snowy was barking. And she was coming, backing up ever so slowly, even though that thing—whatever the hell it was—sat there, nestled in the rock, dirt, and sand.

The disgusting, fleshy mass seemed to react to her feelings, blowing itself up and then deflating, as if to say, *Did you see what I did to your town?* That thought pissed her off all the more, and she actually fought back the urge to show it that she wasn't afraid, and continued to back toward the wall, to escape.

To run away.

She knew that it wasn't running away, that this was something far bigger than she and her friends.

But it still felt somehow wrong to leave the thing there, untouched—mocking her with its awfulness.

She imagined it laughing at her, amused by all it had taken. Flashes of her father filled her head, and an overwhelming sense of sadness turned to a burning anger, and she heard her father's voice.

When she was a little girl, she and her dad used to watch DVDs of old cartoons that he'd loved as a little boy. One of his, and eventually her, favorites was Popeye the Sailor Man. She used to watch with wide-eyed amusement as the weirdly muscled cartoon sailor fought the villainous Bluto, a can of spinach helping him to save the day.

Right then and there, as she fought for her life against the swarm that had no right to exist, she heard her father's voice, quoting the famous words of the cartoon character just before he ate his spinach and vanquished his foes.

"That's all I can stands. I can't stands no more!"

Sidney found herself grinning.

She couldn't have agreed more. She stepped forward a foot or two, hearing her friends continuing to scream for her, but she didn't have the time to explain. She had to concentrate on what she was going to do.

"This is for my father," she said, hauling back the spear before letting it fly with all her might.

The makeshift javelin flew through the air and pierced the center of the organism. She grinned as she watched the writhing, fleshy mass react, its body convulsing wildly as spurts of internal fluid shot up from where it had been punctured, the ends of the thick hairs protruding from its mass throwing off even more crackling discharge.

"Take that, you ugly son of a bitch," she said, then whipped around and raced for the wall, using the momentum of her run to jump and begin her climb.

"C'mon," Cody screamed from the edge of the cliff above her, the ground beneath his feet beginning to give way.

"Get back!" she shouted at him, seeing that the ledge wasn't going to hold.

The ledge crumbled where he was standing, and he jumped back just in the nick of time.

The exhaustion truly hit her then, those multiple adrenaline surges that she'd experienced since the horrors began no longer having any effect.

But all she needed was a little bit more.

She was careful as she grabbed, giving the handholds a little pull before hauling her aching body up. Glancing up to the ledge, she saw the anticipatory faces of Cody and Rich, each one ready to grab at her as soon as she was close enough.

And then she noticed Isaac.

He was standing behind them, a look on his face that filled her with dread. He was completely emotionless as he stared at her, his mouth hanging slack. His lips were attempting to move, to form words, as if he were trying to tell her something, that strange internal struggle that the poor soul had been fighting since the nightmare began still going on.

The words at last came flying from his mouth in a terror-filled roar. "Watch out! It's coming!"

Sidney hadn't a chance to question or even to prepare. She felt an incredible pressure around her ankle, yanking her savagely from the face of the wall.

And she had been so close.

CHAPTER **SIXTY**

Sidney caught a glimpse of what had grabbed her before she fell—a thick, veined tentacle that had emerged from beneath the fleshy skirt of the organism.

How dare you think you could hurt me, she imagined it saying in a horrible, wet-sounding voice as she fell to the ground. She landed on the soft corpses of the monsters they had killed, hitting her face against the wall.

The animals—the mockeries of life that filled the cave—moved away as she was dragged past them, as if somehow they knew that she was no longer for them.

Oh no, she had riled up the big boss now, and anything that was going to be done to her was going to be done by him. . . . *Her? It?*

Her friends were screaming, and she tried to pull the tentacle from around her leg, but it was wrapped so freaking tight. And then she remembered her knife, and she reached down to her belt loop hoping—praying—that it was still there. It was, and she'd barely pulled it free before reaching the body of the monstrosity.

It was even worse to look at up close.

She could see the intricate vein work crisscrossing through its fleshy body as it pumped its life fluids. Somehow she could feel the throbbing of its horrible life, feel the electrical discharge from its swelling mass. It actually made the hair on her body stand on end.

The knife was in her hand, and she began to stab at the tentacle entwined about her leg. The thing reacted by gripping her tighter, and she thought that her leg was going to snap.

Sidney was trying not to cry out, though it hurt so very badly, but it didn't stop her from fighting. She was wild, seeing absolute red, pretty certain that she was now more savage than all the creatures in the cave combined. Her jeans and hands were soaked with the slimy blood of the organism, but she continued to hack and cut at the fleshy appendage until she was actually able to wriggle her leg free of its grip just before reaching the alien mass.

Pulling back her leg, she began to crawl across the stony ground, but the entity lashed out at her, wrapping itself about her waist and hoisting her into the air. The inside of the cave flashed by as she struggled in its grasp. She saw that Cody and Rich hadn't listened to her at all, remaining stupidly loyal and returning to the cave floor. The only smart ones she glimpsed were Isaac and Snowy, still waiting upon the ledge.

She wanted to tell them to go . . . run . . . leave her, but her voice was gone.

Sidney feebly slashed at the thick, muscular tendril that threatened to crush her ribs. Explosions of color caused by oxygen deprivation bloomed before her eyes, pressure so great that she thought maybe her head might pop like a balloon, but she did not stop fighting.

Darkness encroached upon her vision, and Sidney seriously believed that she was about to die, sorry that she wouldn't be able to help her friends.

Things went totally black, and she felt herself begin to float away, when suddenly she could breathe again, and she greedily sucked the dank air into her lungs. She wasn't quite sure what had happened, but the surface beneath her felt odd—spongy, clammy. She was reminded of an old pool cover, the water under the skin sloshing about.

And then she realized where she was.

The organism had dropped her on its own fleshy body. There were sudden roars of thunder—*explosions*—within the cave that she came to recognize as gunfire, and through bleary eyes she saw her friends: Cody firing the handgun that he'd gotten from Officer Kole and Rich having found his homemade, bladed weapon once more. It was an amazing sight to see, her friends fighting for her . . . fighting for their own lives and the lives of those who'd managed to survive the savagery of the night.

In a way, they were fighting for the sake of the world.

The mangled tentacle snapped whiplike at them as the twisted animals under the organism's control again advanced.

She had to help her friends.

Struggling to stand upon the moving, uneven surface proved a chore in her current condition. Sidney could feel that the tentacle had done some damage, her ribs likely cracked. The pain was intense, and it was hard for her to breathe, but she had to do something.

The organism seemed to respond to her presence upon it, writhing and vibrating with life, attempting to shuck her from its skin. It was as she fell backward that she saw it, still sticking up from the center of its mass: the homemade spear that she'd thrown.

Sidney crawled toward the protruding weapon, feeling her cracked ribs grinding together with each inch she made. She told herself she would not pass out from the pain. The flesh beneath her began to buck, to expand and contract as if it somehow knew her malicious intent.

So very close now, she threw herself across the undulating surface, rolling across its rubbery skin toward the spear, gripping the shaft as she almost slid past it, and using it to haul herself up to her feet.

From where she stood she could see the entire cave and saw that things were not good for her friends. Cody's gun had run out of bullets, and now he used it as a kind of club, while Rich continued to stab and slash, but his movements—both their movements—were becoming slow and tired as they fought what seemed to be a perpetual onslaught.

Sidney knew that it had to be now. She yanked on the spear, pulling it from the writhing surface flesh with a sickening sucking sound. Gripping the spear tightly in both hands, she plunged the pointed tines down, again and again, into the body of the beast. The organism bucked crazily, its slimy mass moving beneath her like an ocean wave, but she managed to retain her balance, sticking the spear repeatedly into the body of the alien thing, wanting to do as much damage as possible before—

She must have struck something of great importance. As the spear came down again, the metal forks puncturing the pliant surface, she felt something let go, a release of energy flowing up through the fork's tines, through the wooden shaft, and into her own body.

Sidney went rigid.

She continued to grip the spear as her body began to tremble, every fiber of her—every cell—filled with the unknown energy.

As a connection was made.

Her mind was engorged with something . . . *alien*.

Explosions of imagery unlike anything she had ever experienced filled her thoughts.

Suddenly she knew what *it* knew. She and the organism were of one mind.

She saw where it had come from . . . not outer space, but closer and yet so very far away. On the other side of this reality there existed another place.

An alternate reality. Another dimension.

It had been sent by the others . . . those who lived behind the veil.

Those who watched and waited, coveting what they saw in this world.

Planning how to make it theirs.

They had done this before, reaching across the great divide to exterminate their enemies and take the treasures of a vanquished world.

Using the most powerful of storms as cover, they disguised their initial incursion . . . arriving upon the coveted world unnoticed, using the planet's own indigenous life, turning the seemingly harmless lower life forms into weapons. The lesser the brain function, the easier it was for the invading organism to control and manipulate.

Distracted by the storm, the higher species would be taken unawares, softened for what was to follow.

The information rushing into her brain suddenly began to slow, and Sidney felt the connection between her and the organism brutally severed as the others became aware of her presence within the consciousness of their tool of attack.

They were not happy to sense her there, reaching out to capture her mind, to prevent it from returning to its earthly vessel. Their psychic touch was revolting, like squirming maggots upon the meat of her brain.

They were far stronger than she was, and Sidney felt herself being pulled farther into their realm on the other side of the veil. The others were desperate to have her, the information that the organism had shared through their accidental bond dangerous to their agenda.

Her mind was still trapped within the organism, and the others reached out to take her away, to leave behind an empty husk that could do no further harm to them.

Or to their plans for humanity.

Sidney snapped back to her own mind at the sounds of gunfire.

Her eyes felt as though rocks had been taped across them, but she fought to open them and did not quite understand what she saw.

There were others in the cave with them now, men and woman with guns and . . .

Fire.

The organism tried to take her back.

Sidney felt it at the base of her brain, a revolting, alien touch that wanted nothing more than to see her dead.

She realized that she still tightly clutched the spear imbedded in the organism's body. She took a deep breath and forced herself to pull the weapon from the sucking flesh, breaking the organism's hold upon her.

Standing there on the alien organism, she felt the raw emotion of what she had experienced. The knowledge of what had happened and who—or what—was responsible driving her to the edge of insanity.

The others.

How dare they? she thought, her hate-filled gaze like laser beams as she stared down upon the still-living abomination.

"How dare you!" she screamed manically, plunging the spear point deeper, and deeper still.

And with each stab, the link between her and the alien organism was reestablished—a bond made and broken again and again as the twin fork tines came down.

And with each stab she felt it dying.

Until she felt nothing and surrendered to the swarming darkness.

Unable to fight anymore.

EPILOGUE

Sidney dreamed of a sea of red.

Moving through the waters of scarlet at an incredible speed, faster and faster she traveled until she was moving so quickly that she tore through the crimson surroundings of the environment, punching through to the other side.

There was a sound like the blaring of the loudest horn announcing the end of the world.

A sound that told them she had arrived.

Sidney awakened with a start, not really sure who, or where, she was.

"Hey there," she heard a familiar voice say. "You okay?"

Her immediate thought was *No, no I am not okay. Nobody is,* but she managed to hold her tongue as she glanced over to see Doc Martin sitting by her side, gently holding her bandaged hand.

Sidney shot up, ready to leap from the cot where she was lying.

"We have to get out," she said, eyes darting about the room, searching for any signs of animal or insect life.

"Hey, calm down. It's over," Doc Martin said, standing up from her seat and gently pushing Sidney back down. "You've got to take it easy. You've been through a lot."

Sidney looked around, taking in her surroundings. She was in a large tent. There were other cots lined up around her, but they were empty.

"Where are we?" she asked.

"Stanley Airfield," Doc Martin said. "They've set up a temporary camp for the survivors and—"

"Who?" Sidney wanted to know, suddenly remembering the cave and the people with the guns who had come in.

"Some branch of the military, I imagine," Doc Martin said with a shrug. She fished through the pockets of her blood-covered smock and removed a crumpled pack of cigarettes. "They aren't too keen on talking about it."

"Snowy," she said suddenly, struggling to sit up again. "My friends . . . Cody, Rich . . . Isaac . . ."

"They're fine," Doc Martin said. "Getting checked over in another part of the camp. It's amazing that you all made it through. You're lucky to be alive . . . we all are."

Sidney remembered the cave and how she didn't really believe that any of them would make it out.

"How did they find us?"

Doc Martin puffed on her cigarette, careful to blow the smoke away from her. "I guess they've been investigating similar events in other areas," she explained. "Something to do with zeroing in on some weird signal they started to pick up. They tracked it to the caves."

The image of the pulsating organism filled Sidney's mind, and she remembered how she had been touched by that very signal.

And what it meant.

The front of the tent parted, and a dark-skinned man reading something from a tablet stepped in. There was a woman behind him holding a leash, and at the end of that leash . . .

"Snowy!" Sidney shrieked far louder than she'd intended.

The woman released the leash, letting the dog come to her. Snowy bounded up onto the cot excitedly, licking Sidney's face and head and anything else that she could reach.

"How's my girl?" Sidney asked, going through the motions of checking her over for any signs of injury as she petted her.

"She looks good," Doc Martin said. "I gave her a once-over when they brought you all into camp."

Sidney embraced the dog, pulling her into her arms. The dog obliged, falling into her. If Snowy could have somehow become part of her at that moment, they would have merged together in a single organism.

Images of the twisted animals that had inhabited the cave filled her thoughts, and she found herself suddenly very afraid.

"Miss Sidney Moore," the dark-skinned man then said, looking up from his tablet. "May I call you Sidney?" he asked.

"Sure," she said.

"I'm Dr. Gregory Sayid, and this is my head of security, Ms. Langridge."

Langridge smiled at her and Snowy. "Somebody's glad to see you," she said.

Sidney pulled the dog closer, burying her face in her neck and taking in her comforting smell, even though she seriously could have used a bath.

"I was wondering if you wouldn't mind answering a few questions?" Sayid asked.

Doc Martin suddenly stood up from her chair.

"That's my cue," she said. "I'll catch you later on."

"Don't go too far," Sidney called to her.

Doc Martin turned at the entrance to tent and smiled. "I'll just be a yell away," she said before going outside.

Dr. Sayid was staring at her, and she realized that he was waiting for her response.

"Sure," she said. "Go ahead."

"Excellent." He looked down at his tablet again, his fingers tapping the screen.

"You and your friends—"

"I'd like to see them," she interrupted.

"Excuse me?" he asked, looking up.

"I'm sorry," she said. "You mentioned my friends, and I'd really like to see them."

He stared at her and then nodded. "Of course," he said. He turned to Ms. Langridge, who'd been standing by. "Brenda, would you mind?"

She nodded before leaving the tent as well.

"Thank you," Sidney said.

Sayid nodded and smiled, then went back to the handheld screen.

"Sidney, it's my job to gather information about what happened on Benediction, and I was wondering if you might share any personal observations as to what occurred here during the storm."

What she'd experienced linked to the organism filled her mind. Where should she begin? There was so much to explain.

She was about to begin when Cody stepped into the tent. Sidney couldn't help herself, and she bounded from the cot to wrap her arms around him.

"It's so good to see you," she whispered. She was doing everything in her power to hold back the tears.

"What about me?" She heard Rich's voice and released her ex-boyfriend to throw herself into the arms of one of her closest friends.

"It's good to see you, too," she said, squeezing him as tight as she could.

She lifted her head to see Ms. Langridge holding open the flap of the tent so that a nervous-looking Isaac could duck his head and enter.

"Isaac," she said, opening her arms to hug him, but he stepped back, eyeing her cautiously.

"Glad to see you alive and well," she said to him, feeling slightly embarrassed at her overt emotion.

"Yes, it's good that you're not dead," Isaac told her.

"I'd say that's very good," Rich said, looking around to see if everybody agreed.

Sidney was so glad to see them again, alive and, from the looks of it, relatively in one piece. There were plenty of bandages, and even some stitches, but nothing that wouldn't heal over time, she imagined.

"All right then," Sayid said, interrupting their moment. "I've already interviewed your friends, and now it's your turn, if you'd be so kind."

Sidney nodded, returning to the cot with Snowy practically glued to her side.

"I'm ready," she said, sitting down.

Sayid lowered his eyes to the tablet. "When was it that you realized that something was wrong?"

Her thoughts flashed back to the deafening crack of thunder when Cody and Rich were retrieving the sailboat. She knew now, through her connection to the organism, that it wasn't thunder at all, but the arrival of . . .

Sidney was about to answer when she became distracted by a man who'd come into the tent, stopping at the entrance. They all looked in his direction.

"Borrows?" Ms. Langridge asked.

"I need to speak with Dr. Sayid at once," the young man said, and Sidney picked up the anxiety coming off the man in waves.

Sayid smiled at her as he stood up from his chair, turning his attention toward the man.

"What is it?" he asked.

"A storm," the man said.

Sayid's posture went rigid.

"Where?"

The man held out his own tablet, running his fingers over the smooth surface to share what information he had. Ms. Langridge drifted over to see as well.

"It's Boston, sir," the man named Borrows said, barely able to restrain his intensity. "And it bears all the landmarks of the storm that hit Benediction, only . . ."

They all had turned their attention to the young man.

"Only this is much bigger."

Sidney felt as though she might throw up. "I know what it is," she then said, her voice causing them all to turn toward her. "It's an invasion."

Ms. Langridge stepped forward.

"How do you know what—"

"This is just the beginning," Sidney told them, her words filled with dread and warning. "They come in the storm."

They come in the storm.

THE END?

ACKNOWLEDGMENTS

As always, copious amounts of love to my wife, LeeAnne, for all that she does, and for putting up with my nonsense. Love and thanks also to Kirby, for inspiring me to write a book with a killer French bulldog as a character.

Special thanks also to Michael Strother for his energy and enthusiasm on this book; to Howard Morhaim for having my back; to Liesa Abrams for just being who she is; and to Dr. Kris Blumenstock for my veterinary stuff. Thanks to Thomas Fitzgerald and Seamus, Dale Queenan and Allie, Barbara Simpson and Mugsy, Larry Johnson and Mel, Nicole Scopa, Frank Cho, Mom Sniegoski, Pam Daley, Dave Kraus (miss you every day), Kathy Kraus, and the swarm of creepy-crawlies down at Cole's Comics in Lynn, Massachusetts.

We're going to need a bigger boat.